Praise for Rhyannon Byrd

"No one writes lip-biting sexual tension and sizzling romance like Rhyannon Byrd."   —Shayla Black, *USA Today* bestselling author

"With a Byrd book, you know you will get plenty of sizzling sensuality as well as molten emotion."   —*RT Book Reviews*

"Filled with love, lust, loyalty, betrayal, sensuality, and heady romance. Readers will find themselves reaching for a Kleenex and fanning themselves all at the same time as they devour this page-turner."   —*Night Owl Reviews*

"Combines passion and suspense with a touch of deadly danger guaranteed to keep you reading until the very last page."   —*Joyfully Reviewed*

"Hold on to your iceboxes, girls! This one is a scorcher!"   —*A Romance Review*

Take Me Under

Rhyannon Byrd

HEAT BOOKS | NEW YORK

THE BERKLEY PUBLISHING GROUP
Published by the Penguin Group
Penguin Group (USA) Inc.
375 Hudson Street, New York, New York 10014, USA

USA I Canada I UK I Ireland I Australia I New Zealand I India I South Africa I China

Penguin Books Ltd., Registered Offices: 80 Strand, London WC2R 0RL, England
For more information about the Penguin Group, visit penguin.com.

This book is an original publication of The Berkley Publishing Group.

Library of Congress Cataloging-in-Publication Data

Byrd, Rhyannon.
Take me under / Rhyannon Byrd.—Heat trade paperback edition.
pages   cm
ISBN 978-0-425-26293-1 (pbk.)
I. Title.
PR6102.Y73T35   2013
823'.92—dc23   2012051549

PUBLISHING HISTORY
Heat trade paperback edition / June 2013

PRINTED IN THE UNITED STATES OF AMERICA

10 9 8 7 6 5 4 3 2

Cover design by Springer Design Group.
Cover photography by Shutterstock.

Take Me Under

Prologue

Three years earlier . . .

"I THOUGHT YOU DIDN'T SCREW AROUND WITH MARRIED WOMEN."

Ben Hudson rested his back against the patio wall of the crowded restaurant and scowled at his younger brother. "Mind your own damn business," he muttered, irritated that Michael had noticed the stares he kept directing through the mass of people. As a homicide detective in Miami, Ben had worked hard at learning how to hide his reactions. But at the moment his training wasn't enough to cover the fact that he'd spotted a woman he'd like to fuck. Hard and rough and repeatedly, if his cock had anything to say about it. Which it didn't, considering the lady had a husband and was off-limits.

"And I don't screw around with them," he tacked on more for his benefit than Michael's, thinking the verbal reminder couldn't hurt. He knew damn well what kind of shit could be stirred up when spouses strayed from their commitments, and he wanted no part of that kind of life.

Michael propped one shoulder against the wall and gave a quiet laugh. "Uh-huh. Your lips are saying one thing, Ben. But your eyes already have her stripped and spread."

Choking back a dry curse, he tilted his bottle up to his lips, enjoying the icy burn as the beer slid down his throat. He tried to take his eyes off the woman in question, but it wasn't happening.

"Just because I like the look of her doesn't mean I'm planning to do anything about it." He kept his voice low, mindful of the fact they were surrounded by listening ears. "You know me better than that."

"Yeah, I do." Michael's pale green eyes, a shade lighter than Ben's, zeroed in on the brunette. "But I also know that a woman like *that* is probably worth breaking a rule or two."

Ben gritted his teeth, hating that Michael had noticed the same things he had. At first glance, she was just another pretty face at a party that was currently packed with plenty of pretty faces. It was his cousin Gary's thirtieth birthday, and friends and family of both Gary and his wife, Connie, had been invited to the celebration that was taking place at McClain's Beach House. McClain's was one of Moss Beach, Florida's most popular restaurants, with a prime location right on the waterfront. The floor was usually dusted with sand, but it only added to the restaurant's laid-back, kick-up-your-feet atmosphere, and the food was always excellent, which meant the place was always busy.

Tonight was no exception. People kept moving around the covered patio area, obscuring his view of the woman who stood out from all the others like a shiny new penny. But he couldn't put his finger on what it was exactly that set her apart. He just knew that he couldn't take his fucking eyes off her. When a guy he recognized as Gary's old college roommate turned to the blonde beside him, it cleared the way between Ben and the woman again. Only this time she looked a little to her left and stared right back at him. Big, dark eyes blinked, locked with his, and held. The look couldn't have lasted for more than a few seconds before she quickly looked away again, but it was enough to make his dick go hard and his skin go hot. Fuckin' A.

"Oh, shit." Michael choked back a laugh. "You should see your face, man. If you sport wood in front of Gran, I swear I'll never let you live it down."

Since there was no use denying how close he was to doing just that, Ben decided to find out how much Michael knew about the mystery woman. He hadn't made it to Gary and Connie's wedding earlier that year, since he'd been wrapping up a case at the time, but Michael had been there. Odds were good that his brother might have met the woman at the wedding. "You know her name?" he asked, taking a fresh beer from one of the waiters who strolled by.

"Reese Leighton, though she was a Monroe before she married the Yankee lawyer who has his arm wrapped around her waist. She's one of Connie's older sisters, but I think only a year separates them."

Huh. He wouldn't have guessed the two women were related. Connie was tall and blond and stacked, and this woman . . . wasn't. Not that he gave a shit.

Reese. An unusual name, but it fit her. She was an unusual woman. Beautiful, but not in a classical way. Long, dark hair that looked thick and soft fell over feminine shoulders bared by a stylish black sundress, contrasting sharply with skin that was creamy and pale. She was probably only around five-five, slimmer than his usual taste, but curvy enough that she didn't look like a toothpick. Instead, she looked warm and soft and like something that should be under him. He couldn't tell exactly what color her eyes were from that distance, only that they were dark, her gaze sharp with intelligence when she'd held his stare. Her mouth could only be described as lush, with a full lower lip that begged for the nip of his teeth, and he could see that there was a spattering of freckles sweeping across her cheeks and the petite bridge of her nose.

It was the damn freckles that got him.

It wasn't that they made her look too young for a guy his age. He wasn't into robbing the cradle like a lot of the men he knew who'd hit their thirties. There was just something about that sprinkling of freckles that looked so damn sexy on her. Ben wanted to touch his mouth to them, one by one, and work his way down from there, over her breasts and her stomach, until he'd buried his face between her legs and learned if her pussy was even half as delicious as she looked. If it was, it might be hours before he came up for air.

And he really needed to get his brain onto a new train of thought before he did something stupid, like make an ass of himself in front of his family and friends. Reminding himself that he did *not* hit on married women, he glanced at Michael. "What else do you know?" he asked, the words gritty with lust. He'd have blamed his reaction on a lack of sex, only he'd been sleeping with one of the traffic cops back home on a casual basis for a few months now. And he'd never been the type of guy not to get sex when he wanted it. That wasn't bragging, just a simple fact. He was tall and stayed in shape, and women had always seemed to like his dark hair and green eyes. But he thought it was more of an attitude thing. When he wanted something, he went after it. He didn't let shit stand in his way.

But this was the first time Ben could remember really wanting a woman who he knew he couldn't have. He didn't care for the feeling; but he also couldn't stop his gaze from sliding right back to her.

Michael thought about his question for a moment, then gave him an answer. "I think Gary said she's a schoolteacher—special needs if I remember right—and she and the jackass husband live up in Boston. They don't get down here all that often because of his work, and he doesn't like her to go places without him." Michael smirked, shoving the shaggy strands of his dark hair off his brow. "Can't say that I blame the guy. If I had a wife like her, I don't think I'd let her out of my sight." He paused, staring at the woman—at *Reese*—before saying, "She's easy on the eyes, but it's more than that. She's got that whole shy, earthy vibe thing going on that's such a fucking turn-on. The kind that says she'd be hot enough to melt your cock off, but doesn't actually have a clue how sexy she is. She's just . . . naturally got it, without even trying or being all stuck-up about it."

Taking another long drink of his beer, Ben swallowed and slid Michael another glare. "Stay away from her," he warned, knowing that Michael was capable of doing something stupid. At twenty-five, the guy was still at that age where he let his dick make most of the important decisions in his life.

A sly smile curled Michael's mouth. "Don't worry, man. I'm smart enough to know when it's time to play it cool, instead of pushing my luck."

Ben grunted in response, ignoring the interested looks being sent his way by a glitzy redhead over by the patio bar. He didn't recognize her, which meant she wasn't family, but he wasn't going to take the bait. No sense picking up one woman when he knew he wouldn't be able to take his eyes off another one.

"What do you know about the husband?" He studied the blond male, thinking he looked a little too polished. All styled hair and gleaming teeth. He was tall, but slender, with a look that said he thought he was slick shit.

"Just that he's some Ivy League lawyer," Michael said. "You

know the type. All cock, no balls. Thinks he's God's gift to the world and that we're all backward hillbillies. Self-righteous prick."

"He doesn't deserve her."

Michael nodded. "You're right about that. I hate to gossip, but . . ."

Ben lifted his brows, waiting . . .

His brother lowered his voice. "Gary told me that Connie suspects he's been cheating on Reese since before they got hitched a few years ago."

His lip curled. "Why doesn't she leave the dickhead?"

Michael shrugged. "They're not sure that Reese knows, and no one wants to be the one to hurt her if she doesn't." Michael gave him a long look, then said, "You sure you don't want to make a move on her? Sounds like you'd be doing her a favor if you did."

He shook his head, burying the driving urge to approach her. She was married, and as long as she had that rock glittering on her finger, he wouldn't touch her. Hell, even if she wasn't married, it wasn't like they could get anything going. They were both only visiting Moss Beach. He had his job in Miami and she lived up in Boston. Logistics alone would keep him from making what would no doubt be a big-ass mistake. He couldn't afford to get his head tangled up about a woman, much less one he didn't even know. Christ, for all he knew, she could be a total bitch.

And yet, the instant she turned her head again, locking that dark gaze with his, her face flushed with color, Ben knew that was bullshit. This lady was no bitch. His intense reaction to her tonight made him uneasy, but he knew damn well what he'd do if she ever became free. If that happened, he *would* make a move on her. He doubted there was anything or anyone that could stop him. There'd be future events like this one. Their families were tied together now through Gary and Connie's marriage, which meant they would cross paths again.

If given the chance, he'd fuck Reese Leighton six ways to Sunday and make it count. Hell, it'd probably even take more than a week before he could get this particular woman out of his system. But once he had, Ben had seen enough men in this situation to know the smartest thing he could do was to get his fill, then cut his losses and walk away before any serious damage was done.

And when he did, he'd never look back.

1

Present day

WEARING NOTHING BUT A TOWEL, THE COCONUT-SCENTED BODY LOTION that she'd bought for the beach, and some splashy red polish on her toes, Reese Monroe walked into her new kitchen and took a split-second glance at the tall, muscular male standing with his back to her at the counter. Then she screamed bloody murder, terrified that the crazy-assed stalker she'd been hoping to ditch had followed her from Boston to Moss Beach. At the sound of her bloodcurdling scream, the dark-haired man instantly dropped the things in his arms, spun around, and held up his hands in a way that was obviously meant to put her at ease. But it wasn't helping. Now that she could see his face, Reese was horrified to realize he wasn't a stranger or stalker at all. Oh, God . . . she actually knew this guy!

She also knew this was one intruder who would never physically hurt her or intentionally try to frighten her. Still, her scream got louder, and he winced from the ear-piercing shriek.

Ben Hudson wasn't only the local sheriff in the popular beach town—he was also her brother-in-law's cousin and a friend of the family. And he was a great guy. The kind who danced with little blue-haired grannies at weddings and played touch football with all the kids at family get-togethers. Hard, tough, and probably a little mean when dealing with criminals, but the kind of man who would *never* harm a woman. He was also, hands down, the most gorgeous male Reese had ever laid eyes on. There wasn't even a close second.

So she was no longer screaming from fear. Now she was screaming from pure, overwhelming embarrassment. When she'd pictured running into Ben now that they were both living in Moss Beach, it sure as hell hadn't been looking like this, wrapped in a threadbare towel with her hair hanging in wet ropes around her freshly scrubbed face. She looked like a drowned rat and he looked . . . damn it, even better than the last time she'd seen him, which had been nearly six months ago. His brown, sun-streaked hair was a bit longer on top, as if he hadn't had it cut in a while, and there was a glint in his green eyes that hadn't been there when she'd run into him at Gary and Connie's Christmas party. A sharp sense of anticipation, as if he was looking forward to something he wanted. A lot.

Knowing Ben, he probably had a hot date that night. Thanks to her brother-in-law, Gary, Reese was plenty aware of Ben's wild reputation with women.

But what was he doing *here,* in her new home? She shook her head in confusion, wracking her brain for an answer, but her tired mind couldn't come up with a single explanation that made any sense.

Before she could manage to stop screaming long enough to ask him, Reese caught his heavy-lidded gaze slipping down her barely covered body, and embarrassment got the better of her. Without a single word, she turned, fleeing toward her bedroom in the back of the small, cozy beach house she'd only just moved into earlier that day. Slamming the door behind her, she pressed her hands to the cool wood, panting from shock and a dizzying spike of adrenaline. God, what a ridiculous wuss she was! Yes, she had never found it easy to be around guys like Ben, preferring mellow betas who didn't make her pulse race with nerves—but that didn't mean she had to go running from him like a ninny. Damn it, at twenty-eight she should have more poise than that. More self-possession. At least enough to ask him to sit down and wait while she put on some clothes.

Maybe it was just the stress of the divorce and the move and the long drive from Boston to Florida taking its toll—not to mention the freak who had been screwing with her life the past few months. She knew she should probably cut herself some slack, but it was galling to think about how she'd just reacted. Reese had wanted to start over in a new place where she could rebuild her sense of security and confidence. Instead, she was hiding out in her room while the mouthwatering Ben Hudson was standing in her kitchen. Why he was there, she didn't know. She hadn't even gotten a good look at what he'd dropped on the kitchen counter. But she was never going to find out what he was up to until she went back out there and talked to him.

Taking a deep breath, she started to push away from the door when a soft knock sounded on the other side, making her jump. "Hey, you okay in there?" he asked, the husky timbre of his deep voice all but melting her on the spot. The slight Southern twang only cranked the sexy to a dangerous level. Really, the guy should come with a freaking warning or something.

Reese nodded in response to his question, realized he couldn't see her, and managed a breathless, "Yeah . . . I'm okay."

"I'm sorry I scared you, Reese. I didn't expect you to be here. I saw your mom yesterday, when the movers were delivering your stuff, and she said you wouldn't be making it to town until this evening."

And so he'd taken it upon himself to spend what was probably his lunch hour breaking into her new home to hang out in her kitchen? This was like some kind of bizarre dream. And since when did Ben chat with her mother?

Wait a minute . . . He'd talked to her mother? *Well, crap.*

A horrible suspicion settled in her gut and her face burned. If her mother had put him up to this—whatever *this* was—Reese had little doubt she'd find herself headed for hell. A daughter who strangled her mother, even when it was deserved, was sure to burn for all eternity. Given the murderous rage pouring through her system, she'd probably end up so crispy she crackled.

"Reese?"

"I'm all right, Ben. I just . . . I need to get dressed," she forced from a dry throat, hoping he'd get the hint and go away.

"Okay." The low rumble easily filtered through the door. "I'll be in the kitchen. We can talk when you're ready."

She winced, thinking she would rather face off against her ex again than make friendly conversation with this man. Not that she didn't like Ben. He just flustered the hell out of her. She had no trouble talking to his too-cute-for-his-own-good younger brother, Michael, but when it came to Ben . . . *Whew.* It was crazy and embarrassing, but the few times she'd been around him in the past, she'd felt like a blushing virgin every time he looked at her. It was something in his eyes, or maybe the shape of his mouth. Something primitive and overwhelmingly sexual that made her breasts ache and her sex clench. Then there was that slow, deep drawl that stroked the surface of her skin, teasing everything womanly in her into a hot, frothing mass of nerves and need.

Her ex, Drew, had never managed to make her feel that way, even in the early stages of their relationship, when she'd thought they were crazy about each other. And by the end, Drew had merely treated her like a prop to wear on his arm to maintain a good public image, saving his sexual appetite for women he'd said—after she'd discovered him cheating—were not only more satisfying than Reese, but a hell of a lot more fun.

It'd been a huge blow to her ego. One she was still trying to pick up the pieces from, so that she could put herself back together again. Whenever she thought of the years she'd wasted with Drew Leighton, it made her want to scream . . . and curse . . . and take a baseball bat to his precious BMW. Better to focus on the fact that she'd finally broken away from the miserable jerk, ready to start living on her own terms.

And a woman living on her own terms doesn't hide in her own home. Even one on the run from a sicko stalker. So get a freaking backbone!

Right. So Ben Hudson made her nervous. So what? She'd deal with it, and find out exactly what he was doing in *her* house.

Tossing the towel aside, Reese maneuvered her way through the stacks of moving boxes, and grabbed a clean pair of panties and jeans from the duffle bag she'd thrown on the foot of her mattress. She shimmied her legs into the denim, then grabbed a bra and her favorite black tank top. Ripping a brush through her damp hair, she took the time to slick on a little lip-gloss, then forced herself to go back out there. If she spent too much time getting ready, he'd think she was primping for him, and she was already embarrassed enough. No sense in piling more mortification on her shoulders.

When she came back into the kitchen, Reese found the hunky sheriff placing a carton of milk in the small refrigerator nestled in the far corner of the room. A quick glance at the dark granite countertop showed the plastic bags she'd missed before, and she realized he was putting away groceries. What on earth?

"I figured you'd be beat from the drive," he offered in response to her unspoken question, placing another carton of milk in the refrigerator door, "so I stopped by the store and grabbed you a few things."

"Did my mother put you up to this?" She crossed her arms over her chest, the defensive stance matching her tone.

Closing the refrigerator door, Ben turned to look at her. His green eyes narrowed the tiniest bit as he matched her stance, crossing his muscular arms over a wide chest covered in a black polo shirt that sported the local sheriff's department logo on the upper left side. He leaned back against the counter, focusing on her with an unsettling intensity. One that went all the way down to her bones, making her shiver. She went hot and cold all at once, waiting for him to speak.

"Put me up to what?" he finally asked, the corner of his mouth twitching, almost as if he was fighting back a smile.

"Did she, um . . ." Crap. Reese suddenly realized how stupid she'd sound if she accused this man of letting her mother fix them up. He'd no doubt find the idea laughable. If she'd given herself a second to think about it, she'd have realized that he'd probably only brought her the groceries because he thought of her as something like a little sister. Someone he needed to look out for and help get back on her feet.

There was no way he could know about her stalker problem, because she'd intentionally kept the information from her family. Only a handful of people in Boston and the local police department who'd done the investigation were aware of what she'd been going through. But she had also recently been through a nasty divorce, and she knew Ben had probably heard plenty of gossip about *that* particular bit of news. Did he think the divorce had left her reeling and broken?

Aside from having a wicked reputation with women, Reese knew Ben had a thing about taking care of people who needed help. She was just going to have to make it clear to him that she *wasn't* one of those people. The idea of him pitying her, or thinking she was a wreck because of Drew, made her cringe.

With a deep breath, she decided to get the conversation back on track. "Look, I appreciate the groceries, Ben, and I don't mean to sound ungrateful, but how did you get in? I locked the front door before I jumped in the shower." And she'd checked it twice, just to be sure.

"I used the master key." He gave an easy shrug. "I would have knocked, but like I said before, I didn't think you were here yet."

Her brow scrunched with confusion. "You have a master key to my house?" Weird. Was that some local sheriff thing? He got to carry that wicked-looking gun holstered under his arm, handcuffs, *and* a set of keys to all the local houses? And how rude would she sound if she demanded he hand over the key that unlocked *her* door?

Dragging her gaze away from his chest, where it seemed to have gotten stuck, she found him studying her expression, his dark brows drawn together in a frown. "Uh, yeah. Look, Reese, didn't your mother tell you?"

She could sense from his tone that something bad was coming, and a knot formed in the pit of her stomach. "Tell me what?"

"I'm the landlord your mom signed the lease with. I own this place, as well as the one next door. That's where I live now. Bought both beach houses last year, after winning the election."

She blinked, certain she must have misheard him. "My mother rented this place for me . . . from *you*?"

"Yeah. That isn't going to be a problem, is it?"

"No," she lied, her calm tone belying the fact that she was definitely going to commit a deadly sin. Not even her undying love for the woman who had brought her into this world was going to keep her from wringing the lady's neck.

What in God's name had her mother been thinking? Reese had trusted her to find a pretty, peaceful place she could rent in the idyllic little beach town, while she still had her hands full in Boston, handling her scum-sucking ex and all that other nasty crap that had been crashing down on her. Just a few hours ago, sweet, beautiful, newly remarried Mom had been waiting on the doorstep of the picturesque beach house to greet a tired, travel-weary Reese when she arrived at her new home.

She'd thought the smile on her mom's face had been because she was happy to see her middle daughter out from under an unhealthy marriage and getting on with her life. Thought she'd been thrilled to have her living in the same town, close at hand. But no. Now she knew the truth. That happy twinkle in her mom's big blue eyes had been devious anticipation. All that'd been missing was the diaper and arrow, and the woman would have had the whole Cupid vibe down to a freaking T!

Damn it, her mother had to have noticed how nervous she got around Ben. It's not like Reese had been all that great at hiding it. And what had she done? The traitor had gone and rented her a place right next door to him!

Oh, no, strangulation was too easy. She was going to have to find a way to kill the woman that would be long and painful.

Reese was contemplating the various possibilities, when she noticed Ben still studying her. Collecting herself as best as she could, she pasted on a smile. A phony one, but she hoped he wouldn't notice.

It didn't work.

He not only noticed, he called her on it. "You're a lousy liar, Reese."

The bottom of her stomach dropped out. "It's, um, nothing personal, Ben. I just . . ." Damn it. She couldn't think of a single thing to say that wouldn't make her sound like an idiot. Even now, her heart was racing with a force that felt like pain.

Ben had always had this effect on her, which was one of the main reasons she got so nervous around him. She played it safe . . . and he'd always been too dangerous for her tastes. Too . . . everything. Until a year and a half ago, the guy had been a homicide detective in one of the most violent cities in the country. He was a serious badass who didn't let anything or anyone stand in his way. From what she'd heard, he liked to work hard, play hard, and fuck even harder. Those were Connie's words, not her own, but she knew they were true.

She also knew his rough edges would have most women panting after him like adoring little puppies, but they just made Reese feel out of her element. She wasn't some feisty, sophisticated maneater who could give Ben a run for his money. Instead, she was an introverted schoolteacher who was just crawling out from under an ugly divorce after what had turned out to be an even uglier marriage. About the only excitement she felt ready to handle these days were some quiet walks on the beach and an overindulgence of chick flicks.

And if her previously lax sex drive had suddenly decided to revolt on her simply because Ben Hudson had been sweet enough to stock her fridge and bless her with his sexy presence, she could tough it out. She wasn't going to be driven to idiocy by her glands, for God's sake. Which meant throwing herself at Ben's feet and begging for a piece of his seriously fine ass was *not* going to happen.

No matter how badly I want it to . . .

The dangerous thought had her blushing again, and it suddenly occurred to Reese that she'd just been standing there for the past minute or so, eating him up with her eyes . . . imagining what he looked like naked. And he knew. There was a kinda crooked, knowing grin on his lips as he watched her watching him.

If there'd been a hole in the ground, she'd have dived into it headfirst.

"I . . . uh . . ." Reese searched for something to say, her gaze darting around the room, but the situation had fried her brain. Or maybe that was just Ben.

"Where's your car?" he asked, changing the subject this time, when it became apparent she didn't have any idea what to talk about. She breathed a small sigh of relief, surprised that he hadn't pushed her for an explanation about why she wasn't comfortable with him living so close. Or maybe he just didn't care. She couldn't imagine her thoughts and feelings were all that important to a guy like Ben. He probably thought of her in the same way he thought of all the other plain, nice women in town. Women who were friendly acquaintances, but who were never going to make a blip on his sexual radar.

Trying to convince herself she didn't particularly want to be a blip on Ben Hudson's radar—which was a complete and total lie—Reese answered his question about her car. "It broke down about five miles up the road. I had to call and have it towed, but the guy from the garage was nice enough to drop me off."

"Dave?"

She nodded. "That's right."

"Well, if I'd seen your car outside," he told her, rubbing a hand across his hard jaw, "I sure as hell wouldn't have just let myself in."

"I'm sorry I reacted like that." She forced herself to hold his gaze and stop fidgeting. "With the screaming and all."

"Don't be. I'm sure I'd scream if I found some strange guy

unloading groceries in my kitchen." The corner of his mouth twitched again. "Especially if I happened to be bare-assed naked at the time."

"I wasn't naked," she argued with an embarrassed laugh. "I was wearing a towel."

"Come on, Reese." There was a bit of the devil in his glittering gaze. "The least you can do after splitting my eardrums is play along with my fantasy."

"About you stumbling upon some strange guy in your kitchen?" she snickered, arching her brows. She was surprised by how easy it was to tease him. And how much fun.

"Smart-ass," he shot back, the slow smile on his lips kicking her pulse even higher. Uncrossing his arms, he pushed his hands in the front pockets of his jeans, the casual position doing incredible things to his broad shoulders and his muscular bod. She wanted to ask how often he had to work out to look like that. Wanted to ask if the bump on his nose was from a fight or an old sports injury. If he'd always been this gorgeous, or if he'd grown into his rugged good looks as he got older . . .

She was saved from embarrassing herself when he asked a question of his own. "So, are you happy with the place?"

She nodded again, leaning her hip against the old-fashioned kitchen sink. "I love it. The hardwood floors and French doors are incredible. The whole house is beautiful."

"Good. I had a feeling you'd like it."

He had? The few times she'd been around Ben, he'd always been nice to her, but had more or less kept his distance. It seemed strange that he would think he knew her well enough to have any idea of her personal tastes.

"You seem . . . different," she murmured, surprised that she'd let that little observation slip out. She was usually better at keeping her thoughts to herself.

"You mean friendlier?"

"Um . . ." She hedged, not wanting to be rude.

"It's okay. It's true that I've never been all that talkative around you, but only because it put me in a bad mood."

She blinked again, wondering what he was talking about. "What put you in a bad mood? *Me?*"

He gave a masculine snort and shook his head. "It wasn't you. It was the fact you were married to that worthless prick and I couldn't do what I wanted."

Baffled, she asked, "And what was that?"

Her toes curled against the kitchen floor at the sound of his low, husky laugh. "Why don't you come out to dinner with me tonight and we'll talk about it then?"

Reese was embarrassed by the wide-eyed, deer-caught-in-the-headlights look she knew had just crashed over her face. He wanted her to go to dinner with him? She shook her head, thinking she must have heard him wrong. Men like Ben Hudson didn't date women like her. The conversation didn't make any sense, unless her mother really *had* put him up to this.

She stood up just a little bit straighter and scowled. "Whatever my mother might have told you, Ben, I don't need a sitter. I'm perfectly capable of taking care of myself."

The corners of his eyes crinkled with his look of confusion. "What are you going on about now?"

"My mother asked you to take me out, didn't she?"

This time, he was the one who blinked. Then he laughed, hard and deep. "You think I'm asking you out because of your mom?"

Shivering from the way that husky laugh affected her, Reese chewed on the corner of her lower lip. "Well, that's what this is all about," she said slowly. "Isn't it?"

His grin was boyishly crooked. "I like your mom, Reese. She's a great lady. But I'm not in the habit of letting her fix me up."

"I know you don't *need* to be fixed up. I only . . . I mean—"
She was definitely floundering here. "You, um, probably agreed
just to be nice."

His lashes lowered a little as he held her stare. "You really
think I'd do that?" he asked, his voice soft. "Ask you out because
I felt sorry for you?"

Wishing she was better at reading him, she managed a brief nod.

"Well, I hate to break this to you, but I'm actually not that nice
a guy." She heard the unspoken "when it comes to women" easily
enough, but didn't pay it any attention. She knew damn well that
Ben would have found it hard to tell her mother no.

"You're a lawman," she stated, as if that was explanation
enough. "Being nice to women is part of your job description."

"Only I'm not asking you out as the sheriff." He pushed away
from the counter, coming a little closer. "I'm asking you out as
a man."

"One I happen to know already has plenty of women waiting
to go out with him."

He frowned, but he didn't deny it. Ben might be a lot of things,
but at least he wasn't a liar like Drew. Instead, he simply said,
"You're the one I want to have dinner with. And it doesn't have a
damn thing to do with your mother."

With her pulse roaring in her ears, Reese licked her lips, unable
to believe what she was hearing. "What's going on, Ben?"

"Go out with me tonight," he coaxed, the look in his eyes even
darker than before. "Let me take you to dinner, and I promise
you'll be able to ask me anything you want."

"I . . . I can't." Breathless words, threaded with panic.

"Why not?"

She struggled for a valid reason, but couldn't come up with a
single one that didn't make her sound pathetic or crazy. "Just . . .
trust me when I say it wouldn't be a good idea."

He cocked his head a bit to the side. "You gonna let that jackass you were married to control the rest of your life?"

Shock skittered through her system. She had no idea how to respond to such a personal question from a man she didn't really know all that well. She had no idea what to think about any of this. "My decision to stay home tonight has nothing to do with my ex. I'm tired and I need to unpack."

He took a step closer, bringing a warm masculine scent with him that was so freaking good she had to bite back a moan. "Then I'll bring dinner over and help you."

He was so tall, Reese had to tilt her head back to hold his stare. "That's a nice offer, but I . . . I think it would be best if I have some time alone."

"From the way I see it," he countered in a soft rasp, "you've been alone long enough."

She sucked in a sharp breath, rubbing her hands over her upper arms, as if to ward off a chill. Which was odd, seeing as how she was burning up inside. "I think you should go now, Ben."

The look on his face said he didn't like being shut out, but Reese didn't have any other choice. She was too rattled to deal with him and the things he was saying . . . the way he was making her feel. There were too many raw emotions pressing in on her, weighing her down. Mountains of emotional baggage she didn't know how to cut loose, so that she could grab on to this unexpected, inexplicable offer of pleasure. He wouldn't even have to touch her. Just sitting across from him in a quiet restaurant, free to stare at him for as long as she wanted, would be more than she'd had in . . . in what felt like a long, wasted forever. But she couldn't do it. As much as she wanted that fresh start to start *now*, she couldn't shove past the walls that were pinning her in.

He didn't push her. But he didn't back down, either.

"I'll give you some space tonight," he told her, the look in his dark eyes hard with challenge, "but I'm only going to ask again tomorrow. And one way or another, Reese, you're going to say yes."

"To dinner?"

That bottle-green gaze settled on her mouth, and his voice got rougher. "For starters."

Reese stood frozen in place, breath locked in her lungs as he turned and left the kitchen. The front door opened and closed a few seconds later.

For a moment, she didn't move. Then she twisted around, looking out the tiny window over the sink just in time to catch a glimpse of him as he climbed into a big, black truck. She gripped the edge of the counter, watching as he backed out of the driveway and disappeared around the high wall of colorful hydrangea that shielded the two houses from the road.

Long after he'd driven away, Reese still stood at the window— her chest tight, heart pounding—wishing so badly that she'd had the courage to say yes. To dinner. To just spending time with him . . .

And to whatever the hell else Ben Hudson might want from her.

2

Ben knew a man was in deep shit when he was sitting across the table from one beautiful woman, but couldn't get another one out of his head. Granted, he wasn't fucking Brit Cramer. They were just friends. But he'd never had trouble giving her his complete attention before.

He probably should have passed when she called and asked if he wanted to meet her for dinner at McClain's. But he'd been wearing down his floorboards at home, too wound up by the knowledge that Reese was right next door. He couldn't calm the hell down, and that wasn't like him. No matter how shitty or stressful his life got, he'd always been able to kick back at the end of the day and enjoy some downtime. It was what kept him sane. But ever since he'd heard that Reese was getting divorced, he hadn't been acting like himself. Learning that she was determined to put some serious miles between her and that Ivy League ex of hers by relocating to Moss Beach had been a shock to his system. It'd messed with his mind.

Hell, it had him so twisted up inside he felt like a fucking pretzel.

And now that she was so close, he wanted her so badly he could taste the hunger. A seething, gut-burning craving that had been growing for three frustrating years, cranking higher every goddamn time he saw her . . . talked to her. Since that first night he'd met her at Gary's birthday party, he'd compared every woman he got involved with to Reese, and they came up lacking. It was as if she'd marked him or some weird shit like that, rewiring his brain.

And she'd never had a clue . . .

He shook his head, unable to wrap his mind around that bizarre revelation. Even her ex had known. The guy was an ass, but Drew Leighton hadn't been blind. Ben knew the man had sensed his primitive interest, and so the hotshot lawyer had made it a point to stick close to Reese whenever Ben had been around. Perceptive guy.

Just not a very smart one.

From what Ben had heard, once they were back in Boston, Drew had found it more fun playing with the women he worked with than with his wife. At the start of the new year, Reese had finally found out about Drew's philandering—word in her family was that she'd literally caught the idiot with his pants down—and she'd filed for divorce the next day. According to Gary and Connie, the divorce had gone fairly quickly because Reese didn't want anything but her personal savings. It took class and backbone to walk away from the life she'd had, but he shouldn't have been surprised. She was one of the classiest women he'd ever known.

And now she was here for good . . . his for the taking. The sooner the better, if he had anything to say about it, before he caused himself some kind of permanent damage. It'd been weeks since he'd had sex, and he was aching in a bad fucking way.

"Ben!"

He jolted at the sound of his name, and found himself staring into Brit's laughing face. A quiet curse crept past his lips. Damn, he'd spaced out right in the middle of her telling him about her latest dating disaster. And from the suspicious look in her hazel eyes, she had a good idea where his mind had wandered. Christ. Talk about awkward.

He might be a rough-edged son of a bitch, but he wasn't so much of an ass that he wanted Brit to feel ignored. She was a friend, damn it.

"Sorry," he offered, reaching for his beer.

She made a little snorting sound, lips curled in a wry smile. "I'm not mad. I was just a bit worried you were in the middle of a heart attack. You looked like you were in pain."

He choked back a laugh, thinking about the pain in his balls. "I've just got a lot on my mind tonight, but I promise not to keel over dead on you before dessert."

"You want to tell me about her?" she asked, taking a bite of her Caesar salad.

Oh, hell no. He wasn't buying that deceptively casual tone. The hairs on the back of Ben's neck stood up, signaling danger. He knew he was about to get grilled.

Refusing to go down easily, Ben lifted his brows. "Her?"

She took a sip of her white wine, studying him over the rim of the glass. "The woman who has you looking like you just swallowed a bellyful of frustration. What's the story, Hudson?"

Yeah, he knew that tone. Brit was a top-notch therapist who had helped scores of people with their issues. Ben respected the hell out of her intelligence and her sense of compassion—but that didn't mean he wanted her doling out any advice on the way he lived his life. Not that it ever stopped her.

"Don't start," he groaned. "I've had a shitty week. I'm not up to having my head examined tonight."

As dramatic as it sounded, it was true. On top of thinking about Reese every damn minute of the day, he'd dealt with a number of local crises in the county, from an illegal meth lab and dog-fighting ring to a couple of bone-chilling domestic violence cases. He really didn't want to talk about it—any of it—but Brit wouldn't let it go. She pressed until she got a brief overview of the events, if not any of the gritty details. But she'd worked with law enforcement officers and victims long enough to know how ugly things could get.

"You know, I thought you moved to the Gulf to take it easy," she grumbled with a fretful sigh. "But now you're busier than ever."

What did she want him to say? He wasn't an idle person. If there were things to be done, Ben wanted to be doing them. And the area, while beautiful and popular with tourists, had been in desperate need of a decent sheriff. Sure, he still had a lot to learn, but he was a damn sight better than the corrupt jackass he'd replaced. And he'd hired some great staff who worked their fingers to the bone, eager to make a difference.

A glance across the table showed that Brit was still waiting for him to say something. Leaning back in his chair, he pushed his free hand through his hair and made a conscious effort not to snap at her. "You know I like to keep busy."

"The doctors—" she started to say, but he cut her off.

"The doctors can kiss my ass." More than once, Ben had regretted telling Brit what his surgeons back in Miami had said after the shooting—the one that had prompted his move to Moss Beach. He didn't regret taking the bullets that had saved Ryan

Houghton's little girl—would do it again in a heartbeat—but the recovery had been a bitch. "That was two years ago. I'm fine now."

"Maybe, maybe not. You wouldn't admit it if you weren't, would you? Stubborn idiot."

Though he was used to her concern, Ben was too short on patience to deal with it tonight. "Stop acting like my mother, Brit."

Irritation flashed through her eyes. "Someone has to. If I don't, then you'll just keep—"

"Goddamn it, leave it alone!" he barked, slamming his beer bottle back on the table. "If I wanted your advice, I'd damn well pay for it."

She blinked, cast a quick glance around the restaurant to see if they'd attracted any curious stares, then frowned. "I didn't mean to piss you off," she murmured a moment later, making him feel like shit for losing his temper with her. "I just don't like seeing you like this. But I'm sorry for butting in."

"No, I'm sorry," he forced out, scrubbing a hand over his gritty eyes. "I'm in a crappy mood and you don't deserve it. I'm acting like a dick."

A smile twitched at the corner of her mouth. "Yeah, okay. I'll give you that one."

Ben shook his head and laughed. "You're too good to me, you know that?"

"And that's one of the things I love about you," she said, fighting a grin. "For such a hard-ass alpha, you're never afraid to say something mushy."

"That wasn't mushy. I just—"

"Stop scowling. It's not the end of the world to have a decent streak, you know. You may be *almost* as gorgeous as Christian Bale, but you—"

Ben cut her off with another husky laugh. "What is it with you and Christian Bale?"

"As if I need to explain." Stifling a shiver, she flicked her wavy red hair over her shoulder and theatrically fanned her face. "The man is freaking sex on legs."

"Well, if he ever visits Moss Beach," he drawled, smiling at her antics, "I'll make sure to detain him long enough that you get an introduction."

Her shoulders fell. "That's a sweet thought, but don't bother. He's married."

"Ahh." Enough said. Ben knew they shared the same view on infidelity.

"But just because I can't have Christian doesn't mean you can't get lucky in the love department," she murmured. "This woman you're thinking about *is* single, right?"

Ben gave a hesitant nod. "Divorced. And it's not love. It's . . . complicated."

"I'm sure it is," she said, hiding her smile behind her wineglass. "God knows you never do anything the easy way."

His tone got drier. "Thanks," he muttered, finishing the last bite of his steak.

"Speaking as your friend," she went on, "I think it's about time you got off your ass and went after her. You've been wound up about this mystery woman for far too long."

There were times when Brit's ability to read him freaked the hell out of Ben. "I haven't been—"

"Save it, Sheriff. I'm a trained professional. I know what I'm talking about."

He started to argue, then accepted defeat with a sharp sigh. "Shit."

She laughed softly. "So who is she?"

Wishing he had something stronger than his beer, he said, "One of Connie's sisters."

Her eyes widened with surprise. "The one who lives up north?"

Ben gave another nod as he slouched back in his chair, fiddling with the spoon that sat beside his plate. "She lived up there with her husband. Got divorced a few months ago and just moved down to Moss Beach."

The look of shock on Brit's face when he glanced her way again was almost funny. "Ohmygod, she's the woman renting your other house, isn't she?"

He fought the urge to squirm in his seat like a criminal under interrogation. "Yeah. Her name is Reese Leighton. Actually, she's taken her maiden name again, so she's a Monroe now."

Brit seemed to take a moment to process, then asked, "What does she think of you?"

He shrugged, the question making him restless. "I don't really know. We have chemistry, but she's gun-shy."

Brit grinned. "And you're not known for being patient."

What the hell did she think was so funny? "I've been patient for three fucking years. I'm at my limit."

He could see the wheels turning in her head. "But Reese doesn't know that, does she?"

"I don't know what she's thinking." He stared sightlessly at his empty plate, replaying the scene with Reese from that afternoon through his mind. "I would have thought it was obvious. Her ex picked up on it right from the start. But she doesn't seem to think she's the kind of woman I'd date."

"So she's shy and a little low on self-confidence. Did the ex screw around on her?"

Ben responded with a jerky nod, his jaw tight. "He's a total prick."

Brit leaned forward and braced her crossed arms on the table, her expression sincere . . . but serious. "Ben, if there's a chance you could really feel something for this woman, then I say go for it and don't let anything stop you. I love you and I want you to be happy. But . . . and I hate to say this, but if you're just planning on fooling around with her and moving on, then you need to take a step back and really think about what you're doing. She's already been through enough."

He choked back a low curse. "You never know. A hot affair might be just the thing she needs to get back on her feet."

"And if it isn't? If she falls in love with you? What then? And how is it going to work with her living right next door to you? Have you thought about how she's going to feel when you bring another woman home with you?"

"I don't bring women to my place. I go to theirs," he muttered, rolling his shoulder. "And I plan on parting as friends."

"God, Ben," she said on a quiet laugh. "Sometimes you just don't think. How is she—"

He cut her off with another scowl and a growled response. "You don't think you're jumping ahead here? The woman isn't in love with me, Brit."

"You're right." Her eyes narrowed. "And you never know. Maybe it'll be *your* heart that gets broken. And if that happens, how do you think you're going to feel watching *her* bring the next guy home?"

"I'll handle it," he ground out, while inside his gut was churning. The idea of some other man shoving his cock inside Reese's firm little body made him see red. He'd never been the jealous type, but he knew damn good and well that he'd want to take apart the first guy who even looked at her with interest. Which meant he was in one hell of a screwed up situation.

He didn't want to keep her forever—but he didn't want any other man keeping her, either.

Fuck.

Maybe renting the beach house to Reese hadn't been his brightest idea, but damn it, he'd seen it as the perfect opportunity to gain access to her, and he'd grabbed it. And it's not like there was any use in second-guessing the decision at this point, because he wouldn't do it differently, even with Brit's warnings. He'd deal with that other shit later, if it became an issue. He couldn't worry about it now, when he couldn't stop thinking about how to get Reese where he wanted her. Which was on her back, with her legs spread, and *his* cock buried so deep inside her she could taste him at the back of her throat. He wasn't known for holding back when it came to sex, but he had a feeling that Reese was going to push even his own limits. Once he finally got his hands on her, she'd be lucky if she could walk the next day.

Hell, he was so jacked up, he might not even let her out of bed for the first week.

The waiter came and cleared the table, taking their order for two coffees and a couple of slices of McClain's famous cheesecake. As soon as he walked away, Brit asked, "So what's she like?"

"Beautiful. Smart. Funny." There was a wealth of gruff pride in his voice, as if Reese was already *his* to brag about. An odd reaction on his part—and one that he'd sure as hell never experienced before. "She works as a special needs teacher, or at least she did. I'm not sure what she plans to do now that she's relocated to Florida."

A speculative gleam started to burn in Brit's eyes. "She sounds like someone I'd like to have as a friend. And in case it never occurred to you, that's a big departure from the norm, seeing as how your girlfriends usually just grate on my nerves."

"They weren't my girlfriends. Those women were just . . ."

She raised her brows. "Your bimbos? Fuck-buddies?"

His chest rumbled with a gritty laugh. "I get the point. You think I'm a man-whore."

She blinked with mock innocence. "I never said that!"

"You say it all the time," he responded in a wry drawl.

Brit scrunched her nose. "Hmm . . . I do, don't I? Guess it must
be true."

They were still grinning when the waiter delivered the coffee
and desserts. Brit swallowed a bite of cheesecake, then got right
back on topic. "So, have you thought about how Reese is going to
react to your . . . um . . ."

"My what?"

She blew out a short breath. "Look, I'm not judging, Ben. But
it's no secret that your sexual activities are . . . well, rumored to be
a bit on the wild side. Granted, you've toned things down since
taking the job as sheriff, but still . . . Emotional issues aside, have
you considered how compatible the two of you will be sexually?"

"You sound like a freaking therapist," he muttered.

"I *am* a therapist. But I'm talking as your friend. You're going
to feel like shit if you—"

"Leave it." He didn't want to continue this conversation, her
words hitting a nerve. He knew the odds were high that Reese
would be uncomfortable with a lot of the things he'd want from
her. He wouldn't push her—but he wouldn't let her shy away from
him, either. Getting his fill was going to require a lot of hot, sweaty
hours between the sheets . . . or anywhere else they happened to
end up. He couldn't promise that he wouldn't shock her at times,
but he damn well planned to make sure she enjoyed every second
of her time with him. He'd never wanted to make any woman
come as badly as he wanted to watch and feel Reese coming apart
in his arms, shivering and screaming and blowing his ever-loving
mind.

Brit waited until they'd finished their desserts before making
another comment. Pushing her empty plate aside, she studied his
expression as she said, "I don't think it's going to be easy, but I
hope it all works out. I'm keeping my fingers crossed that you
won't be a jackass and let her slip away."

Ben locked his jaw, knowing that Brit wouldn't understand how he could be happy with the idea of a sexual fling and not want something more than that. But it was exactly what he wanted. He'd seen too many doomed men go down the romance and relationship road to ever make the same mistake himself. If his parents' fucked-up marriage hadn't persuaded him to avoid getting too serious with any one woman, his older brother's shitty experience would have convinced him that Hudson men were better off on their own. Fewer complications that way, and a hell of a lot less damage.

Still, something about the situation with Reese told him he should be on his guard. There was just something about the way he wanted her that kicked him a little too hard in the gut, making him edgy and a little uneasy. He wasn't one of those guys who claimed bachelorhood was the life, then turned around and married the first woman who wrapped him around her little finger. Ben knew what he was capable of . . . and what he wasn't. And he didn't need to pay for a therapy session with Brit to have his personality profiled when he already knew what she'd say. That his rocky childhood had stunted his ability to place emotional trust in another person. That what happened to his older brother, Alex, had then compounded his fear of emotional intimacy. He'd heard it all before, as well as her theory that he put his life on the line so often because he didn't care all that much about living. Which he thought was bullshit. He didn't want to die. He just couldn't stand scumbags walking around hurting innocent people, when they should be suffering behind bars.

And just because he couldn't stomach the concept of marriage didn't mean he was in the wrong. It was just a part of who he was. The idea of a wife and kids would be his worst fucking nightmare.

And that's just another line of bullshit, Hudson.

Taking a deep breath, he tried to force the irritating voice inside his head back into silence, knowing better than to listen to it. But the damn thing wouldn't shut up.

You're just afraid to let yourself care, because you don't want to be screwed over. Because you're terrified of finding someone, and then losing her.

Ben choked back a guttural curse, wondering what the hell was wrong with that. There were times when the world could be a miserable cesspool of violence and danger. Psychotic assholes prowling the night, picking their victims at random. No order to the chaos. Almost impossible to protect against it. Jesus, just the thought of falling in love with some woman, marrying her, and putting babies in her belly made him break out in a cold sweat. How the fuck would he deal with the worry without smothering the ones he loved and driving them bat-shit?

So you'd be protective? murmured the voice. *That's not a bad thing. And think of all the good that could come from it . . .*

He started to shrug that aside, when his gaze landed on the young family sitting at the next table over. Pregnant mom, glowing in that way that only an expectant mother could. Proud dad helping his curly-haired toddler get a grip on his sippy cup, while giving his wife a private smile. They looked ridiculously happy. In love. Blissed out and mad for each other, unabashedly excited about the future and their little growing army of rug rats.

See what I mean? the voice prodded. *They don't look like they're suffering the torments of hell.*

Yeah, all right, so he could see the good when looking at this family. But that didn't mean it was a scenario that would work in his own life. He was a Hudson, after all. His dad had tried, again and again, only to crash and burn. And Alex had barely survived his shot at love and marriage. In each situation, Ben had been the one to pick up the pieces when everything went to shit. The one who forced them to keep on going, refusing to let them slide into a slow, whiskey-flavored death, stubborn bastard that he was. And he'd learned from the experience. He might die old and alone, but at least he wouldn't have let a woman drag his balls through the wringer and tear his bloody heart out. As badly as he wanted her, he wouldn't even allow Reese to have that kind of power over him.

Not now. Not ever.

But hell, he thought, scrubbing his hands down his face. *Why am I even doing this to myself?* There was no reason for him to be crunching this emotional shit through his mind in the middle of McClain's, getting wound up by Brit's advice and a damn voice in his head. The last thing in the world Reese would be looking for, after coming out of a crappy marriage, was to get serious with anyone. If anything, she should be on the prowl for a rebound fling, and that he could *easily* provide, once he got past her defenses.

It was a perfect scenario . . . so long as he could get Reese to agree.

Ben was still lost in thought, when Brit's voice suddenly cut into his private musings for the second time that night, bringing him back to the moment. Almost as if she'd been reading his mind, she gave him an apologetic smile, and said, "I know you're a good guy, Ben, but just . . . don't make Reese any promises you can't keep. Make sure she knows what she's getting into, right from the start. Even if it means you lose your chance with her."

3

Ben squinted at Brit across the table, a little surprised by her words. He thought she knew him better than that. "You really think I would ever lie to get what I want from a woman?"

Her tone was wry, and maybe even a little sad. "You're a male, aren't you?"

He shook his head. "You're gonna eat those words one day," he shot back, hoping he'd be there to see it when some brave man finally broke through her shields and rocked her world. Ben would love the guy, just so long as he treated Brit like a queen.

After they'd finished their coffees and walked outside, into the humid, sea-scented night, he kissed her on the cheek, agreeing to meet her at the beach party her practice was throwing the following day, then headed home. As he pulled into his driveway, Ben could see the lights on in Reese's house through the flower-covered trellis that separated the two properties. He parked the truck, wondering if she'd thought about him that evening. Had she regretted not taking him up on his offer for dinner? Or was she so wrapped up in starting her new life that she hadn't even given him a second thought?

He wanted to go over there, just to see her. Talk to her. But she'd looked so freaked out that afternoon, he reckoned he should give her some time. He didn't like it, but he also didn't want to push her to the point that she panicked and shut him out completely. Not that he'd let her, but he was trying to get on her good side, damn it. It wasn't going to help his cause if he started acting like a bullheaded jackass.

Resigning himself to the fact that he wouldn't be able to see her until tomorrow, he climbed out of his truck and set the alarm.

As he made his way to his front door, Ben gave a soft laugh, recalling the look of shock that had settled over Reese's face when he'd told her he was her new landlord. As soon as he'd learned her mom was looking for a place for her to rent, he'd suggested the beach house. But he hadn't realized the woman would keep that information to herself. He'd figured she had put the lease in her own name to keep Reese's ex from being able to track her down, which was fine by him. He didn't want the bastard bugging her. Drew Leighton might have screwed around on his wife, but Ben had no doubt the prick was missing her now that she'd bailed.

The night air was warm and thick as he singled his house key out from the others on his key chain, the roar of the surf a soothing backdrop to the nearby sounds of late-night beach parties and blaring music. Making a mental note to call one of his deputies if the music hadn't let up by midnight, Ben unlocked his door and started to head inside, when he heard something that sounded like breaking glass.

What the fuck? This wouldn't be the first time that a group of drunken partygoers had wandered up from a beach bonfire onto the patio that ran the length of both houses in the back. The last time it'd happened, he'd found a couple of local teens going at it on one of his lounge chairs. They'd had the crap scared out of them when they realized they'd trespassed onto the sheriff's private property, and had taken his warning seriously not to let it happen again. But the beach attracted so many partiers during the summer months, there was no telling who it might be this time.

Pulling his door shut, Ben made his way around the side of his house, hoping Reese hadn't heard anything. He didn't want her wandering outside and having to deal with a bunch of shit-faced teens. They were harmless enough, but who knew what they might say to her?

The moon cast a silvery glow over the long patio as he climbed up the two steps that led to the raised platform of wooden planks. A rustle in the hedge that ran along Reese's side of the patio signaled the departure of whoever had made the racket. Ben figured they must not be too drunk, if they were smart enough to make for cover, instead of heading straight out to the beach, where he could have easily seen them. He looked around, spotting a few empty beer bottles on one of the tables, but didn't see any broken ones. Then he turned toward Reese's house and muttered a curse.

Son of a bitch. The idiots had thrown one of the bottles, breaking a long pane of glass in the French doors that led to her living room.

He was walking over to take a closer look when he heard her voice. "Ben? Is that you?"

Shifting his gaze, he caught sight of her as she came around the far corner of the house, a heavy hammer gripped tight in her right hand. "Yeah, it's me," he called out. "You okay?"

"I'm fine." Looking relieved to see him, she quickly set the hammer down on the corner of an oversize flowerpot brimming with dahlias, crossed her arms over her chest, and headed toward him. Her dark gaze flickered between him and the shattered pane in the door. "What happened?"

"Summer break," he said, eyeing her getup. She had on a gray cotton nightshirt and a pair of white, unlaced Converse high-tops. It was an odd combination, but looked adorable on her, those damn freckles on her face only adding to her appeal. "I think some of the kids from one of the bonfires were on our patio," he added, his voice a little gruffer than before. "Looks like they tossed a bottle and it broke your door."

She seemed worried . . . and maybe a little nervous about running into him. "Did they leave any kind of message?" she asked, scanning the patio with a troubled look.

"A message?"

"Yeah." She brought her gaze back to his and wet her lips. "Like a note or something?"

"Reese, this wasn't someone who knew you. It was just some kids screwing around. You don't need to be scared."

Taking a deep breath, she asked, "Does this happen a lot?"

"Naw. They've wandered up here a few times, but they've never caused any damage to the property. I'll have the patrols increased on the beach for the next few weeks. That should keep things calm."

She caught her lower lip in her teeth as her gaze shifted toward the damage, but he could sense her watching him from the corner of her eye. "I'm sorry about the door."

"Don't worry about it," he told her, wondering if she could feel that strange current arcing between them, like an electrical pulse in the air. "I can call someone out to repair it tomorrow. I'm just glad you weren't hurt."

A slight shrug sent the scoop-neck shirt sliding off one smooth shoulder, streams of moonlight reflecting off the pale luster of her skin. She looked so silky and soft it was killing him, his hands itching at his sides to reach out and grab hold of her.

"It just startled me," she was saying, careful to keep her arms crossed over her breasts. "I was getting ready for bed when I heard the noise."

At the mention of bed, Ben's gaze took another heated sweep over her body, settling on the bare length of thigh revealed beneath the nightshirt. Her legs were sleekly muscled and toned, and he wondered if she'd be taking runs on the beach. If she did, he had every intention of going along with her.

She cleared her throat into the breath-filled silence, drawing his hot gaze back up to her face. "What about your date?" She cast a quick look over his jeans and white polo shirt. "Is she waiting back at your place?"

"She isn't here," he replied, pushing his hands in his pockets. "And it wasn't a date. I just had dinner with a friend."

"Oh . . . well, I hope you had a good time."

He sighed, knowing damn well what she was thinking. "You can stop looking at me like that, Reese."

"Like what?" she asked, sounding wary . . . and a little confused.

"Like I've just screwed around on you."

A flurry of emotions raced across her face, those dark blue eyes suddenly shocked big and wide. "I don't know what you're talking about. We're friends, Ben. At least I hope we are. You're obviously free to sleep with whoever you want."

"I didn't sleep with her." Tension bunched across his shoulders, climbing up the back of his neck.

Her gaze skittered away, bouncing off random pieces of patio furniture, before settling on the distant crashing waves of the sea. She swallowed hard, her voice tight when she spoke. "Well, that's, um, not really any of my business."

"Look at me, Reese."

She made a sharp sound of exasperation, but finally locked her narrow gaze with his. Ben closed the distance between them until she had to crane her head back to hold his stare, the slight breeze blowing several strands of dark, gleaming hair across her cheek.

"I may be a lot of things, but I'm not a liar. If I said I didn't fuck her, then I didn't fuck her."

She blinked up at him. Took a single step back. "I . . . I'm going to head on to bed now. I'll, uh, see you . . . around."

Ben stopped her retreat by reaching out and grabbing her upper arm. "You can't sleep alone with a broken door."

Chin raised, she struggled to pull her arm from his grip, but he wasn't letting her go. "It's a safe town," she argued, glaring up at him. "You said so yourself."

"We're still on the beach, and the coast is always going to have its share of trouble. I've scheduled to have an alarm put in, but the installation isn't until next week. So it's smart to be careful, Reese. A single woman living on her own can't afford to take any chances."

Beneath that impish spray of freckles, her face went pale. "Are you trying to scare me?"

Ben kept a firm hold on her arm. "No. I'm not saying lock up and hide. And this *is* a safe place to live, or I wouldn't have leased you the beach house. But it's stupid to take any chances. I'll bunk down on your couch tonight, and we can get the door fixed tomorrow."

"Oh . . . that's not necessary. I can just go stay with my mom for the night," she said in a rush, renewing her efforts to free her arm. He didn't want to hurt her by gripping too tightly, so he grabbed the short sleeve of her shirt instead.

"There's no reason to go worrying your mother," he said in a low voice, fisting her sleeve in his hand.

She sent a stunned look from his hand to his face. "Really, Ben, this is ridiculous." Her voice was even tighter than before. "I can take care of myself. And I'm sure you have someplace else to—"

"Damn it, there isn't another woman waiting for me," he ground out, frustration searing through his veins. "I was out with a *friend* tonight. Her name is Brit Cramer and I expect the two of you are gonna hit it off great when you meet. Brit and I have been friends for a long time now, but we've never dated. End of story." He tugged on the sleeve, pulling her a little closer. Close enough that he could scent the toothpaste on her breath. See the gold flecks shimmering in the midnight blue depths of her eyes. "And even if I had been out on a date, I wouldn't have slept with the woman. You wanna know why?"

Her eyes flared—but with panic, not fear. "I think you should go—"

"Don't." Ben grabbed on to her other arm, holding her in place. "Stop telling me to leave the second we start talking about something that makes you nervous."

"Everything you say makes me nervous!" she burst out, her body trembling beneath his hands.

He took a deep breath, struggling for patience . . . for sanity, when all he really wanted was to take her down to the ground and make her come. *Hard.* As many times as it took, until she lost that strained look on her face and the tension drained from her muscles, leaving her mellow and melting and eager for more.

But it's not gonna happen tonight, you oversexed jackass. So get it together before you freak her out.

Striving for a measure of control, he managed to say, "I'm sorry about that. I don't want you to be nervous around me. That's the *last* thing that I want."

"Why are you doing this, Ben?" She licked her lips, breathing hard. "Is this some kind of challenge thing? You're making a play for me because you think you can't have me or something?"

He narrowed his eyes. "Stop being so damn cynical. Is it so hard to believe that I want you simply because you're you?"

"Ah, yes." Her laugh was brittle. "It is, actually."

Ben pulled her closer, hating the pain he could see clouding her eyes, like a shadow falling over a flame, dulling the glow. "I plan on spending a lot of time with you, Reese. And yeah, I want to fuck you. But I'm willing to wait if that's—"

"Wait? Wait for what?" she demanded, cutting him off. Her cheeks burned with color.

It took a moment for Ben to figure out what he wanted to say. "For you to realize that it's something you need as badly as I do."

"Wow. I, uh, suppose I should be flattered," she said dazedly, blinking up at him. "But, God, Ben. Your ego is unbelievable."

Desperation knotted his stomach. "That's not ego talking. It's fact. There's something between us. I felt it the first time we met, and it's gotten stronger every damn time we've been in the same room together. I know this is a shitty time for you, but we'll figure it out. Just . . . don't shut me out."

"This is crazy," she argued, wetting her lips again. "For all we know, we don't even have any chemistry."

Ben gave a harsh laugh. "That's such bullshit," he grunted, yanking her up on her toes and pulling her against him.

"What are you doing?" she gasped, wriggling in his hold, her nipples pressing thick and tight against his chest. He'd known she wasn't wearing a bra, but feeling the proof nearly killed him.

"One kiss, Reese." His pulse was roaring, his dick so hard he could have hammered nails with the damn thing. "Just one, and I can guarantee you won't ever throw that ridiculous excuse in my face again."

Before she could protest or tell him no, Ben lowered his head and took possession of her soft mouth, pouring three long years of need into a kiss that was deep and hard and explicit. Her lips were sweet and plump beneath his, her mouth deliciously hot, like melting honey. He swept his tongue against hers with raw hunger, licking and teasing, making the kiss as sexual as it could be. Sensing her shock, he tried not to push too hard too fast, but it wasn't easy. She tasted like sin and felt like something that belonged in his arms, her firm little body shivering against him, cranking his lust up to a dark, dangerous level. It was so fucking perfect it was scary.

No chemistry? Like hell. They burned so hot he was a hairsbreadth away from pumping his cum out in his pants like some sex-starved virgin.

"Okay!" she panted, tearing her mouth away as she struggled for breath. "You . . . you made your point."

His laugh was low and rough. "Not nearly." He caught her mouth again so that he could go back for a deeper taste, bending her head back, the feel and flavor of her making him crazed. His control started to slip away in a heated rush, sliding through his fingers, but he couldn't stop. Taking her mouth in another blistering kiss, Ben buried one hand in the back of her hair and shoved the other into the back of her panties, palming her ass. Her skin was silky and smooth, cool to the touch, and he made a thick, primitive sound in the back of his throat, nipping the lush swell of her bottom lip.

"This is a mistake," she gasped as he lifted her higher, her legs automatically wrapping around his waist. Her arms curled around his broad shoulders, holding tight, eyes bright with a wild blend of excitement and panic as she locked her gaze with his again. "I mean . . . we're neighbors, Ben."

"We are. But it's too fucking good to be a mistake," he growled against her lips, fighting for control, knowing he couldn't push this too far tonight, no matter how badly he wanted to. She'd just retreat and hide from him, or slap his face and tell him to get lost. She might still be finding her feet after her divorce, but Ben had no doubt that Reese could be tough as nails when she needed to be.

He was playing with fire, but he couldn't pull back before having just a little more of her.

Damn it, there was so much that he wanted. He needed to have his mouth on that soft, freckled skin. Needed the shirt out of his way so that he could lift her up and taste her nipples. Lick and suck on them until she came so hard she screamed. He was hard and aching to the point of pain, ready to throw her onto the nearest flat surface and fuck the living hell out of her—but he choked it back, blood pounding, allowing himself nothing more than a tighter grip on that beautiful heart-shaped ass.

Then his grip slipped lower, her tender sex pressing hot and wet against his callused palm, and Ben couldn't stop his thumb from stroking between those firm ass cheeks. She gave a sharp cry against his mouth when the pad of his thumb rubbed across her tight little hole back there, so he did it again. She cried out a second time, wriggling in his hold, and he muttered a rough curse, imagining how good it was going to be when he took her there. She'd likely fight him on it, but Ben wasn't going to let her hide behind her embarrassment. She might be shocked, but the way her hands had just tangled in his hair, her mouth wild beneath his, told him she instinctively liked it. He stroked her again, wanting to push his thumb into the puckered entrance, but held back. There was another hole he wanted inside even more, and he dipped his thumb lower, swiping it across the slick surface of her vulva.

"*Ben!*" She broke away from his mouth to drag in shivering gulps of air as he rimmed the tiny opening with the callused pad of his thumb. Her vulva was hot and drenched, a little swollen, and impossibly tender. She was so wet her juices were slicking across his hand, slippery and warm, his cock so rigid and full he could have gone off with little more than a stroke. When she tightened her legs and rubbed against him, his damn eyes nearly rolled back in his head.

"You have the softest, wettest little cunt," he breathed into her ear. Pushing the top of his thumb inside her, Ben tested the delicate opening, a hard shudder wracking his body, muscles clenched so tight they ached. "I want my tongue in here," he growled, slipping his thumb a bit deeper, knowing damn well he was treading a dangerous line, playing hard and fast with his control.

Have to keep it together. Can't scare her off. Just need to keep her on the edge . . .

Burying his face in the crook of her shoulder, he scraped his teeth along the sensitive tendon at the side of her throat, unable to get enough of her taste . . . her scent. With her strong, cushiony little pussy muscles clamping down on his thumb, he asked, "You like coming in a man's mouth, Reese?"

She moaned, tilting her head to the side to give him better access, and he couldn't stop himself from shoving his thumb all the way inside, thrusting it deep. A sexy cry jerked from her throat, all those plush inner muscles closing in slick and tight around him, causing another powerful surge of blood to rush straight to his cock.

"I'll take that as a yes," he whispered in her ear, wishing he could strip her naked, tie her up on her bed, and taste every single soft, shivering inch of her right the fuck *now*. "When you're ready, I won't hold back on you, Reese. I'll have my mouth between your legs, giving this sweet pussy a deep, slow tongue-fuck every god-damn chance I get. I'll eat you out so often, you'll find yourself creaming every time I look at you."

She made a breathless sound of need, digging her nails into his shoulders.

Knowing he'd reached his limit, Ben forced himself to pull his thumb from her snug grip—but couldn't resist stroking the slick pad across that other sensitive hole again. "And sometimes, after I've spent hours buried in your juicy little cunt, I'll even fuck you here."

She jolted in his grip, limbs tensing with shock. "No. You don't really—"

"Shh." Using the hold he had on her hair, Ben forced her to meet his stare. "Don't look at me like that," he said, taking in her fiery blush and scandalized gaze. He rubbed a little harder with his thumb, deliberately stroking the tight, sensitive flesh. "It might sound strange to you now, but I promise that when I get my cock in here, you'll love every second of it."

Her face got redder, eyes dilated until the blue was nearly overwhelmed by a glittering sea of black. "I haven't ever . . ."

"I know you haven't," he growled. "But you *will*."

"I . . . uh . . . please, just put me down," she said shakily, suddenly struggling to get out of his arms, pushing against his shoulders. With a rough breath, Ben pulled his hand from her panties and lowered her until her feet touched the ground. She stumbled back, coming up against the rear wall of the house, right beside the French doors, the broken slivers of glass crunching under the rubber soles of her shoes. While he stared, she slumped there against the white planks of wood, panting, face still flushed, the look in her dark eyes wary and nervous.

His dick felt strangled inside his jeans, so he reached down to adjust the angle, and her gaze followed his movements, mouth parting when she got an eyeful of the thick bulge trapped behind the button fly. She shook her head with a frantic movement, long hair swishing over her shoulders. "You must be crazy . . ." she started to say, the rushed words lost in another gasp when he moved toward her.

Ben took her hot face in his hands, tilting her head back, his thumbs stroking across the burning warmth of her blush. "I swear I won't hurt you." He touched his thumb to the edge of her kiss-swollen lips, his gaze focused and hot, heart hammering in his chest like something trying to pound its way out. "But I won't let you hide from me, either."

"Jesus, Ben, where did this come from? You hardly know me."

It took considerable effort, but he managed to drag his gaze off her ripe, fuckable mouth and back up to her glittering eyes. His breathing was ragged. "I know you, Reese. I've been watching you for three goddamn years. Since the moment I met you, I've just been waiting for the right time."

She swallowed, her pink tongue flicking nervously over her lips. "But I didn't . . . I never . . ."

"I don't know how you missed it. Everyone else knew damn well what I wanted. *Everyone.*"

Her brows drew together with a frown. "Even Drew?"

"Yeah, that arrogant shit knew. Dumbass bastard. I'd fuck you right in front of him if we got the chance, just to show him what he's missing."

She lowered her gaze, a bitter laugh on her lips as she stared at his chin. "I doubt he'd think he was missing much."

"Don't," he grunted, the guttural command jerking her gaze back to his. "Just because he was too dickless to handle you, to give you what you needed, doesn't mean shit. It's going to be good between us, Reese. It's gonna be fucking incredible."

Pulling her lower lip through her teeth, she asked, "What do you want, Ben?"

He rubbed his thumb over her freckled cheek, unable to get enough of how soft her skin was. "Just you," he said in a low voice. "That's all I'm after."

Doubt clouded her eyes as she met his stare. "But for what? You want a one-night stand? An affair? A fling?"

He fought back a grimace, Brit's warnings echoing inside his head. "Do we have to put a label on it? Why can't we just enjoy each other for as long as it lasts?"

She looked as though she didn't know what to say, and while he didn't like it worth a damn, Ben sensed it was time to ease off and give her some space. "We can talk about it more tomorrow," he said, taking a step back. "You must be exhausted. Let's go inside and get to bed."

Her mouth dropped open, and he grinned as he reached out to tap it shut. "I'll sleep on the couch, Reese. All I need is a pillow and a blanket."

"Uh, right. Okay." She started to walk away, one hand pushing a lock of hair behind her ear.

"Be careful of the glass," he cautioned.

"You, too," she said, stopping to look back over her shoulder. She stared at him in the hazy moonlight, her expression curious . . . but wary. His pulse quickened, and he had to shove his hands in his pockets to keep from reaching out and grabbing hold of her again.

Quietly, she said, "I can't really believe this is happening."

Ben locked his jaw, not trusting what he might say. He didn't know what expression he wore at that moment, but whatever it was, it didn't scare her off, thank God. With a shy smile tucked into the corner of her mouth, she turned her head and walked inside, the movement of her hips beneath the cotton shirt drawing his eye.

Lust burned like a grass fire under his skin, along with a dangerous surge of emotion he didn't dare look at too closely.

Keep it simple. Fuck her out of your system, and then get on with your life.

Right. It was sound advice, but as he followed Reese inside, something that felt like fear twisted in his gut at the thought of her slipping out of his reach. He flinched, wondering what the hell was wrong with him.

Just get your fill of her, and then you can move on.

Just get what you need, and everything will go back to normal . . .

Ben repeated the mantra again and again, forcing the words through his cramped mind . . . and hoped to God it would be that easy.

4

Burying her face in her pillow to avoid the Florida sunshine pouring in through the slanted shutters, Reese moaned as Ben's words from the night before came back to her. His language had been shocking—but she'd have been lying if she'd said it hadn't been sexy as hell. She'd never had a man talk like *that* to her before, so raw and unrestrained, but she'd liked it. Those wicked words had just seemed so right coming from Ben's mouth, his provocative tone deep and dark and wildly erotic. And the longer they'd fooled around, the stronger his accent had gotten, until his words were melting together in a smooth, rumbling drawl. Even when he'd been growling at her.

She still couldn't believe that he'd kissed her. Couldn't believe that she'd been in town less than twenty-four hours, and he'd already had his hand in her pants!

She also couldn't believe that at this moment, Ben Hudson was in her house, in the other room, sleeping on *her* couch. Her heart raced at the thought of getting up and facing him, but taking a deep breath, she forced herself to look at the situation logically. Despite what he'd said about being interested in her for a long time now, Reese knew it was probably just a line. The guy was good with women, which meant he was good at telling them what they wanted to hear. She didn't think there was anything malicious in what he'd done, claiming an interest that likely had more to do with her being nearby and available than any long-term attraction. If anything, she should probably be flattered that he was interested in her at all, since she knew she wasn't his usual type. "Tall, blond, and stacked" was how Connie had described the women she'd seen Ben with over the years. The description might have fit her younger sister to a T, but it was worlds away from Reese.

When the phone she'd only just plugged in last night suddenly rang on her small bedside table, she quickly grabbed it, hoping the sound hadn't woken him. Before she could even say hello, her sister's bright voice filled her ear. "Morning, sunshine! How was your first night in the new place?"

"Interesting," she replied, thinking Connie really needed her husband back in town. Gary had spent the past few weeks overseas for work, and Connie was clearly at loose ends without him if she was up this early. Normally she was a late sleeper and Reese was the one calling to wake *her* up.

It took Connie no more than two seconds to pick up on the nerves in her voice. "Interesting how? What happened?"

Clutching the phone against her ear, Reese sat up and pressed her back against the bare wall she'd pushed her mattress against. "Well, some kids that had been partying on the beach threw a bottle at my French doors, shattering the glass."

"Those immature jerks! Are you okay?"

"I'm fine. Um, Ben Hudson, who lives next door, came over and . . . Wait, did you know he was my new landlord?"

Connie's tone went from worried to amused. "Of course I knew. Now go on."

"Oh. Well, Ben heard the glass breaking and came over to check on me. He, um, didn't want to leave me alone with a broken door, so he's, uh, sleeping on my sofa."

There was silence for all of five seconds, and then a rapid burst of words. "Wait a minute. Are you telling me that big ol' bad Ben Hudson, sex god extraordinaire, is sleeping over? Oh-my-freaking-god! You little hussy!" Connie squealed, laughing with delight.

Reese frowned. "Calm down, you lunatic. He's sleeping on the sofa, not in my bed."

"Well, did you offer it to him?"

She spluttered for a moment, trying to get her words out. "Are you crazy? I only just . . . we don't even . . . God, Connie. Of course I didn't offer! You're nuts!" she hissed, hoping like hell that Connie didn't ask if anything had happened between them. Reese wasn't sure she could pull off a convincing denial when she was already so keyed up on adrenaline.

"Hmm," Connie murmured, sounding suspiciously thoughtful. "You know, on second thought, honey, maybe it's a good thing you didn't fall right into bed with him. I mean, it's such a shame about his . . . well, you know."

She blinked, clutching the phone even closer to her ear. "What are you talking about?" she asked, a thousand awful scenarios running through her head. Did he have some horrible STD . . . or some life-threatening condition, like a faulty heart? "What's wrong with him?"

"Haven't you heard? Ben suffers from PDD."

Her mind raced, trying to place the acronym. "PDD? What's that? What does it stand for?"

"It's short for Panty Dropping Disease," Connie proclaimed in a bubbly voice. "The instant women set eyes on him, they drop their drawers. I can't believe you've never heard of it."

Reese drew in a deep, shuddering breath, then exploded in another quiet hiss. "You jerk! I thought you were being serious!"

Connie snickered. "Sorry. I couldn't resist. You're still so easy to tease, Reese."

"Glad you find me so amusing," she muttered.

"Hey, you know I love you. I want you to be happy and have some fun, which is why I'm thrilled that Ben's smart enough to be paying you attention. Just . . . just watch yourself around him, okay?" Something in Connie's tone had changed. "Guys like Ben can be a blast, as long as you know what to expect."

"Trust me, I know the score." Which was why she doubted anything could come from his surprising flirtation. She was so unbelievably tempted, but couldn't help seeing it as a potentially massive catastrophe. No matter how badly she wished otherwise, she wasn't programmed for a gritty sexual fling. And that's definitely what he'd been putting on the table with his shocking sex talk. Smoothing her hand over the top of the light blanket she'd used to fight off the chill of the air conditioner, she added, "I still can't believe Mom rented this place from him. What was she thinking?"

"Well, once Ben heard you were moving down, he wouldn't take no for an answer."

Her breath caught as she thought of what that meant. "Wait a minute. Are you telling me that Ben's the one who told Mom about the beach house?"

"That's right. He thought it might be perfect for you."

"Why?"

"What do you mean why? Don't you like it?"

"It's not that. I just wouldn't think that a single man like Ben would want some stuffy schoolteacher living so close to him."

"Hey, don't talk like that," Connie snapped. "You're not stuffy."

"You have to say that because you love me," she said with a smile in her voice. "But I've been told otherwise."

"By who? That asshead Drew? That evil little bastard!"

"Yeah, well, he's an evil bastard who isn't my problem anymore, so don't waste your time cursing him."

They talked for a few more minutes, making plans to get together for lunch the next day, and then Reese finally got off the phone. Before they hung up, Connie made her promise to call and let her know if anything juicy happened with Ben that morning.

Hah! As if, she thought, making a strong effort to convince herself that she wasn't incredibly tempted to dive right in. She had to be smart about this, damn it. She couldn't go gunning for him like a sex-starved maniac just because the guy was the hottest thing she'd ever seen or heard or known.

Climbing out of bed, Reese pulled a soft gray cardigan over her sleep shirt and headed to the bathroom. After brushing her teeth and running her brush through her hair, she debated hiding out in her room until she heard Ben start moving around in the living room or sneaking to the kitchen to make some coffee. Her mouth watered at the thought of a hot cup, making the decision for her. Creeping down the hallway, she tried to be quiet as she made her way past the entrance to the sitting room, but he called out to her just as she went past, his voice deliciously husky from sleep. "Reese?"

"Sorry," she murmured, peeking around the edge of the archway. He lifted his dark head from the far end of the sofa, and her heart raced as she got a good look at him. The light blanket she'd given him to sleep with was wrapped around his lean hips, his powerful chest completely bare. Hard muscles were packed under his tanned skin, his body so long that his feet hung over the other armrest. She tried not to fixate on how big they were, remember-

ing the old adage about big hands and feet meaning a guy would
be big in other places, as well. "I didn't mean to wake you."

"You didn't. I heard the phone ring." He looked sleep rumpled
and sexy as he stretched, his jaw dark with stubble and his hair
falling over his brow.

"You didn't need to sleep on my sofa, Ben."

"'S that right?" He swung his feet to the floor as he sat up,
shoving a long-fingered hand through his tousled hair. One of his
dark brows lifted in a wry arch as he held her gaze. "You were
gonna share the bed with me?"

"No," she said, relieved she'd been able to keep her tone even.
"But you didn't look very comfortable. You could have gone home
and slept a lot better in your own bed."

"Doesn't matter. I wasn't about to leave you here alone with
that glass busted." He jerked his chin toward the French doors
that led to the patio, the shattered pane on the left letting in an
early morning breeze.

"I'm not in any danger here." More than ready to stop looking
over her shoulder, Reese willed herself to believe it. "And like I
said last night, I could have gone over to my mother's."

His sculpted lips turned down in a frown. "I didn't want you
having to go to your mother's. I want you to feel at ease here."

"Well, that's sweet, but it's not your job to give me peace of
mind."

He gave her a kinda crooked, sexy smile. "I thought I made it
clear last night that I'd like to give you a hell of a lot more than
that."

A soft laugh slipped past her lips. "Are you trying to embar-
rass me?"

"No." His lashes lowered a little over his eyes. "I was just hoping you might have given it some thought."

"I . . . did."

"And?" he prompted.

"Well, I guess I'm still having a hard time believing that the, um, pleasure you're offering would be worth the . . . stress."

There was so much heat in his heavy-lidded gaze, she felt burned. "You won't know that until you try me out, Reese. You might find it's worth the restless night we both just had."

It wasn't so much his words as his tone, but suddenly all the pieces started clicking together. She'd been so close to coming last night. If he'd touched her clit, she'd have gone over screaming. But he hadn't, and now she was pretty sure she knew why. He *wanted* her on edge, aching for it, unable to get him out of her mind.

Moving into the archway, she crossed her arms over her chest and held his stare. "Why didn't you make me . . . *come* last night?" Once the words were out of her mouth, she couldn't believe she'd found the guts to say them, but was feeling pretty proud of herself. And pretty irritated, too.

He went still, but didn't look away, his gaze locked hard and tight with hers.

"Were you . . . You did it on purpose, didn't you? To keep me on edge?"

He moved to his feet, his cut abs rippling with the movement, arms hanging loose at his sides. The guy was so freaking sexy it should have been illegal. Instead of denying her accusation, he simply raised a hand to scratch his dark jaw and asked, "Is it working?"

Reese bit her lip, hating that he could look so calm when she was shaking apart inside. And then she lowered her gaze, staring at the rigid bulge trapped inside his jeans, and something inside her loosened at the proof that he was on edge, too. There were no other women here, which meant that breathtaking erection was all for her, and she almost licked her lips, the thrill surging through her veins as intoxicating as a drug. "Yes. It's working."

He made a thick sound, and she watched as that firm ridge got even bigger, the head poking out from the top of his waistband. Dark, flushed, and gleaming, it was as round and full as a ripe plum. He didn't move toward her, but he fisted his hands at his sides, squeezing until ropy veins stood out beneath the golden skin of his forearms and biceps, his hard, masculine beauty making her want to do crazy, irresponsible, stupid things. Like walk across the hardwood floor, drop to her knees, and try to take that massive thing inside her mouth, suckling and tasting, doing everything she could to drive him mad, until he exploded against her tongue and cursed something dirty in that deep, decadent voice that made her melt.

But whom was she trying to fool? All he had to do was look at her and she melted, her sex going moist and warm and ready.

The question was, did she feel like being used?

Obviously, it wasn't a situation any woman would seek. But then, it wasn't every day that a woman like her got the chance to get down and dirty with a guy like Ben Hudson. Could she really just walk away and tell him no, without finding out what it would be like? It seemed like such an impossible feat, because she wanted to experience the reality of being under him, that long hard body pressing her down, with a desperation that bordered on craving. Wanted to know what it felt like when he pushed that big cock into her body and fucked her into one screaming orgasm after another. She might get her heart bruised when he left, but would the pleasure be worth it?

She wished to God she knew the answer.

It wasn't easy, but Reese somehow forced her gaze away from the heavy head of his cock and back up to his gorgeous face. Rubbing her hands over her arms, she said, "I keep telling myself that I just need to tell you no, but I *want* to say yes. I . . . I just don't know if I could do a casual relationship. I've never had a fling in my life, Ben, and things are pretty crazy for me right now."

A notch formed between his dark brows. "I thought we agreed not to label it."

"We did?"

He nodded, his gaze sharp. Determined. "No labels. We can make our own rules as we go along. And I know you're just getting settled here. I won't take up too much of your time. Outside of the bedroom, you can have as much freedom as you want."

"And *in* the bedroom?"

Something dark and intense moved through his eyes. "I won't lie to you. I don't play nice when it comes to sex. But I swear I'll never hurt you. I just want to make you come so hard you scream."

Wryly, she admitted, "I'm really not much of a screamer."

"Maybe not yet," he said. "But you could be. Whatever it is that'll make you lose control and let go, Reese—that's how I'll give it to you."

She stared, wanting very much to believe him. "That's a bold claim."

"When you want proof"—he gave her a slow, sexy smile—"just say the word."

There was a wild woman inside her who wanted to tell him that yes, she was ready *now*, but the worst interruption in history came when someone started knocking on her front door. She jumped, startled, and took two steps back. "I have no idea who that could be."

He checked the watch on his thick wrist. "It's probably a little early for the glass repair company."

"You already called them?"

Turning a bit to the side, he nodded as he reached over to snag his shirt off the back of the sofa. "I could get called in to work at any time, and I don't want to leave you alone until that door is fixed."

Before she could comment, another knock sounded, along with her mother's voice shouting through the door. "Reese? Aren't you up yet? It's almost eight o'clock!"

Her wide eyes locked with Ben's, and she felt her face flame with color. "That's my mom."

His lips twitched. "I know. Go answer the door, Reese."

She could tell by the twinkling in his eyes that he was enjoying her discomfort. With a hot glare, she turned and headed down the hallway. Hating that she felt embarrassed by the thought of her mom finding a man in her house, as if she were some underage teen, she took a deep breath and opened the door.

Her mother stood there in yoga pants and a tank top, still looking beautiful and far younger than her age. She had the same blond coloring that Connie and Cami had, but with Reese's blue eyes instead of their brown ones. Before Reese could get the first word out, her mother breezed into the house, her blond hair swinging in a ponytail. "Morning, sweetheart. I was in town for coffee and thought I'd come to see how—Oh! Um, wow. Am I interrupting anything?"

She knew, by the stunned look on her mother's face, that she'd caught sight of Ben. Sure enough, when Reese looked over her shoulder, she found him standing in the hallway, arms crossed over his chest, shoulder propped against the wall. He'd pulled his shoes and his polo shirt back on, hiding anything she wouldn't have wanted her mother to see, thank God. But he still looked all mellow and sleep-tousled, as if he'd just rolled out of bed. Another one of those slow, suggestive smiles curved his mouth, and she blasted him with a glare again before looking at her mom.

"Of course you aren't interrupting anything," she said a little too brightly, thankful that Ben's shirt was long enough to conceal his erection. "There isn't anything to interrupt."

Ben's smile melted into a sexy smirk. "Morning's still young, though."

It wasn't easy to get her next words out through her gritted teeth, but she managed. "Ben slept on my sofa."

"Oh?" Her mom's eyebrows had risen nearly to her hairline.

Ben finally took mercy on her, though it was a little late in coming. "I'll put on the coffee while you explain, Reese. Mrs. Thompson," he said with a nod, using her mom's married name. He pushed away from the wall and headed into the kitchen.

Her mom blinked a few times, then slowly turned her stunned gaze on Reese. "What's going on?" she whispered with false concern, doing an incredibly crappy job of trying to hide her excitement.

Reese scowled. "Don't even try that innocent act," she snapped. "I can't believe you didn't tell me he was my new landlord!" And the conversation pretty much deteriorated from there, with her mother trying to look contrite, but failing miserably. For some inexplicable reason, the woman obviously thought the idea of her newly divorced daughter hooking up with the town stud was a stellar idea. Go figure.

When Reese came into the kitchen a few minutes later, after sending her mom on her way with a promise to call her that evening, she found Ben waiting for her. He was leaning back against one of the counters, the dark hair hanging over his forehead only adding to his bad-boy image. He might be the sheriff of this beautiful, upscale county, but she wasn't fooled. Yeah, he was a respectable guy, but he was also rough and wicked and wild. It was like having a beautiful predator lounging in her kitchen, making her feel like the proverbial mouse.

He appeared to calmly be drinking a cup of coffee—until she noticed the long fingers wrapped around his mug were white with tension. Did he think she was going to kick him out? And would it really bother him so much if she did?

With those strange thoughts running through her head, something she wasn't ready to put a name to spread through her chest
in a warm, kinda soothing rush. She could see how hard he was
trying to hold on to his control, and it made her own nervous tension easier to deal with. But she was still irritated by how he'd
handled the situation with her mother.

"What exactly was that?" she demanded.

He set his mug on the counter. "What was what?"

Tossing her hands up in frustration, she said, "You do realize
that my mother now thinks we're sleeping together, right? She'll
have told half the town by lunchtime!"

He whistled under his breath. "She works fast, huh?"

"She's not the only one," she muttered, knowing everyone was
going to assume that she'd thrown herself at Ben, when it was
actually the other way around. But how could she expect anyone
to believe that shocker when she could hardly believe it herself?

He lifted his hands, as if claiming innocence. "Hey, I've been
golden. I might have kissed you last night, but I kept it tame,
despite how badly I'm dying to fuck you."

She shook her head with disbelief. "You call that tame?"

He closed the distance between them, crowding her against one
of the counters, all six plus feet of sexy, sleep-tousled male. "As
soon as you're ready, let me know."

Reese stared up at him. "Ready for what?" she asked a little
breathlessly.

His eyes gleamed with wicked heat. "The untamed version."

She gave a nervous laugh, needing caffeine if she was meant to
handle him this early in the morning. "What I'm ready for right
now is coffee and food. Thanks to your grocery shopping, I can
offer you some Cheerios and milk."

He cocked his head to the side and smiled. He was so gorgeous
she thought it might actually hurt to look at him for too long, like

staring at direct sunlight. But she couldn't look away as he said, "I'd rather just have you."

She blushed as she started to respond, but was cut off by the beeping of the phone he'd attached to his belt. "Don't you need to answer that?" she asked, when he just stood there, staring back at her.

"No." He leaned forward, gripping the counter on either side of her hips, caging her in. "I can tell from the notification tone that it's a text from work."

"You can?"

His face was right over hers now. "I can."

"But don't you need to—"

"Shh." His lips brushed against hers, tempting and warm. "I don't want to talk about work or my phone, Reese. So just shut up and let me kiss you."

Her voice was little more than a whisper. "I already let you kiss me. Last night."

Her eyes slid closed, but she could feel him smile against her mouth. "Then let me do it again. I get better with repetition."

She laughed, unable to believe she could be so turned on when he'd barely even touched her. Then she gasped as his hands slipped under the hem of her sleep shirt and settled on her hips. "I thought we were going to have breakfast," she said, gripping his biceps.

"But you were complaining earlier about how I left you hanging last night." He kissed the corner of her mouth. "I think we should take care of that first."

Reese moaned, almost sobbing with anticipation, until he finally took her mouth in a deep, eating, toe-curling kiss. The guy did things with his tongue that should have been outlawed, and she drowned under the onslaught of heat and excitement, her heart tripping as he suddenly moved his right hand, shoving it down the front of her panties. Rough fingertips softly stroked her damp folds, separating them, brushing over screamingly sensitive flesh. He made a hard, guttural sound and pushed one big finger inside her, her hips jerking as she felt that heavy penetration roll through every part of her, blindsiding her senses.

"You're already drenched," he groaned against her lips, sending another long finger in beside the first. The pressure was full and hot, his fingers curling with expert skill to rub against that hypersensitive bundle of nerves inside her. The feeling was so intense she had to break away from the kiss, gasping for breath.

"*Ben*," she panted, shivering from the top of her head down to her toes. Her brain was shot, but her body was so happy that she just didn't give a damn.

"Three fingers now," he said in a low rumble, grazing his teeth down the side of her throat.

She was already so stretched around him, so full inside, the idea of taking more snapped her out of the pleasure-haze fogging her brain, jerking her back to awareness. "You must be joking," she gasped, grabbing hold of his wrist with both hands when he started working that third digit in beside the others. "That's too much."

"Shh. Don't panic." He caught her earlobe in his teeth, biting gently as he worked that third finger inexorably deeper. "You can take it."

"No, I can't."

He pulled back his head, looking her right in the eye. His stare was deep and measuring, smoky and hot. "You *have* to. Because one way or another, I *am* getting my dick in you, Reese."

"I saw enough of you earlier to know that you're big, but are you saying that you're as big as three fingers? Your fingers are huge!"

The corner of his mouth twitched, and he shook his head.

She blew out a relieved breath. "I didn't think so."

Leaning down, he nipped her bottom lip. "I'm bigger."

Her eyes went wide. "Seriously? You're joking, right?"

Very slowly, he took his fingers out of her and pulled her hand to his crotch, pressing her palm against the rigid flesh pushing against his fly. He held her hand close to the base, and her breath sucked in on another sharp gasp. The first words that popped out of her mouth caught her completely by surprise. "You actually thought you were getting this thing in my ass?"

He blinked, and then his head went back as a deep, rumbling laugh surged up from his chest, making her face go hot.

"It's not nice to laugh," she muttered.

"I know, I'm sorry. But you keep taking me by surprise." He lowered his head to look at her, another crooked grin flirting with those firm, sensual lips. "I like it."

She couldn't stop from rolling her eyes. "So glad you find me hilarious."

"I find you refreshing," he told her, his voice husky and low. He seemed to be searching for what he wanted to say next, while his gaze moved slowly over her face. "Genuine. Different from what I'm used to. Almost innocent."

Pulling her hand from beneath his, she said, "I was a married woman, Ben. I'm not innocent."

The heat in his green eyes got a little hotter, making her oblivious to the chill of the air-conditioning vent blowing down on them from above. "Just because you've had sex doesn't mean you're experienced." His gaze narrowed a little, and there were tiny lines that she found ridiculously sexy crinkling at the corners of his eyes. "I have a feeling you've only ever been served a fairly vanilla menu."

Her brow arched, even as her pulse rushed. "And you're not a vanilla kind of guy? Is that what you're saying?"

"'Fraid not, honey." He lifted his hand to her face, watching as he rubbed his thumb against the corner of her kiss-swollen mouth, her lips still tingling. She could smell her salty scent on his fingers, and it made her insides clench. "I should probably stay the hell away from you, but I'm not going to. I want you too badly."

Her reply was soft. "And what about what I want?"

He lifted his gaze, locking her back in that warm bottle green. "Tell me, Reese. You wanna be fucked hard and rough? Want your sweet little pussy licked for hours on end, my tongue sinking inside you, deep and slow?" His nostrils flared as he pulled in a short breath, that rough voice getting even rougher. "Whatever it is you want or need, I'll give it to you."

She wanted to ask, *And what if I want it slow and easy, like you're making love to me?* But she didn't dare. The last thing she needed was to look like some lovesick divorcée. If she did this thing with Ben—and that was a BIG if—she was going to keep her eyes wide open and her emotions locked down as tightly as she could. It would be about pleasure, about what she knew would be incredible sex, and nothing more. She wasn't going to lose her head over him, and she sure as hell wasn't going to lose her heart.

"Hey, you in there?" he asked.

She licked her lips, blinking him back into focus. "Yeah, I'm here. I was just trying to decide how to handle you . . . us . . . this thing we have between us."

Satisfaction smoldered in his gaze. "At least you're accepting that it's going to happen."

"I haven't actually accepted anything yet." Knowing damn well that she was playing with fire, and more than a little surprised by how much she enjoyed it, Reese arched her brow again. "Maybe I'm just trying to decide how to tell you I'm not interested."

"Like hell," he said with a husky laugh, suddenly taking her mouth in another hard, devastating kiss. One that was over far too quickly for her liking this time. He had his hand buried in her hair, and he tilted her head back even more as he tugged on the strands, the slight sting on her scalp only making her burn hotter, until she could feel the fire all the way down in her belly. "I meant what I said, Reese. I'll give you whatever you need. You just have to let me know what you want."

Beautiful words—but she knew they weren't true. He'd give her sex, maybe even friendship, but that's all.

It's better than nothing.

She didn't know where that pragmatic thought had come from, but she couldn't argue with it. Not now, when he was standing in front of her looking like sin incarnate. Wanting to push him, to shake him up like he was shaking her, she pressed her palm over his erection again and tightened her grip, rubbing him through the denim. "You know what, Ben? This thing of yours is ridiculously proportioned. Kind of like your ego."

A flush shaded the crest of his cheekbones, his eyes hooded and dark. But a devilish grin kicked up the corner of his mouth. "It's only ridiculous if I don't know how to handle it."

"Do you?" she asked, unable to keep an answering grin off her lips.

"Take me for a test drive and decide for yourself."

Her grin instantly twisted with regret. "If I tried, I don't think I'd even know what to do with you."

"It's easy. Just throw me down and fuck me till my eyes roll back in my head and I'll be putty in your hands."

"Is that right?" she asked, muffling an embarrassing giggle.

There was something spellbinding about the way he was smiling down at her, his lustful look edged with some intriguing emotion she couldn't put a name to. "Well, you know what I'm like. As much as I'd enjoy it, I'd rather be the one doing the throwing," he admitted with another husky laugh. "And the fucking."

She swallowed, and tried to remember why this was such a bad idea. "You make it so hard to do the right thing, Ben."

"Then just do me instead." Curving his hand around the nape of her neck, he held her hard and tight as he took her mouth in another one of those *Is the world spinning out of control?* kisses. From the far corners of her pleasure-hazed mind, Reese was aware of him curling his other arm under her bottom and carrying her through the narrow archway that led into her dining room. She felt the cold surface of her small table hit the backs of her legs, and then he was laying her down . . . coming down over her, his hard chest crushing her breasts while his mouth ate at hers in a way that was wild and raw and outrageously sinful.

She didn't remember doing it, but she had both hands fisted in his hair now, her tongue rubbing hungrily against his as he shoved his hand back into the front of her panties, then quickly shoved two of those long fingers back inside her. She was so wet she could hear the sound of his fingers thrusting, and she arched her back, pushing her breasts harder against him as he brought his thumb into the action, working her clit. Her heart pounded, thoughts as tangled and fractured as her breaths. She was already tightening, trembling, ready to come out of her freaking skin. Then he hooked his fingers and rubbed that sweet spot deep inside her—and that was it. With a breathless cry on her lips, she started coming, hard, her sex convulsing around his pumping fingers, gripping him tighter . . . and tighter.

"That's it," he groaned, lowering his head and biting her nipple through the thin shirt, then sucking it hard. "Let me hear it, Reese."

She gasped, keening, unable to hold in the raw sobs as he suddenly pushed a third finger into her. He was stretching her to a point just shy of pain, but she didn't care, the thick penetration hurtling her into a deeper level of orgasm that made her close her eyes, throw her head back . . . and scream so loud it probably shook the rafters.

Holy. Freaking. God.

It could have lasted an hour, or a mere handful of seconds. Reese had no idea, all sense of her surroundings and time completely annihilated beneath the bursts of mind-shattering ecstasy. When she finally blinked her eyes back open, she had no idea how long she'd been caught in that . . . whatever the hell *that* had been. An orgasm-induced meltdown? A head-spinning trip to another dimension? Whatever it was, the sensations had been so intense she felt as if she'd been permanently . . . changed. As if he'd left some kind of indelible mark on the very center of her universe. On her entire concept of her body and her self and what she was capable of feeling and experiencing.

Damn it, she'd known getting a taste of Ben Hudson would be dangerous. The guy was too freaking addictive for his own good!

"You have freckles on your thighs." He was bracing himself on his left arm, his dark gaze burning with heat as it swept over her pale skin, before focusing in hard and tight on her sex. He pushed his fingers in a little deeper, making a low sound in his throat. "Christ, you even have a few little freckles on your cunt. That's so fucking sexy, Reese."

She wet her lips, searching for her voice. "You like freckles?"

"On you? I fucking love them," he said roughly, carefully pulling his fingers from her still softly pulsing flesh. She wanted to protest, wanted to keep him inside her, a part of her, but the words quickly caught in her throat when she saw him lifting his hand. Her jaw dropped as he put his drenched fingers in his mouth, a visceral, breathtaking look of hunger on his rugged face. Then he sucked on them, taking in every bit of her taste, before slowly pulling them out. "You're so damn sweet," he growled, exploding into movement as he gripped the sides of her panties, wrenching them down. But they'd only just cleared her knees when there was a loud knock on her front door.

"Oh, God," she said hoarsely, her voice still wrecked from screaming. "That's going to be the repair guy, isn't it?"

He nodded as he took a harsh breath, looking as though he was bracing himself for something painful as he straightened. Reaching down, he grimaced as he rearranged himself in his jeans. "He has the worst timing in the world," he ground out, still staring between her legs. "I wanted to get my mouth on you. I should have fucking tasted you last night when I had the chance."

With a soft laugh, she drew her legs together. "It, um, won't kill you to wait."

"Feels like it," he muttered, shoving both hands back through his hair.

It was probably unfair of her, considering he'd just given her such an awesome orgasm, but Reese couldn't resist teasing him a little. "You'll survive."

"That's debat—"

The ringing of his cell phone cut her off, the tone a rapid beat that repeated itself, and this time he didn't ignore it. "Damn it, that's our emergency signal. I need to take this."

She sat up and pulled her cardigan across her chest, then smiled at herself. Her shot at modesty was a little ridiculous when her panties were still past her knees. "You take your call and I'll get the door," she said, wondering if there was a graceful way to hop off the table while pulling up her underwear.

He nodded, finally dragging his gaze back up to her face. "Put on some sweatpants before you go anywhere near that door. That shirt is too damn short."

She gave him a jaunty salute. "Sure thing, officer."

He laughed as he leaned in for another quick kiss, then turned and walked into the kitchen. She could hear Ben on his phone as she hopped down from the table, yanked up her panties, then quickly ran and pulled on some sweats. It didn't take long to let in the repair guy, an older man named Frank who had an easy smile, and make sure there wasn't anything that he needed. He got to work on clearing out the jagged pieces of glass that were left around the edges of the door frame, and she went back into the kitchen.

"Something's come up at work," Ben said, hooking his phone back onto his belt as he turned around to face her. "I've got to head in for a bit. But I wanted to ask if you'll go to a beach party with me this afternoon. I should be back by one, but if I'm not, I could meet you there. I think it's getting started around twelve thirty, just down the beach from us."

"Is everything okay at work?" she asked, deliberately ignoring the bit about the party. After what had just happened between them, she needed some time to figure out what the heck she was doing. For a woman who had serious reservations about having a purely sexual fling, she seemed to be doing a pretty good job of it so far. "Did something happen?"

His face had that kind of closed expression that could only belong to a cop. "One of my deputies was patrolling the beach a little while ago and found a teenage girl. She was barely conscious, but it looks like she was beaten last night and then left behind one of the dunes, where she couldn't easily be seen."

"Ohmygod." Reese covered her lips with her fingers. "Is she all right?"

"She's at the county hospital. Chris, the deputy who found her, said she was banged up pretty badly. I need to get over there."

Thoughts spinning, she ran her hands over her chilled arms. "Of course. I'll walk you out."

She started to move around him, but he caught her arm. "Reese?"

Distracted, she said, "Yeah?"

She could feel him waiting for her to lock her troubled gaze with his. "What's going on, honey?"

She shook her head. "What do you mean?"

"You look scared to death," he said with a frown.

"I'm fine. I just feel bad about what happened."

He wasn't any better at hiding his frustration than she was at hiding her fear. "You don't tell the truth very often, do you?"

Her chin kicked up a notch. "I'm not a liar."

His gaze got a little sharper. "You can trust me, Reese. You don't need to keep things from me."

Shaking her head again, she said, "Really, I'm okay. You need to go, Ben."

He pulled her closer, one hand splayed at her lower back, while the other lifted to her face, brushing her hair back. "Not until you give me an answer about the party."

"Oh . . . I uh—"

"Come on and just say yes. It'll be fun. McNamara Clinic is throwing it, and they're a good group of people. It's where my friend Brit works as a therapist. There'll be an open bar and a big crowd, so we won't stick out. We can blend right in."

"Um, wouldn't I be intruding on your time with your friend?" she asked, hedging. She knew damn well that Ben would be the focus of attention for nearly every woman there, which just sounded . . . stressful.

"She's my *friend*. Like a sister. And you wouldn't be intruding on anything. She wants to meet you, and I want you there with me."

"Well, that's really nice of you, Ben. You're being very, um, neighborly."

He bit back a smile, but she could tell he was amused. "Call it what you like. Just say that you'll come."

Reese knew she'd be nervous if she went, but it was probably a better option than sitting at home and worrying herself sick over the idea that trouble might have followed her here. Ben Hudson in a pair of swim trunks had to be about the best distraction she could think of, and there was no denying how safe he made her feel. "Okay. I'll think about it."

"You do that. I'll be back as soon as I can." He released her and headed for the doorway, then stopped and turned back, looking a little guarded. "You're not going to run off on me, are you?"

"Run off?"

His expression bordered on grim, but there was a touch of a grin on his incredible mouth. "Just remember that if you try to leave, I'll track you down. So you might as well stay put."

She almost snorted. "What? Are you going to handcuff me if I don't?"

Something dangerous and male darkened his eyes. "You ever been handcuffed before, Reese?"

Realizing he wasn't joking—that he *liked* the idea of handcuffing her during sex—she started breathing a little faster. "Are you really into that kind of thing?" she asked.

The corner of his mouth kicked up as he walked back to her, and she could just hear his voice over the hammering that had started in the sitting room, the jarring sound mirroring the hammering of her pulse. "Not usually, though I'm definitely eager to see your sweet little ass tied up and spread for me." He must have read something in her expression, because he added, "I'm not a control-freak misogynist, like a lot of other assholes out there. And I definitely believe that women have a hell of a lot more brains than men. But when it comes to sex, I like to be the one in charge."

She was about to tell him that he liked to be bossy when it came to *everything*, but he suddenly had both hands in her hair and was kissing her senseless again, his tongue thrusting against hers, driving her wild. She didn't know how long the kiss lasted, minutes . . . hours . . . days, but when he pulled back, his voice was like gravel. "I *will* see you on the beach."

Oh yeah, definitely bossy. "Ben, I'm—"

"Just be there, Reese. We'll sort everything else out later." Then he gave her another quick kiss, and left.

Reese stood in the middle of the kitchen, eyes closed, arms wrapped tight around herself. She refused to follow after him like a lovesick puppy, no matter how tempting it was. It took a little effort, but she finally cleared the sexual haze from her mind and got her thoughts focused on what she'd learned from Ben about the teen-ager who'd been attacked. Did the girl have anything to do with her? Or was it just coincidence? She was so uncertain about what to do, and the damn lust still messing with her head wasn't helping.

"I'm just being paranoid," she finally muttered under her breath, pouring two cups of coffee. She took one mug to Frank, then headed back to her bedroom to get dressed and unpack some more boxes. She was still working through the first box when she heard the sound of Ben's truck starting up, and listened as he drove away. Her cell phone buzzed a moment later, signaling a text message, and she lunged for it, wondering if it would be from Ben. As she swiped her finger over the screen to pull up the message, she realized how stupid she was being. Ben didn't have her number. It was probably her sister, wanting to know how the morning had gone. Or even her mom. But as the text popped up on her screen, Reese realized it was from neither. The number was blocked, and there were only five little words staring back at her, chilling her blood.

i saw you with him

~~~~~~~~~~~~~~~~

5

As Reese made her way down to the beach a little after one, a colorful tote bag hung from her shoulder, and there was a smile on her lips. Not even the disturbing text she'd received that morning—either by accident or on purpose—had been able to overshadow her nervous excitement about seeing Ben at the McNamara Clinic's beach party.

We'll sort everything else out later . . .

Gaah! Had more frustrating words ever been spoken in the English language? Reese was fairly sure they hadn't. How was she meant to stay levelheaded when Ben was all about having fun in the now, and worrying about the consequences later? When he was all about pleasure and satisfaction and just going with it.

Shaking her head, she smiled a little broader as a soft laugh slipped past her lips. They were as different as night and day, and yet, the moments she'd spent with him since yesterday had been some of the best in her life. As worried as she was about getting

hurt, being in his arms had been wonderfully exciting. Even free-
ing. Then she remembered what had taken him away from her that
morning, and her smile fell.

She hoped the girl who'd been attacked was okay. The situation
was a stark reminder of how something dangerous and ugly could
happen at any moment, and for the first time since she'd learned
that Ben was her new landlord and next-door neighbor, Reese was
actually thankful he was so close.

Looking back, she really should have sensed what her mother
was up to, and as she scanned the beach for the party, she mentally
replayed one of their first conversations about the move. She'd just
let herself into the apartment she'd moved into after leaving Drew,
her arms full of grocery bags, cell phone wedged between her
shoulder and ear while her mother said, "And then my friend
Sarah and I went into town for lunch, and guess who we ran into?"

"Who?" she'd asked, locking her door behind her and flicking
on all the lights. After the past few weeks, she couldn't shake the
feeling that someone was shadowing her every move. She was only
half listening to her mom until she heard her say, ". . . that hunky
Ben Hudson. Did you know he's the sheriff here now?"

"Yeah, you told me," she'd murmured, an image of Ben's hand-
some face immediately filling her mind.

"He asked after you like he always does."

Yeah, right, she'd thought, rolling her eyes. More like her mom
had probably talked the poor guy's ear off about her middle
daughter, boring the hell out of him.

"I told him you were holding up great after the divorce."

"You what?" Reese had screeched, mortified. "Mom, what
were you thinking?"

Now, three months later, she knew *exactly* what her mom had
been thinking. But she was grateful for the fact that he lived within
shouting distance. If the person who'd sent her that creepy text

turned out to be the same one who'd been stalking her in Boston, she had no doubt that Ben would flatten the jackass if he ever tried to mess with her.

You don't know it's a he, an inner voice pointed out. *The police didn't think it was Drew, which means it could be anyone.*

That was true. And the jerk in Boston had never texted her, either. So maybe today was just a fluke. God, she hoped so. But she still planned to do the smart thing and talk to Ben about it.

Trying to decide between the two large groups of people she could see on the beach, one to her right and the other off to her left, Reese shivered as a chill ran down her spine. She had the strangest sensation that someone was watching her. Not Ben, but someone . . . else. She hadn't seen anyone on her way down from her patio a moment ago, but she couldn't shake the feeling that she was under someone's gaze. In several places, thick, glossy bushes ran parallel to the beach, creating a natural barrier between the sand and the residential gardens and patios that went along the coast. Was someone hiding in the tropical bushes, spying on her from there?

This is ridiculous. I'm just creeping myself out, she muttered to herself, trying to sound convincing. Still, she knew she'd feel safer in a crowd, so she decided to try the group off to her right, hoping to catch sight of Ben. She realized she'd chosen wrong after asking a cute guy in Hawaiian swim trunks if the party was for the McNamara Clinic. He gave her a friendly smile as he told her it wasn't, then invited her to join their get-together anyhow. She politely declined, a little stunned by the interest in his dark eyes as he looked her over. Where was this coming from?

Maybe it's the Florida sunshine, she mused, shaking her head as she went back in the other direction.

Slipping off her flip-flops, Reese bent down and looped the straps over two fingers, holding them as she made her way over to the other group, which looked to be at about thirty to forty people already. She could hear Lana Del Rey playing from someone's sound system, and it was clear that Ben's friend's medical practice had put a lot of money into the catering. A wicker bar had been set up on the far side of the party, shielded by a massive palm frond umbrella, while three young chefs cooked seafood on several oversize grills, a half-dozen or so tables set out with what looked like enough food to feed a small army.

When she was only twenty yards or so away, she caught sight of Ben. The guy had his back to her, but she was positive it was Moss Beach's sexy sheriff. He was talking to a tall, stunning redhead dressed in a dark green halter top and skirt, and Reese frowned, feeling a little sick inside. The temptation to cut and run swept through her, but before she could execute the move, the redhead pointed her way. Ben instantly swung around, waving one hand high in the air to catch her attention.

She stood still as he started toward her, debating what to do. Then she blinked, taking a good long look as he came closer, her tongue pretty much stuck to the roof of her mouth. Holy cripes, he was gorgeous. His body was hard and cut, like something right out of that *300* movie, and she was pretty sure her mouth was hanging open, eyes glazed with lust. He must have taken a shower before coming down to the party, because his hair was still damp, the bright sun picking out the golden glints in the chocolate brown strands. He used both hands to slick his hair back from his face, and didn't stop striding forward until he was standing right in front of her. Like that morning, she had to tilt her head back to see his face, and almost wished she hadn't. There was so much heat in his eyes, she felt burned in a way that no amount of sunscreen was going to help. Then she remembered the way he'd made her come and cry out on her dining room table, an image flashing in her

mind of how he'd looked when he'd been staring at the most intimate part of her body, and she damn near went up in flames.

Cool it the heck down!

"Hey," he said, with just enough drawl to make the word sound
deliciously suggestive. "I was worried when I got here and couldn't
find you."

She gestured toward the party she'd just come from. "I came
down at one, but wasn't sure which get-together was your friend's."

He nodded, those green eyes taking everything in. "What's
wrong?"

She clutched the strap of her tote with her free hand, scrunch-
ing her toes in the warm sand. "Nothing. I just feel a little awkward, not knowing anybody."

"You know me."

"Not well, though."

"You'll know me a lot better by the end of the day," he said
with conviction, taking her sandals from her and grabbing her
hand. "Come on, we'll just sit and relax for a bit in some of the
chairs down by the water before I start dragging you around to
introduce you to everyone."

As they made their way down to the shore, where the waves
were softly lapping at the white sand, Reese watched him from the
corner of her eye. Despite the breathtaking scenery of the Gulf
Coast, it was impossible to look anywhere else. His beautiful body
was bare, except for the loose black swim trunks that hung off his
lean hips. He had those mouthwatering muscles there at the base
of his abdomen that guys who are really in shape can get, and she
ran her tongue over her bottom lip, wondering what it'd feel like
to lick him there.

"What?" he asked, when she gave a quiet snort.

"You, in those trunks." She found it nearly impossible to take her eyes off the sexy trail of dark hair that whorled around his navel before heading south. "It hardly seems fair. Are you trying to give all the women heart attacks?"

There was a wealth of satisfaction in his deep voice. "You like?"

"You're flaunting," she murmured, lifting her gaze. "It isn't right."

He turned his face a bit to the side, but she still caught his grin. "I'm wearing what every other guy here is wearing."

She gave another quiet snort. "Like that matters. They don't look like you."

"It could all be yours," he purred, waggling his brows at her. "Just say the word."

"You're so warped." She tried to sound stern, but inside she was secretly delighted by how playful he could be. Yeah, he was beautiful to look at, but the more time she spent with him, it was becoming clear that there was a hell of a lot more to Ben Hudson than his wicked reputation and impressive occupation.

"Warped?"

She fought back a smile. "That's right. Warped."

He scratched his jaw. "I think the word I would use is *horny*. Or *needy*. Even *aching*." An edge of wryness crept into his tone. "At the moment, I'm feeling all of those things and more."

The temperature was in the high nineties, but Reese still felt herself shiver. "Are you planning on doing this all afternoon?"

"Doing what?"

"Driving me crazy. Because if that was your plan, then you need to back off a bit. I don't want to jump you in front of all these people."

The look in his eyes was so hot, she felt singed. "If I took you somewhere private, would you jump me then?"

She started to respond, when someone squealed his name.

Looking over her shoulder, Reese could only blink at what she saw running toward them. Blond, bouncy, and massively top-heavy.

God save her. They might be hundreds of miles from the West Coast, but they'd just been spotted by freaking Malibu Barbie.

OH SHIT. BEN MENTALLY BRACED HIMSELF AS STACY PETERS RAN toward them, her chest barely contained in a minuscule neon pink bikini. No way in hell was this going to be good. He could already feel Reese's tension ramping up, her hand pulling away from his, and he reacted quickly. "Hey, Stacy. I'll catch up with you a little later," he called out, hoping to stop her in her tracks. "We're heading down to the water for a bit."

"Don't be too long," she shouted, giving him what she probably thought was an attractive pout. But it looked a little scary with all that shimmery pink lipstick smeared on her silicone-puffed lips.

"Who's the girl?"

"Her name's Stacy," he replied, settling his gaze back on Reese's face. She hadn't put on a stitch of makeup, her cheeks flushed, lips naturally rosy and plump. She looked so delectable, he just wanted to toss her over his shoulder and carry her back up to her house, where he could strip her out of that little black sundress and see what she was hiding underneath. Knew that when he took her mouth, she'd taste warm and sweet the way she had that morning, instead of like a tube of lipstick.

"Let's sit here," he said, pulling two of the low-slung beach chairs closer together, facing them toward the party. All he needed was someone like Stacy sneaking up on them and dropping into his lap before he could stop her.

"Did you date her?" She gazed at him impassively as she sat down, as if she didn't care one way or the other. But he knew it was bullshit.

"No, I didn't."

She smoothed the short skirt of her dress over her thighs, then tucked a windblown strand of hair behind her ear. "She can't take her eyes off you."

"Don't worry about her," he murmured, wondering if he was going to look ridiculous if he scooted his chair even closer to hers. Only a few inches separated them, but he couldn't shake the unfamiliar compulsion to stay glued to this woman like a fucking shadow.

"In other words, mind my own business?"

A frustrated sigh surged past his lips, but he still found himself giving her an explanation. "She works as a receptionist for one of the doctors at McNamara. We met last year and she was hoping to start something—" He paused for a moment, before saying, "But we didn't."

"Why not?"

He leaned back in his chair and shrugged. "I couldn't do it."

With a smirk, she said, "You know, they have medication for things like that."

"Smart-ass," he laughed, shaking his head. "My equipment works just fine, which you'll soon learn for yourself."

She kept her gaze on the growing crowd as she responded. "Since the jury is still out on that one, I'll take your word for it."

Ben started to ask her if she wanted the proof right then, but changed his mind. He enjoyed teasing her, but sensed that now wasn't the time. "Anyway, what I meant was that I couldn't start something with her when I knew she was expecting it to be more than it was."

"Meaning she wanted more than a fling?" she asked, turning her head to look at him.

His comfort level headed toward sub-zero temperatures. "Yeah."

She looked confused. "If you steer clear of relationship girls, then why are you . . ." It sounded like she was searching for the right words. "Pursuing me?"

With another uneasy shrug, he said, "I told you before, you're different."

"Actually, I'm pretty average. I think it's just that I was married." She nodded, her expression almost triumphant, as if she'd finally solved an irritating puzzle. "You were interested because I was someone off limits." Waving her hand between them, she added, "You know what I mean. One of those 'you wanted me because you couldn't have me' things."

"You can think whatever you want, but it's bullshit." His tone was flat. "I have a little more maturity than that."

Did he? When it came to his work, it was obvious he did. But Reese wasn't so sure about his interactions with the women he dated.

Before she could launch her next salvo, the tall redhead she'd seen him talking to earlier called his name, waving at them, the friendly smile on the woman's face putting her at ease. This wasn't someone like Malibu Stacy, looking to score the sheriff for herself. In fact, the woman's attention was on her, instead of Ben. As she headed their way, they both moved to their feet.

"Reese, this is my friend Brit," Ben said when she reached them, making the introductions. "She's the one who invited us to the party."

Brit shook her hand. "It's nice to meet you, Reese. I've heard so much about you, I feel like we're already friends."

"Thanks. It's nice to meet you, too," she murmured, surprised by how comfortable she felt. When Ben had described his friendship with this woman last night, and again this morning, she thought for sure that she'd pick up a different vibe between them if she ever actually met Brit Cramer. But she didn't.

Brit took a sip of her mojito, the sunglasses pushed up on her head keeping her hair from her face. With a smile, she said, "I know your sister Connie and her husband. I've also met your mom. She's something else."

Reese laughed. "I know what you mean. She can be a bit over-the-top at times."

"I think she's great. An absolute riot."

"Not to be rude," Ben said, his tone in complete contradiction to his words as he gave his friend a pointed look. "But shouldn't you be getting back to the party?"

Brit's own tone was cheerful, her smile bright. "Actually, I have a feeling they're doing just fine without me."

"Cramer," he growled.

"*Hudson*," she drawled, stretching out the syllables.

"Damn it, I—"

"Yeah, I know," she said, cutting him off as she raised her brows. "You want her all to yourself. But tough. Just get lost for a bit, okay? I want to chat with Reese."

Mild panic shone in his eyes. "Why?"

She waved her hand at him like someone shooing away a pest. "I don't have to give you any reasons. Just run along."

Reese fought the urge to smile when Ben turned toward her, his expression a dark blend of masculine frustration and resignation. "I guess I'll go and grab us some cold beers," he muttered, while Brit slipped into his chair. "Just don't believe anything she says. This woman lies through her teeth."

"Oh for God's sake," Brit huffed. "Stop worrying and just go!"

As Reese sat back down, she watched Ben make his way across the sand, acres of muscle rippling beneath all that golden skin, and she noted every female head that turned to follow him. A knot formed in her stomach when a tall blonde grabbed hold of his arm at the bar, plastering herself against his side as he waited for the bartender to pull their beers. "Does that happen everywhere he goes?" she asked sourly, wondering what she was doing there. The past twenty-four hours had been such a whirlwind, her sense of reality at the moment seemed as steady as the shifting grains of sand beneath her feet.

"Don't worry about her," Brit murmured, patting her arm. "She's all plastic smiles and fake lashes."

The sour feeling spread. "Isn't that what men want these days?"

"Some. And maybe Ben, too, for a time. But he's gotten bored with it. You know, I've seen them come and go over the years, Reese, but he's never fixated on one woman the way he's fixated on you."

She forced herself to look away from Ben and the blonde, and brought her stunned gaze back to Brit. "I'm not sure what he's told you, but Ben and I don't really know each other all that well."

"But you have a connection. A lot can be built on that."

Reese gave a dry laugh. "So far he's made it clear that he's only interested in boinking like a couple of bunnies."

Brit coughed and laughed at the same time, then sent Reese an apologetic smile. "Sorry, that just took me by surprise."

She could feel her face heating. "Me, too, if I'm honest. I don't normally just blurt things like that out." With a frown, she added, "He's got my head all muddled."

Brit took a healthy drink of her mojito, and said, "It sounds to me like Ben's trying to stick to his comfort zone."

"It's some comfort zone," she murmured.

"Yeah, well, I can already tell it won't work with you. Without a doubt, he's different with you, Reese. The way he talks about you. The way he looks at you." Her dimples appeared as she grinned. "If you let him into your bed, I bet my life's savings he'll even stay the night."

She couldn't conceal her surprise. "He doesn't normally spend the night with the women he sleeps with?"

Brit snorted and rolled her eyes. "Are you kidding me? He'd be terrified of giving one of them the wrong idea."

"And they're fine with that?" she asked, remembering all the lectures her mom had given her and her sisters when they'd become adults and headed out into the world on their own. In Catherine Thompson's world, if a man didn't respect you enough to spend the night with you, then your foot needed to connect with his ass as you kicked it out the door.

"If they're not," Brit said, "then he doesn't touch them."

"But I'm not . . . I've never . . ."

Another smile curved Brit's lips, her hazel eyes soft with understanding. "I know. That's not your speed, right?"

Reese nodded, her confusion only mounting.

"And it isn't sending him running." Brit sounded as if she wanted to pump her fist in the air, celebrating a long-awaited triumph. "It's that connection pulling the two of you together. I put a lot of faith in things like that. And like I said before, a lot can be built on it, if you give it a chance."

The wind picked up with a sudden gust of energy, and Reese held her hair out of her face as she studied the other woman's expression. "Would you take a risk like that?"

"I'd like to think I would." Brit's smile turned wry. "But I'd have to find a guy who made me want to first."

Shifting a little in her chair, Reese said, "I hope this doesn't seem too, well . . . Ben said you hadn't, but I was just wondering if the two of you ever dated?"

A hard laugh instantly slipped past the redhead's lips. "God, no. We met a few years back, when he was still working in Miami and I helped him out with a case. It was strange, but right from the start we were like two bickering siblings." She smiled a little, before adding, "I'm really lucky to have Ben in my life. He's a great guy, but . . . well, closed off in a way, if you know what I mean. I've despaired about the women he dates for years, Reese. You have no idea how excited I am that he's finally interested in someone I'm looking forward to hanging out with."

It took her a moment to process everything Brit had said. Closed off how? Did she mean emotionally? Why? Reese wanted to ask for an explanation, but this hardly seemed like the right time and place. And just like Ben had predicted, she *was* enjoying Brit's company. "We should do lunch sometime soon."

Brit's smile was warm. "I'd love to." Pulling her phone from the pocket of her skirt, she said, "If you give me your number, I can give you a call after I've gotten my schedule for next week."

"That sounds great. I just need to check my phone to make sure I've got my new number right," Reese said, reaching into her beach bag for her new smart phone. She'd gotten the new phone and number last week, just before she'd moved, wanting to cut ties completely with Drew. Pulling up the number, she gave it to Brit, then put Brit's number into her contact list.

Ben came back just as she was entering the last digit, holding a beer in each hand. "You two exchanging numbers already?"

"We're going to do lunch," Brit said cheerfully.

With a scowl on his rugged face, he cut his gaze toward Reese. "How come she gets a lunch date, but I can't even get you to agree to go out to dinner with me?"

"Um, well . . ."

Brit slid him a wry smile as she moved back to her feet. "Maybe I'm just more charming than you are, Ben."

His response was a sarcastic snort that got him socked in the arm, one of the beers nearly spilling over the rim of the glass.

"I need to do the rounds now before McNamara tracks me down," Brit said, "but it was lovely to meet you, Reese."

"You, too," she replied, smiling as she listened to Ben tell the redhead to find some hot guy and get laid. Brit laughed as she walked away, and he slipped into the vacated chair, handing Reese one of the beers.

"Thanks."

He reached over, running his finger along the bridge of her nose. "You should put some more sunscreen on soon. You're already getting pink."

She took a sip of the frosty beer. "That's the downfall of being too fair."

His dark gaze moved slowly down her body, hot with appreciation. "I like your fair skin."

"I'd rather be dark, like you," she said, admiring his hard chest and shoulders.

"I like the dress, too, Reese." He eyed the short hem on her thighs. "You got bikini bottoms on under there?"

"Yes." She fought back a grimace, wondering where he was going with this. Did he think she was going to take the dress off and walk around in her bathing suit in front of all these people? Not freaking likely!

"What about a top?" Shifting his attention up to her shoulders, he said, "I don't see any straps showing under the ones for the dress."

She swallowed, shifting restlessly in the chair, toes digging into the warm sand. "The top is strapless."

He reached down and fingered the skirt, his tone more serious than teasing as he whispered, "Take this off and let me see."

She blanched, sinking her teeth into her lower lip. No way in hell did she have the confidence to strut around in front of Ben Hudson in nothing but a bikini. "I don't think so."

"Why not?"

The words were out of her mouth before she could stop them. "Because I look flat-chested compared to someone like Stacy."

Green eyes bright with humor, he shook his head and laughed.

"Honey, even Pamela Anderson looks flat-chested compared to Stacy."

She couldn't help but laugh along with him. "You're probably right," she admitted, her pulse racing a little at the smoldering look he was suddenly giving her breasts.

"If you ask me, you're just the right size."

"*Riiight*," she scoffed, finding his claim hard to buy. But the deep rumble of his voice and his hot stare were damn compelling. If she hadn't listened to Drew complaining about her chest size for so many years, she just might have believed him.

"I'm serious, Reese." His voice got lower, huskier, reminding her of how he'd sounded that morning, when he'd been touching her. "I can't wait to get my mouth on your bare breasts. Make you come just from sucking on you."

Oh, wow. If her face got any redder, she was pretty sure she'd catch on fire. She was floundering for something to say back to him, when her attention suddenly snagged on a round scar on his shoulder that she hadn't noticed before. But it was hard to miss anything in the bright sunshine. "What happened there?" she asked, nodding toward the scar.

"Forget about it," he grunted, rolling his shoulder as he leaned back in his chair. "It's just an old bullet wound."

6

REESE'S JAW NEARLY DROPPED TO HER CHEST, HER BLOOD GOING COLD at the thought of Ben being hurt. She knew he'd had a dangerous job in Miami, and that he likely faced danger from time to time in his role as county sheriff. But she hadn't let herself think about some bastard actually firing a weapon at him. "I don't believe this. How did you get shot?"

"Someone fired a gun and I was too slow to dodge the bullets," he joked in a tight voice, and she sensed the unspoken message. He didn't want to talk about it. But she wasn't ready to just let it go.

"When did it happen?" she asked, spotting a second scar as she swept her gaze over his chest, this one a bit closer to his heart. He'd nearly been killed and she'd never even known. The idea made her head spin.

He took a long drink of his beer before answering her question. "A few years ago."

That was around the time he'd left Miami, and she wondered

if the two events were related. "It didn't hurt when you picked me up?" she asked, biting her lip.

He laughed. "You'd have to weigh more than a feather for it to bother my shoulder."

"A feather?" She rolled her eyes. "Hardly, but it's nice of you to say so. Drew always thought I was too heavy."

His own eyes darkened with surprise and a sudden blast of anger. "That fucked up sack of shit," he ground out under his breath. "What the hell? Was he blind? Did he want you anorexic?"

She blinked, a little stunned by his vehement reaction. But she made a quick recovery before he could press her for more information about Drew, since it wasn't a topic she wanted to discuss any more than he wanted to talk about his scars. She didn't even know why she'd brought him up. "If you're not busy this afternoon," she said, changing the subject, "can we talk after the party?"

He shifted toward her again, leaning his elbow on the chair's plastic arm. "Let's talk now."

"No, there's no rush. I just . . . I need to ask your opinion about something."

His direct, steady gaze made it clear she had his complete attention. "You can ask me about anything. Just let me know when you're ready to go."

They finished their beers, then spent the next hour eating and walking together in the surf. They didn't engage much with the other people at the party, aside from Brit, which earned them some killer glares from the women who couldn't take their eyes off Ben. But Reese tried to shrug it aside and enjoy herself. It felt good to be outside in the heat, the breeze blowing in off the turquoise water cool and refreshing, the sand soft beneath her feet. And being with Ben . . . wow. The guy was . . . not what she'd expected. Oh, she'd known he was gorgeous and smart and funny. Had surreptitiously watched him enough times over the years when they'd been at the same get-togethers to get a gist of the basics. But she'd never known how good it felt to hold his hand and just talk to him, about everything from movies to football to places they'd like to visit one day.

They'd just made it back to their chairs, where she'd left her sandals and bag, when she heard her phone ringing. She was tempted not to answer the call when she pulled the phone out of the inside pocket in her bag and saw Drew's cell number displayed on the screen. She wondered how he'd gotten her new number. And what in the world did he want? Suddenly worried that something might have happened to one of her friends up in Boston, she swiped her finger across the screen and put the phone to her ear. "Drew? What is it? What's happened?"

She could feel the intensity of Ben's stare against the side of her face as she listened to her ex's furious outburst. "What the fuck, Reese? You moved!"

With her free hand pressed over her ear to block out the music, she asked, "Why do you sound surprised? My lawyer informed you I was relocating."

Drew's voice was biting. "But I didn't think you'd actually go through with it. Damn it, Reese. What the hell are you thinking? Do you have any idea how this makes me look? I've been telling everyone we were going to reconcile, and you leave the fucking state!"

She tried to keep her tone even, mindful of the party going on around them, but it wasn't easy. Frustration made her want to scream like a banshee. "First of all, I don't know why you would tell anyone we were going to reconcile, when there isn't a chance of that ever happening. And we got a *divorce*, Drew, which means there was no reason for me to stay in Boston. What exactly did you think was going to happen?"

"I don't know," he growled. "I just . . . I miss you, damn it. I thought you'd stay here and we'd have a chance to work things out. I didn't think you'd be stupid enough to move down to that little Podunk town where your mother and sister live. I told you I didn't have anything to do with that shit that happened at your apartment, but instead of listening, you fucking run. This is the dumbest goddamn thing you've ever done!"

Pinching the bridge of her nose, she blew out an angry breath. "Get help, Drew. You need it. And please don't call me again."

"What was that about?" Ben asked, the instant she ended the call. It was impossible to miss the guttural edge to his voice, but she knew his anger was directed at Drew and not her.

"I have no idea," she murmured, slipping the phone back into her tote. "He must have had too much to drink." He'd never been much of a drinker before, but she knew from some of their mutual friends that Drew had been hitting the bottle pretty hard since the divorce.

"What did he say?"

She gave a stiff shrug. "Just nonsense, really."

"I don't like him calling you." His words were clipped, and he looked as surprised by the gruff admission as she was.

"Trust me, I don't like it, either." Pulling her bag over her shoulder, she started walking down the beach, away from the party. She needed to be on the move, too much frustration and nervous energy pumping through her system to sit still.

Ben kept perfect pace at her side. "Did you give him your new number?"

She nearly stumbled as she turned her head to glare at him. "Of course I didn't! I want nothing to do with him!"

"Sorry," he muttered, shoving a hand through his hair. "I just can't stand the jackass. I don't know why you stayed with him for as long as you did."

She kept walking, the music fading a bit as they left the party behind them. After a moment, she said, "I don't take marriage lightly, or I would have left him a long time ago. But I had every intention of honoring my vows. So long as he honored his."

"Which he didn't, because he's a damn idiot."

"Thanks. You might not say that, though, if you ever saw the receptionist he's sleeping with." Her tone was wry. "Lizzie's a tall, stacked blonde with the body of a centerfold."

"I don't care what she looks like. There's no way in hell she's sexier than you."

Reese shook her head as she laughed. "You know, I had no idea law enforcement guys could be such smooth talkers."

He reached out and grabbed her hand, spinning her around to face him as he pulled her to a stop. "It's not lip service, Reese. I mean every word."

Her breath caught at the heated look in his eyes and that rough, sexy tone. She needed to pull herself together and put some space between them before she did something crazy, like fall for the sexy stud, but she couldn't find the strength to look away. Didn't want to, really, when looking at him was so much more thrilling than running.

They were standing at the edge of the surf, the water warm as it rolled in over their bare feet. She parted her lips, no idea what she was going to say to him, when she found herself being pulled into his arms, against that rock-solid chest. He lowered his head, his lips brushing across hers as he shifted her a bit to the side, putting his back to the beach, his broad shoulders shielding her from anyone who might be looking. The kiss was warm and slow and deliciously tempting, drawing her in, coaxing her to surrender.

"Kiss me back," he urged, rough and low, and she realized he was waiting for her to take the initiative. His hands moved into her hair as the wind blew it around her shoulders, tiny grains of sand dancing against her legs as her own hands lifted, gripping his powerful biceps. His sun-warmed skin was hot and sleek against her palms as she slipped her tongue past his lips, exploring his mouth with tentative strokes. It was still so new, kissing a man who wasn't her husband, and she was still searching for her footing in this wholly unexpected situation. But she wasn't going to let it stop her. She rubbed her tongue against Ben's, loving the way his muscles bunched beneath her hands as a low groan rumbled deep in his chest. The distant sounds of music and the sea receded, her head filled with the soughing, erotic cadence of their breaths. His strong hands curved around her head, angling it back at a sharper angle, while his mouth turned almost violent in its need, taking more . . . demanding it. Despite the raw sexuality of the kiss, Reese had never felt so . . . well, cherished, as weird as that sounded. Almost needed . . . and God, was that a dangerous road for her fantasies to travel. Ben Hudson wasn't the kind of man who needed anyone.

"Reese, let's leave the party and go up to your place." He pulled back a little, his face close to hers, his green eyes burning with heat. "I want to be alone with you."

Her mouth opened and closed twice before she managed to say, "Not yet. I'm not . . . I'm still not ready to have sex with you."

When he started to respond, she put her fingers over his lips, silencing him. "And I still need to talk to you, remember?"

"Right." He took a deep breath, then slowly let it out. "What did you want to talk about?"

Not wanting to do this out in the open, she asked, "Do you mind if we go up to the patio?"

"Not at all. Just let me say bye to Brit first."

A few minutes later, Reese did her best to ignore the death-ray looks coming from Stacy and a few other women as she and Ben left the party, walking up to their houses together. Focusing on what she wanted to tell him, she tried to decide where to start, hoping he didn't . . . God, she didn't know. Think she was some wack job? Or worse, see it all as some ploy to get his attention? She couldn't see Ben doing either of those things, but then, she didn't necessarily trust her judgment much when it came to men. There'd been a time when she'd thought Drew was the best thing that could have ever happened to her, and look at how that had turned out.

But with a little jolt of surprise, Reese realized she had a hell of a lot more faith in the man walking beside her.

IT DIDN'T TAKE LONG FOR THEM TO REACH THE RELATIVE PRIVACY OF the back patio that ran the length of both houses. Ben watched as she set her bag down on one of the chairs, then made a kind of restless movement with her hands, before crossing her arms. It was obvious she was nervous, her voice a little husky as she locked her gaze on his and said, "It's probably nothing . . . I mean, I'm sure it's nothing, but I figure it's better to be cautious than stupid, right?"

He gave a slow nod, not liking the tremor of unease he could hear in her quiet tone, and more than a little surprised by how protective he felt. He liked looking out for people—hell, it was a fundamental part of his job. But the feeling was deeper with Reese. More . . . intense. It was all he could do to keep his hands at his sides, instead of reaching out and pulling her into his arms.

"First, I need to give you some background. No one in my family knows about this, so please don't tell them."

"You can trust me, Reese."

She studied his expression, then took a deep breath. "A few months ago, I had some . . . trouble up in Boston. It began when I started getting the weird feeling that someone was watching me. At first, I thought it was just my imagination, but then something happened. I came home one day after work and found a . . . a butchered cat in the middle of my bed. There was a note next to the animal's body that said my time would come."

He cursed under his breath, the guttural words rough in his throat. "Did the police have any suspects?"

She nodded. "Yes. But they couldn't—"

"That's why you asked me about a note last night, isn't it?" he ground out, suddenly cutting her off. "You were worried that whoever threw that bottle through your door did it on purpose, weren't you? Fuck, Reese. I can't believe you didn't tell me. What the hell were you thinking?"

"Well, we don't know who threw the bottle last night. It probably *was* just some kids who'd had too much to drink. But before we start arguing about it," she snapped, "I have something else to tell you."

Ben could feel his heart beating even faster, while a boulder-size lump of dread settled in his gut. "What is it?"

She rubbed her hands over her arms, as if she were chilled, when the temperature had to be climbing. "A few weeks after the cat incident, a woman was found nearly beaten to death in my apartment building. She wasn't able to give any details about her attacker, and the police couldn't find any kind of connection between us, but it definitely freaked me out. There wasn't any note left near her body, like there was with the cat, but . . . I don't know. It just didn't feel right. So I got the heck out of there."

"You did the right thing."

With those simple words, he could sense some of her tension easing. "So you don't think I was just being paranoid?" she asked, searching his expression.

"Not at all." Aware that his anger wasn't going to help the situation, Ben tried for a calmer tone. "I've been in law enforcement long enough to know that you should always listen to your gut. Now tell me about the suspects."

"The police in Boston compiled a list. Not a long one, but there were three possible suspects that they looked into, after asking me to give them the names of anyone who might have a grudge against me or who I might have pissed off. Things like that."

"Who were they?"

"Drew, obviously, because of the divorce. Then there was the father of one of the students I taught a few years ago. I reported him to the state for suspected abuse, which turned out to be true."

"And the third name?" he asked, hoping the bastard father was rotting away in prison somewhere. Though knowing the justice system these days, the jackass was probably already paroled.

"A creep one of my friends broke up with after I found out he was cheating on her with another one of the teachers at our school. I told her about the affair, and he blamed me for the end of both relationships."

"What did the police find when they looked into things?"

"They cleared Drew. Seems he had a solid alibi with his receptionist, Lizzie. My friend's jerk of a boyfriend died from an overdose two years ago. And a car had hit the parent of my student, killing him instantly, the day before the cat was left on my bed. Weird timing, but it couldn't have been him."

Scratching the stubble on his jaw, he asked, "What about one of Leighton's former opponents in the courtroom? Did the police look into any of them?"

"He works mostly in corporate law. So he's gone up against a lot of assholes, but not necessarily the profile type the cops were looking for."

His mouth pressed into a flat line. "They should have been looking at everybody."

"I would have felt better if they had, but after they'd checked out the three names I'd given them, they said there was nothing more they could do until a new lead came in. They didn't even have any partial prints they could use, which means he probably wore gloves when he broke into my apartment and left the cat. So I packed up and moved here, hoping to leave it all behind me. But . . ."

He grabbed her chilled hand, rubbing his thumb over the delicate points of her knuckles. "But what?"

"I don't know," she said tensely. "It just seems that some weird things have been happening since I got to town. First there was that bottle, which was probably nothing. But then you told me about the girl who was found beaten on the beach, and this morning, after you left, I got a strange text on my phone."

"Let me see it."

She pulled her hand from his and turned, rummaging in the bag for the phone, before turning back around and handing it to him. Ben made a low sound in his throat as he read the text, furious that someone would deliberately try to frighten her. He knew the bottle and the teenage girl probably had nothing to do with her, but the text was definitely meant to draw a personal reaction.

"I know it could have been sent to me by accident. I mean, I haven't had the number long. But it's still creepy."

"It could be Leighton," he said, handing the phone back to her. Despite the alibi her ex had given the local PD in Boston, his gut told him the guy was somehow involved. He probably thought he could scare the crap out of her, and she'd go running right back into his arms. "He called you on this phone," he added, "so you know he has the number."

"But the text didn't come from his cell phone," she pointed out, slipping the phone back into her bag. "It was a blocked number."

"He could have used another phone, Reese. Burn phones are easy to pick up these days, and he would know better than to send the text from his own number."

"I guess. But it . . . it seems unlike him to put so much effort into something. Drew's the kind of man who pays people to do things for him."

"Well, that's always a possibility." His voice got a little grittier. "He could be paying someone to keep an eye on you. Maybe even do his dirty work for him."

Reese sucked in a sharp breath, realizing he was right. But there was still something that didn't feel right about it. As much of a bastard as Drew was, she found it difficult to believe he could be so vindictive. Maybe if *she'd* been the one cheating, but damn it, he was the one who had wrecked what was left of their marriage. Not her!

"Since we don't know for sure what's going on," he said, drawing her from her thoughts, "I think it's better to be safe than sorry." It was probably just her hormones, but the hard edge of authority in Ben's deep voice was already making her feel better. "I'm going to call the alarm company and have them move up the installation date."

She'd been thinking the same thing. "That would be great. But I think I should pay for the alarm."

His gaze narrowed. "Like hell you will."

"Ben, it would make—"

"I'll pay for the fucking alarm, Reese. So drop it."

"Fine," she said tightly. "I also wanted to ask if you think I should hire an investigator."

He shook his head. "Not when I can look into things for you. I've got more resources at the station than an investigator will have. Even one as good as Alex."

She knew from the bits she'd heard over the years that Alex Hudson's career as a detective in Orlando had fallen apart after the end of his marriage. Since then, the dark, quiet Hudson brother had worked as a private investigator, specializing in cases in Southern Florida. She knew he'd earned a kickass reputation for himself, but was glad Ben hadn't suggested she hire him. Alex's arctic personality had always made her extremely uncomfortable.

Ben went on, saying, "I'll try to get the alarm company out tomorrow, but it might not be until Monday or Tuesday. Hopefully I'll be able to stay with you most nights, but I get called out for work whenever there's an emergency. When that happens, I want to know that you're protected."

"Stay with me?" She blinked, wondering where he'd gotten *that* idea. Yeah, she wanted his advice, but she hadn't expected him to think she needed to be watched over like a child. "I don't need a protector, Ben. That's not why I confided in you. I just wanted you to know what was happening, so that you could maybe help me keep an eye on things."

"I'd rather keep an eye on *you*."

"Well, that's not going to happen. I can take care of myself."

He shook his head again, beginning to sound more than a little frustrated. "And if things get worse?"

"Then I'll ask for your advice about what I should do next. But I won't expect you to solve my problems for me."

"It's my job to keep people safe, Reese."

"You wouldn't offer to sleep over at any other woman's house. Brit told me that's not your MO."

He looked pissed. "Brit needs to mind her own damn business, because I don't have a fucking MO," he snapped. "And we can keep going around in circles, but this *is* going to happen."

"What exactly do you mean by *this*?"

"You and me. Spending time together. In *and* out of bed. And don't look so damn surprised. I plan on sticking close to you until we figure out what's going on with your ex and that text, but you know there's more to it than that. I've been honest about what I want from the moment you hit town."

"And to think that I thought what I've told you might actually scare you off," she shot back, on the verge of stomping her foot like a child. And wouldn't that be embarrassing!

He came a little closer, his expression a mesmerizing mix of humor, anger, and intensity. "I don't scare easily, Reese. It pisses me off that some jackass could be deliberately trying to screw with your head, but it doesn't make me want you any less. I want you more every damn second that we spend together. That hasn't changed."

She swallowed, feeling dazed by everything that was happening. Like she was caught up in a rockslide that she couldn't stop. It was such a strange sensation, wanting this man so badly when he was driving her so crazy. Somehow, she found enough composure to say, "I'm not letting you spend the night with me again, Ben. And despite what happened between us this morning, I still haven't agreed to anything."

"But you will," he said quietly, suddenly giving her the cockiest smile she'd ever seen. "You'll do it because you deserve to just sit back and enjoy yourself for a while. To celebrate the fact that you got rid of that prick jackass you were married to and lose yourself in as many screaming orgasms as you can take."

God, she was as bad as Pavlov's dog. All he had to do was give her the *I-want-to-eat-you-alive* look he was giving her at that exact moment, and desire consumed every other emotion in its path. "You're so damn arrogant," she said in exasperation, wondering what on earth she was going to do with him.

"It's only arrogance if I can't deliver."

"You're that sure of yourself?"

"I am." His green eyes darkened with challenge. "Come on, Reese. Use me for some fun. For pleasure. Use me for whatever the hell you need." He reached out, brushing his thumb along the edge of her jaw. "I'm daring you to."

Her eyes went huge. "You're *daring* me to take what I want from you?"

"You're damn right, I am."

"You're so freaking crazy," she whispered, giving a nervous laugh as she turned her head to the side. "This isn't something you can rush, Ben. I need more time to—"

"Screw that." He caught her chin, making her look at him. "Time isn't going to solve anything. It's just going to make it easier for you to shut me out."

"No. I just . . . I need to know what I'm doing."

"That's where you're wrong," he argued, gripping her shoulders. "You just need to go with your gut."

"And take your dare? Say to hell with everything else and just take my pleasure from you?" She made a short, sharp sound of frustration, jerking out of his hold. "God, Ben. Open your eyes. I'm not some dominatrix. I'm a freaking schoolteacher! I don't tie men up and suck them dry!"

There was a single instant when she could see just how surprised he was by her outburst, and then a husky laugh rumbled up from his chest. "That's not what I meant"—his lashes lowered a little over the glittering heat in his eyes—"though it certainly makes for an interesting visual."

"I'm serious," she muttered, glaring at the gorgeous jerk. She couldn't believe he was laughing at her!

"So am I." He stepped even closer, his body nearly touching hers as she tilted her head back. "If you're willing to trust me, I swear you won't regret it."

"Aren't you listening? I don't know how to tell you what I want or need!"

"Then let me be in charge. Hell, that's what I'm more comfortable with, anyway. All you'll have to do is lie back and feel good. Just leave the how up to me."

She licked her lips, breathing fast. "The how?"

"How it happens between us." His eyes got even darker, and

his voice dropped. "If you trust me, I'll fuck you in the ways I know will make you come the hardest . . . the longest. After everything that you've been through—all the shit you've been dealing with—*that's* what you need, Reese. You need a man to spend his time on you, learning you, controlling your pleasure. To get under your skin and make you come till you can't even see straight. Until you can't even remember your name."

She reeled, feeling those husky words roll through her like a smoky shot of whiskey, rich and warm and provocative. She didn't think she'd ever get used to the way he talked to her. And then she thought about what he'd said. Really took a moment to think about what it meant—realization coming like a smack between the eyes as she thought back to their conversation that morning about handcuffs. Breathlessly . . . and a little hesitantly, since she wasn't really sure how she felt about it, she asked, "Are you a Dom?"

His brows rose. "You're familiar with the BDSM lifestyle?"

"I . . . read."

"Is that right?" His mouth twitched, as if he was trying not to smile. "Well, to answer your question, I don't practice the lifestyle the way a lot of people do. But that doesn't mean that I'm not dominant in bed."

She ran her hands over her arms again, barely able to control her breathing. It was more than a little surprising to discover how turned-on she was by the idea of him liking to take control in the bedroom. "And . . . and what if I want more than just screaming orgasms?"

There was a heavy pause, before he finally asked, "What kind of more?"

She shrugged, stung by that pause. "There's no telling. Women are complicated creatures, Ben. Surely you know that."

He stared down at her, studying her eyes, making her feel as if he were trying to look inside her mind and dig out the answer he wanted. Then he finally said, "If that happens . . . who knows? I guess you'd have to be willing to work for it."

His answer shocked her as much as everything else that had happened between them. She hadn't expected anything but a flat-out refusal, the question more of a test, if anything, to see just how strongly the idea of a relationship would make him freak. She knew damn well that a guy like Ben would never settle down. But instead, he'd voiced his response so that it almost sounded like a challenge.

Or even another dare.

"I TOLD YOU I DON'T SCARE EASILY," BEN ADDED, READING THE SURPRISE in her eyes. Hell, he'd even surprised himself with that one. But he wasn't going to worry about it now. There'd be plenty of time for that later, when he wasn't watching her pull that bitable lower lip through her teeth again, making him desperate for another taste of her mouth.

Burying his hands in her hair, Ben slipped his tongue past those soft lips as he pulled her closer, taking instant possession. It was one of those wild, *can't-breathe-through-the-need* kind of kisses. The kind he'd only ever known with Reese, and now that he'd discovered how good they could be, he was completely addicted.

But as sweet as her mouth was, there was something he needed even more. And he was done waiting for it.

With a low growl, Ben broke away from the kiss and lifted his head. Loving how quickly he could turn her on, her breaths already quickening as she gripped his biceps, he looked right then left, deciding that the small walkway on the side of her house would afford them the most privacy. Taking one of her hands in his, he quickly pulled her behind him, into the narrow, secluded passage. Then he turned and pressed her against the side of the house, the air heavy with the lush scent of bougainvillea and the delectable woman in his arms. She jolted with shock as he dropped to his knees in front of her, shoving her sundress up to her waist. "Hold it," he growled, his lips moving against the smooth skin just beneath her navel as he pressed his face against the soft swell of her stomach.

"I thought we were waiting," she gasped, digging her free hand into his hair. But she didn't push him away. She held on for dear life, and Ben took a deep breath, her warm scent making his mouth water as he dredged up every ounce of control he possessed and gave her the chance to tell him no or to fuck off and leave her alone. When she didn't say anything, just stood there, panting and trembling, he tugged on the ties at the sides of her black bathing suit bottoms and let them drop to the ground.

"Spread your legs for me," he told her, the gritty command thick with lust. He wanted to lay her down and spread her wide, looking until he'd had his fill. Take in all the plush, intimate details. But if he gave her too much time to be shy, he'd lose her. Hell, at this rate, he wasn't even sure his heart could take it. It was already pounding like a bitch in his chest, and she was moving too damn slow.

With a guttural sound of impatience, Ben hooked one slender thigh over his shoulder and shoved his face against her. His tongue plunged greedily through her slick folds, before rubbing against that tiny opening. It was swollen . . . slippery . . . perfect. She was melting into hot liquid, so drenched she was making his face wet, her sweet, salty flavor making his dick so hard he was in some serious pain. But he was having too much fun to stop, the feel of her tender sheath closing around his tongue as he pushed it inside her so incredible it nearly killed him. And when she started to pulse, his damn eyes nearly rolled back in his head.

The woman had the most edible little cunt he'd ever tasted, and Ben went at her with everything he had, her raw moans and sharp cries driving him on, until she suddenly crashed over the edge. She went silent then, not even breathing, her pale throat arched as her head went back, her body caught in a powerful, wrenching climax that nearly made him come right along with her, her hips pumping against his face. She was unraveling him, each sweet, wrenching pulse of pleasure rushing through him like it was his own. He was tied into her, feeding on the same sensory loop, his tongue still plunging and stroking as he pressed his face harder against her, trying to suck up every hot, decadent drop.

"I told you I wouldn't be able to keep my mouth off you," he growled, no clue where he finally found the strength to pull back. With his eyes squeezed shut, he lowered her trembling thigh off his shoulder and gripped her hips, his forehead pressed against her quivering belly as he breathed in hard, ragged gusts. She was his for the taking, ripe and ready and needing to be fucked—but somewhere in the back of Ben's mind, he knew she would freak if they took things any further right then. Christ, he had to have the worst timing in the world, but at least he'd made his point. No way in hell could she doubt how good they were together. When he finally got inside her, the sex would probably be so intense it destroyed them.

He swallowed, tasting her in his mouth, her lush scent still filling his head, and knew he needed to put some space between them before it was too late. "Damn it," he snarled, surging to his feet and taking a quick step back, his chest heaving as he struggled to catch his breath. Running his tongue over the edge of his teeth, he watched as she let go of her dress, the skirt falling back into place and covering his new favorite spot in the world. "I'm trying to be good, but it's fucking impossible around you, Reese."

A goofy, adorable grin curved her lips as she lowered her gaze, eyes glued to the rigid erection straining inside his swim trunks. "Am I really so tempting?" she asked softly.

"You have no idea," he grunted, wiping the back of his wrist over his damp mouth. It was still taking a herculean effort to keep his hands off her. If he'd ever been this painfully hard before, he'd blocked it from his mind. And he'd never seen her look so beautiful, her expression soft . . . relaxed, almost dreamy.

He pushed both hands back through his hair, then crossed his arms over his chest and gave her his best *I-don't-want-another-argument* stare. "You're having dinner with me tonight."

"No, I'm not," she replied, still a little breathless, and obviously missing the whole meaning of the stare. "This . . . what happened . . . it was lovely, Ben. But I told you before, I need time to think."

He didn't think it was possible for him to feel more frustrated than he'd already been, but he did. "You're overcomplicating it, Reese."

Her chin went up, some of that beautiful flush fading from her cheeks. "I'm not trying to. But I've never done anything like this before. It might be commonplace for you, but this is a big deal for me."

He scowled. "And you don't think it will be a big deal for me, too?"

Bending down to pick up her bikini bottoms, she said, "Whether it is or it isn't, you can't deny that you're a lot more comfortable with casual relationships than I am."

He clenched his jaw, knowing better than to argue the point as she straightened, that bright blue gaze locking with his.

"Please. Just . . . a little more time. Okay?"

He took a deep breath, struggling for patience, Brit's words from the night before ringing through his head again. Jesus, had it only been yesterday that he'd first told Reese he was interested in her? Maybe he *should* back off and give her a little room.

Lowering his arms to his sides, he said, "Fine. But I'm not giving up."

Another one of those shy, beautiful smiles curved her lips. "It probably means I'm crazy, but I'm glad."

"You are such an evil little tease," he groaned, fisting his hands to keep from grabbing her again.

She snorted in response, as if she thought he was joking. The woman had no idea how the things she said and did affected him, which he normally would have been thankful for. But when it came to Reese, her lack of awareness got under his skin. Made him feel crazed, as if it was his mission in life to make her understand just how fucking incredible she was. And the fact that some bastard was out there, trying to scare the hell out of her, made him want to thrash the fucker to within an inch of his life.

Ben couldn't take his eyes off her as they walked back to the patio to grab her bag, then around the side of her house again, to the front door, since she'd left her French doors locked. He didn't even trust himself to put a chaste kiss on her lips, knowing he was working on a hair trigger where she was concerned. Instead, he forced himself to give her a lecture about locking up and calling him if she needed anything or got another one of those damn texts. Then he turned and walked away, before he did something pathetic and desperate, like drop to his knees and start begging.

Letting himself in through his front door, Ben grabbed a beer from the fridge and sprawled in one of the chairs that faced his back patio, watching the late afternoon clouds blow in off the water. Reese's question about what he wanted out of a relationship with her kept looping through his mind, but there was no easy answer. He just knew that he wanted her, badly. Knew that since they'd first met, he'd compared every woman he came into contact with to Reese, and they'd all come up lacking. That he thought about her too damn often, and when he'd heard she was leaving her husband and relocating to Moss Beach, he'd known exactly what he was going to do. That he would go after her with everything he had, doing everything in his power to get his fill of her.

Rubbing his thumb over his bottom lip, his beer went forgotten as he thought about the intoxicating taste of her mouth. He could have gone on kissing her forever, which wasn't like him. Kissing wasn't normally his thing, considering there were always more exciting things he could be doing when he had a woman in his arms.

But he had to admit that he couldn't get enough of kissing Reese . . .

Brit had once told him that a kiss was one of the most romantically intimate experiences a couple could share, because it put them face to face, engaging each of their senses in the closest proximity possible. Even with your eyes closed, the other four were all in use, making you hyperaware of the person you were tangling tongues with. Which was probably why he'd always sped through the act so quickly. Women got dangerous ideas when you lingered on things that were too intimate and romantic. Best to avoid that sinkhole.

But it didn't feel like that with Reese. *He* didn't feel like that. He wanted to lose himself in the slick, tender textures of her mouth. In those petal-soft lips and her warm honeyed taste. It all blew his fucking mind.

Then he'd gone and put his mouth on her pink, pretty little pussy, and he'd nearly died. He'd never known anything that intoxicating in his life. Hadn't gotten nearly enough of it. Would have been happy to spend hours, days, even weeks with his mouth buried between her soft thighs, wallowing in those juicy folds.

Last night, it'd been damn near impossible to keep his ass planted on her couch, instead of following her into her bedroom. Today, that sense of need and anticipation was even worse. He was edgy . . . restless. He'd never, in all his thirty-four years, been this wound up about a woman before, and Ben knew if he gave himself too much time to think about how she affected him, it was going to screw with his head.

Instead, he stood up and carried his beer into his office, firing up his laptop. He'd give her the time she'd asked for tonight and spend the hours focusing on what she'd told him. With any luck, by tomorrow morning he'd have a better idea of what had gone down in Boston . . . and what part her bastard ex had really played in it.

7

SITTING IN A COMFORTABLE BOOTH WITH A WELCOME STREAM OF COOL air blowing down on them from above, Reese was glad she'd agreed to meet Connie for lunch at the best Mexican restaurant in town. Despite it being Sunday, the place wasn't too packed, and the food was delicious. They were washing down a platter of nachos with ice-cold sweet tea, when Connie started reminiscing about some of the crazy things they'd gotten up to in high school.

"Do you remember when I'd just started my freshman year and you dared me to go over to Corey Handler's house dressed up like Britney Spears and perform that dance from her video?" Corey had been the star quarterback of the football team and the cutest boy in Reese's junior class.

"Oh my God," Reese gasped, setting her tea down as she laughed. "I'd completely forgotten about that. Didn't he end up asking you out?"

Connie's smile was wry. "Yeah, only Mom said no way in hell."

She took a sip of her tea, then grinned as she reached for another chip. "But I was glad I'd done it, because you and I had such a blast setting the whole thing up. You were always so much fun back then."

Back then? Reese's smile fell. "Gee, thanks."

Her sister flushed. "I'm sorry. I didn't mean it like that. It's just that—"

"Don't worry about it. I know what you meant."

She honestly did understand, though she wouldn't have been able to say that before. But with each day that she spent out from under the oppressive thumb of her marriage, Reese could see how much it had changed her a little more clearly. Could see how much of herself she'd given up trying to make Drew happy. Trying to be the wife that he wanted and fit into his mold for the "ideal" woman. She didn't know how it'd happened. Couldn't understand why she'd *let* it happen. But she thanked God that she could see it now.

"Say what you like about Ben," Connie murmured, as if she could read her mind, "but he'll be good for your ego."

She rolled her eyes, wondering how many times her sister was going to mention the guy. "Be realistic, Con. How will watching him walk away when he's through with me be good for my ego?"

There must have been something in her voice, because Connie's expression changed, her brow creasing with worry. "Wait a minute. Are you . . . Do you have *feelings* for Ben?"

"Of course not," she said a little too quickly, hoping it was true. The last thing she needed was to fall for a guy like Ben. She might as well leave her heart out on a stake to cook in the summer sun.

"If you're not falling for him, Reese, then what's the problem?"

"There's no problem," she said, trying for a more casual tone. "I just don't want to get hurt. I mean, who's to say how I might come to feel about him if we start seeing each other?"

Connie gave her an understanding nod. "So be smart and pull away before you get too far into him."

She scrunched her nose. "That sounds so . . . crass."

Her concern forgotten, Connie shot her a dazzling smile and waggled her brows. "Ben's a big boy. He won't mind being used. God knows he's done it enough times himself. So have your fun with him, and be the one who walks away first."

She pressed her hand against her stomach, just the thought of doing something like that making her feel a little queasy. "I don't know if I can do that, Con."

"Sure you can. It won't be easy, but I have a feeling it'll be worth it. You need some fun in your life, sis. Need to mix things up in a wild way." Connie dropped her voice to a dramatic drawl, doing the eyebrow thing again. "And from the things I've heard about our sexy sheriff, he'll be just the guy to do it."

Jeez. Even Connie thought she needed to have some fun. Did everyone think she was a walking mausoleum? It was starting to get embarrassing. "I have to think about it."

"Just don't think too long. The sooner you jump into the pool again, the sooner you'll realize how many opportunities are out there."

"I don't need a man to be happy," she argued, the idea of wading through some endless dating pool making her cringe.

Reaching across the table, Connie patted her hand. "I know that, Reese." A wry smile twisted her sister's mouth. "But you can't get away from the fact that some things are just a hell of a lot more fun when you've got one around."

They both laughed, and Connie excused herself to go to the ladies' room, giving Reese some time alone with her thoughts. She'd enjoyed their lunch, but her sister's words from earlier kept niggling at the edge of her mind, making her tense. After living for so many years with Drew trying to shape her identity, she was still coming to grips with who she was and what she wanted. Still trying to understand how she could have let it happen.

It was just so weird, how you could look back and watch your life play out like a movie. There were times when she didn't even recognize the actress playing her in most of the scenes. Who was that woman? The one who'd let a crap husband walk all over her? The one who'd pasted on a false smile and pretended to love her life, simply because she was too embarrassed to admit that she'd made more wrong choices than right ones? Sometimes, the frustration with the way she'd lived still bubbled up inside her with so much force, she felt like burying her head in her pillow and bawling her eyes out. But it wasn't going to solve anything. The answer was to finally start living on her own terms. To take back control. To start having some fun, like everyone kept suggesting, and stop worrying about where everything was going.

Then why in God's name aren't you taking Ben up on his offer?

She scowled, wondering when that annoying voice in her head was finally going to shut up.

I'll shut up when you start listening to me. You want some fun? Some pleasure? That guy is ready to offer it, with a no hassle guarantee.

True. Ben hadn't asked her for anything more than her body, though she still wasn't sure why he wanted it. But she was the one complicating things. Worrying she wouldn't be able to keep herself from developing feelings for him.

And would it really be the end of the world if she did? If her divorce had shown her anything, it was that she was tough enough to take a hit and keep on ticking. She might be bruised, but damn it, she wasn't broken! She'd just have to keep her eyes open and the facts sharp in her mind. Remember that they were together for pleasure . . . not forever.

While the restaurant buzzed with activity around her, Reese sat at the table completely lost in thought, determined to make a decision where the sexy sheriff was concerned. And in the end, it was Ben's dare that did it. Not because she couldn't turn one down—but because she always had. Despite being fun-loving when she was younger, she'd never been the wild one. Oh, she might have dared her sisters to do crazy things, but she'd never done them herself.

She was going to do one now.

After all the talk of handcuffs and domination, she was a little nervous about what he'd want from her, but it'd have been a lie if she'd said she didn't want him. The fact that she melted into a shivering state of bliss every time he touched her was proof enough of her attraction, as was the way she could never tell him no. She had the resistance of a gnat around the guy, so wasn't it time she started enjoying his efforts for a change, instead of worrying it all to death?

You bet your stubborn ass, it's time!

After Connie returned to the table, they paid the bill, then made their way out to the sweltering parking lot. Her Toyota had been delivered from the auto shop that morning, and she was thankful for the freedom to get around. Wanting to pick up a few new things for the beach house, she stopped by one of the local garden centers and stocked up on houseplants, as well as some flowers, pots, and four hanging baskets for the patio. Declining any help out to her car, Reese pushed the heavy cart into the afternoon sunshine, and started across the warm asphalt. As she turned down the third row of cars, a strange chill traveled down her spine, making her pause. She stood still, hands gripped around the cart's handle like claws, trying to pinpoint the source of the uneasy sensation, but none of the other customers loading their vehicles were paying her any attention. Shaking her head, she set off again, her jaw clenched with irritation.

Great. Just what I wanted to turn into: a paranoid head case!

There'd been no further texts on her phone, which meant the one from yesterday had probably been a wrong number. Creepy, but most likely meant for someone else. Or nothing more than a stupid prank. She just needed to pull up her big-girl pants and stop getting spooked by her shadow. Enough was enough!

Still, despite her determination to just chill, Reese couldn't shake the bizarre feeling that she was being followed as she drove home. She found herself looking repeatedly into her rearview mirror, trying to determine which cars were taking the same route, as if she had a clue what she was doing. The last suspense film she'd watched with Drew flashed through her mind, twisting her stomach into knots. She found herself replaying the scene where the psychotic killer stalked the heroine on her way home from the store, and it hadn't ended well for the girl.

Oh, honestly! Get a freaking grip!

Jaw set, she cranked up the radio and focused on simply getting home in one piece. Ten minutes later, she was pulling into the small drive that led to the beach houses, and was surprised to see Ben's truck parked in front of his place. When she'd left that morning, he'd already been gone.

Filled with so much nervous tension she was about to snap, Reese changed her jeans for a pair of cutoffs and started to unload the car. She'd just stepped onto the patio with the last of the hanging baskets, when she caught sight of Ben jogging up the path that led down to the beach.

"Hey," he called out, looking entirely too edible in a sweaty gray T-shirt and black running shorts.

She looked at his sexy, sculpted mouth, remembered where it'd been the day before, and felt the heat rise in her face like a fever. "Um, hi. Did you have a good run?"

He nodded, looking around at all the colorful flowers. "You went shopping?"

"After I met Connie for lunch. We ate at Casa di Pico."

"I love that place. Best chips and salsa in town." He picked up a small towel that he'd left on one of the chairs, using it to wipe his face and neck as he walked over to join her. "I heard from the alarm company. They're going to be out tomorrow morning at nine."

"That's great. Thanks for calling them."

"Not a problem." He pushed his damp hair back from his forehead, and she almost gasped at the sight of his biceps bunching under his tight, dark skin. If the man were any more masculine, he'd be freaking lethal. She already felt light-headed. Either the heat was getting to her, or he was so gorgeous it was messing with her equilibrium.

"Reese?"

"Hmm?" she murmured, jerking her attention back to his rugged face.

"I said I need to grab a shower, but do you want to sit out here and have a drink after I'm done?"

"You're sure you have the time?" she asked, hoping he'd say yes as she set down the basket she'd been holding by the others.

He tossed his towel over a broad, muscular shoulder, and a damp lock of hair fell over his brow as he smiled. "Wouldn't matter if I didn't. You're more important than anything else I could have going on."

She grinned, trying to remember to keep things light. "I bet you say that to all the girls."

"The hell I do." He cocked his head a bit to the side, looking as if he couldn't decide between kissing her . . . or spanking her backside for doubting him. "And just so we're clear on this, Reese, while I'm fucking you, I won't be fucking anyone else. I don't see the point in sleeping with one woman when I wouldn't be able to stop thinking about another one."

She swallowed, pulling in a deep breath of his scent, and even sweaty the guy smelled incredible. Hot and musky and wonderfully male. It was a scent that called to her on a primitive, visceral level, and before she'd even realized the words were coming out of her mouth, she said, "But you're not fucking me, Ben."

"Not yet." His smirk was unbelievably sexy. "But admit it, I'm making progress. And I just got you to say the f-word."

She laughed, some of her earlier tension easing. "Actually, I'm glad we ran into each other. There's something I want to talk to you about."

Concern knitted his brow. "Did something else happen? Did you get another text?"

"Oh, no. Nothing like that." She didn't bother mentioning that strange feeling she'd had in the parking lot at the garden center, knowing it was probably just her imagination. She was wound up too tight, which meant her mind would definitely be playing tricks on her.

"Then what did you want to talk about?"

She took another deep breath, and forced herself to just say it, before she lost her nerve. "I've decided that I'm done complicating everything. I'm ready to take you up on your dare and, um, use you for a . . . a fling."

She could tell she'd taken him by surprise, but he didn't say a damn thing in response. He just stood there looking all hot and intense, his dark gaze focused on her so sharply she felt like he was trying to get inside her head.

"That's what you wanted, isn't it?" She sank her teeth into her bottom lip, heart pounding so hard it hurt.

The heat in his eyes sent chills racing over her body. "I don't see the point in having to label everything, but you can call it whatever you want," he finally responded, the quiet words raw and gritty. "All I care about is that I get to fuck you hard and deep and as often as possible."

"Then . . . okay. That's what I want, too. Um, I mean to do to you." Oh, God. If she'd ever blushed this much, she'd blocked it from her memory.

He started prowling toward her. "You plan on fucking me hard, Reese?"

"Y-yes."

"I think I can handle that." The smile that curved his wicked mouth could only be described as dangerous. "But I get to fuck you first."

Laughing low in his throat, he pulled off his damp T-shirt, caught her around the waist, and jerked her against his hot, sweaty chest. His head swooped down, his mouth taking hers in a kiss that was wild and hard and outrageously explicit, his tongue thrusting in a way that nearly melted her bones. When he finally let her take a breath, he nipped her jaw with his teeth, then put his mouth close to her ear. "Can I use your shower?"

"Y-yes."

He set her back on her feet and grinned. "Don't move," he ordered her, and she stood there in a daze, watching him run over to his house. He disappeared inside, then came rushing back out, a clean pair of sweats thrown over his shoulder . . . and an entire freaking box of condoms in his hand!

Reese knew her mouth was hanging open because he tapped it shut, turned her toward the French doors, and gave a playful swat to her bottom. "Lead the way, sweetheart. And be quick."

She looked over her shoulder, loving the hunger she could see in those heavy-lidded eyes. "In a hurry, are you?"

"Woman, you have no idea," he said with a playful growl. "Now go!"

She stifled a nervous laugh as she made her way through the French doors, the rooms of the house cool and shadowed. He'd barely even touched her, and already her breaths were coming in sharp, tight bursts, her pulse racing with excitement. She was still scared to death of the risk she was taking, but needed him too badly to turn back now. He was giving her an outlet for all her pent-up emotions and frustration, and by God, she was going to take it. She no longer cared if it was a smart or stupid move. If she was going to end up hurt or heartbroken. All she wanted was to lose herself in this man and give herself over completely to the need. To this blistering, heady urgency thrumming through her veins, shivering across her skin. She wanted to pull him to her and hold him tight, demanding he fuck her harder, faster. Wanted to be wilder, more outrageous and demanding, than she'd ever been before.

And she wanted him to do the same. Wanted him to let go and really have at her. Wanted him to show her just how badly he deserved his reputation as a man who could make a woman scream in pleasure and forget her own name, reducing her to a quivering mass of erotic sensation.

"Get your clothes off," he said in that low voice, as soon as they entered the bathroom. "I want to see every inch of you."

"I will if you will."

His mouth quirked up at the corner, his dark gaze smoldering and hot as he tossed the condoms and his sweats on the counter, then reached for the waistband of his running shorts and shoved them down. At that moment, Reese was pretty sure her jaw hit the floor, watching him take off his clothes one of the most exciting experiences of her life.

She'd seen pictures of muscular models and athletes. She knew what a powerful male body could look like. But, wow. Just wow. Nothing she'd ever seen in print had prepared her for the sight of a tall, deliciously naked Ben Hudson. The guy was un-freaking-believable. Rugged and hard and tough, but heart-stoppingly beautiful. Lean, but packed with strong, sleek muscles. Broad shoulders, narrow waist, powerful thighs. Ripped abs, perfect pecs. And if she followed that sexy whorl of dark hair around his navel, she got a mouthwatering eyeful. She'd known he was big, had felt him pressed against her, even felt him against her palm, but the visual in her mind hadn't been anything like this. He was longer . . . broader . . . the dark skin ridged with a thick mapping of veins. He looked . . . well, fairly intimidating, but she refused to cower like a trembling virgin. She knew it was probably going to hurt a bit when he shoved that massive thing inside her, but it would be worth it. She didn't doubt it for a second.

He jerked his chin toward her frilly tank top and she finally shook herself out of her daze. Wishing she could do this without blushing, she pulled off the tank top, then quickly unhooked her strapless bra before she lost her nerve.

He stared at her breasts, then slowly lifted his gaze. "Now the rest."

"Okay," she whispered, watching as he reached into the shower and blindly started the water, his eyes never once leaving her. Her hands shook as she worked her shorts and underwear down her legs, kicking off her sandals before stepping out of the soft-washed denim cutoffs and panties. Slipping the silver hoops from her ears, she set them on the counter then turned to face him, her hands fidgeting at her sides.

His jaw worked as he pushed the shower door open wider, nostrils flaring as he sucked in a sharp breath. "Get in."

She brushed past him, stepping into the shower, her back pressed against the wall as he followed her in and pulled the frosted door shut.

"It was hell staying away from you last night." His voice was deep and rough, thick with things she'd never even heard before. But she liked them. A lot.

"It was hell for me, too," she admitted.

Satisfaction burned like a molten flame in his eyes. "Good."

She took a quick breath of the damp air, steam rising up around them like a sensual cloud. It felt as if she'd stepped into some kind of provocative dream world, and she hoped to God she didn't wake up before the finish. "This is probably a good time to tell you that I've only ever been with my husband."

"*Ex*-husband."

"Right." She could feel the erotic weight of his gaze like a physical touch as it moved over every inch of her flushed skin, but couldn't manage to take her own eyes off his stunning erection. "I just wanted you to know . . . I'm not very . . . I mean, you'll, uh, probably have to teach me . . . some stuff."

His laugh was low and wicked as he crowded her against the tiled wall. "Christ, you're trying to kill me, aren't you?"

She smirked as she tilted her head back, staring up into his gorgeous face. "You look tough enough. I don't think you're in any danger of expiring."

"And that just shows how little you know," Ben murmured, bracing one forearm beside her head. With his other hand, he grabbed her wrist and lifted, pressing her palm against the center of his chest. "My heart's beating like a jackhammer, Reese."

A shy smile bloomed across her mouth, her big eyes dazzling and bright. She was so damn beautiful. So fucking perfect and sweet and soft. He just wanted to fall on her like a madman, but knew the more comfortable she could get with him, the better it would be for her. And, God, did he want it to be good. He wanted her addicted to it, to *him*, so that he could have her whenever he wanted. He needed that constant access, because who knew how long it would take before this knot of need in his gut finally eased. Before he'd finally have his fill. If he never did . . .

No. He didn't want to think about that. Not now, when she was staring up at him with those big blue eyes, her cheeks flushed, lips rosy and slick.

Forcing himself to take a step back, he grabbed her shampoo bottle. "Turn around. I'll do your hair."

Reese blinked at the unexpected command, but did as he said. She let her head fall back on her shoulders as he started up a rich lather, the coconut scent of the shampoo drifting to her nose. She'd expected things to be hot and fast, but he was obviously trying to ease her into the encounter. She almost thought about lodging a protest, her body so needy she felt like she might combust at any moment, but then he started massaging her scalp with those strong fingers, and she forgot all about complaining. And when he murmured for her to turn around and reached for the body wash, she was more than ready for what came next.

Oh, yeah. This was heavenly. His deliciously hard, hot body vibing with need before her, while his big, skilled hands lathered her up.

But it was the look on his face that really undid her. That hard, thrilling, *I-want-to-shove-you-up-against-the-wall-and-fuck-your-brains-out* look.

Needing to touch him, she started to reach for the body wash, but he caught her wrist. "What?" she asked. "Don't I get a turn?"

He blew out a ragged breath, letting her wrist go as he shook his head. "It'll take too long, and I'm nearly at the breaking point already."

She would have found that difficult to believe, given his experience and the hoards of beautiful women she knew he'd been with, but the hard cast of lust on his face was proof of just how on edge he was. So she simply stood under the water and rinsed off as she watched him quickly lather up that breathtaking body. When he was done, he didn't bother switching places. He simply stepped under the spray of water with her, lifted her up with his hands around her waist, and pressed his hot face between her breasts.

"Ben?" she breathed out, feeling the tremor that ran through him.

"I've waited so damn long to get my hands on you," he groaned, turning his head to lick one nipple, before shifting his attention to the other. Then he pulled his head back and watched as they pulled tighter, his voice little more than a guttural croak. "You're so fucking beautiful, Reese."

She gasped as he suddenly pushed her against the tiled side of the shower, lowered his head, and greedily took one of those sensitive nipples into the blistering heat of his mouth. "My, um, breasts could be bigger," she whispered, her eyes closing as she turned her head to the side and bit her lip.

"They're perfect," he growled, hating the insecurity he could hear in those quiet words. Didn't the woman know he was fucking starved for her? That he was terrified he would never get enough? That he'd never get his fill?

Keeping her pinned against the wall, Ben licked and sucked and teased until sharp, pleasure-thick cries were climbing up her throat, her hard little nipples throbbing against his tongue. Her hands dug into his hair, pulling him closer, body trembling against him. But she still kept her head turned away, damp strands of hair sticking to her rosy cheek.

"Look at me," he ground out, his deep voice rough with command. "Look at me, Reese. Right this fucking second."

She took a shuddering breath, turned her head, and opened eyes that were burning with a need as desperate and urgent and violent as his—and Ben's control snapped.

WITH ROUGH, HURRIED MOVEMENTS, BEN TURNED OFF THE WATER AND pulled Reese out of the shower, quickly snagging a fluffy white towel from the shelf and using it to dry them off. It took no more than a handful of seconds before he was carrying her into the bedroom and tossing her into the center of her mattress, along with a couple of foil packets from the box of condoms.

With the late afternoon sunlight filtering in through the slanted shutters and spilling across the bed, Ben crawled over her, his heart pounding in his chest like a drum. Shoving her legs apart with his knee, he knelt between her sprawled thighs, the sight of her under him, where he'd wanted her for so damn long, making him ache. Holding her heavy-lidded gaze, he reached down and stroked his fingertips over the plump folds of her sex, wanting her to know exactly how juicy and slick she was. Then he pushed two big fingers inside that pink little hole, loving the way she held him. The way her breath hitched and her eyes went wide, that lush lower lip caught in her teeth. She looked like a pagan goddess with all that creamy, freckled skin and silky hair spread out around her head, and all he could think was *now*. He had to get inside her *now*, damn it, before he fucking lost it.

Breathing in ragged gusts, Ben sat back on his heels and quickly reached for one of the foil packets. His hands shook as he sheathed his cock in the thin latex, before settling back over her and bracing his weight on one arm again. Then he gripped the heavy, rigid shaft, angling it away from his stomach. Shaking a drop of sweat from his brow, he rubbed the swollen head around her tender opening, getting himself wet, then slowly started to force his way inside, her sharp gasp making him clench his jaw. She was hot and slippery and tight as a fucking fist, and he wanted to slam himself inside her so badly he could taste it. But he had to make this good for her, damn it. Had to control his own primitive urges and make sure she was right there with him.

"You're so wet," he growled, watching her juices cream around his thick rod as he worked it in deeper, forcing his way past that deliciously tight resistance. "You're fucking drenching me."

"Sorry," she said breathlessly, hands gripping his biceps in a death grip as he braced his weight on both arms.

"Don't be. I love you like this. All juicy and shiny and slick." He lifted his head, eyes locked with hers as he pulled out on a slow slide, and she cried out as he pushed back into her, her hips writhing as she tried to take him deeper.

"Feels incredible," she moaned, her head tipping back as she closed her eyes. "I feel so *full*."

Shit, she was completely undoing him. And she was about to get a hell of a lot fuller. "Take more of me," he ground out, his body burning with heat, muscles coiled beneath his tight skin as he tried to hold still.

"I'm trying," she panted, breathing hard. "But I can't."

"You can, baby. I know you can."

She groaned, lifting her knees a little higher as she arched beneath him, and more of his thick flesh slipped inside, throbbing and hard. Gripping her jaw, Ben waited until she'd opened her eyes, before saying, "Now take another inch, Reese. I dare you."

"You and your damn dares!" she shouted, suddenly laughing as she swatted at his chest.

"Look at you already beating on me. I knew you'd be a little hellion," he teased, grinning, and just like that, she relaxed enough to take the next three inches of his cock. And oh, God, it was sweet. He'd never known anything like this, the white-hot, blistering lust wrapped up in this tender, unfamiliar emotional thing they had going. She was so goddamn plush inside, so cushiony and snug and wet, he felt like he was sinking his dick into some kind of sexual nirvana, the excitement he could see shimmering in her big blue eyes only intensifying the sensations.

Looking down, Ben watched as he gave her another slow, grinding thrust, his broad shaft stretching her wide. Time passed by in a provocative haze, his entire world narrowing down to this bed and the woman beneath him, his rolling hips working him in inch . . . by inch. Finally, he was packed up deep inside her, only the top two inches of his cock, where he was thickest, still visible. He wanted to grit his teeth and ram them in, feel her hot little cunt hugging every throbbing inch of him as he went balls-deep, but knew it would be too much. He'd already given her even more than he gave most of the women he slept with, and she was the tightest he'd ever had. No matter how good it would feel, he'd rather have his fucking balls crushed than hurt her.

Then she blinked up at him, her beautiful eyes glowing with passion as she whispered, *I love this.* And he fucking lost it.

The next thing Ben knew, he had his hands curled around her wrists. Tightening his grip, he lifted them over her head, pinning them against the pillows, and put his face close to hers. "I'm sorry," he snarled, his hips already pulling back. Then he let go, burying himself in her tight pussy as hard and as fast as he could, his body hammering into hers again . . . and again. He gave her everything but those final inches, thankful for that last scrap of sanity that kept him from going too far. But she was screaming loud enough to wake the dead, and he hoped to God it was in pleasure, because he was bound by this driving rhythm, unable to pull out, to slow down. Then he felt her legs wrapping around his waist, her heels digging into his ass, and Ben knew he was gone. With a hoarse, guttural roar on his lips, he started coming, the pleasure ripping down his fucking spine with such devastating force it nearly turned him inside out. He cursed and shuddered and blasted himself into her until everything went mindless and black, his lungs heaving as his arms gave out and he collapsed, crushing her beneath him.

For a long time he just lay there, wrecked, his mind completely blown. All he knew was the feel of the soft, lush body trapped beneath him, the most mouthwatering scent in the world filling his head with each of his deep, ragged breaths. And then reality slowly started to creep back into the edges of his consciousness, and he thought, *Shit*. He'd just completely lost control. Had taken her hard and rough. Even harder and rougher than he normally screwed, and it'd been their first time together. What the fuck had he been thinking?

He hadn't. At least not with anything but his dick. And that *always* led to trouble.

Lifting his head, Ben tried to get his bearings, but his damn brain was still spinning. When he'd come, he'd gone into some kind of strange physical state, hyperaware of every wrenching pulse as his cum had blasted into the condom. He'd been riding pure sensation, heart pounding, head thrown back as he'd roared like an animal.

Then he'd lowered his head, staring back down into Reese's hazy gaze, and the sensations had multiplied in an endless rush, until he'd blacked out like some kind of junkie. What the hell? The woman had turned him into a rutting madman, and with dawning horror, Ben realized he couldn't recall her own climax. Son of a bitch! Had he missed it? He hoped to God he hadn't left her hanging. All that intense build up, and he wasn't even sure if he'd carried through on his talk. What a fucking prick!

"If you give me another chance," he rasped, letting go of her wrists so that he could brace himself on his elbows, "I swear I can make it better for you."

She covered her face with her hands, but he knew she was smiling. He could feel it, as if that lighthearted burst of emotion was his own. "Make it any better," she said in a muffled voice, "and it might kill me."

Despite the sickening weight of guilt still churning in his gut, Ben suddenly felt like smiling, too. "You liked it that rough?" he asked with surprise, taking her left hand and pressing it to the bed so that he could see her face. A precious, blushing face that made him want to kiss her again.

She lowered the other hand, her soft lips pressed together as she shook with laughter. "Do we really need to have this conversation?"

"'Fraid so," he said huskily. "I can't read your mind, honey."

"Could have fooled me," she drawled.

A slow smile kicked up the corner of his mouth, his chest tight with emotions he was doing his best to ignore. But there was no ignoring how good this moment felt. "God, I've wanted you under me for so damn long."

She blinked up at him again, and her smile turned deliciously shy. "I never knew," she whispered, tracing the shape of his brows with a delicate fingertip, before stroking the stubble on his jaw. "Why didn't you tell me?"

"You were another man's wife," he said, thinking that he'd never realized how sexy a blush on a woman's cheeks could be before. Cute little freckled cheeks that he couldn't resist touching with his mouth. "No matter how badly I wanted you," he explained, brushing his lips across her smooth skin, "I wasn't going to butt in where I didn't belong."

Her tone was wry. "Trust me. I didn't belong in that marriage either."

Drawing his head back, he caught her gaze. "I was hoping you'd figure that out. And when you did, I was planning on making an ass of myself."

She looked curious. "And just how did you plan to do that?"

"By making sure you noticed me," he admitted, loving the way she'd started running her fingertips down his back.

Quietly, she said, "I always noticed you, Ben."

"Bullshit," he snorted. "You hardly ever said more than two words to me."

Her long hair slipped over the sheets as she tilted her head and shrugged. "Only because you scared me."

A crease wedged itself between his brows. "I scared you?"

"Not in a bad way," she explained, blue eyes dark and serious as she stared back at him. "You just . . . you made me feel things that I wasn't comfortable feeling."

A slow smile curved his mouth. "So you *did* notice me."

"I even dreamed about you sometimes." The admission was soft . . . and hesitant. "To be honest, I thought about you a lot, Mr. Hudson."

"When?" he pressed, his heart starting to beat a little harder.

Her blush got deeper. "When did I think about you?"

"Yeah."

A nervous laugh slipped past her lips. "I don't remember."

"Then I'll help jog your memory," he told her, reaching down to hold the condom in place as he carefully pulled out, loving the way her body fought to hold him inside. She winced a little as he moved onto his side, and he knew she had to be sore after the way he'd lost it. Turning so that he could toss the rubber into the small wastebasket beside the bed, Ben rolled back and braced himself on an elbow, his body pressed along the side of her smaller, delicate one. "You ever touch yourself while thinking about me?" he asked, resting his big hand across the soft swell of her belly.

Her eyes went a little wide as she gazed up at him. "I'm uh . . . not really comfortable talk—"

"I don't care if you're comfortable. I only care about making you feel good. About giving you what you need. So answer the question."

Her disgruntled look was adorable. "How will my answer tell you what I need?"

Stroking his thumb across the sensitive skin just beneath her breast, he said, "If it's a yes, then I want to know what you thought about. What you pictured in your mind. Moonlight and romance? Or me putting you against a door and giving it to you hard? Did I get my mouth on you? Tongue-fuck you? Cock-fuck you?" Propping his head on his hand, he grinned. "These are things I intend to find out."

"Well, I don't think we've known each other long enough to—"

"Stop stalling, beautiful, and just answer the damn question."

"You're so freaking bossy!" she huffed.

"When it comes to making you come, you're damn right I am."

"You have that part covered. Trust me." She shifted a little, and her eyes went wide again when she felt his already hardening shaft pressed against her hip. "God, Ben. Is that normal?"

"Not usually." It was a little embarrassing to feel the heat in his face, but she was looking at him like he was some kind of erection mutant. "It must be you."

"Oh." She pulled her lower lip through her teeth, and his cock started throbbing, as if he hadn't just blown like a fucking volcano. "Do you want me to . . . ?"

His mouth twitched as he fought back a smile. "Do I want you to what?"

Her lashes lowered a little, shielding her gaze. "Um, you know."

"Come on," he coaxed, his tone teasing and soft. "Say it."

"Why?"

He leaned down and nipped her chin. "Because I *really* want to hear you talking about my cock."

She shoved at his shoulder, choking back an exasperated laugh. "Just answer the question! Do you want head or not?"

"Oh, I want it," he replied in a husky rumble, catching her hand and pulling it down to his rigid hard-on. He'd expected her to be shy about touching him, but she wasn't, his breath sucking in on a sharp gasp when she took hold and squeezed, her thumb rubbing a slow circle over the slick head.

With heavy-lidded eyes, Ben watched as she brought her thumb up to her mouth, licking away the drop of pre-cum he'd given her.

"Jesus," he hissed, the erotic sight shredding his control. "You're pushing me, Reese."

"Good." There was a wealth of satisfaction in that single word, a triumphant spark in her eyes that was sexy as hell.

Ben gave her a hard, dark stare, taking her measure. "You sure you're ready for this?"

She smirked. "Bring it on, Sheriff."

His eyes narrowed a little. "Then roll over and get your little ass in the air."

Her own eyes went round. "*What?*"

"You heard me." He let his fingers play in the tidy little triangle of damp curls at the top of her mound while he waited for her to make a move. When she just lay there, watching him, her breaths coming soft and fast, he smoothed his hand up over a perfectly shaped breast. Then he trapped her nipple between his finger and thumb with just the right amount of pressure. He wasn't hurting her, but he definitely had her attention, her eyes dilating as a soft gasp fell from her lips. "Don't make me tell you again," he said with a husky edge of command.

"Fine. But I thought I was going down on *you*," she grumbled under her breath, shifting over to her front the second he let go. Without even waiting for him to tell her, she pressed the side of her face into the bedding and lifted onto her knees.

Ben closed his eyes at the mouthwatering sight, then slowly opened them. "You'll get your turn," he growled, moving onto his knees behind her. "My dick is at the ready whenever you feel like sucking on it—but right now I want more of *this*." He used his knees to spread hers a little wider and grabbed her hips, jerking her ass higher. Then he used his thumbs to spread her rosy cheeks, looking his fill. Her cunt was opened up like a juicy peach, her anus a tight little rosette that made him groan.

She gasped his name, trembling as he ran a thumb over the puckered entrance.

"Shh. Don't panic. I just want you to get comfortable with me touching you here."

Chill bumps raced over her skin, and her voice shook. "I d-don't think that's p-possible."

"It'll happen," he assured her with a groaning laugh. He pushed in a little with his thumb, just testing her tightness, and bent down low near her ear. "One day soon, I'm going to take you here, Reese. I'm going to spread these round little ass cheeks, lube you up, and bury every inch of my cock into this tight little hole."

"Oh, God," she moaned.

He gave another gritty laugh, slipping his fingers down to her swollen, slippery folds. "And once I'm in this sweet ass to the hilt, I'm going to give you another dare."

Her voice shivered with excitement. "Like wh-what?"

Pressing his lips to the back of her neck, he said, "I'll dare you to fuck this deluxe little pussy with your favorite dildo. The bigger, the better."

"Ohmygod! I don't even have one of those!" she protested, her face turning pinker beneath the silky wisps of hair falling over her cheek.

"Really?" When she nodded, he nipped her shoulder. "Then we'll have to go shopping first."

Her laugh was muffled by the bedding as she buried her face in it. "No way!"

"Come on, sweetheart. We both know if I dare you, then you can't say no. It's your weakness," he whispered, kissing the tender side of her throat as he kept up the slow thrust of his fingers in that slick sheath. "And I really want to see you fuck this tight little cunt while I'm fucking your ass. I don't think I've ever wanted anything more."

Reese groaned with mortification, and he laughed, his breath warm against her ear as he nuzzled his nose against her hair. "You don't need to be embarrassed," he told her.

Her voice was still muffled. "Who said I'm embarrassed?"

He gave another one of those deep, husky laughs as he pulled back, trailing a fingertip down the sensitive line of her spine. "You're blushing over every inch of this beautiful skin."

"Sorry," she grumbled.

"Don't be sorry, baby." He pressed his lips to the base of her spine, the sweet kiss so at odds with the way he ran his thumbs down the crease of her buttocks, then pulled them apart again, completely exposing her to his gaze as he kneeled behind her. She knew he was staring at her. Could feel the blistering heat of his gaze like a physical touch. "You're beautiful, Reese. Especially here," he rasped, rubbing his thumbs over her slick, puffy vulva. "And here," he added, his voice a little rougher as he stroked his thumbs on either side of her anus.

She shivered, surprised by how much she enjoyed him touching her there. It was embarrassing, but she'd have been lying if she'd said it wasn't hot as hell. He pressed one of his thumbs right over the puckered opening again, stroking it, and she wriggled her hips, heat rushing beneath her skin, no doubt turning her an even brighter shade of pink. But she didn't care. She just wanted to feel . . . more . . . *there.*

"Ben?" she whispered with a thread of panic, wondering what the hell was happening to her.

"Stop thinking and just enjoy it," he murmured in a low voice. And then, without any warning, she felt him shift behind her, and something wet and soft stroked right over that tight, sensitive flesh. *Holychrist!* She couldn't believe he'd just . . . licked her. There! Something sharp and thick crawled up from her throat, the sound purely sexual and desperate, and he groaned, licking her again, before she felt the pressure of his thumb pushing in once more.

"Ben!" she breathed out, shaking, shivering, then pressing back, taking the tip of his thumb a little deeper as he lowered his head, that wicked tongue lapping her vulva, before pushing inside her . . . her *pussy.* He growled low in his throat, his mouth going at her a little harder, his thumb pressing a fraction deeper, and she couldn't fight it. Another scorching orgasm slammed into her, knocking the breath from her lungs, her cries raw and violent as she pulsed around his clever tongue, drenching him. She got lost in the madness, barely aware of him moving, shifting, but it all crashed into a blinding focus when he slammed back into her, the stretching pressure of that massive shaft driving into her catching the last spasms of the orgasm and hurtling her into something that made her freaking claw at the sheets, it was so overwhelming and incredible.

"You okay?" He pumped into her with another thick, heavy lunge, his ridged cock head rubbing against that hot spot deep inside her that made her whimper and gasp. "Answer me, Reese. I'm not hurting you, am I?"

"No!" she moaned, the pleasure obliterating whatever soreness she might be feeling. "Just don't stop!"

"Thank God," he growled, driving hard and deep, and then he was right there with her. He made a thick, primitive sound deep in his chest, his strong hands gripping her hips as he pumped into her, the violence of his release letting her know that she hadn't fallen into that breathtaking chasm alone. Even after the surreal burst of sensation, residual pulses of pleasure continued to pull low moans from their throats, their chests heaving as they tried to remember how to breathe.

When their heat-glazed bodies had finally stilled, he collapsed onto the mattress beside her with a guttural groan, and she lowered her trembling legs, stretching out on her front. Resting her face on her crossed arms, Reese watched him deal with the second condom, then roll back toward her, his expression impossible to read. He looked satisfied, but intense, his dark gaze narrowed. Her thoughts still spinning and dazed, she found herself focusing on the fact that he had unbelievably long eyelashes for a man. She'd never noticed before, but it was impossible to miss when they were tangling together at the corners of his eyes.

Rubbing his callused palm down her spine, he stared into her eyes and said, "He never fucked you worth a damn, did he?"

She shivered again, needing to close her eyes to collect herself, but she couldn't. The intensity in those green eyes held her, drawing her in, the raw force of his hunger making her feel more feminine than she ever had before. Even more than when she'd been a lithe twenty-three-year-old and Drew had taken her to the Caribbean. He'd promised to make love to her on the beach in the moonlight, but he'd gone off drinking with some other lawyers every night, then crawled back into bed in the mornings stinking of alcohol and smoke and cheap perfume. She'd bought his lies, because she hadn't thought she could afford the truth.

But Ben seemed determined to show her that she could take anything. There were no boundaries. No limits.

She had to swallow to clear the lump of emotion in her throat before she could respond to his question. "No, he didn't."

Instead of pity, which she would have hated, he gave her one of those smoldering looks that said he was thinking about everything they'd done together . . . and everything they were going to do. "Want me to kick his ass for you?"

She pressed her lips together to hold in a giggle. "You know, I just might take you up on that offer."

"I hope you do. I've been wanting to smash his pretty face from the moment I set eyes on him."

"I wouldn't mind smashing his face, either. But I'd rather not talk about him. He's old news."

"Fair enough. Why don't we grab another shower and make some dinner. Then crawl back into bed together." He gave her a crooked smile as he patted her bottom. "If you're lucky, I might even let you catch some sleep later."

Flustered, Reese sat up and grabbed for the top sheet, clutching it to her breasts as she stared down at him. "Don't get me wrong, Ben. This . . . what's happened . . . it's been lovely. *Wonderful.* But I still don't think it would be a good idea for you to stay the night."

He rolled to his back, his brow already creased in a scowl. "Why the hell not?"

"Because I think it's important that we keep things as . . . as uncomplicated as possible."

"Jesus, Reese. You're actually serious, aren't you?"

She nodded, biting her lip.

With a low curse on his lips, he rolled into a sitting position at the side of the bed, his muscles bunching and flexing with breathtaking beauty as he moved to his feet and headed for the bathroom. When he came out, he was wearing the clean sweats he'd brought over, his running shorts thrown over his shoulder.

"Ben, wait," she pleaded, when he started to walk out of the room.

He stopped in the middle of the floor and slid her a shuttered look that gave nothing away. "What?"

She moved to the edge of the bed, putting her legs over the side. "I just . . . I didn't mean to piss you off," she whispered, feeling sick inside. How had everything gone so wrong, so quickly?

He shoved his fingers through his hair, his dark eyes blazing with a volatile mix of anger, frustration, and disappointment. "Then stop pushing me away every time I get close to you."

Taking a deep breath, she tried to explain. "I wasn't expecting you to want to stay. That's not how I thought these things work. You know that Brit told me you don't spend the night with the women you date. And we're not even dating. We're just . . . sleeping together."

Wondering what the fuck Brit had been thinking, Ben popped his jaw. "First off, Brit needs to keep her nose out of things that don't concern her. And secondly, what I've done in the past has no bearing on what's going on now."

"Okay." But it was clear she was confused.

His breath left his lungs in a sharp, angry burst. "Stop putting me in some damn box, Reese."

"I just don't want to expect . . . too much."

"Yeah, well, it's insulting as hell that you expect too little. You're worth more than just a quick fuck and a have-a-nice-life."

Holding the sheet in a death grip, she said, "Maybe this was a bad idea."

The quiet words turned his hot fury into something cold and chilling. "You might make me angry as hell, but we're not done with each other," he growled as he headed back toward the bed. "Not by a long shot." Gripping her upper arms, he yanked her up and crushed her mouth against his in a kiss that was hot and hard and relentless, wanting to brand her in a way that would tell every other jackass out there exactly whom she belonged to. The unfamiliar compulsion reeked of possession, and he abruptly ended the kiss and let go of her, wondering what the hell he was doing.

Jerking back from the bed, Ben's voice was little more than a snarl as he reminded her to lock up behind him.

Then he turned and got the fuck out of there.

9

MONDAY MORNING, BEN SAT BEHIND HIS DESK AT THE STATION IN A foul mood that was getting fouler by the second. He loved his job, loved the county and the people he worked with, but this morning everything and everyone were testing his patience. He felt like he'd had his skin peeled back, every nerve left raw and exposed, his head still reeling from those too short, too intense moments he'd spent in Reese's bed. He'd been sitting there brooding for too damn long when he caught sight of one of his deputies walking past the open door to his office. "Hey, Ryder," he called out. "You got a second?"

The tall, dark-haired deputy stuck his head around the doorway. "Sure. What's up?"

"Come on in and shut the door."

Scott Ryder had been with the department for about nine months now, and had worked some top-secret government job before that. He was a genius with computers, and Ben knew if there was anyone in the department who could get the answers he wanted, it would be Ryder. "I need you to do some research for me," he said, after the deputy had taken a seat in one of the chairs that faced his desk.

"On what?" Ryder asked, bracing an ankle on the opposite knee.

"I need a workup on a lawyer up in Boston. I already got the basics down this weekend, but I'm looking for more."

Ryder's brows lifted with interest. "Am I looking for anything specific?"

"His ex-wife is a friend of my family. She just moved down a few days ago and is renting the beach house next door to mine. I need you to—"

"Wait a minute," Ryder said, interrupting him. "Are we talking about Reese Leighton?"

Ben leaned back in his chair, his gaze locked hard on the deputy's rugged face. Even with his shaggy hair and the scar that slashed from his temple to the middle of his right cheek, Ryder was a good-looking guy. He gave off a hard, sometimes dangerous vibe, but then, there were a lot of women who went for that kind of thing. Ben just hoped Reese wasn't one of them. "You know her?" he asked, wondering what their connection could be.

"I've met her a few times," the deputy explained, his tone curious. "Pretty girl."

"She's twenty-eight," he grunted. "Hardly a girl."

Ryder looked like he was suddenly trying to hold back a shit-eating grin. "That's true. But then, she has that soft look of innocence about her. Know what I mean?"

"Just do the damn report on Leighton and let me know what you find."

"Sure thing," Ryder drawled, his dark eyes laughing as he lowered his foot to the floor. He leaned forward in his chair, elbows braced on his parted knees. "But are you going to tell me what I'm looking for?"

Shit. Jealousy was making him act like a fucking idiot. "Reese had some trouble with a stalker up in Boston after her divorce. The local PD cleared her ex, but I want to know if he's really clean or just good at covering his tracks. He's still harassing her with phone calls, and now she's gotten a strange text from a blocked number on her cell. If another text comes up, I'll bring her phone in and have the IT guys look at it. It could be nothing, but I want to know if this bastard has picked up a burn phone that he's using."

All traces of humor vanished from the deputy's eyes. "Has anything happened since she got to town?"

With his elbow braced on the arm of his chair, Ben rubbed his jaw. "Someone threw a bottle through one of her French doors on Friday night, but you know what it's like here during the first weeks of summer break. It could have just been some kids getting out of hand."

"Could have been. But we also had that assault on Friday night."

"I know," he said, rubbing his hand over his mouth. "Has the girl been able to give us any more details?"

Ryder shook his head. "Nothing yet. He came up on her from behind, so she never even got a look at his face. All we know is that he's around six feet and heavy with muscle."

They caught up on a few other department issues, and then Ryder headed out on a call, leaving Ben alone in his office again. He leaned back in his chair and stared at the ceiling, trying not to think about yesterday. But it was impossible. He could hardly think about anything else. He'd known it was going to be good between him and Reese, but Christ, he hadn't had a clue it would be so explosive . . . or mind-blowing. He tried to tell himself that sex that good would knock anyone for a loop, but he was still edgy over the way he'd reacted. He'd wanted to cling to her, for God's sake. Hold her in his arms and drift off to sleep with her soft little body wrapped around him, and how many shades of fucked up was that?

He hadn't liked getting kicked out of her bed, but Ben knew that it'd been for the best. If he'd stayed, there was no telling how far things would have gone between them. He wasn't ready to cut and run—far from it. But he definitely felt like he needed to watch his step where this woman was concerned. She was so goddamn different from anyone he'd ever been involved with. Unique. Refreshing. That strange combination of adorable and sexy that made him so fucking hot, he was surprised he hadn't come away with burns.

The way he felt about her, around her, was different, too. And that had him wound up more than anything.

Normally, at this point the attraction would already be on the decline for him. Once that initial lust was slaked, Ben had never felt it to the same degree again. But that wasn't the case with Reese. He didn't know if it was because he'd wanted her for so long and hadn't been able to have her, or if it was simply something about the woman herself. About the two of them together. Chemical? Biological? Whatever the fuck it was, his normal standard operating procedure wasn't in play.

Instead of easing, his goddamn need was even worse.

Instead of bringing relief, he'd been left in a world of hurt, because he wanted more. Needed it. Was going out of his fucking mind thinking about it. He'd always curled his lip at addicts, thinking they just needed to man up and face the music. But he was getting a humbling lesson. He was just as susceptible as those poor bastards. He just hadn't found his drug of choice before. And now that he had, he was jonesing for his next hit.

Thankfully, his day got damn busy, and he was saved from sitting in his office, brooding about Reese. After a meeting with the mayor, he had a scheduled visit at a county youth detention center, where he taught the kids basketball, and then some work at the courthouse. It was four before he was back in his office again, only to find he'd had another call on his private line from Sanchez, his old partner in Miami. The guy had been trying to call him for a few days now, but Ben had been doing his best to avoid him. Not that he didn't want to talk to Sanchez. Tony was a good friend and they hadn't caught up in forever. But it sounded like there was a new development with the Houghton case, and Ben was finished with all of that. After the media had turned their backs on the police department, painting the drug lord out to be some kind of tragic hero, just because the guy knew whose pockets to grease, the DA had caved to public opinion and plea-bargained a lesser sentence. Ben had still been laid up in a hospital bed at the time, full of holes that a PCP-dosed Houghton had drilled into him, and he'd decided then and there that he was done with the bullshit. Whatever was going on back in Miami, he wanted no part of it.

What he did want was to talk to Reese, and he couldn't hold off any longer. Pulling her number up on his BlackBerry, he put the call through.

After two rings, she answered. "Hey," she said, sounding a little breathless, but happy to hear from him. "You having a good day?"

Wondering what she was doing, he said, "It's been busy. And I've been distracted."

"By what?"

"You." He swiveled his chair around, staring out his office window at the park trees swaying in the breeze. "I thought maybe you'd let me take you for a walk on the beach when I get home. Maybe even fool around a bit behind the dunes."

"Sounds . . . sandy," she murmured, and he could hear the smile in her voice.

"What if I promise to keep you so distracted, you don't notice the sand?"

He loved the husky sound of her laughter. "Tempting. But it'll still be daylight then. I'd hate to be responsible for the esteemed sheriff of Moss Beach County getting arrested for indecent exposure and lewd public behavior."

Ben sighed with defeat. "Then if you're not going to let me have my way with you on the beach, come out to dinner with me instead."

"Oh. Um, tonight's not really good for me. The thing with the alarm company took forever, and now I'm really running behind. I hate living out of boxes, but I'm hoping I can have the kitchen finished up before going to bed."

"We can unpack together after dinner. I'll even do all the heavy lifting."

She gave a quiet snort. "You're such a guy."

"After yesterday," he drawled, "I'm hoping that's something you're happy about."

"Oh, definitely."

Ben wondered if she was biting her lip and blushing. He'd figured she'd be shy after everything they'd done together. Hell, he'd have been willing to bet on it, and it made him grin. But his grin fell as she said, "But I really don't feel like going out tonight."

Shit. Maybe he'd read her wrong. Was she trying to avoid being seen with him in town?

Tired of dancing around the issue, he asked, "What's going on, Reese? Are you embarrassed to be seen out in town with me?"

"What? No! Why would you even think that?"

Ben rolled his eyes. "What the hell am I supposed to think? What's the big deal about us going out to dinner together?"

"I don't know." Her quiet voice was tense. "I just . . . It's me, Ben. You know I'm not good at this . . . at whatever we're doing. I'm trying to keep things straight in my head. Going out like that with you—it will make it more difficult. Make it feel like we're . . . well, like we're dating, and that's not really what we're doing."

No. They were just fucking. He should have been happy she was accepting the limits of what he was willing to offer. But he wasn't. Instead, he hated that what they had was being labeled and put in a damn box. Hated this arbitrary list of what they could and couldn't do together. Screwing like a couple of minks, acceptable. But eating together in a restaurant, denied.

"You went to Brit's barbecue with me," he pointed out, trying not to sound like he was snarling.

"That was before we started sleeping together."

"Fine. I'll find something else to do. Just . . . be careful tonight."

"Yeah. You, too."

He hung up and leaned back in his chair, scrubbing his hands down his face. Damn woman was twisting him into knots and he didn't like it. Knowing he'd just be knocking on her door if he went home, Ben called his brothers and asked if they wanted to meet him at the Hoop, a local sports bar where they often grabbed meals together. When he got to the bar, Mike had already snagged them a table. They ordered a couple of beers while waiting for Alex to arrive, and Ben brought Mike up to speed on the things Reese had told him about Boston.

"I've got Ryder doing a check on the ex," he explained in a low voice, making sure they couldn't be overheard. "If anyone can dig up dirt, it's him. But this is personal. If I need it, you gonna back me up?" Mike worked for the DEA and was a serious badass in his own right.

"Yeah, I'll back you up." His brother grinned, saying, "But I can't see you needing it against the Yankee lawyer."

"One-on-one, yeah. But I don't trust him. He's got money, which means he's got options."

Mike's grin fell. "You think he might hire someone?"

"I don't know what to think at this point. But I'm sure as hell not ruling anything out. And I'm not going to let my ego get the better of me. If the shit hits the fan, I want your help."

"You don't even have to ask, man. You know it's a given."

"Thanks."

His younger brother winked at a cute server as she walked by, then shot a curious look at Ben. "I'm surprised you're not with Reese now. If she was mine, I'd be stuck to her like white on rice."

He gave a frustrated sigh, slumping back in his chair. "She may look all cute and clueless, but the woman has a stubborn streak a mile long."

His brother laughed. "She kicked you out on your ass?"

"More or less," he admitted with a scowl.

Mike ran his tongue over the edge of his teeth and smiled. "I knew there was a good reason I liked her."

"You think this is funny?" Ben growled.

"Not the part about some dickhead screwing with her life," Mike clarified, wiping the foam off his top lip after taking a drink of his beer. "But I'd be lying if I said I wasn't going to enjoy seeing a woman finally give you a run for your money."

"A warning, Mike." Ben's voice was quiet, but hard. "I'm not in the mood for your shit tonight."

His brother opened his mouth, no doubt ready to make another smart-ass comment, when his gaze shot over Ben's shoulder and he grimaced. "Shit."

Ben sat up a little straighter. "What is it?"

Mike reached for his beer again. "Alex looks rough tonight."

Looking over his shoulder, Ben watched as his older brother cut his way through the crowded bar. He didn't look drunk, thank God. But the guy didn't look like he was in a good place, either.

He hated seeing Alex this way. Before he'd met Judith, Alex had been full of life. Always laughing, smiling. Now the guy looked like his face might crack if he so much as grinned. He'd managed to stop drinking, and work was going well for him, but Ben knew damn well that inside, where it counted, Alex was still carrying too many scars.

It was a sobering thought, reminding Ben why he liked to keep things casual and light. Why he didn't let himself get twisted up over a woman. *Ever.*

Of course, that'd always been easy. Until now. It was just Reese who screwed with his head and made him feel like a fucking addict. Every place he put his mouth on her, she tasted warm and sweet. Her lips. Her breasts. But the juices that spilled between her soft little thighs were what nearly killed him, they were so incredible. He wanted that slick honey in his mouth again. Wanted the feel and the warmth of it on his lips, sliding over his tongue. And, damn it, he wanted back inside her. Wanted that crazy feeling of being . . . Hell, he didn't even know how to describe it. All he knew was that he wanted it so much that he ached.

And she'd blown him off.

Shit.

Reaching for his beer, Ben gritted his teeth, determined not to spend his night thinking about the frustrating female. Instead, he was going to hang out with his brothers, find out what was bothering Alex, and do his best to keep a certain little stubborn schoolteacher out of his head.

REESE STARED AT THE SMALL SCREEN ON HER PHONE AND BLINKED. When she'd heard the text alert go off, she'd lunged for the phone, which had been sitting on the kitchen counter, hoping it might be Ben. He still wasn't home—yes, she'd been listening for his truck—and she had no one to blame but herself. He'd asked to spend the evening with her, and like an idiot, she'd turned him down again.

Shaking her head, she focused her mind back on the problem at hand. Instead of a text from Ben, which would have made her night, she was staring at another message from a blocked number.

i love the flowers

A shiver slipped down her spine, and she quickly headed for the front door to make sure it was locked. Yeah, she'd felt reasonably comfortable blowing off the first text as a fluke, considering she'd only just gotten to town and the number was new. But this was too freaky. She'd spent the later part of the day hanging all her new baskets along the back of the house, as well as filling the new flower pots she'd bought at the garden center. Whoever had sent this new text might have been watching her, and she shuddered, pacing the floors of her house, too restless to sit still.

Despite how badly she didn't want it to be true, it was becoming more and more likely that someone was sending her these texts on purpose. But who? God, who had she pissed off so much that they felt the need to try to scare the shit out of her?

Forget tried, muttered her inner voice. *If it's not the nightmares, it's this crap. I've had enough!*

Reese winced, another queasy shudder wracking her frame as she thought about the cat nightmare she'd had last night. It'd been the same as all the other times. She woke up gasping, drenched in sweat, arms flailing blindly as she tried to fight off the shadow crawling over her, while she lay in a sea of mutilated cat bodies. When she'd jerked herself out of the nightmare, she'd wished like hell that she'd had Ben there beside her, his hard chest to cuddle against. But it'd been her own fault that she hadn't. She was the one who'd sent him home, as if not sleeping beside him was going to help her keep some kind of perspective. Not likely. She hadn't been able to stop thinking about the gorgeous lawman the entire day.

Moving into the sitting room, she glanced at the French doors, wishing she'd already ordered the vintage bamboo blinds for them that she'd found online. Despite the longer summer days, it was after nine and her patio was barely lit by the shadowy moonlight. As she moved farther into the room, wanting to double-check that the doors were locked, she could have sworn she felt a set of eyes following her movements from the darkness.

Okay. So there were really only two options here. Run from the room screaming and call Ben, begging him to come over, when she'd already refused to go out with him tonight. Or stop letting this asshole screw with her emotions and let him know she wasn't going to be so easily cowed. And she could do that by going out there and giving him a dose of his own medicine.

And if it *was* Drew out there, she was going to beat the living shit out of him!

Setting down her phone and picking up the hammer she'd left on the coffee table after hanging a framed Klimt print over the fireplace earlier, Reese took a deep breath and headed for the French doors. With a flick of the lock, she ripped the newly repaired doors open and stepped out into the humid night, scanning the shadowy bushes that lined the patio. The air was warmer than inside the house, where the air conditioner was running. Sweeter. Heavier. She stared into the sultry darkness, lungs working, fueled by rage. Her fingers tightened on the hammer, ready to swing in defense if anyone tried to screw with her. She was so tired of this nauseating feeling weighing her down. Just wanted to be left the hell alone so that she could get on with her life!

Was it Drew watching her from the cover of darkness? Was he really that sick? Or was it some other jackass screwing with her? The same one from Boston? Or someone new? And why *her*? What had she done to draw some wack job's attention?

A minute went by, then two. Reese stood there just outside the doorway, glaring into the shadows, daring whoever was out there to come forward. When another minute passed with nothing but the rapid sound of her breathing to fill the air, she lowered her shoulders, wondering if she was losing her mind. Then she caught the sound of Ben's truck driving onto their shared driveway, and everything low in her body clenched tight, her thoughts momentarily scrambled, her fear nearly forgotten.

Not wanting to look like she was out on the patio waiting for him, Reese hurried back inside, pulling the French doors shut and then quickly locking them. Thinking Ben would head straight into his own place, she turned to make her way back toward the front of the house, where she could set the alarm. She nearly jumped a foot when she heard someone rap on the glass. Spinning around, she let out a sharp breath of relief at the sight of Ben standing there on the back patio.

Oh, thank God.

Still carrying the hammer, Reese opened the doors. Without a word, she flicked her gaze over his tall body, taking in the casual white button-down shirt with its sleeves rolled up on his forearms. It had been left open at the throat, and made his shoulders look a mile wide. Then she took in the worn-in jeans and the scuffed boots on his big feet. The guy looked good in anything he wore, but she especially loved him like this, when he had this sexy, rugged, I'm-comfortable-in-my-own-skin thing going on. He could have given Jude Law a run for his money in those cologne ads any day of the week.

And the fact that he was a lawman—a badass who spent his life protecting people and putting the scum of the earth behind bars—only made him sexier. She wanted so desperately to cling to him, but that would be a disaster, driving him away faster than anything. Despite his protective instincts, she knew Ben wasn't the kind of man who could ever handle being tied down or shackled by commitment.

But, God, it was tempting. He looked so hard and capable and strong. Looked as if nothing in the world could break him.

"Hey," she murmured, being the first to break the weighted silence that had settled between them. And then she heard herself ask, "Did you go out straight from work?"

Ben fought the urge to smile, uncharacteristically pleased that she'd noticed he hadn't been home. Normally, that kind of attention from a woman would have driven him bat-shit. But not with Reese.

Answering her question, he said, "Yeah."

She flicked another look over his clothes. "Don't sheriffs have to wear those little outfits?"

He rolled his eyes. "I'm not a freaking clown, Reese. I don't wear a fucking outfit."

"You know what I mean. The whole uniform thing."

"Yeah, well, that's one of the great things about being in charge. I don't have to wear anything I don't want to," he said in a low drawl, crossing his arms over his chest before propping his shoulder against the doorjamb. He let his heavy-lidded eyes do a slow pass over her own little getup, liking the way she looked in the skimpy tank top and cutoffs. Of course, he liked it better when she was wearing nothing at all. Bringing his gaze back up to her face, he finished his explanation, saying, "And I usually keep some extra clothes at the station."

"Did you, um, have a good time tonight?"

With a nod, he said, "I grabbed some burgers and beers with Mike and Alex."

"Oh!" she gasped, giving a little cough. "Well, that's great that you guys get to, uh, hang out like that."

Reese had tried to hide her relief at the news that he'd merely been out with his brothers, but she must not have done a very good job of it, because a frown started to weave its way between his dark brows. Then he growled a really pissed off sounding question at her.

"What the hell did you think I was doing?"

10

REALIZING SHE'D INSULTED HIM WITH HER SURPRISED REACTION, REESE was ready to tell Ben she was sorry, but he cut her off before she could get a single word out.

"I told you yesterday that I don't juggle women. How many times do I have to say it, Reese? And remember that *you're* the one who turned *me* down tonight. Not the other way around."

"You're right," she said in a rush, holding up her hand. "I'm sorry. I really wasn't trying to accuse you of anything. I swear it."

He didn't say anything in response. Just pushed away from the doorjamb and came inside, pulling the door shut behind him.

"Please lock it!"

Ben froze at the sound of panic in her voice. Grinding his jaw, he studied her tense expression, then lowered his gaze, taking in the hammer she was holding in her fist. He'd assumed she'd been hanging pictures around the house, but now he realized she was holding the damn thing like a weapon. "What the hell's going on?"

Setting the hammer down on the coffee table, she said, "I just got a little spooked right before you got home. I . . . well, I felt like someone was watching me."

His eyes went wide, anger surging through his system in a blistering rush. "And you didn't call me?"

She gave a little laugh as she brought her gaze back to his. "I'm not going to bother you every time I get spooked, Ben."

"Just tell me what happened," he forced through his gritted teeth, wanting to shake some sense into her.

"I . . . I had a weird feeling that someone was watching me through the glass."

His gaze cut to the hammer, then back to her. "Did you go outside with that thing?"

"Um . . ."

His quiet voice lashed with fury. "Answer the fucking question, Reese."

She bristled, chin up, shoulders back. "Yes, okay! I went outside! But only because I was pissed after getting another one of those stupid texts!"

"What'd it say this time?"

She grabbed her phone off the coffee table and handed it to him. "Here, see for yourself."

He thumbed the screen on, hitting the messages icon, and read. *Son of a bitch.*

"I want to take your phone into work with me tomorrow," he told her. "See if our IT guys can make anything of it."

"Okay. But I really doubt that it's Drew, if that's what you're still thinking."

Ben gave her a hard stare. "Why?"

"I don't know," she whispered, rolling her shoulder. "It just doesn't seem his style."

His chest shook with a grim, humorless laugh. "Yeah, well,

you'd be surprised what a shredded ego can do to a man's sense of style."

"But his ego should be fine. He's the one who cheated on me!"

"And you're the woman who left his ass," he said, slipping her phone into his back pocket. "If you don't think that fucked over his ego, then you don't know jack shit about men."

Her eyes narrowed. "Did you come over here just to insult me?"

Closing the distance between them, Ben put his arms around her and pulled her against his chest. Resting his chin on the top of her head, he stroked a hand down her spine, sliding the other under her hair to curve around the back of her neck. "I'm sorry. I don't mean to bark at you. I just want this asshole to leave you alone."

"Me, too," she mumbled into his shirt.

He brushed his lips against the tender parting in her hair. "I'm going to have the Boston PD keep an eye on Leighton."

She tensed, then gradually relaxed as she exhaled a slow breath of air. "All right. But if he's in Boston, how would he even know about the flowers to send that text?"

"People have their ways, Reese. And he's got to know you pretty well after living with you for so many years. He probably figured one of the first things you'd do was buy flowers."

Drawing her head back, Reese locked her gaze with his. "You're right. I guess I'm just not thinking straight." She covered her mouth with her hand as she yawned, then immediately blushed. "Sorry. I didn't mean to be rude."

His lopsided smile was unbelievably beautiful. "With the stress you've been under, I'm surprised you can even stay on your feet." He moved his hand to her face, his touch gentle as he rubbed his thumb under her eye. "You look exhausted."

"Gee, thanks."

"Exhausted, but still incredibly beautiful," he clarified in that soft, rough-as-sin voice that always rolled through her like a provocative lick of heat. Her insides clenched, and she was secretly thrilled by the twinge of discomfort she still felt deep inside from the powerful way he'd taken her. The passion between them the day before had been nothing short of explosive, and from the moment she'd first opened her eyes that morning, she'd savored every sensual ache that reminded her of just how possessive he'd been.

"Come on," he rumbled, turning her toward the hallway and swatting her bottom. "It's bed for you, sweetheart. You're beat."

"We still need to lock that door." She sounded a little breathless, but then, it was impossible not to be excited by the idea that he might join her in bed for a bit before heading home. God only knew she wouldn't be able to tell him no if he touched her. She'd been dying for his touch all freaking day, the need always simmering just beneath her surface, like an electrical current that couldn't be switched off.

"I've got it." He walked back to the French doors, then looked back at her over his shoulder as he opened them up again. "Stay right there. I just want to take a quick look around outside."

Reese started to shout for him to stay where he was, but he was already gone, pulling the doors shut behind him. She paced from one side of the room to the other, hating the idea of him going out there and facing some unknown danger in the darkness because of her. Didn't the crazy man know that it'd kill her if anything happened to him? It didn't matter that she knew he was tough enough to handle whatever this sicko jerk might try, if there really was someone out there. But he wasn't invincible, damn it. The bullet scars on his body were proof enough of that.

He came back a minute later, though it'd felt like a lifetime. "If anyone was out there, they're gone now," he said, twisting the dead bolt into place, before making his way back to her. Completely clueless about how badly he'd just worried her, he asked, "You've locked everything else?"

She nodded as she drew in a deep breath, still too upset to speak, and he took her hand, pulling her along behind him as he headed for her bedroom. He let go when they reached the bed, leaving her standing at the foot as he moved to the far side, where a small table sat between the mattress and the wall. Unlike the table on the right side of the bed, where she had a small reading lamp and some books, this one was empty. She had a vase that she planned to put there, along with a few picture frames, but hadn't unpacked them yet. Ben, however, seemed ready to claim the table as his own.

She watched him with a notch between her brows as he emptied the pockets in his jeans, setting his wallet, their phones, and a handful of coins on the table. Then he opened the small drawer, reached back under his shirt, pulled his gun from his waistband, and placed the weapon inside the drawer before closing it.

Rolling her lips together, she said, "Um, Ben. What are you doing?"

"Getting ready for bed." He didn't look at her as he sat down on the side of the mattress and started untying his boots. Then he took them off along with his socks, unbuttoned his shirt, and tossed it on the top of the pile.

"I don't understand."

"I'm staying the night." He moved back to his feet, undoing his belt as he turned to face her, and her mouth started to water at the sight of those hard, chiseled abs. "You can bitch and moan about it all you want, Reese, but it isn't going to change my mind. Not when it's clear that you can't be trusted."

"Can't be trusted?" She forced her attention back on his rugged face and frowned. "What on earth are you talking about?"

Undoing the button-fly on his jeans, he said, "You didn't call me when you got another message, even though I'd told you to. And then you went outside when you thought someone might be out there, with nothing for protection but a fucking hammer." With his unbuttoned jeans hanging low on his hips, he made his way around the foot of the bed, not stopping until he was standing right in front of her. Instead of getting louder, his voice was becoming ominously quiet. "So I don't give a shit if you want me here or not. Tonight, your ass is sleeping next to me, where I know you'll be safe."

"This . . . this is nuts!" she argued, throwing up her hands. "Of course I *want* you here. That's not the issue. And the only reason I didn't call you the second that text came through was because I don't want you to think I'm clinging to you. I can't think of anything a guy like you would hate more, even if you *are* in the habit of taking care of people. And I hate it that you think I'm some helpless, feather-brained little idiot!"

"I don't," he said roughly, the corner of his mouth suddenly twitching as he tried to hold back a smile. The frustration that had tightened his expression a moment ago was easing, the look in his eyes almost . . . tender. "A little naïve maybe. And too intrepid for your own good. But never helpless, Reese. You're too fucking smart for that."

She turned and moved to her side of the bed, then sat down with her back to him. "I wasn't trying to piss you off. I just don't want to smother you." Her voice was small . . . tight.

Following after her, Ben didn't stop until he was standing right in front of her again. Reaching down, he lifted her chin with his fingers, a wry grin on his lips. "If you'd stop arguing for two seconds and open your eyes, you'd see that I'm the one coming after you, Reese. Not the other way around."

She blinked up at him. "Only because you think I need you here."

"I *want* to be here," he said, tucking a strand of that soft hair behind her ear, then sliding his hand to her jaw. "If I was only worried about your safety, I'd send you to stay with your mom or Connie."

"Oh."

"I'm here because I couldn't stop thinking about you last night. Or this morning. You've been in my head all goddamn day, and it's only gotten worse as the hours wore on. Mike ribbed me about it the whole damn time we were together tonight." Cocking his head a bit to the side, Ben studied her through his lashes. "Just out of curiosity, who did you think I was out with?"

Her gaze skittered away. "I, uh, I don't really know."

Lowering his hand to his side, he said, "Well, it was just me and Mike and Alex, until some of the guys from work joined up with us. But I wasn't out with any women."

"I believe you," she said, fiddling with a thread on the cuff of her shorts. "But it doesn't mean that women weren't still hanging all over you."

He gave a frustrated snort. "And like I've said before, I'm not some horny twenty-year-old prick, Reese. I know how to keep my cock in my pants."

Her gaze shot back to his. "You sleep with a different woman every week!"

"That's bullshit. Yeah, I've been around the block a time or two. But I'm not a serial womanizer. Before you, the last time I slept with a woman was over two months ago."

She looked stunned, and more than a little skeptical. "Why'd you stop seeing her?"

Shoving a hand through his hair, he said, "Because we were only having sex because we were lonely." And because he hadn't been able to get Reese out of his head. But he wasn't going to admit that out loud.

"You were lonely?" It was clear from her tone that she thought he was feeding her a line.

"What? You think I can't get lonely?"

She shook her head, that plump lower lip caught in her teeth. "Of course I don't think that. I . . . I've just never thought of you that way." No, she just pictured him as some kind of roving Superdick, ready to leap into any woman with a single bound. He didn't know whether to be insulted, or to laugh his ass off. "I mean, it's not like you're hurting for opportunities, Ben."

"Maybe not. But despite what you seem to think, I don't sleep with every woman who makes me an offer. And when I say that I won't be seeing anyone else while we're together, I mean it."

"Okay," she whispered, her expression difficult to read. Before he could figure it out, she looked down at her hands as she rubbed them over her thighs.

"And?"

"And what?"

He bent down so that he could see her face beneath the fall of her hair. "You won't be seeing anyone else, either. Right?"

She looked at him and frowned. "Are you serious?"

"I know I say this a lot, Reese. But just answer the damn question."

"Who would I see?" she asked, the strap of her tank top slipping off her shoulder as she shrugged. "I don't even know any other men here," she added, tilting her head back as he straightened.

"Well, they know you," he told her, remembering the comments that had come from a few of his deputies after Mike had let it spill that Reese was his new tenant. And Ryder had already known.

"What are you talking about?"

Feeling like a jealous fool, Ben said, "Scott Ryder was talking about you tonight."

Her brows lifted with surprise. "The deputy?"

"Yeah. How do you know him?"

She looked a little flustered. "I've run into him a few times with Connie, when I've been here visiting. She's friends with one of his neighbors. But we've only talked a few times. That's so strange that he would remember."

"Oh, he remembers," he muttered under his breath.

She gave him an exasperated look and rolled her eyes. "It doesn't mean anything, Ben."

He shook his head, wondering when she was going to start getting it, the fact that she was beautiful and that men wanted her. Grabbing her chin, he said, "I want to make sure that we're clear, Reese. While we're together, we're exclusive."

She blinked and took a shaky breath. "Have you ever asked that of a woman before?"

For a moment, Ben considered refusing to answer the question, knowing it would only make him look like a jackass. But he wanted honesty between them. And there were already so many things he wasn't willing to give her. Christ, the truth was the least she deserved.

Shaking his head again, he said, "I haven't. I've been asked, but I've never agreed."

"Then why now?"

He rubbed his thumb along the tender swell of her lower lip, watching her through his lashes. "Because for as long as this lasts," he said quietly, "I want you all to myself."

A shiver moved through her, those big eyes dark with emotion. There was surprise there in the deep blue, as well as wariness, and what was hopefully at least a touch of happiness. "Wow," she whispered, her slender throat moving as she swallowed. "Talk about giving mixed signals, Ben. Saturday you dare me to have a raunchy sexual fling with you, and now you want me to promise that I won't date anyone else?"

"You're the one who called it a fling, not me." He worked his jaw, his body hard with tension. "And I'm giving you more than I've ever given any other woman. Can't we just leave it at that?"

For a moment, she simply stared up at him, making him feel as if she were seeing right through him. As if she could understand this maddening need twisting him up inside even better than he could. He was starting to sweat, thinking she was going to tell him to take his commitment-phobic ass out of her house and never come back, when her lips finally curled in a small, soft smile. "Yeah, we can leave it there for now."

A ragged breath of relief burst from his lungs, and he pulled her to her feet, wrapping her in his arms as he buried his face against the side of her throat. "You're not going to regret this," he vowed in a low, determined voice. But he wasn't sure which one of them he was trying to convince. Him? Her? Both? Shoving the irritating thought from his mind, Ben focused on getting her where he wanted her. Which was under him, open and soft and wet, coming so hard she saw stars or God or whatever a woman saw when she was screaming the fucking roof down.

"And now on to the night's entertainment," he whispered, nipping her tender earlobe.

She stifled a giggle. "Oh yeah? What's that?"

He drew his head back so that he could see her face, his hot gaze locking with hers. "First, you need to get naked. Because I'm getting ready to lay down another dare."

Her brows lifted. "You know, I thought I was the one who was supposed to be using *you*."

Ben moved his hands down to her firm little ass and squeezed. "You're supposed to be having fun, getting off, coming so often you can't think straight. And since I know what it takes to get you there, we're not going to argue about who's in control tonight. Understood?"

She nodded, looking . . . intrigued. Flicking her tongue over her bottom lip, she asked, "So what's the dare?"

"Not really what you would call a dare this time," he clarified, gripping the hem of her tank top and slowly pulling it up. "I just want to see how many times you can come in a man's mouth."

He couldn't see her face as he pulled the top over her head, but he could hear her gasp. And looking down, it was clear her nipples had just pulled tight beneath her stretchy little strapless bra. Tossing the shirt aside, he reached for the button on her shorts. "You got any stockings?"

She blinked, going adorably pink. "Um, yes."

"Where?"

"Top right drawer of my dresser," she said, stepping out of her shorts and panties after he wrenched them down. For a second, her hand fluttered in front of the sexy ringlets at the top of her mound, as if she wanted to cover herself. Ben opened his mouth, ready to stop her, when she took a quick breath and reached behind her back instead, undoing the bra.

"Lie down in the middle of the bed," he said in a thick voice, his granite-hard dick somehow getting even harder as he stared down at her pale, beautiful body. He had to force himself to move away and head to the dresser, his mouth already watering at the thought of getting her under his tongue.

Minutes later, Ben gave a low growl as he knelt between her sprawled thighs, knowing damn well that he'd never seen anything this provocative in his life. He'd tied a black silk stocking to each of her delicate wrists, then secured her right wrist to her right ankle, repeating the process on her left side. Now, she was naked and bound, completely at his mercy, but she wasn't panicking. Her dark blue eyes smoldered with heat as she watched him through her thick lashes, her pink-tipped breasts rising with each of her excited breaths.

"God, you look beautiful." He leaned over her, sucking hard on each of those plump nipples until they were shiny and wet, then pulled back to admire the view. With his pulse roaring in his ears, Ben lowered his gaze over the feminine curves of her body, until he was staring at the lush, glistening folds of her cunt.

"I haven't been able to stop thinking about this," he rasped, running his index finger through her slippery folds, before pushing her open with his finger and thumb, completely exposing the delicate, intimate details. "You're very pink, Reese." He stroked the callused tip of his finger over her swollen clit, then slipped it down to her vulva, circling the plush, tiny opening. "I don't think I've ever seen anything that comes close to being this pretty. And you smell so fucking sweet."

She gave a throaty moan, a voluptuous rhythm to the way she was rolling her hips, teeth sunk into that succulent lower lip as a rush of color rose up under her skin. She was vibrating with desire, the look in her eyes carnal and hungry and dark, so goddamn beautiful it made him ache. He pushed two big fingers up inside her, her snug sheath clinging to him . . . pulsing, and her voice cracked as she gasped his name.

"That's it," he groaned, already settling down on his elbows. "I want to hear your voice shake like that when I've got my tongue shoved up inside you and you're coming all over my face. You understand?"

"*Yes!*" she cried, and with a wicked smile on his lips, Ben gripped her ass, lifted her to his mouth, and licked her. She arched, straining against the bonds as he worked his way higher, lashing her clit with his tongue, then suckling it soft and slow, before lashing it again. His chest shook with a gritty laugh when she started cursing under her breath, saying things he would have been willing to bet she'd never said before. Unable to wait any longer, Ben lifted her higher, thrusting his tongue deep in her cunt, eating at her like he was starved. She gave a breathless cry, then started coming in a sweet, warm rush, trembling so hard she shook the bed.

"So fucking incredible," he growled, pressing his face closer, wanting to feel every second of it, his tongue thrusting deep, trying to take in as much of that slick juice as he could get. He stayed with her until the very end, putting his mouth back on her clit, rubbing it hard with his tongue, before going lower and pushing back inside. He could eat her like this forever and still not get enough, something about the act with Reese wiping his mind, until the only fucking thing he knew and needed was *her*. A scary-ass feeling, but he couldn't pull away, still licking and sucking, until she finally tried to buck him off, gasping, her voice shivering as she said, "Wait! Just . . . give me a second. It's too much."

"I can't. Your taste is fucking unreal." He touched his tongue to one of the freckles close to her clit, and gave another growl. "Christ. Even your freckles are sweet."

"Ben, seriously, *please*. I just need . . . a . . . second."

Nowhere near ready to stop, he frowned as he lifted his head, wiping his wet mouth on his shoulder. He didn't say anything as their gazes locked. Hell, at that moment, he didn't trust anything that might have come out of his mouth. The woman had blown his goddamn mind. But there was still a small shred of sanity that reminded him to untie her before she got too uncomfortable.

"Thanks," Reese whispered, watching as he unknotted the first stocking, then reached for the second one, his hard expression etched with hunger. A husky moan slipped past her lips as she stretched, and the next thing she knew, Ben's powerful body was pressing her into the mattress, his hands buried in her hair, and his mouth crushing hers.

She could taste herself on his lips, salty and sweet. The erotic exchange was melting her down, layering heat on heat as her body burned for him. She was molten and needy, thighs already spreading wide for him, ready to give whatever he wanted from her . . . to accept whatever he wanted to do to her. She was aching and empty, just waiting to be filled . . . completed. She'd never had sex like this, had never even known it existed. That it could happen to her. That she could feel like this. But she reveled in it, loving the way it made her feel about him . . . about herself.

"Where are you going?" she asked, when he suddenly pulled away from her and climbed off the bed.

"Condom." His voice was hard . . . raw, biting with urgency. "Get ready, because I need to fuck you."

She nodded, even though he wasn't looking at her as he headed for the bathroom, where he'd left the box. She wondered if he was feeling as shattered as she was, then lost the thought as she watched him walking back into the room, to the foot of the bed. All day long, she'd been convinced that she must have been embellishing him in her mind whenever she'd thought about yesterday, but no. No way. He really *was* that freaking beautiful.

He'd already stripped down to a tight pair of black boxers that left little to the imagination. Reese blinked, staring at the blatant proof of his hunger, the black cotton hugging his heavy testicles and rigid cock. Then he tossed a foil packet onto the bed and dropped the boxers, and she dropped her jaw. He was so breathtaking, standing there all hard and rugged and muscled, that she damn near forgot her own name.

Unable to resist, she crawled to the edge of the bed on her hands and knees, leaned forward, and ran her tongue over his massive cock from root to tip.

"Jesus Christ, Reese!"

"Sorry. I couldn't wait anymore. I wanted to know what you taste like," she whispered, wrapping her hand around his thick base and going back for more. She loved the rough grunt that he gave, his breath catching as she wrapped her other hand around him, pulling the heavy shaft toward her, so that she could cover the swollen head with her mouth. He was so big, so hard, that it wasn't easy. She stretched her lips, determined to take more of him, and focused on breathing through her nose as she rubbed the underside of his burgeoning flesh with her tongue. Somehow, the timing and technique all clicked together for her, and she was able to take another couple of inches. The veins beneath his soft skin pulsed as he cursed, his long fingers digging into her hair, curling around her head.

She'd never managed this so well with Drew. But then, she was starting to realize a simple truth when it came to sex: Want trumped duty any day. And she wanted so damn much from this man.

"Enough," he grated, glaring down at her. "You're going to make me come and I need to fuck you first."

"But I'm not done yet," she complained, holding his molten gaze as she sucked him in again, using her hands to massage the inches she couldn't fit in her mouth.

His head fell back on his shoulders, his breath hissing past his lips as he cursed another dirty, graveled string of swear words.

"I never understood how women could like this so much," she whispered, running her lips along his broad shaft. Then she flicked her tongue over the slick, flushed head, taking the salty drops of moisture there into her mouth. "But I think I get it now."

"Reese." There was a wealth of meaning in that harsh word.

"Shh. This is supposed to be about me getting pleasure, right? And this is what I want. I want more of this right here. More of *you*."

"Hell," he groaned, shoving the heels of his palms against his eyes as he let her pull him back into her mouth. But he only lasted another handful of seconds before pulling her off, saying, "Damn it, you can make me come in your mouth next time."

"What's wrong with now?"

"Because I said so," he growled, picking her up under her arms and tossing her back on the bed. He pulled the condom on and came down over her quickly, pinning her beneath him and spreading her legs.

"You're so damn bossy!" she said with a laugh.

He didn't smile, his green eyes shadowed and dark. "I warned you about that."

"So you did," she murmured, fighting back a smile. There was a hardness in him, a kind of raw, intense focus, but it didn't scare her or turn her off. She loved it when he was playful and fun, but she loved this rough, aggressive side of him, too. Especially when he gripped the back of her neck, took her mouth in another ravaging kiss, and rammed that magnificent cock inside her. It took a few hard, pumping lunges before he was packed in deep and tight, her body clenching around him, already pulsing.

"No. Don't close your eyes," he growled, muscles rippling beneath the hard stretch of his skin as he sat back on his heels and gripped her hips. Wrenching her lower body off the bed, he pulled her along his shaft, the erotic position revealing his penetration in shocking, explicit detail. It looked so brutal, but spellbinding. She could hear how wet she was, the air filled with the moist, slippery sounds of sex. Could see the slick juices she left gleaming on his dark shaft every time he pulled back, then thrust that huge beast back inside her.

"Ben . . ."

"I know. It feels so fucking good." His voice was rough and low, jaw clenched as he forced out the guttural words. "All those snug little muscles inside you, rippling around me, squeezing me so fucking tight. It's like you were made for me."

His husky words and thrusting body shot her into another mind-shattering climax, her throat still hoarse from her cries when she finally blinked his gorgeous face back into focus. It was clear from his breathtaking expression that he was nowhere near being done with her, and her heart gave an excited jolt.

"Again," he growled, swiveling his hips so that he stroked that sweet spot deep inside her. "I want to see it again."

"See it?" she panted.

"The way you look when you come around my cock. I can't get enough of it."

Holding her hips in a bruising grip, he powered into her in a hard, relentless rhythm that just kept getting faster. It was raw, bordering on violent, but she loved it. He was grinding himself over that cluster of nerves inside her again and again, his skill with her so perfect she didn't even need his fingers on her clit to make her go over. She started screaming somewhere in the middle of it, when the spasms started deep inside, then shot out through every part of her body. He went wild then, her reactions fueling his aggression, and she wouldn't have changed it for anything in the world. This was Ben losing control, lost in her, needing her, and her hunger matched his, feeling just as sharp and visceral. She wanted to claw at him, sink her nails into his tight ass and tell him to fuck her harder, but she couldn't stop screaming long enough to do anything but shiver and come, her body milking that massive shaft until her orgasm had bled into one endless explosion of dark, devastating pleasure.

Gasping for breath, she stared up at him through a shimmery wash of tears as he came. She loved the way he had his head thrown back, his strong throat working as he swallowed, rugged muscles bunched tight beneath his sweat-misted skin. Making love with him was the most amazing, mind-blowing thing she'd ever experienced, and as she closed her eyes, all she could think was *Oh, God. How am I ever going to live without this when it's over?* Would she go through the rest of her life aching for it, feeling empty without it, like a broken cup that could never be full?

"Jesus, Reese. Why are you crying? Did I hurt you?"

She quickly opened her eyes to find him staring down at her with a tense expression, his dark eyes shadowed with fear. "No!" she whispered. "I'm fine."

Confusion creased his brow as he carefully pulled out of her, lowering her back to the bed. "Then why the tears?"

Swiping at her wet cheeks with her fingertips, she said, "I don't know. I think it felt so good I just got a little overwhelmed. I'm sorry for crying all over the place."

Ben stretched out on the bed beside her, bracing himself on an elbow. "No need to be sorry," he offered quietly, catching one of her tears with his thumb as it slipped over her temple. "Tears don't scare me."

She gave a watery giggle. "That's probably a good thing, then."

Knowing he probably looked uncomfortable as hell, he said, "Reese, I—"

She put her fingers over his lips, silencing him. "Stop worrying, Ben. No, you didn't hurt me. And no, I'm not getting all clingy on you. I know the score. It's just that . . . just that that was a pretty powerful . . . experience."

"Yeah," he agreed, unable to get enough of the way she was looking at him. "It was for me, too."

A soft smile curled her mouth. "Thanks. That means a lot to me. But you really can relax, okay? I swear I'm not expecting you to give me anything more than this."

Son of a bitch. He should have been relieved that she was letting him off easy. That she was happy to enjoy the mind-blowing sex, without expecting more from him emotionally. It should have been the perfect goddamn situation. But as he stared into her beautiful eyes, those dark lashes glistening with tears, he wanted to tell her that it was bullshit. That a good time in the sack wasn't all he had to give. That there was more, surprisingly *much* more.

But the dangerous words were choked up inside him, unable to work their way out.

Deciding that he really wasn't giving her a choice tonight about letting him stay, Ben got rid of the condom, lifted the covers over them, and pulled her against his chest. She stayed tense for a few moments, no doubt carrying on some internal debate about whether she should try to kick him out or just give in and accept the fact that he wasn't going anywhere. Slipping his hand down her spine, he was ready to keep smoothing his way down to his new favorite place in the world, when she suddenly gave a little satisfied sigh and snuggled closer. Her breath was soft against his chest, head resting on his biceps, tucked up under his chin, a slender, feminine arm wrapped around his waist, holding him tight. He'd never cuddled like this with a woman before. Had never known how good it could feel, or how right, when the woman was someone like Reese. Her soft, curvy body was nestled against his, her mouthwatering scent flowing through his head, a sense of ease settling over him that he hadn't felt in . . . Christ, he didn't think he'd ever felt anything like this.

He should have been worried or freaking out, trying to keep his fucking head on straight, instead of getting mixed up in something that was getting dangerously . . . complicated.

But at that moment, it felt so good Ben just didn't give a damn.

11

BEN SQUINTED AGAINST THE EARLY MORNING SUNSHINE GLARING OFF the highway, wishing he hadn't forgotten his sunglasses. It hadn't been easy to drag his ass out of Reese's bed when the five a.m. call had come in on his cell. There'd been a nasty head-on collision on the interstate, out on the edge of town, and three people were dead. One of the trucks involved had been carrying a heavy load of gasoline, and both vehicles had gone up in flames too quickly for anyone to escape.

Considering how the accident had taken place, he wondered if the driver who'd veered into the oncoming lanes had been drinking, or if there'd been another factor that made him lose control. Hopefully the coroner would be able to shed some light on the situation, giving the victims' friends and loved ones a better sense of closure. It was a miserable situation, and for the first time that he could remember, Ben found himself wondering how he'd react if one of the victims had been someone he had a personal connection to. Hell, what if it had been *Reese* in one of those cars? He couldn't imagine the rage that would consume him, or the kind of raw, gaping hole her death would leave inside him. He shuddered, not even wanting to follow that particular trail of thought. He was barely dealing with this stalker shit as it was. If he started thinking about something bad happening to her, he'd lose it. Big time.

As he'd left her house that morning, he'd made her promise to lock the door behind him and keep the alarm set. But it didn't make him feel any better. He wanted her by his side. Wanted her close enough that he could protect her if any fucker ever tried to harm her.

When he finally made his way into the station, he dropped her phone off to Toby in IT, then ran into Ryder, who gave him a preliminary report on Drew Leighton. Sitting at his desk, Ben flipped through the pages, impressed with Ryder's work. He didn't know why the guy was working as a deputy, when he could have had a position with any private-sector security firm in the country, but figured it wasn't his place to pry. If Ryder wanted to spend his life working for the sheriff's department, he was damn glad to have him.

The report on Leighton made for some interesting reading. On the surface, he looked like your all-American prep boy, his background not dissimilar to that of Miami drug lord Ryan Houghton. Growing up, they'd both had their share of mansions, private schools, and pricey beach houses in Martha's Vineyard. Leighton came from some serious money, and was in good standing with Boston's social elite. But when you looked a little deeper, you could start to see just what a controlling, arrogant prick he really was. When he was seventeen, his girlfriend's parents had filed a report against him for harassing their daughter when she'd tried to end the relationship. According to Ryder, he'd had to dig deep for the information and call in some favors, but he'd managed to uncover the unsavory details. It seemed that Leighton had spent a lot of time and money trying to bury the various skeletons in his closet, and Ben remembered hearing that the hotshot lawyer was considering running for public office.

There were more instances of suppressed complaints during his university years, and even a few from the first law firm where he'd worked. Ben couldn't help but wonder what kind of husband the bastard had been, then cursed, realizing he really didn't need to wonder at all. With a scowl on his face, he recalled the way Reese had wanted to rush out of bed that morning and get ready before having coffee with him. When he'd asked her what the hurry was, she'd tried to brush it off as nothing, but he'd pressed until she'd finally admitted that her ex would make fun of her in the mornings, delivering snide comments about her wild hair and lack of makeup. From the sound of things, the jackass had constantly complained about her looks and figure, urging her to go on diets and have cosmetic surgery, systematically doing everything he could to dismantle her self-esteem. It made Ben so angry he wanted to track the smarmy fucker down right then and there, and teach him a lesson about what happened to misogynist assholes who bullied women.

He was still reading through the report when his phone buzzed, signaling an incoming text. Glancing at the screen, he laughed when he saw a message pop up that Reese had sent from her tablet.

Laid down for nap, but bed cold w/out u. Thx for last night! Best sleep I've had in ages, even if we didn't sleep much. ;)

A husky laugh rumbled in Ben's chest as he thought about how he'd awakened her during the night not once, but twice. Even then, he'd still wanted more. No matter how many times he had her, it just got better. Hotter. More intense. But it'd been fun, too.

Except for when she'd cried.

Despite what he'd said at the time, her tears had definitely freaked him out. Not because she'd been emotional, but because of how they'd affected his own damn emotions. He'd done his best to make the rest of the night as lighthearted as possible, and was proud of the results.

After the second round of sex, they'd spent a long time just laughing and goofing around under the covers, which was new for him. Yeah, he enjoyed a good time as much as the next guy, but when it came to fucking he kept it hard and sweaty. He didn't linger in bed and laugh with women. But Ben had enjoyed the hell out of those playful moments with Reese. And she'd seemed to enjoy him just as much. Not just his dick, but his jokes and the things he said. Just . . . *him*.

He liked that she seemed interested in him for more than just the things he could do with his cock. Liked every damn thing about the woman, which just highlighted how dangerous this situation with her could become. If he wasn't careful, he could get addicted to more than just the sex, and then he'd really be in deep shit. After such a crap marriage, he figured the last thing she was looking for was another serious relationship—and he sure as hell wasn't capable of pulling one off. Which meant that as far as Ben could tell, he had two choices: Walk away and stop things now, before he got in any deeper. Or keep working on getting his fill of her, and hope to God that it eventually happened.

The first choice probably made more sense, but he knew he was still banking on the second. He had to get there at some point, right? And walking away from her now . . . No, he just didn't see that as something he could do. Not when there was still so much that he wanted from her. So much that he needed.

He started to text her back, then decided that he'd rather just tell her what he wanted to say in person. He'd worked through lunch, so he could head out early without feeling guilty. Hell, he'd started so early because of the accident that morning that he could have kicked off an hour ago, but he'd been hoping the IT guys would finish up with her phone. Leaving a message with them to call as soon as they had any info, Ben grabbed his keys and headed home. He parked the truck in front of his place, but didn't bother going inside, heading straight over to Reese's.

When she didn't answer the door after he'd knocked a few times, he started to get worried. "Reese!" he shouted, trying to see through the frosted pane of glass in the top of the door, but the hallway was nothing more than a distorted blur.

"Use your key!" came her shouted reply from somewhere inside the house.

"Where the hell are you?" he called out, after letting himself in. She'd given him the alarm code that morning, which he used to disable the system, before prowling down the hallway.

"I'm back here in the bedroom."

He found her curled up under a lightweight blanket in the middle of her bed, a pillow clutched to her chest as she lay on her side, long hair gleaming against the white sheets, lips curved in a soft, kinda shy smile.

"Shit," he grunted, pulling his hand down his face. "You scared the hell out of me."

"Sorry. I know I'm being lazy, but this just feels too good to move." She had the windows open and the shutters cracked, letting in a cool breeze. There was a storm forming out over the Gulf, a light rain already falling. Her bed had that soft, cozy look that came in the late afternoon on a stormy day, the sheets rumpled, the woman in them too delectable not to touch . . . and devour.

Hunger settled low in his body, making him hard and thick. "Well, now that I know you're okay, I hope you weren't planning on climbing out of that bed anytime soon." He liked the way her dark eyes started to go all hazy with arousal, that potent sexual energy that always burned him to a crisp already arcing between them. "Because I intend to keep you there for hours."

She arched one of her feminine brows. "Aren't you meant to be at work?"

He shook his head. "I needed to get out of there." Setting his gun and holster on the top of her dresser, Ben pulled his shirt off and started unbuttoning his pants. "Couldn't concentrate worth shit this afternoon, because all I kept thinking about was coming home and getting back inside your sweet little ass."

She snuffled a soft laugh under her breath, a mesmerizing light in those dark eyes as she rolled to her back, stretching out under the blanket. "Far as I recall, you still haven't *had* my ass."

"We'll get there. I'm just breaking you in slowly," he replied in a husky drawl, enjoying their sexy banter. She might be shy, but she was a far cry from timid. "And in the meantime, I sure as hell can't get enough of the rest of you."

That light in her eyes got brighter, the deep blue shining with humor. "I think you're obsessed with certain female body parts, Sheriff Hudson."

He laughed as he kicked off his boots. "So long as they're *your* female body parts, then I'd have to agree. God knows there aren't any others who have ever gotten in the way of my work before." He got rid of the rest of his clothes, then prowled to the foot of the bed. "Tell me, Reese. Have you put something in my water? Slipped me some kind of drug? Because I seem to be suffering a serious addiction to your tight cunt . . . and that smart-ass mouth . . . and those beautiful breasts." He crawled onto the end of the bed, and his voice got rougher. "To be honest, there isn't a single part of your gorgeous little body that I'm not dying to get my mouth on."

She snorted as she propped herself on her elbows, a soft blush on her freckled cheeks. "You'd think you've been sex deprived."

"Well, there's sex and then there's *sex*. I haven't had anything like this in . . ."

Her eyebrows lifted. "In . . . ?"

"Honestly?" he murmured, blowing out a rough breath. "I've never had anything like this."

Her smile was so beautiful it made his heart skip. "You like that?" he asked.

She did this shy, shrugging thing with her shoulder. "It's always nice to feel a little special."

He reached under the bottom edge of the blanket, grasping her ankles. "You're definitely that. I've never stayed so primed and ready. Doesn't matter how hard I have you, I just want you harder the next time. Harder, deeper, longer."

She was still smiling, but there was a shadow of suspicion creeping into her gaze. "Are you sure this isn't just your way of keeping an eye on me?"

He gave a low laugh. "I don't have to do that by keeping you in bed."

Her mouth twitched. "That's true."

"Then again," he breathed out, a crooked grin on his lips as he ran his callused palms up the slender length of her calves, taking the blanket with him. "I think it'd be hot as hell to fuck you in my truck. Or at my office."

Surprise widened her eyes. "You have sex at the station?"

"I haven't before. But I would if you were there."

She smiled again, the color in her face getting a little warmer as he pushed the blanket up to her waist, revealing smooth thighs and a tiny scrap of white cotton panties. With an appreciative moan, Ben fisted the blanket in his hand and tossed it to the floor, leaving her lying there in nothing but those minuscule panties and a thin tank, her nipples making two hard little points beneath the soft cotton.

"Mmm, would you look at this," he murmured, grasping the

sides of her underwear and pulling them down, then trailing his rough hands back up the delicate skin on her inner thighs and shoving them apart. His gaze went heavy as he stared at the pink, glistening folds of her cunt, watching as he pushed two big fingers inside the snug opening. "You're already dripping in juices, Reese. What exactly have you been lying here thinking about?" He lifted his hot gaze and locked it with hers, waiting for her response.

Reese's lashes lowered, her face on fire—but she didn't look away. "You," she whispered, thinking he had to be the sexiest man who'd ever been created.

His eyes got darker, and before she could draw her next breath, he came down over her, taking her mouth, eating at it. The kiss was deliciously raw and explicit, mirroring the breathtaking strokes of his fingers inside her sex. It was ridiculous, how quickly he could get her going, her body responding to his touch like a marionette being controlled by its master. She was already on the verge of climax, the dizzying pressure of his thumb against her clit making her gasp, when he suddenly pulled away and ripped open the top drawer of her bedside table, where he'd stored the box of condoms last night.

With a wicked smile on his lips, he tossed a few of the foil packets on the bed by her hip and got rid of her tank top. She thought he'd take her then, but he obviously wasn't done playing, his teasing smiles and husky laughter driving her wild. Her blood was like fire in her veins, skin so hot she was surprised she didn't steam. The way he turned and positioned her in increasingly shocking, erotic positions, her body open and exposed to him, both physically and emotionally, was more seductive than anything she could have ever imagined.

With his clever fingers playing between her legs, and his mouth dragging kisses across her stomach, he said, "I can't get enough of this. Having you under my hands and mouth. You're so soft inside. So sweet. It's like touching a piece of heaven."

"I didn't know you were spiritual," she murmured, a dreamy smile on her lips as she ran her fingers through the thick, silky locks of his hair.

He lifted his head, locking that molten gaze with hers again. "I'm not. But I'm thankful as hell for you."

She gave a dry laugh. "Wow. With lines like that, no wonder you get laid so often."

Reese knew the words were a mistake the instant she said them. He immediately jerked away from her, a pissed off look in his eyes as he knelt between her legs and scowled. "What the fuck was that for?"

"I don't know," she whispered, biting her lip. "I wasn't trying to piss you off."

He snorted. "Really? Because it felt like you just launched a fucking grenade in my face."

"I know. I'm sorry. It's like I have this . . . I don't know, some kind of defense mechanism that just kicks in."

"Well next time try not to kick me in the face with it."

She probably didn't look very graceful, but she managed to scoot back and brace herself against the wall, grabbing a pillow to cover the front of her body. Feeling ashamed, embarrassed, and more than a little frustrated, she said, "I'm sorry that I said what I did, but it's not easy when you . . . when you say things like that to me. I thought this was just meant to be about sex, and then you go and say something that completely messes with my emotions and it confuses the hell out of me. You can't have it both ways, Ben. That's not how it works, and I don't appreciate you playing games with my head."

"I'm not playing some stupid game with you," he ground out in a raw voice, muscles bulging with tension as he shoved a hand back through his hair, his huge cock still rock-hard and straining toward his navel. "I'm just trying to be honest with you. I'm trying to tell you that being inside you, that having any part of my body inside yours, feels different than it's ever felt for me before. And I want the chance to enjoy it. So stop worrying everything to death and just fucking deal with it."

Slapping a hand against the mattress, she demanded, "And exactly how am I meant to *deal* with it?"

"By lying back and letting me do what I want. By giving in and just enjoying yourself. By just . . ." He broke off, making a hard, thick sound of frustration. "By just lying back and letting me make you feel like the goddamn queen of the universe! Is that so fucking much to ask?"

If he'd been facing a mirror, Ben had no doubt that his expression would be just as surprised as hers. He didn't say things like this to women. Ever. If he was in bed with a woman, he expected to get as much as he gave. An even physical exchange, keeping the balance, with as few emotions involved as possible. But it was so different with Reese. God knew he loved having her hands on him, and her hot little mouth. Loved it more than anything he'd ever done with any other woman. But he fucking *craved* giving her pleasure. Touching her. Tasting her. Sinking deep inside her.

And he was done with this maddening conversation.

Pulling her back under him, Ben ripped the pillow out of her hands, shoved her legs apart and went back down on her, burying his face against the drenched folds of her cunt. "You make me feel like a goddamn addict, Reese. I can't ever get enough of you— even when you make me so fucking mad I could spit nails."

She fisted her hands in his hair, holding him to her as she arched in pleasure. "Are you going to punish me for it?" she gasped, her breath catching as he gave a wet, voluptuous lick to her clitoris, then softly suckled.

"Maybe," he grated. "In fact, I just might fuck you until you can barely walk. Until every breath makes this tight little pussy ache."

He quickly sheathed himself in a condom and moved over her, his dark eyes drilling into hers as he forced his way inside . . . then started to move, pumping himself into her with those thick, heavy lunges that made her tremble and cry out. Putting his mouth close to her ear, he said, "I'm going to ride you raw, baby, but you won't care. It's going to feel so good, all you'll be able to think about is getting me back inside you. Keeping me here, packed up tight and deep, screwing into you so hard you go hoarse from your screams . . ."

And that was exactly what happened. By the time Reese could open her eyes, they'd gone through two condoms, the storm had already passed, and she felt deliciously well ridden, but surprisingly refreshed. Climbing out of bed, she definitely felt a few twinges and aches as she slipped on a T-shirt and jeans. But after such an onslaught of pleasure, she was buzzing with too much adrenaline to stay indoors.

"Come on," she said, the wrecked, raspy sound of her voice putting a silly grin on her lips as she walked to the end of the bed and ran her finger along the bottom of his foot. "Let's go for a walk on the beach."

He yanked his foot away with a grunt, definitely ticklish. "Get your ass back in bed," he grumbled, his impressive cock finally taking some downtime as he rolled to his back and stretched. "It's time for a nap," he added, his eyes already closed.

"But I love going outside after a storm," she said, moving to the side of the bed so that she could get a better look at him. She wished she had the guts to snap a picture of him like this, his hard, outrageously masculine body sprawled across her white sheets, tanned skin stretched tight over all those mouthwatering muscles. Swallowing to clear the lump of lust in her throat, she went on, saying, "And we could watch the sunset together. It'll be fun."

"You're just saying that because you got to sleep all day," he groaned, covering his face with a pillow.

She gave a soft laugh. "I did not. And I don't want to go by myself, but I will if I have to."

"Can't you just stay here?" he asked, glaring when she tugged the pillow away, tossing it to the foot of the bed. "You're forgetting that I'm older than you." A sexy smirk lifted the corner of his mouth. "I need sleep if I'm going to keep up with your man-hungry appetites."

"Hmm . . . you do make me hungry." She smiled . . . and ran the tips of her fingers up the inside of his muscular thigh. "If you come with me, I promise I'll make it up to you later."

Shaking his head, Ben gave a low, gritty laugh. "You already think you know how to control me, don't you?"

"Maybe." With an impish grin on her lips, she used her fingertip to draw little circles on the top of his thigh that were driving him crazy, the confidence he could see in her flushed expression and those bright eyes somehow making her even more beautiful than she already was.

Knowing he didn't stand a chance in hell against her, he surrendered with a rumbling groan of defeat. "Fine, I give in. I'll drag my wrecked ass out of bed for you."

And Ben was glad that he did. There was something to be said for walking on the beach after a storm, the air crisp and cool, with a beautiful woman at your side, her hand in yours. And when she smiled . . . Christ. He could get drunk on it, on that sweet curve of her mouth and the tender warmth in her eyes. And those damn freckles. It didn't matter how many times he kissed them across her nose or her chest, or between those sweet little thighs, he just wanted to do it again . . . and again.

When the wind started to pick up, they finally turned and began to head back. There were already a few bonfires going, most of the groups college-aged, though a few were made up of older couples. He was cutting a quick look over the groups, just to make sure nothing looked like it was going to get too out of hand, when something caught his eye.

Apparently sensing his tension, Reese squeezed his hand. "What's wrong?"

"That guy over there," he rasped, distracted, his focus on the tall, dark-haired male who was standing off to the side of one of the groups farther up the beach. He was wearing a T-shirt and shorts, like most of the other men, but he didn't look like he was there to kick back and relax. His vibe was too alert. Too focused. And while he'd looked away the second Ben had spotted him, he could have sworn the bastard had been staring at Reese.

"What about him?" she asked.

"I don't know. I swear I've seen him somewhere before, but I can't place it."

"Maybe the barbecue on Saturday?"

He cut her a sharp look. "Did you see him there?"

"I think so. Or someone who looked a lot like him," she said with a shrug. "The guy was hanging around near the bar, but I don't think I saw him talking to anyone."

He looked back toward the group again, but the man was no longer there. "Shit. Where the fuck did he go?"

"He's probably just someone who's moved here recently." Her tone was deliberately mellow, as if she was trying to chill him out. "There are houses up and down the beach, Ben. You can't know everyone."

"True," he muttered, still scanning the beach. "I just didn't like the way he was looking at you."

She tugged on his hand until she had his attention again, then waggled her brows. "You never know, stud. He might have been looking at *you*."

His mouth twitched with a reluctant grin. "Smart-ass."

"Hey, you're nice to look at," she drawled. "I'm sure I'm not the only one who's noticed."

He squeezed her hand. "You're the only one I care about."

He immediately stilled for a beat, as if a little stunned to have heard those unexpected words slipping off his tongue, and he wasn't the only one. Reese knew her own surprise, along with too many other confusing emotions, had to be showing on her face, so she quickly looked away, staring out over the water. She was still trying to figure out how to respond, when his phone rang. He took the call after seeing that it was from Toby, the IT guy who had her phone, and they continued walking up the beach, toward their houses, while he talked.

"Any news?" she asked, after he'd thanked Toby and ended the call, slipping the phone back in his pocket.

They'd reached the patio, and he turned toward her, a grim expression on his rugged face as he rubbed his jaw. "They were able to trace the number the texts were sent from to a disposable phone that was bought somewhere in Boston."

Dread slithered through her body, sickly and cold. "Are they sure?"

"Yeah."

She closed her eyes for a moment, then forced them back open. "Shit."

"There's no way to trace the exact purchase point, but it's not looking good for your ex, honey."

"I guess not."

She sounded distracted, lost in thought, and Ben didn't blame her. He knew she'd been hoping for something that didn't link back to Leighton. Hoping to get her mind off the jackass, he said, "Why don't you come over to my place for dinner, then stay the night with me?"

Her startled gaze shot to his. "Oh, that's, uh, really sweet of you, but I don't think it would be a good idea."

"Why not?" he demanded, wondering what kind of infuriating excuse she was going to lob at him this time.

"Because it wouldn't be smart."

"Smart?" he bit out, and Reese thought he not only sounded pissed, he looked it. "What the hell isn't smart about it?"

"I know I sound crazy, and I'm sorry. I just . . . I don't want this to get more confusing than it already is."

He clenched his jaw so hard it looked painful. "You're the one confusing it, Reese. No one else."

"I'm sorry," she said again, wishing there was a way to make him understand. But he was speeding ahead with this thing like they had miles of open road before them, while she kept waiting for the brick wall that came out of nowhere. *Splat.* He might be able to just get up and walk away from that kind of wreckage, but not her. Not with the way her emotions were getting all tangled up over him. Clearing her throat, she added, "I just don't think it's a good idea for me to get too comfortable over at your place."

He blew out a sharp, frustrated breath. "You are the most stubborn, bullheaded woman I've ever known."

Her response was dry. "Well don't hold back, Ben. Just tell me how you feel."

Forcing the words past his gritted teeth, he said, "Fine. If you don't want to succumb to the danger of actually setting foot in my house, we can go out to eat."

"I don't—"

"Christ!" he exploded, shoving a hand through his hair as he glared down at her. "What is it now? Are you . . . is this about *me*?" He shook his head, a shadow of something that looked almost vulnerable creeping into that dark, piercing gaze, as if she actually had the power to hurt him. "For the last fucking time, Reese, are you embarrassed to be seen out in public with me?"

"What? No, of course not. That's ridiculous!"

"Then we're going out tonight," he said in a low, *do-not-fuck-with-me* tone. "I'll grab a shower at my place and pick you up in an hour."

His hard gaze dared her to disagree, and she was tired of fighting about it, when what she wanted was to be with him anyway. If she ended up a heap of emotional road kill, she'd have no one to blame but herself. She'd probably never even want to look at another man again, but hey, at least she'd have gone out enjoying herself. "Fine," she murmured. "I'll be ready in an hour."

He gave a low grunt, apparently satisfied with that response, and followed her to her door, waiting for her to get inside and turn off the alarm. "And just for the record," she called out, when he'd already started walking back down the pathway, "you're the bossiest man *I've* ever known!"

Reese didn't quite catch his muttered response, but she could have sworn it was something along the lines of ". . . *you'd better get used to it.*"

As she closed the door and turned the lock, she couldn't help but grin.

IT WAS ONLY TUESDAY NIGHT, BUT MCCLAIN'S WAS PACKED. AS BEN SAT across from Reese at one of the tables by the front wall of windows, he thought about how much things had changed since last Friday, when he'd been eating here with Brit. He'd spent the entire meal thinking about Reese, wondering how he was going to get his hands on her—and now she was here with him, looking more beautiful than ever. She'd always been stunning in his eyes, but there was something about her tonight, something soft and vibrant in her expression that he couldn't recall ever seeing before. Despite the fact that some wacked-out jackass was screwing with her life, trying to scare the hell out of her, she looked flushed with happiness. So fucking gorgeous he just wanted to keep staring, soaking in the sight of those bright eyes and rosy cheeks. He liked to think it was the way they'd been burning up the sheets together that had her looking so full of life, but he knew it could just as easily be the fact that she was finally out from under the stress of an unhappy marriage.

"What?" he asked, when he caught her staring at him over the rim of her wineglass. "Do I have food on my face?" They'd shared an order of fried calamari and were waiting for their entrées to arrive.

"No," she replied with a warm smile. "I was just thinking that you clean up pretty well, Sheriff Hudson."

"Thanks." He took a drink of his Scotch, then grinned. "I was tempted to come in one of my 'little sheriff outfits,' but figured the shirt and jeans would be a better bet."

She laughed, sipping her wine as she cast an appreciative look over the restaurant, then focused those beautiful blue eyes back on him. "This is nice. The two of us being out together."

He gave a husky laugh, his tone dry. "It took long enough to get you here."

Reese could feel the color rising in her face, but was saved from having to respond when the waiter delivered their meals. They talked as they ate, with Ben answering her questions about his work (and carefully avoiding any she asked about his childhood), while she filled him in on the teaching job she would start at the end of the summer. They'd only just dug into their desserts when a stunning brunette left her seat at the bar and approached their table. She was a little wobbly on her stiletto heels, the calculating gleam in her kohl-rimmed eyes telling Reese she was looking to cause trouble.

"*Ben,*" the woman purred, running her hand over his shoulders as she practically sat on the arm of his chair. "Cindy and I have been waiting for you to come back over and party with us again." She slid a catty look toward Reese, before saying, "There's no one in this town who can keep up with two women the way you can, Sheriff. It's like you were built for it."

Reese had to choke back a gasp, feeling instantly chilled, in shock, as if something rank and slick had just been tossed in her face. The coldness was leaking all the way down to her bones, and she set her fork down before it slipped from her icy fingers.

For his own part, Ben looked seriously pissed, and maybe even a little panicked, no doubt worried about how she was going to react to the woman's taunting. Did he think she was going to cause a scene? If so, he was wrong. Reese was too stunned to do anything but sit there and look like she'd just been slapped in the face with a fish. Keeping his dark eyes locked with hers, he spoke in a quiet, guttural rasp. "That's enough, Denise."

"Oops, sorry," the woman giggled, covering her mouth with her hand as she stumbled back a step from his chair. "I guess you wanted to keep that little threesome a secret, huh?"

You conniving little bitch, Ben thought, wishing he could wring Denise's neck. She knew exactly what she was doing. Turning his head, he slid her a narrow, furious look of warning that he hoped would shut her the hell up. "You've obviously had too much to drink tonight. Have Daryl at the bar call you a cab and go home."

"Oh, don't worry about me, Sheriff. I'll be careful." As if completely oblivious to his anger, she gave him a blinding smile and leaned down to kiss his cheek, before whispering for him to call her.

As the leggy brunette strolled away from their table, Reese

drained the last of her wine, then carefully set down the glass. Quietly, she asked, "Do I even want to know?"

His nostrils flared as he rubbed the woman's lipstick off his face, jaw clenched so tight she was surprised it hadn't cracked. "This isn't important, Reese."

She shook her head, lips curving in a wry smile as she wiped her mouth and set her napkin on the table. She didn't even look at him when she spoke, her gaze focused on the dark seascape beyond the window. "Maybe not to you, but it is to me. I knew your past was . . . colorful. But hearing that you slept with both her *and* her friend, at the same time, definitely puts a new spin on things. Especially when it gets slammed in my face like that."

"You need to let it go," he said, forcing the graveled words through his teeth.

She smirked. "I know."

Ben struggled to rein in his temper, knowing damn well what she was thinking. "Not me. Not *us*," he said in a low, furious tone. "I'm talking about that troublemaking little bitch. She meant less than nothing to me and I wish to God that I'd never touched her."

"And not long from now, you'll probably be sitting here with some other woman . . . or hey, maybe even *two* of them . . . saying the same thing about me."

"Fuck," he growled, fisting his hand on the top of the table to keep from slamming it against the rustic wood. "You're making a big deal out of nothing."

"That's the problem, Ben." She turned her head, locking that dark, turbulent gaze with his. "It's not nothing for *me*. I tried to do it your way, but I can't. I'm not good at separating sex from emotion. And after tonight, I'm *glad* I'm not that way."

"I never asked you to do that."

"You did," she argued, giving a tired, bitter laugh. "You just don't even realize it."

They finished the meal in tense silence, neither of them saying a single word until the check was delivered. Then she tried to give him money for her portion of the meal, and he nearly bit her head off. After that, she let him pay the damn bill and they drove home.

"You going to let me stay with you tonight?" he asked in a gritty rasp, meeting her at the front of his truck.

"Actually," she murmured, crossing her arms as she held his stare, "I was thinking I'd just like to have some time alone."

He took a step toward her, but stopped when she immediately stepped back. "Look, I get that you're upset about what happened, but I don't like you sleeping alone right now." His voice was low and tightly controlled, as if he was trying to keep a firm grip on his temper. "Just because that burn phone was bought in Boston doesn't mean we've got a handle on this thing. We still need proof that it's Leighton. And I'm still waiting to get a fix on his exact location, which means the asshole could be anywhere. Hell, even if he *is* in Boston, I'm not convinced that he's in this alone."

She lifted her chin. "I understand what you're saying. But I refuse to be too frightened to stay in my own house by myself. And it's not like I'm stranded here without help. You're right next door, and I can use my landline if I need to call you. And I also have the alarm now."

A fierce scowl creased his brow, that tight control beginning to show its cracks. "What exactly is going on here, Reese? Is this some screwed-up way for you to punish me for what happened tonight? Yeah, I have a past, and there are parts of it that I'm not particularly proud of. Hell, there's a lot of it, like Denise, that I don't want getting anywhere near you, and I'm sorry that it happened. I can't change how I've lived my life until this point, but it's the *past*. It has *nothing* to do with the two of us. With what's happening right now."

Rubbing her pounding forehead, she said, "I'm not trying to punish you, Ben. I just need some time to think."

He looked ready to erupt, a muscle pulsing in the hard set of his jaw, but managed to hold his tongue long enough to walk her to her front door. But as they stood beneath the muted glow of her porch light, he couldn't hold back any longer. "This is fucking bullshit. I can feel you pulling away from me."

"I'm not." She unlocked the door, went inside, and disabled the alarm. She could feel him vibing his hot, angry male energy behind her, waiting to be dealt with. To get everything out in the open and thrashed into some kind of resolution. But she wasn't up for it tonight. Her thoughts were in chaos, emotions zinging all over the place, only making her headache worse. She was a mess, and she really did need some time to figure out what the hell she was doing.

Turning to face him, she met his hard, simmering stare, and held her ground. "I'm just trying to make the right decision about how we go forward from here."

He prowled into the entryway, his big, muscular body taking up all the space, towering over her, the overwhelming force of his presence nearly sucking up every ounce of oxygen. "And putting distance between us is the right decision? You have some jackass out there who's trying to scare the shit out of you, who's probably the same bastard who left a dead cat ripped to pieces in your apartment, and you think the smart thing to do is stay here alone?"

"That's why I have the alarm," she said, striving for a calm tone, when she was anything but. "I don't want to fight with you, Ben. I just . . . I need to set some limits or boundaries or whatever you want to call them on things between us so that they don't get too confusing. That's what I've been trying to explain to you from the start."

Spearing his fingers through his hair, he muttered, "I wish to fuck you would stop trying to analyze everything to death and just enjoy yourself."

She opened her mouth, but before she could respond, he

brushed past her, saying, "I'm going to check the house. Wait here."

He came back a minute later, that muscle still pulsing in his jaw. Without saying a word, he curved his hand around the back of her neck and yanked her against him, taking her mouth in a devastating kiss that was raw and angry and full of breathtaking hunger. When he finally pulled back, she was panting and flushed, her eyes widening when she saw the satisfied gleam in his hot, heavy-lidded gaze. "You might be pissed at me, Reese. You might not even be able to stand the sight of me right now." His voice got lower, vibrating with the intensity of a vow. "But when you're lying alone in your bed tonight, you know what, sweetheart? You're still going to miss the hell out of me."

Then the arrogant jackass turned and walked away, slamming the door behind him.

12

AFTER SPENDING THE MORNING BROODING ABOUT BEN AND UNPACKING the last of her moving boxes, Reese was glad when Connie called and asked her to lunch with one of her friends. The woman's name was Rachel Linden and she worked at the same elementary school where Reese would start teaching at the end of the summer. They ate at Casa di Pico again, and she really enjoyed the petite brunette's company. In her late-twenties, Rachel was sweet and smart, with a wonderful sense of humor, and it was easy to see how she and Connie had become friends. The three of them hadn't stopped talking since they'd sat down, the conversation effortlessly flowing from one topic to the next. As they snacked on nachos and empanadas, Rachel shared some hilarious stories about the school, as well as a few about Connie that Reese planned to use for ammunition later on. They'd just decided to make plans for a girls' night out the following week when Rachel's phone started ringing.

"Ohmygod, I'm sorry about that. I forgot to put this thing on vibrate," she said, reaching into her purse for the phone. When she glanced at the screen and paled, all the color draining from her face, Connie and Reese both set down their forks.

"I'm really sorry, but I . . . I have to go," Rachel murmured, slipping the phone back in her purse.

"Is everything okay?" Connie asked, touching her arm.

"Fine," she obviously lied, her dark eyes troubled. "There's just . . . something I have to take care of." She scooted out of the booth, then dug into her purse for some money. "This should cover my tab," she said, offering Connie a twenty.

Connie held up her hands, refusing to take the folded bill. "Don't worry about it, hon. Today was my treat."

"Oh, um, thanks. But I owe you one." With a strained smile on her pretty face, she looked at Reese. "It was nice to finally meet you. We'll definitely have to plan for that girls' night out soon."

Returning her smile, Reese said, "I'll be looking forward to it."

They both watched as Rachel left the restaurant, and then Reese brought her worried gaze back to Connie. "Is she okay?"

Her sister frowned. "I hope so. I know she's been having some trouble with an ex, but it's not easy getting information out of her." She directed a wry look at Reese. "Reminds me of someone else I know."

Reese ignored the taunt. "I hope she'll be all right."

"You and me both," Connie muttered, reaching for her drink.

They finished their food in thoughtful silence, until Reese finally asked, "So when does Gary get home?"

"Next week. I can't wait!" her sister said with excitement, before giving Reese a mischievous look from beneath her lashes. "By the way, I've told him all about how you're falling into Ben's lecherous clutches."

She nearly choked on her iced tea. "What? Why? There's noth—"

Connie waved her manicured hand in the air. "Oh, get off it. I knew you'd succumbed to the sexy stud the second I set eyes on you today."

Reese collapsed against the back of the booth, her breath leaving her lungs in a soft *whoosh*. "How did you know?"

Connie cocked her head to the side and smiled. "It's just something in your face, and your eyes. You look like there might be something bothering you, but under that, you're still all lit up like a Christmas tree." Waggling her brows, she lowered her voice and asked, "So was he really good?"

"Was who good?"

They both gasped at the sound of that deep male voice, eyes wide as they looked up and found Ben standing at the end of their table. He wore one of the black sheriff's department polo shirts that she'd seen him in last Friday morning and khakis, his gun holstered under his arm, dark hair tousled from either the wind or his fingers.

Reese swallowed a mouthful of lust, thinking he got more gorgeous every freaking time she saw him.

"Hey," she said faintly, surprised by how badly she wanted to throw herself at this man. Just as he'd predicted, she'd missed him like crazy last night, and not just because of the sex. Yeah, the sex had been part of it. But she'd also missed the weight and the warmth of him lying beside her. Missed the feel of his strong arms wrapped around her, holding her close.

Clearing her throat, she asked, "Are you here to meet someone?"

His eyes darkened as he gave a curt shake of his head. "Just stopped in to grab a quick bite. The station's only around the corner."

"Oh."

Jerking his chin toward the table, he said, "I'll let you both get back to your lunch. Nice seeing you, Connie."

Looking completely fascinated by the undercurrents that were simmering between the two of them, her sister murmured, "You too, Ben."

Reese had thought he'd walk away then, but he didn't. Instead, he angled that impossibly tall, muscular body in her direction . . . and gave her a scorching look that was so full of hunger, she practically melted. "Will I see you tonight?" he asked.

She licked her lips, her heart beating so loud she was amazed everyone couldn't hear it. "Um, sure, if you want."

"Oh, I definitely want," he said in a low, guttural rumble, bracing one hand against the back of the booth as he leaned down and claimed her mouth in a hard, possessive, bone-melting kiss, his other hand framing her jaw. And then he was gone, leaving her sitting there with tingling lips and burning cheeks, gasping for breath.

Eyes wide with shock, Connie watched him as he made his way across the restaurant. Then she looked at Reese and blinked. "Wow. For a minute there, I thought he was going to take you right on the freaking table. What on earth are you doing to the poor guy?"

"Me?" she breathed out, quickly reaching for her iced tea. "I'm not doing anything. He's the one . . . the one who can't . . ."

Connie laughed. "Yeah, I get it. He can't keep his hands off you." Leaning forward, she lowered her voice and asked, "So what's your secret?"

"Nothing!" Reese squeaked, wishing she could dump the cold tea over her head and cool the heck down. This was so embarrassing! "I'm just . . . you know . . . I'm just *me*." Which was why none of this made any sense. How could a guy with *his* wild reputation be so interested in someone like her? It boggled the mind.

And wasn't that a huge part of the problem right there? She was falling for this guy hard and fast, knowing damn well that she could never be enough for him. That before long, he'd end up getting bored and moving on.

No doubt reading the pain on her face, Connie reached across the table and patted her hand. "Oh sweetie, you're not *just* anything. That ass Drew really did a number on you, didn't he? But you're so beautiful Reese, inside and out, and Ben knows it." The waiter brought their check to the table, and Connie gave him her credit card. As he walked away, she looked at Reese again and finished what she'd been saying. "If you ask me, I think Ben knows how lucky he is to be with you. And if he's smart, he's going to do everything he can to make sure you feel the same way about him. Which definitely includes blowing your mind in the sack."

Biting her lip, Reese said, "I really like him, Con. But things are pretty . . . well, complicated between us. We had a big disagreement last night."

"Oh no. What happened?"

Fiddling with the edge of her napkin, she said, "We went out to dinner at McClain's and ran into some catty woman he'd slept with." Just thinking about it put a sour feeling in the pit of her stomach. "Needless to say, it wasn't an ideal situation."

Connie leaned back against the booth, her expression an odd mixture of humor and understanding. "Hell, Reese. Considering Ben's reputation, I think you'd run that risk in just about any restaurant in town."

Her shoulders slumped. "I know. That's why I didn't want to go out to eat with him in the first place. I had a feeling something like that would happen."

"So you got upset?"

Reese nodded, feeling nauseous. "She was all over him, talking about how he'd had a threesome with her and one of her friends and how amazing he was. It was awful."

Connie winced. "Ouch. I think hearing something like that

would have upset any woman." Her sister took a deep breath, then slowly let it out, as if gathering her courage. Then she gave Reese a wry grin, and said, "But if it makes you feel any better, I had some similar trouble when Gary and I started going out. On our third date, I found out that he'd been big into ménages before meeting me, and I had to deal with more than a few of his old lovers when we were out together. But the way I see it, you can either let those women come between the two of you, or put them in their place. If Ben still wanted them, he would have stayed with them. But he didn't. They're old news. You're the new news."

"Yeah. And one day in the not so distant future, I'll be the old news, too."

Connie pursed her lips, her head cocked to the side again . . . but she didn't immediately say anything.

"What?" Reese asked, giving her a wary look.

"I don't know," Connie said, shrugging a little. "It's just that, before seeing how he is around you today, I'd have probably agreed with you. As wonderful as you are, I wasn't sure that Ben had it in him to realize how lucky he is that you're interested. But now . . . I think I would have been wrong about him."

Terrified to get her hopes up, Reese repeated one of their late grandmother's favorite sayings. "I can hope for the best, but it's smarter to prepare for the worst."

Connie gave a soft laugh. "Well, just so you know, he's sitting at a table over there, facing the mirrored wall, and he hasn't been able to take his eyes off you since he sat down."

Just like that, Reese's blush came back in full force. "God, I wish I could just figure him out. But he's so damn confusing."

Connie snorted. "He's a guy, isn't he? They're always a lot to handle when they see their bachelor days slipping away from them."

The waiter brought Connie's credit card back to the table while

Reese was still sitting there, blinking, stunned into silence by what Connie had just said. As her sister slipped the card back into her wallet, she went on, saying, "I'm going to head on home, but you should get over there and keep the poor boy company while he eats. I think Mom and I are planning to drop by your place in the morning with a few housewarming gifts, but if you're not at home, I'll know whose door to knock on," she finished with a wink.

Shaking her head, Reese said, "It isn't like that, Con. We're . . . we aren't spending the night together."

Connie's face fell. "Oh."

She wondered if her smile looked as unsure as it felt. "It's better that way."

"His idea?" Connie asked, lifting her brows.

Reese exhaled a shaky breath. "No. Mine. It's actually one of the things we argued about last night," she murmured, feeling bad for not telling Connie the whole truth. But she didn't want her family worrying about this crazy stalker business. Knowing her mom and Connie, they'd probably board a plane to Boston and try to confront Drew face-to-face.

"Oh . . . well, in that case," Connie was saying, sliding a sympathetic glance at Ben, "I think you should cut the guy some slack, sis. He looks like he's got it bad." Sliding out of the booth, she slid her purse strap over her shoulder, then gave Reese a hug after she'd scooted out of the opposite side. "Just remember that anything worth keeping is definitely worth fighting for," Connie whispered in her ear.

Reese ran those compelling words through her mind as she waited for Connie to reach the door, knowing her sister would give her a little wave before she left. With her pulse beginning to roar in her ears, Reese waved back, then took a deep breath, turned, and started working her way through the crowded restaurant, heading for Ben's table. She was nervous and dangerously hopeful, her heart pounding like crazy as she considered the idea that Connie might actually be right. Maybe she *did* need to fight for what she wanted. To let all those bitchy Denises stay in the past, where they belonged, and focus on going forward.

A year ago, she would have never had the courage or the confidence, but she was different now. Her will had been forged in the burning ashes of her divorce and the madness that had stalked her afterward—that was *still* stalking her—and she knew that she could face whatever life threw at her . . . and maybe even put up a decent fight for what she wanted in the process. Even if what she wanted was a tall, dark, devastatingly sexy badass. One who seemed determined to work his way under her skin, making her crave his touch and taste and scent. Making her ache for every crooked smile and heated glance.

There was no guarantee that Ben would ever return her feelings. Brit had told her that he was "closed down," and she didn't know if she had what it would take to break him open. But she wasn't ready to turn her back on them without even trying. She'd be smart, holding on to those boundaries that they'd talked about, but she wasn't going to scurry off and hide.

Yeah, they might eventually find that brick wall coming at them from out of nowhere, but today was a new day, and Reese could suddenly see that there was another option besides slamming into the thing headfirst.

If she fought for him hard enough, they just might be able to smash right through it . . .

And reach the other side.

Two days later, despite a couple of heated arguments, Ben still hadn't managed to change Reese's mind about letting him sleep over again, her determination to keep those "limits" on their relationship impossible to crack. He also hadn't managed to get any closer to getting his fill of her, the need continuing to dig its way deeper into him each day, impossible to ignore. He didn't know how to explain it, or how to make her understand where he was coming from without revealing far more than he was comfortable with. All he knew was that when he was with her, he had this overwhelming feeling that he was *exactly* where he was meant to be. Yeah, she drove him crazy at times, too fucking stubborn for her own good, but she made him feel better than he had in . . . Hell, she made him feel better than he *ever* had. But like an idiot, he didn't have the balls to tell her.

Sitting at his desk, he stared out the window at the windblown trees, thinking about the conversation they'd had last night, before he'd headed home. They'd been lying on her sofa, wrapped around each other, still damp with sweat from a deliciously long, grinding fuck, when she'd said, "I'm sorry I didn't feel like going for a walk down on the beach tonight." They'd been sticking close to home, since he hadn't wanted to risk another disaster like the one with Denise. At least not until he had this thing with Reese on steady ground, and knew they could handle the shit from his past without it driving another wedge between them.

"No need to be sorry." His voice had been rough with satisfaction. "There's nothing in the world I'd rather be doing than what we just did."

She'd laughed, but then went quiet as she'd snuggled back against him, hands wrapped around his forearms as he held her close. Eventually, in a soft voice, she'd said, "He told me I was boring."

"What?"

She'd drawn an unsteady breath. "He said he was bored. Drew did. That he loved me, but that I wasn't exciting enough for him."

"I take back what I said before," he'd ground out, so furious he could have snapped the fucker in two. "He's not just stupid, he's a

moron." A moron they'd learned was currently at a legal conference in Northern California with the receptionist Reese had
caught him banging.

Smiling at him over her shoulder, she'd said, "For such a badass,
you're awfully sweet, Sheriff Hudson."

"That's just 'cause I'm trying to put you under my spell," he'd
teased, his voice still rough with anger. But he wasn't going to take
it out on her.

"Why?"

"Why what?" he'd asked, distracted by the way she was looking at him, her eyes all glowing and soft.

"What do you want out of this, Ben?" She'd sat up and turned
toward him, tucking a glossy strand of hair behind her ear. "I
promised myself I wasn't going to ask you that question, but this
week has been so overwhelming and . . . *intense*. I just . . . I need
at least a glimmer of what's going on in your head."

Panic had instantly lodged itself in his throat like a boulder.
Instead of answering, he'd bent one of his arms behind his head,
and had asked, "What do *you* want out of it?"

Taking a deep breath, she'd held his gaze as she spoke. "I . . . I
know that I don't want to get hurt. But I don't want to walk away
from you, either."

"Then don't."

When she'd realized that was all he was going to say, she moved
to stand up, but Ben had caught her wrist and tugged her back
down to the sofa, pinning her beneath the hard weight of his body.
Pushing her hair back from her face, he'd stared down into her
stormy eyes and struggled to find the right thing to say before he
completely fucked things up. It took him a few moments, but he'd
finally told her, "I don't know how to have these kinds of conversations, Reese. I know I'm not any good at this, but if you can just
be patient, I promise I'll try not to screw it up."

"I'm not trying to pressure you," she'd said, staring up at him like she was trying to solve a puzzle. Trying to get inside his head and figure out what his fucking problem was. If he was worth fighting for, or if it was better just to wash her hands of him now and find some other guy who wasn't so emotionally stunted. "I'm just trying to get you to talk to me."

"I know, honey. But you want me to talk about feelings and all that shit, and I . . . I'm not any good at—"

"Just forget it," she'd said, cutting him off. It'd been clear from her expression that she was disappointed. "You don't have to say anything. This was obviously a bad idea. I'm being an idiot."

"No, you're not." He'd lowered his head, kissing his way across a soft, freckled cheek. "You're beautiful and fun and so sexy I can't think straight when I'm around you."

"You're nuts," she'd whispered, turning adorably pink.

His voice rough with emotion, Ben had stared into her eyes, swallowed back his fear, and finally forced out at least a few of the words he'd wanted to say. "I *want* you, Reese. More than I've ever wanted anything. Just . . . give me a chance to prove that to you, okay? To prove that I won't hurt you."

Which could very well be bullshit, he realized in the bright light of day, furious with himself for being such a pathetic bastard. If his track record was anything to go by, there was a good chance she wouldn't come out of this unscathed. Not if he stuck around long enough to do the damage. According to Brit, it was a learned behavior for him: Hurt before you get hurt. One he'd no doubt picked up at an early age, after watching his parents' screwed-up marriage. He could fight it all he wanted, but Ben had a strong suspicion that the harder he fell for Reese, the stronger that instinct would eventually kick in.

But Christ, he didn't want that to happen.

He'd been telling himself from the beginning that she wouldn't want anything serious. That she'd be happy with an exclusive, but short-term arrangement, same as him, until they both decided it was time to move on. But as he'd lain on that couch, staring into those dark blue eyes, he'd had to question if that was really what he wanted. Because the idea of walking away from her made him feel like he'd been kicked in the gut. Somehow, his old lifestyle wasn't some safety line waiting down the road for him. It was a fucking death knell ringing in his ears, because it meant that the best damn thing to have ever happened to him would have slipped through his fingers.

She'd had an early lunch date with Brit at eleven, and was going to meet up with Connie after that to do some shopping for a few new pieces of furniture. Hoping she was done, Ben tried to call her cell phone—he'd given it back to her on Wednesday evening—but it went straight to her voice mail. He left her a message, telling her that he had to finish up some work at the station and to give him a call if she wanted him to bring something over for dinner. Even though they weren't sharing a bed, they were still eating together every night, and then screwing like a couple of minks, until she kicked his ass out when it got late. And he was getting damn tired of that scenario. With any other woman, yeah, it would have been the way he played it. Screw her through the mattress, then head home, where he could enjoy a good night's sleep without someone clinging to him, setting expectations he was never going to meet . . . and didn't even want to. But everything inside him rebelled against the idea of leaving Reese alone.

Just like he had on Monday night, Ben wanted to hold her through the quiet hours of darkness. Wanted to feel the warmth of her breath on his chest, the softness of her skin pressed along his. He just . . . wanted her. Badly. And even though it still scared the shit out of him, there was a part of him that just didn't give a damn anymore. That just wanted to get the woman in his arms and keep her there.

Maybe tonight he'd just wear her out until she collapsed in exhaustion, and she'd fall asleep before she could ask him to leave. If she was prickly about it in the morning, he could always soften her up with his tongue before letting her out of bed. God knew there was nothing he enjoyed more than getting his mouth on that sweet little cunt. He couldn't get enough of the way she felt, the way she smelled . . . and Christ, the way she tasted nearly killed him. It was a goddamn sensory overload every time he went down on her, his body reverting to some kind of primitive state where her pleasure became an insatiable craving, and he was strung out on the feeling. So much so that his mouth was already watering, his dick loaded and rock hard in his khakis, just from thinking about it.

"Cool it, for chrissakes," he muttered under his breath. The station was no place for a fucking hard-on. Not if he wanted to avoid being the butt of bad jokes for the rest of his life.

He put in a quick call to Alex, checking to see if his brother had made any progress with the favor he'd asked him. On Wednesday evening, when he and Reese had gone down for another walk along the shore, Ben could have sworn he'd caught sight of the same dark-haired male he'd seen at the beach on Tuesday. But he'd lost him in a crowd gathering for a big beach volleyball tournament, and hadn't been able to spot him again. Though he couldn't fucking place him, Ben was positive that he knew the guy from somewhere, and so he'd asked Alex to do some asking around to see what he could uncover. But with so little to go on, Alex still didn't have anything for him.

Ben had only just set his cell phone back down on his desk when it starting ringing. Thinking it was Reese, he picked up before the second ring, a smile in his voice as he said, "Hudson."

"Ben, it's Mike. There's been an accident."

He knew, without even being told, that Reese had been involved. The blood drained from his face as he jerked to his feet, his pounding heart trying to lodge itself in his throat. "What happened?" he barked, keeping the phone against his ear as he grabbed his keys and headed for the station's front doors.

Mike's tone was grim. "I was in town, having coffee across the street from where it went down. Reese is on her way to the hospital now, but it doesn't look good, man. She was hit by a fucking car."

13

Ben's stomach roiled, visions of the accident on Tuesday morning still fresh in his mind. Christ, not Reese. The thought of her delicate body caught up in a bone-crushing heap of twisted metal made him want to bellow with rage—but instead, he found himself silently pleading, repeating the same choked words in his head, over and over . . .

Please, God, no. Please don't let her be hurt . . .

Ignoring the worried looks being sent his way as he raced out of the station, Ben sucked in a ragged breath and struggled to find his voice. "What road was she on?" he finally bit out, sunlight glaring into his eyes as he headed for his truck, the phone still pressed against his ear. "Was it a head-on? What the fuck happened, Mike?"

His brother pounded on his horn and shouted at someone for driving like a jackass, then said, "She wasn't in her car. She was getting ready to cross O'Neill Street on foot. I don't know all the details. Just that a minivan knocked her into the air and she came down hard."

"Oh, fuck."

"I'm sorry, man. I'm on my way to the hospital now. I'll meet you there, okay?"

"Yeah, okay." Feeling like he'd had the goddamn ground ripped out from under him, Ben lowered the phone from his ear, shaking so hard he could barely manage to end the call. *Fuck.* She hadn't had another one of those creepy texts since that one about flowers, and now this. Had she been hit on purpose . . . or had it been an accident? And why the fuck was the hospital all the way on the other side of town? Turning his siren on, Ben floored the gas, but the minutes that it took him to reach her were still the longest of his life. He'd seen accidents like this too many times not to know how much damage could be done by a moving vehicle. When it was metal against flesh, the body almost always came out the loser. The thought made him physically ill, but he didn't have time to indulge in any roadside vomiting. He just needed to haul ass and get there as quickly as possible.

He barely remembered parking his truck and running through the hospital corridors. There was nothing but a dark, suffocating desperation churning inside his head until he finally burst into her room, the irritated nurse from reception hot on his heels, and saw for himself that Reese was alive. Hurrying to the side of her bed, he swallowed back his panic as he did a quick visual sweep. "What the hell, baby? Are you okay?"

"I swear it looks worse than it is," she croaked, giving him a wobbly smile. "I'm fine, Ben."

"Like hell you are," he growled, noting the scratches and bruises that covered her arms and face. And those were just the parts of her he could see! Carefully gripping one of her battered hands in his, he asked, "How the fuck did this happen?"

"I don't really know," she told him. "One minute I was walking to my car, waving at Connie over my shoulder, and the next thing I knew there was this awful noise and all the air was shoved out of my lungs, really hard. When I tried to move again, I realized I was lying facedown on one of those strips of grass that line the streets in the center of town."

"Jesus. You're lucky you're not dead."

"Trust me, I know," she whispered, squeezing his hand.

Narrowing his eyes, he asked, "What was the driver's story?" He'd been so frantic to reach the hospital, he hadn't even put in a call to whomever had been on the scene from the sheriff's department. Did they even have the bastard in custody?

"It wasn't the minivan's fault," Connie said, drawing his gaze to the window, where she was standing, arms crossed tight over her chest. Ben had been so focused on Reese that he hadn't even noticed she was there. "The van was just reacting to the asshole in the truck."

His gaze got even sharper. "What truck?"

Connie's mouth was a flat, tense line, her face still pale with fear. "I don't know. It sped off after Reese was hit. But it had been pulling up beside her for some reason, on the wrong side of the road. When the van turned the corner and saw the truck in its lane, the driver swerved, and that's when she was hit."

Ben scowled, wondering why the truck had been pulling up beside Reese. "Did you see who was driving the truck?" he asked Connie. "Or get a license plate number?"

She shook her head as she frowned. "I'm sorry, Ben, but no. The windows were tinted, so I don't think anyone got a clear look at the driver. And once Reese was hit, we were all just trying to help her."

He gave Connie a look that said they needed to talk more later, then looked back down at Reese. Pushing her hair back from her bruised face, he asked, "What have the doctors said?"

"That I'm fine, just like I told you." She struggled to sit up a little higher, until he told her to hold still and reached down, pressing the button on the control panel that raised the head of the bed. She thanked him, then said, "They want to keep me overnight, just for observation. And they're going to do an MRI in a little while, just to make sure everything's okay. But there aren't any real concerns." A wry grin curled the corner of her mouth. "I'm apparently very bouncy."

His chest shook with a breathless laugh. "Well thank God for that," he murmured, leaning down and pressing a careful kiss to her scraped forehead.

A nurse came in with some pain meds and to check her vitals, and after making a quick phone call to the station, Ben joined Connie by the window, deliberately keeping his voice too low for Reese to overhear. Despite having survived the ordeal with miraculously minimal damage, he knew the experience had left her shaken. He didn't want to say anything that would upset her even more at that moment, but he was worried as hell about what the truck had been doing so close to her. Had the driver planned to abduct her? Sideswipe her? Shoot her with a fucking gun? Whatever the reason, his gut told him that she'd been a target, and it made him want to go for blood.

He hadn't been talking to Connie for more than a few minutes, the nurse still busy with Reese, when another nurse opened the door to her room and poked her head inside.

"Ms. Monroe, there's another visitor here to see you. A Mr. Leighton."

Reese's jaw instantly dropped. "What?" she gasped, looking completely stunned.

"You've got to be fucking kidding me," Ben snarled, moving toward the door with a hard, purposeful stride.

The nurse shot a startled look in his direction. "Sheriff Hudson? Is everything okay?"

"It's fine," he barked, his tone sending her scurrying back as he grabbed the door, jerking it wide open. "Tell Mr. Leighton that I'll talk to him in the hallway."

"Ben, no!" Reese protested, trying to lower the safety bar at the side of her bed as the nurse she'd been talking to quickly left the room.

"Don't even think about it," he growled, jabbing his finger at her in an order for her to stay put. "You set one toe out of that bed, Reese, and I'm spanking your ass. You understand?"

Ben didn't wait for her response, more than ready to confront this son of a bitch on his own. Shutting the door to her room behind him, he turned and headed toward the hotshot lawyer, who was waiting a few yards down the hallway, near the nurses' station. Mike stood nearby, back braced against the corridor wall, his dark gaze focused sharply on Leighton, who was dressed in an expensive-looking suit and tie, a young, aggressive looking blonde hovering near his side. Mike had obviously made it clear that Leighton wasn't getting past him, and the guy wasn't happy about it. The lawyer's pretty-boy face was flushed with anger, a scowl wedged deep between his golden brows.

Planting himself in the middle of the hallway, Ben crossed his arms over his chest and locked his hard gaze with Leighton's. "What the hell are you doing here?" he demanded in a gritty rasp, thinking it was a good thing he'd left his gun locked in his glove box. If he found out this prick had tried to hurt Reese, he knew he'd be tempted to shoot him.

Looking thoroughly insulted by his question, Leighton said, "I could ask you the same thing. I happen to be here to see my *wife*."

Ben gave the jackass a sharp smile. "*Ex*-wife. Let's not forget that she divorced your sorry ass."

The lawyer's pale blue eyes narrowed with suspicion. "If I had to guess, I'd say that you're not here in a professional capacity, Sheriff Hudson."

"And you'd be right," Ben drawled, watching Leighton's face get redder as his breathing quickened. The guy looked like he was hanging on to his control by a thread, and Ben had every intention of pushing him further, needing to see just how violently the arrogant prick would react. "And now you're going to tell me what the fuck you're doing in Moss Beach."

"That's none of your business," the blonde sneered, curling her lip as she plastered herself against Leighton's side. Ben would have been willing to bet some serious money that this was the infamous Lizzie, whom Reese had caught her husband screwing. He couldn't imagine what the idiot had been thinking, cheating on his wife with this bitter bitch. She had the curves and a store-bought finish—towering heels, a pricey business suit, and makeup that looked like it'd been professionally caked on—but it wasn't hard to see that beneath the glitz, she was hard as stone.

"I told you to keep your mouth shut if you came with me," Leighton muttered under his breath, jerking his arm out of the blonde's hold. Then he turned his attention back to Ben. "I'm in town because I wanted to make sure that Reese was doing okay after the move. The last time we talked, she sounded . . . upset."

Lowering his arms, Ben took a step closer. "She told you she was fine and to leave her alone."

Those pale eyes went wide, then narrowed again to hot, glittering slits. "You were with her when I called, weren't you?"

Hooking his thumbs in his front pockets, Ben curled his lips in a sly smile. "Reese and I are neighbors now, so we get to spend a *lot* of time together."

A shudder moved through Leighton's stiff frame. His nostrils flared. "You fucking touch her and I'll—"

"You'll what?" Ben pressed, knowing damn well the lawyer didn't have the balls to fight him. It was written all over the asshole's face. Leighton might be pissed, but he was still a fucking pussy. He'd never go up against someone bigger and meaner than he was, but God, Ben wished he would throw a punch so that he could go ahead and wipe the floor with the smarmy bastard.

Ready to cut through the bullshit and start getting some serious answers, he opened his mouth to ask his next question, but was cut off by Reese's tense voice coming from behind him. "What are you doing here, Drew?"

"What the hell?" Ben growled, shooting her a dark look over his shoulder. "Get back in bed, Reese!"

Completely disregarding that sharp bark of command, the stubborn woman started shuffling toward him, arms holding the overlapping sides of a robe closed at the front to hide the thin hospital gown she was wearing. She had scrapes on her forehead and chin, the way she was favoring her right side no doubt the sign of some serious bruising on the left side of her body. But the steely look in her eyes was anything but cowed.

Leighton's next words came out hoarse with concern. "My God, Reese. Look at you. Are you all right?"

"I'm fine." She moved a little closer to Ben's side, but kept her eyes locked on her ex. Ben noticed that she hadn't even spared a glance at Lizzie, who was still hovering near Leighton like a protective pit bull. Voice surprisingly steady, Reese said, "You shouldn't be here, Drew."

A possessive gleam burned in the lawyer's eyes as he held her stare. "I know you're angry, but I'm not going back to Boston until we talk. I miss you and I want—"

"Don't come near me!" she snapped, when he took a step toward her.

Leighton's jaw tightened. "What the fuck, Reese? You're my *wife*."

She pulled her shoulders back. "Not anymore. Which should be evident by the woman you've brought with you today."

"Lizzie came as my friend," he said emphatically. "Nothing more."

A tired laugh slipped past her lips as she shook her head. "I couldn't care less why she's here. I just want you both gone. But first, Drew . . . first I want to know how you got my new number."

His lips thinned. "You gave it to Valerie before you left town. She gave it to me when I asked for it."

"Who's Valerie?" Ben murmured, sliding a supportive arm around Reese's waist, since he needed to hold her, and she looked like a strong wind might blow her over. But he knew she was a hell of a lot tougher than she looked.

Reese glanced up at him as she answered his question. "She's a friend I worked with in Boston who I thought I could trust." Glaring at Leighton again, she added, "I was obviously wrong."

The guy turned a violent shade of red, his furious gaze taking in the way Ben was holding her, before cutting back to her face. "It was just a fucking phone number."

"One that I didn't want you to have, so please don't call it again." She took a deep breath, then quietly added, "And don't text me, either."

"I haven't sent you any damn texts," he bit out, rubbing a rough hand over his mouth. Then his pale gaze slowly darkened with understanding. "This is about more of that stalker bullshit, isn't it? God, Reese. You can keep throwing it in my face like you did in Boston, but I'm not the one responsible." He shoved his hair back from his brow, before muttering, "If the asshole even exists."

Reese stiffened with outrage. "You think I made it up?" she said chokingly. "That it was *me*? That I mutilated a cat to get your damn attention?"

Leighton worked his jaw. "I think you were confused and wanted to come back home." He flicked a contemptuous look at Ben. "Then something changed your mind and you ran."

"I didn't run, Drew. I came here to start a new life. And I think it's time that you left."

"You heard the lady," Ben muttered, jerking his chin toward the double doors at the end of the corridor. "Time to get the fuck out."

Leighton studied them for a moment from beneath a heavy scowl, then smirked. An ugly laugh rumbled up from his chest. "I don't believe this shit. Are you actually letting this asshole fuck you?"

Ben made a low, guttural sound, ready to toss the son of a bitch out himself, but Reese simply said, "I don't owe you any answers, Drew. My personal life no longer has anything to do with you."

Those soft words made the jackass flinch, as if she'd physically struck him. "Like hell it doesn't," Leighton shouted, suddenly lurching forward and grabbing her arm. She cried out, his fingers digging into her bruised flesh, and Ben reacted with a swift surge of rage. With a visceral snarl, he drew back his arm and slammed his fist into Leighton's mouth. The violent force of the blow knocked the bastard off his feet, the lawyer's body making a dull thud as it crashed into the wall behind him.

"You don't lay a fucking hand on her!" Ben growled, trying to gently pry Reese's hands off his arm as she held on, doing her best to hold him back. Leighton's lip had been split open, blood spilling over his chin and throat, soaking into the snowy white collar of his shirt. The noise had caught the attention of the hospital staff, who were trying to intervene, but Mike was holding them back, telling them the situation was under control.

"Ohmygod! Drew!" Lizzie glared daggers at Ben as she rushed

to Leighton and crouched beside him. "I told you this was a waste of time!" she hissed near his ear.

He threw her arms off, using the sleeve of his tailored suit jacket to wipe the blood from his face as he staggered back to his feet. "And I told you I wanted to see my wife. Stay out of it, Lizzie."

She crossed her arms as she stepped back, her face composed into a smooth, expressionless mask that looked fake as hell. "You've seen her, Drew. And her new boyfriend, too. Don't you think it's time we got out of here?"

"*Fine*," he forced through his gritted teeth. "We'll go."

Realizing Reese was now shivering at his side, Ben stopped trying to extricate himself from her grip. Instead, he pulled her against his chest and wrapped his arms around her, holding her close. It was a caring, protective embrace, and he hoped Leighton got a good, long look, because if he ever tried to hurt her again, Ben would go after him until there was nothing left on the ground but a stain. Staring over her head, he locked his steely gaze on the bastard and said, "Before you slink off, I want to know where you were this afternoon."

Voice tight, Leighton asked, "What are you getting at?"

"You know exactly what I'm getting at." Reese went tense in his arms, no doubt bracing herself for the question she'd guessed was coming next. "How did you know to come looking for Reese at this hospital?"

"The clerk at the hotel recognized Drew when we were trying to check in," Lizzie snapped, rushing to Leighton's defense before he could respond. "We only just landed an hour ago and took a taxi instead of renting a car. So it couldn't have been Drew who hit that stupid woman."

"Which hotel?"

"The Davis."

Ben wasn't surprised. The Davis was a privately owned resort

right on the beach, catering to those who could afford its outrageous prices.

Lizzie continued her explanation in a belligerent tone. "The
clerk's girlfriend was in town when the accident happened, and she
called him to gossip about it."

"I've stayed there before, with Reese, when we were here visiting. That's why he thought to tell me about the accident," Leighton added in a raw voice. He looked at Ben with sullen eyes. "I
don't give a shit what you think is going on, I would never do
anything to hurt her. She's . . . just know that I don't plan on letting this go."

"I don't know why," the petulant blonde muttered. "She's
nothing special. Just look at her."

Ben had had enough. "Get this trash out of the fucking hospital, Leighton. Now, before I have you both thrown out. And you
can expect a visit from one of my deputies at your hotel."

"I'll escort them out of here," Mike offered. "You just take care
of Reese."

"Thanks, Mike." Picking her up as carefully as he could, Ben
cradled her in his arms as he carried her back to her room, the
scent of the antiseptic they'd used on her scrapes still lingering on
her skin. There were a few muttered curses behind him, but he
knew Mike could handle Leighton and his mistress. Connie, who'd
been watching the whole thing from the doorway, held the door
open for him, and he carried Reese to the bed, keeping his face
close to hers after he'd laid her down. Then, using his most intimidating tone, he said, "You move again and I'll damn well tie you
down."

Despite the shitty scene she'd just been through, her blue eyes
were shining with humor. "Promises, promises," she whispered,
somehow managing to sound both sexy and adorable at the same
time.

It took everything Ben had to choke back a gritty laugh. "Don't sass me right now, you little hellion. I'm not happy with you."

She rolled her eyes. "I'm not all that thrilled with you, either."

Well, hell. "Are you upset that I hit him?" he asked, straightening to his full height.

"No. Of course not. He had it coming. But I wanted to be the one who busted his lip," she grumbled.

His own lips twitched with a grin. "I'll let you hit him next time."

She smirked. "I'll be looking forward to it."

Pushing a gleaming lock of hair back from her face, Ben asked, "Did you know he was coming here? To Florida?" The last he'd heard, Leighton wasn't scheduled to fly home from that legal conference in California until Sunday.

Her eyes went wide. "What? No! He's been trying to reach me since you gave me my phone back, but I've been ignoring his calls."

Before Ben could respond, Connie joined them, standing on the other side of the bed. "Well, this has certainly been an eventful day."

"Tell me about it," Reese murmured, noticing that her sister still had that pinched look she got when there was something she wanted to rant about, and she knew she'd be getting an earful the next time they were alone. She'd already suspected that Ben had blabbed about her stalker problem when he and Connie had been talking, just before Drew's arrival. But even if he hadn't, her sister would have heard enough from what was said in the hallway to get the gist of the situation.

"Since Ben seems to have you covered here, I'll get out of your hair for a while. But I'll be back first thing in the morning with some decent food for you guys. God knows you can't live off the stuff they serve here."

Reese smiled. "Thanks, Con."

"Hey, we sisters have to look out for each other, right? And speaking of sisters, I'll call Cami and let her know you're okay." A wry grin crossed Connie's lips. "If Mom gets to her first, she'll probably have poor Cam thinking you're already dead and buried."

Reese wasn't as close to Cami as she was to Connie, but she hoped to change that. Cami had hated Drew's guts, which had made it difficult for them to spend time together. But Reese had a feeling her older sister was going to get on great with Ben. "I haven't seen Cami in so long," she murmured. "Tell her I miss her."

"Will do, sweetie." Looking at Ben, Connie added, "Take good care of her."

He nodded, gripping Reese's hand so tightly it almost hurt worse than her other one, which was pretty sore. But she bit her tongue, touched that he was still so upset. It had to mean that he cared at least a little, right? God, she hoped so, because as hard as she was trying to control it, she was falling more for the sexy, complicated lawman with every second that went by.

As Connie opened the door to leave, Reese caught sight of a tall woman in a sheriff's department uniform standing outside her door in the hallway. Looking at Ben, she asked, "Why is there a guard posted outside the door?"

"That's Robin. She's here for your protection."

Her brows lifted. "From Drew?"

Ben shook his head. "I don't think he'll come back. But I don't want anyone getting inside this room without being cleared first. That includes the hospital staff."

She could feel her blood go cold. "You think it was intentional, don't you?"

The look in his eyes was as fierce as his tone. "I think that whoever was driving the truck that caused the accident was up to no good. And whoever it is, I think they have some kind of dangerous obsession with you."

"But that doesn't make any sense," she said, finding the lethal rage in his voice somehow comforting. "I'm not the kind of woman a man would obsess over, Ben. Even one who's bat-shit crazy."

"Like hell you aren't."

Taking a deep breath, she asked, "Do you still think it's Drew?"

"I don't know," he muttered. "But the bastard wants you back, Reese."

She chewed on her lip. "If that's true, then why try to hurt me?"

His voice got rougher, a hard glint in his eyes as he held her gaze. "Because he knows that he's lost you. If he's messed up enough in the head, he might start to think the only solution is to make sure no one else can have you, either."

She shuddered, then winced when the movement sent a fresh surge of pain rushing through her battered body. "Ouch," she whispered.

"Don't do that again," he grunted, his deep voice gruff with worry. "Just lie still."

"Okay." She watched him snag one of the chairs and pull it close to her bedside. As he sat down, she turned her head on the pillow and asked, "What about Drew's alibi with the hotel?"

Rubbing his hand against the hard set of his jaw, he said, "Even if his story about the hotel checks out, I've been saying all along that he could be paying someone to do his dirty work for him. Ryder's been trying to find a money trail, but it might take some time."

Reese wanted to ask him more, but her mom and step-dad, Joe, chose that moment to burst in, full of tears and demands to know what had happened. Thankfully, Ben quickly calmed them down, and it didn't take long for understanding to dawn in her mother's big blue eyes. Reese had been avoiding her mom for days, not wanting to have to answer questions about Ben. Questions she knew would be awkward and intrusive. But the way he stayed glued to her side, his sharp gaze brimming worry and heat whenever he looked at her, had to have made it obvious to her mom that they were involved.

Sometime later that evening, when she and Ben were alone and her eyelids started to get heavy, he leaned over the side of the bed and gave her a brief, tender kiss. "Go to sleep, sweetheart."

"Aren't you going home?" she asked drowsily.

"No," he murmured, sinking back into his chair. "I'm not leaving your side."

A rueful smile touched her lips. "You won't be comfortable here. That chair is about five sizes too small for you."

"I'll be a hell of a lot more comfortable than I would be at home, worrying myself sick over you," he argued in a husky rasp. "And Reese?"

She stared at his deliciously rugged, impossibly gorgeous face from beneath her lashes, and had to swallow to clear the lust from her throat. "Yeah?"

His dark eyes burned with resolve. "From now on, we sleep together. Every night. End of story."

14

THOUGH HER MOTHER AND CONNIE HAD BOTH OFFERED TO TAKE REESE home with them, Ben had made it clear that the best place for her at this time was with *him*. And it was exactly where he planned to keep her.

He pulled into his driveway and turned off the truck's engine, feeling a swift surge of relief at the fact that she was sitting there beside him. For a moment, he closed his eyes, briefly reliving the frantic minutes he'd spent racing to the hospital yesterday, when he hadn't known if she was going to live or die. The closest he'd ever come to feeling that kind of panic had been when he'd found Alex passed out in the middle of his living room floor, barely breathing, nearly poisoned to death by alcohol. Ben had been sick with fear, and yet, at the same time he'd been filled with rage at Alex for acting like such a selfish bastard.

But none of this was Reese's fault. He didn't feel any anger toward her for the hell he'd been through. There was just this cold, burning fear still eating at him from the inside out. It'd been nearly twenty-four hours since her accident, and he still got shaky when he thought about how easily she could have been killed.

By some miracle of fate, her MRI had shown no internal damage. Not even a single broken bone. But two significant things had happened since her accident. The first was another text message that had come through on her phone in the middle of the night. The message had been simple, but unnerving. Six little words that were proof whoever had been in that truck had known who she was.

i didn't mean to hurt you

The second was an attack on Reese's car, which had still been parked on O'Neill Street. Connie had driven past the parked Toyota on her way to the hospital that morning, and had told them the bad news. Ben had arranged to have the car towed to a local garage, and it sounded as if the damage was fairly extensive. Slashed tires, smashed windows, and significant dents in the bodywork, as if someone had taken a sledgehammer to it. He wished to God the city had security cameras posted in that area, but that was something he was still working to get the funding for.

It made him fucking ill to think of some wack job out there being this fixated on her. While he still wasn't ready to put Leighton in the clear, even though the bastard's alibi had checked out, Ben hadn't been able to stop thinking about that dark-haired male he had Alex looking for. Earlier that morning, he'd worked with a department artist to sketch up an image that Alex could use while canvassing the town. Ben didn't know if there was any connection between the unknown man and the shit happening to Reese, but he wasn't going to take any chances. Not when the guy kept showing up. If it turned out to be nothing, then fine. He'd be glad he looked like an idiot for wasting Alex's time. But after yesterday, he wasn't willing to write it off as nothing until he knew exactly who the stranger was.

"Hey, you in there?" she asked, pulling him from his thoughts.

"Sorry," he murmured, taking his keys out of the ignition. "I was just thinking."

"Me, too. And I . . . I'm still not sure that this is the right move, Ben."

He clenched his jaw. "Why not?"

Drinking in the sight of his rugged profile, Reese took a deep breath and tried to explain. "Moving in together, even in the short term, is only going to complicate things between us. And we've probably already complicated them enough. I don't want either of us to feel trapped," she said, when what she really meant was that she didn't want *him* to feel trapped.

Lying in her hospital room last night, Reese had watched as he'd dozed in the chair he'd pulled up beside her bed, and finally faced the terrifying truth of how she felt about him. Despite her fears and knowing there was a strong chance she was going to end up hurt—hurt in a way that was a thousand times worse than her divorce—she was, without any doubt, already in this thing up to her eyebrows, her feelings for Ben deeper than any emotion she'd ever known. Deeper than she'd thought she was even capable of.

And now the gorgeous, complicated man wanted her to stay with him. Part of her wanted to jump for joy, while the other was still waiting for his response to her very logical worry about it being a bad idea.

Quietly, he said, "I don't feel trapped. And I hope you don't, either."

"You'll tell me if it . . . if you change your mind?"

The look in his eyes when he turned his head toward her made her breath catch. It was dark, mesmerizing . . . full of lust and need and heat. "I'm not going to change my mind," he told her, his voice husky and low. Then he climbed out of the truck and came around the front, opening her door for her. "And one of the perks of staying with me is that you get truck-to-bed service," he added with a grin, picking her up and clutching her against his chest.

"You don't need to carry me," she protested, even though she loved the feeling of being in his strong arms. "I might still look a little banged up, but I feel perfectly fine."

"Let's give it a little more time and then see how you feel."

"Hmm. You're not listening to a word I say, are you?"

"I just want to take care of you, Reese." When he looked down at her, there was a devilish light in his eyes as he said, "In bed *and* out of it."

With a smile on her lips, she gave up trying to convince him and simply enjoyed being in his arms. She caught flashes of his house as he carried her through the quiet rooms, and it was even more beautiful than she'd imagined it would be. Dark hardwood floors were covered in off-white rugs, the walls that same shade of white, furniture a mix of coffee-colored leather and rustic wood.

"Any news about my car?" she asked, after he'd laid her on a massive king-size bed. His room was decorated in the same color scheme, with rugged pieces of furniture, and she loved it. Loved the warmth and the masculinity of it, since it reminded her so much of Ben.

Stretching out beside her, he braced himself on an elbow and said, "As much as I wanted it to be Leighton, so that I could go ahead and arrest his ass for vandalism, he's been cleared. It wasn't him."

"How do you know?"

"Because he can't be in two places at the same time. And I've been having him watched since he showed up at the hospital yesterday."

Her eyes went wide. "I had no idea."

He shrugged. "I didn't want you worrying about it."

"So you know it wasn't him because he was . . ." Her voice trailed off, waiting for him to provide the explanation.

"It's still a possibility that he has someone working for him, but he didn't do it with his own hands. He was at his hotel all night, getting shit-faced in the bar."

"I don't know what his problem is," she said with a frown. "He never used to be a big drinker."

Ben snorted. "Yeah, well, we all have our coping mechanisms."

"Have you ever . . . ?"

He gave a curt shake of his head. "No. But Alex took things hard after his divorce."

"Oh no."

"It was pretty ugly there for a while, but Mike and I finally managed to get him back on his feet."

"I've only been around him a few times over the years, but he always seems so . . ."

"Disciplined? Cold?" When she nodded, he said, "It's how he copes now. But he wasn't always like that."

"I'm sorry."

"Yeah," he rasped, brushing her hair back from her face. "Me, too."

Thinking it was a good time to change the subject, she asked, "What about Ryder?"

The instant she said the deputy's name, his brows pulled together in a scowl. "What about him?"

She had to choke back a laugh at his guttural tone. "I was just wondering if he's learned anything new about Drew?"

"No. Nothing yet," he muttered, resting his hand on her stomach, his thumb stroking the soft cotton of her tank top. "But he's been doing some background checks for me on Lizzie Jennings."

"Why Lizzie?" she asked, lifting her brows, and then immediately wishing that she hadn't. The scrapes on her forehead stung like hell every time she did that.

He shrugged his shoulder again. "I thought she gave off a really strange vibe yesterday."

"Has he found anything?"

"Not much. She's moved around a lot, and doesn't have any family. There was a younger brother that she was apparently close to, but he died in a fire at an institution a few years back."

"Oh, God. How awful."

"Yeah, well, that was the last of her family. She's been on her own since she was sixteen, going to school in various places, and then working. There are some significant periods of time where she's fallen off the grid that Ryder hasn't pieced together yet. But he'll get there."

"It sounds like she had a pretty rough start in life. That's probably why she latched on to Drew," she murmured, placing her hand on top of his. "Poor girl."

He gave a stunned, gritty laugh. "Poor girl? Are you shitting me? She's a total bitch, Reese."

Running her fingertips over the back of his large, masculine hand, she said, "But I understand her a little better now. I mean, I can see why she would fall for Drew's 'come with me little girl and let me take care of you,' spiel."

Ben narrowed his eyes. "Was that the spiel he used on you?"

With a soft snort, she said, "No. He knew better than to try that crap on me."

"Exactly how *did* the two of you end up together?"

"You really want to know?" she asked, giving him a puzzled look.

"Yeah," he murmured, lowering his gaze to watch her touching his hand. She was tracing one of the heavy veins that ran under his skin, the featherlight touch of her finger for some reason striking him as incredibly erotic. But he wasn't going to let it distract him from the topic. Clearing his throat, he said, "I really want to know."

Reese could tell that he wasn't quite comfortable being this curious about a woman's past, and it put a warm feeling in the center of her chest to know that Ben's interest in her was new for him. That it set her apart, in at least some small way, from all the other women who had wanted to be a part of his life. "Does this answering questions about our pasts work both ways?" she murmured.

The look in his eyes became guarded. "Let's start with you."

Hmm. Not exactly the answer she'd been hoping for, but at least it wasn't an outright no. It wasn't easy to talk about something so painful, but she made herself do it, hoping it would help him open up with her, as well. "I met Drew my second year in college." A wry smile twisted the corner of her mouth, and she said, "It's embarrassing, but I made the same stupid mistake that a lot of young women make. I was afraid I would never find someone who loved me and wanted to spend their life with me, so I believed the first guy who told me that he did."

Ben hadn't expected her to respond with so much honesty, but if he'd learned anything in the past week, it was that Reese wasn't what he was used to. She didn't play coy or try to make herself out to be anything other than what she was.

He didn't know why her honesty made him feel tense, but it did. Hell, it was probably because he wasn't willing to give her the same, holding close to his secrets like they were going to make a fucking difference. But it was too late for that. He was already so deep into this woman, he didn't even want to try to find his way back out.

"So he told you that he loved you and wanted to marry you?"

he forced from his tight throat, surprised by how bitter the words tasted in his mouth.

Her response was a soft "Yes."

"How long had you been together?"

She cocked her head a bit to the side, eyes curious and dark. "Before we got married, or before he asked?"

"Both."

"We'd been dating for about five months. We were married three months later."

His next question surprised them both. "Do you think you'll want to get married again someday?"

She gave a quiet laugh. "I might. But only if I met the right guy." She studied him for a moment, then said, "You look surprised."

"I guess I am. After what you went through with Leighton, I would have thought you'd be soured on the idea."

She shook her head. "That would mean letting Drew have an effect on the rest of my life, and I refuse to do that. But I'm in no hurry. Right now, I'm just taking each day as it comes." She gave another quiet laugh, her tone dry. "But don't worry. I won't be sending you an awkward invitation to any future wedding. I imagine you hate those kinds of things."

Ben shot off the bed so quickly it startled her. Shoving a rough hand through his hair, he looked down at her and snapped, "Don't say shit like that. Not when you know it's going to mess with my head."

She blinked up at him, heat rushing into her face with a pink flush. "I'm sorry, Ben. I was just . . . teasing, I guess."

"Don't," he ground out, the word rough in his throat. "Not about that."

As Reese watched him turn and leave the room, she bit her lip, wondering why she'd said what she had. She was worried she'd ruined the day, wrecking the easy vibe they'd had going, until he came back in a few minutes later with a glass of iced tea for her, his expression no longer tight with strain. He was obviously making an effort to get things back on the right track between them, and she breathed a small sigh of relief. After he asked if she'd like to take a bath, he went over to her house to get some of her things. She'd thought he'd come back with some soap and maybe her makeup bag, but he practically loaded up her entire bathroom. While she soaked in his oversize tub, he put her things away, clearing a drawer for her in the wooden chest that stood by the sink. For some reason, that simple gesture made her ridiculously happy, as if he was planning on her being there with him for some time, when she knew that had to be all kinds of dangerous for her emotions.

His dark gaze smoldered with heat as he propped his hip against the sink and watched her bathe. But he didn't join her in the coconut-scented bubbles when she invited him to, claiming that he wouldn't be able to keep his hands off her if he did. Reese knew he was worried about how she felt after the accident, but she hoped he didn't plan on behaving himself for too long. If there was anything that would make her feel better, it was Ben's powerful lovemaking.

When she was finished soaking, he helped her from the tub and dried her with a towel, his touch gentle and unhurried, as if they had all the time in the world, and she was glad it was a Saturday, which meant he didn't need to go into work. He towel-dried her hair before brushing it out for her, the soothing strokes making her eyes go heavy, then bundled her back up in his bed. She slid between the sheets naked, watching him strip down to his boxers with a greedy, appreciative gaze, the way all those rippling muscles and long lines of sinew moved beneath his dark skin the most mouthwatering sight in the world. He was beyond gorgeous, so sinful and sexy and strong he looked like some kind of ancient warrior getting ready to fight . . . or fuck.

He crawled into bed with her, bracing himself on an elbow again as she lay on her back, staring up at him from beneath her lashes, fascinated by the heat and shadows in his heavy-lidded gaze. With one of his long legs tangling with hers beneath the covers, he tugged the sheet down to her waist and ran his hand up her side, a dark, decadent rumble in his throat as he curved his long fingers around her breast. Stroking the callused pad of his thumb over her nipple, he watched it tighten and flush with color. For over a week now, her body had been under his touch, and yet, she was no more accustomed to the heady, overwhelming sensation today than she had been that first night. A breathtaking current of awareness still shivered over her skin the instant he put his hands on her, her blood rushing through her veins, pulse quickening until it was a quiet roar in her ears.

"You have the most beautiful tits in the world," he told her, his voice rough and low.

She couldn't help but snicker. "Tits?"

His lips twitched, a mischievous glint in his eyes as he slid his green gaze up to hers. "Tits. Jugs. Melons. Whatever you want to call them, yours are perfect."

"It's lovely that you think so."

"I *know* so."

Reading the doubt in her eyes, Ben lifted his hand to her face, pushing a lock of hair back from her brow. "Seriously, Reese. You're so beautiful. Why can't you see it?"

She shrugged self-consciously. "I'm freckled. And too fair."

"Well, I can't get enough of your freckles," he said in a soft rasp, pressing a kiss to her nose, before pulling back and letting his hot gaze roam over her chest. "And I love the color of your skin."

He pulled the sheet even lower, revealing the pale length of the leg she'd thrown over his. She shivered, but it wasn't from the cold. It was how Ben was looking at her. With so much heat. So much possessive intensity. With a guttural edge to his voice, he rubbed a careful hand over her bruised hip and said, "I love the way our bodies look together. Dark and light. It's sexy as hell."

"You really think so?"

"You're damn right I do." He lifted his gaze back to hers, and there was even more of an edge to his voice as he said, "I still can't believe you put me off for so long."

Reese lifted her brows. "*I* was the one who just invited you to join me in the tub. *You're* the one who said no, Ben."

"I'm not talking about today," he explained, a crooked grin on his lips as he shook his head. "I'm talking about the last three years."

"Oh." She laughed softly. "It, uh, doesn't count as putting you off when I had *no idea* that you were even interested."

He ran a finger down the bridge of her nose, touched it to her chin, then down the front of her throat, sweeping it across her collarbone. "You should have known," he told her, the slow, sensual stroke of his fingertip so at odds with the way he normally touched her. It was still sexual, but there was something *more* to it. Something that felt like . . . like *devotion*, of all things, and her head spun with the thought, her breath trapped in her chest.

"Do you remember the night we met?" he asked, trailing that callused fingertip between her breasts. Her nipples instantly tightened in response, begging for the touch of his hand . . . the heat of his mouth.

She swallowed against the shivery feeling in her throat, and tried to steady her voice. "You mean the night of Gary's thirtieth birthday party?"

"Yeah," he breathed out, watching his finger sweep across the underside of her breast.

She gave a soft snort. "You hardly said two words to me."

The smile he flashed her was brief and sharp. "That's because I was trying to keep from tossing you over my shoulder and running off with you."

"You big liar," she drawled, lifting her hand to his hair, the thick locks silky and warm.

"I swear to God. Just ask Michael. He kept ribbing me about getting a hard-on at a family event." His voice got huskier. "But I couldn't control myself. I saw you standing there in that sexy little black sundress, and all the blood in my body rushed straight from my head to my cock. I spent the whole night light-headed, and horny as hell."

"Well, I doubt you suffered for long. Women were hanging all over you that night."

He caught her hand just as she started to lower it, the look in his smoldering eyes making her melt. "I might have had other women over the years, but I can promise you one thing, Reese. Every time I was with one, I wished it was you."

Oh, God. She didn't know what to think when he said things like that. When he looked at her the way he was looking at her at that moment. For a man who had never had a serious relationship in his life—who'd come into this thing between them offering her some fun and a lot of hot sex—he sometimes said the most incredibly romantic things.

"Ben . . . why didn't you ever say anything?" she asked, fighting to hold back the hot, emotional rush of tears burning at the backs of her eyes.

He let go of her hand, and she watched a flat smile twist the corner of his mouth. "What would have been the point? You belonged to another man."

"I might have been married to him," she said, shaking her head, "but I never belonged to him. He never wanted me like that."

"Which just shows what a fucking idiot he is."

She rolled onto her side, resting her cheek on her hands. "I think that deep down inside, Drew's not a very happy person."

"I don't care what he is, so long as he stays the hell away from you." Exhaling a rough breath, he added, "I hate it that he wants you back."

A small smile touched her lips. "Yeah, well, even if that's true, he can't have me."

"Damn right he can't." Ben pressed a soft kiss to her forehead, then drew his head back, watching his thumb gently coast over her scraped cheek, before making himself pull away.

"Where are you going?" she asked, when he'd moved off the bed and back to his feet. He had to choke back a graveled curse when he caught her staring at the way his hard-on was tenting the front of his boxers, knowing damn well he shouldn't touch her, since she needed her rest. But it wasn't easy when she was lying there all sexy and soft and flushed, looking like she wanted it as badly as he did.

Pulling the sheet up over her, he had to swallow twice before he could answer her question. "It's time for your pain meds."

"But they'll make me sleep," she complained, clutching the sheet against her chest as she sat up.

"That's what they're meant to do," he said with a brief smile, forcing himself to leave the room before he forgot his better intentions. He checked his phone quickly to make sure no one had tried to get in touch with him from work—he'd had Ryder put out a statewide alert for any trucks matching the description witnesses had given at the scene of the accident, and the station knew to contact him if anything was called in—then brought her the pills they'd picked up in the hospital pharmacy and a glass of water. He sat on the side of the bed as she swallowed the meds with the water, then took the glass from her and set it on the bedside table.

"This sucks," she grumbled, sounding adorably miffed as she snuggled back down into the pillows. "I was enjoying talking to you."

Climbing back into the bed with her, Ben stretched out on his back and pulled her close, a deep sense of satisfaction filling him as she cuddled against his side, resting her cheek on the front of his shoulder. "I'm not going anywhere," he told her, loving the way she curled her leg over his thigh as he stroked the feminine curve of her hip. "I'll be right here in bed with you when you wake up. We can talk more then."

"Fine." A soft sigh slipped past her lips, and he could feel her starting to relax, before she quickly reached out and grabbed his hand.

"What's wrong?" he asked, sensing her fear.

She didn't look at him as she answered his question with one of her own. "Are you sure it's safe for you to have me here?"

A frown hardened his mouth. "What are you talking about?"

Lifting her head, she took a quick breath and said, "If someone's trying to hurt me, they could try to hurt you, too."

"I hope the bastard is stupid enough to try. I'm not letting him get anywhere near you, but I'd kill for the chance to get my hands on him."

"No! Ben, I'm serious. I don't want anything to happen to you."

"Trust me. Nothing's going to happen, honey. I know how to take care of myself."

And it was true. She didn't need to waste her time worrying about him. But as she grumbled about how he wasn't taking her seriously, Ben found himself holding her a little closer, a warm glow burning deep in his chest. Yeah, he was a tough son of a bitch who could take care of himself. But he'd have been lying through his teeth if he'd said it didn't feel good, knowing that she cared.

A guy could get addicted to feeling like this, he thought, closing his eyes. And as the lazy sound of the ocean surf rumbled through an open bedroom window, Ben simply enjoyed the feel of her body next to his, in his arms, and thanked God that he hadn't lost her.

REESE AWAKENED FROM ANOTHER NAP LATER THAT NIGHT, DROWSY AND relaxed. Despite being a little sore in places, the pain meds were definitely doing their thing, and this had ended up being one of the most enjoyable days she'd ever had. When the sun had finally set, she and Ben had cuddled up on his sofa and watched an action flick together. Then he'd carried her back to his bed, given her more meds, and held her until she'd dozed back off. She didn't know what time it was now, but he was still awake, sitting beside her in the sprawling bed. He was wearing nothing more than a pair of tight gray boxers, his hair still damp from a shower, so sexy she couldn't have looked away to save her life. He had his broad shoulders braced against the dark wood of his headboard and his knees bent, his attention focused on a massive manila folder that was resting against his muscular thighs. The folder's well-worn pages were illuminated by the soft glow of his bedside lamp.

"What are you reading?" she asked, sitting up and reaching for the glass of water that was sitting on her nightstand.

"It's a case file." There was a warm, sensual look in his eyes as he turned his head and swept that bottle green gaze over her tight-fitting tank top, before lifting it to her face. "One of my deputies brought it over a little while ago. My old partner in Miami had mailed it to the station."

Curling up against the headboard, she took a sip of her water. "Anything interesting?"

It was on the tip of Ben's tongue to blow her off, saying it was nothing important. But he knew that was just reflex. She'd been open and honest with him about her past, and he knew it was time that he started to do the same. But, damn it, he hated talking about this shit. It put a bad taste in his mouth and a sour feeling in the pit of his stomach.

Forcing his jaw to relax, he told her, "It's the file for the last case I worked as a detective."

As if she sensed how new this was for him, she didn't say anything or press him. She just sat there patiently waiting for him to go on, giving him time, letting him set the pace.

"We'd been working with vice to put this son of a bitch named Ryan Houghton away. He's a big-time drug lord who relocated to the area about five years ago, and he's about as far from the stereotype as you can get. We're talking an all-American prep boy, like your ex. Lots of connections up in the Northeast, but he decided he liked the Miami sunshine."

"I can remember hearing Houghton's name in the news, but I never paid any attention to the story," she murmured, setting her glass down, then turning back to him. "I didn't know you were involved in the case, or I would have followed it. What happened?"

"We were investigating Houghton in connection with the murder of another local dealer, and it got ugly. When we went in with a warrant for his arrest, he was doped up on some bad PCP. According to his doctors, he had what they called 'an extreme paranoid episode,' seeing monsters and demons or some shit like that. All I know is that he came out shooting."

Her face went ghostly pale. "At you and your partner?"

"At *everyone* in the goddamn house. He caught his wife in the leg, and I took the hits in my shoulder and chest protecting his seven-year-old daughter."

"Ohmygod." Her blue eyes were wide with shock as she reached out and touched his arm. "He was trying to kill his baby girl?"

He gave a bitter, humorless laugh. "He claims he didn't know what he was doing, but the bastard aimed right at her. Then his legal team fed the media a ton of bullshit, and they managed to sway public opinion in Houghton's favor, making him out to be some modern-day hero who'd been wronged by the department. How they put that kind of spin on it, I'll never understand. But the DA ended up offering him a plea bargain that has him in minimum security with a chance for parole in two years."

"God, Ben. That's awful. No wonder you got the hell out of there."

His smile felt more like a grimace. "When I left, I told my partner, Tony, that I didn't want anything else to do with the department or that fucking case. But he's been trying to get in touch with me about some new development, and I've been ignoring his calls. When this file showed up, I finally called him to find out what he wanted. He said they think a mole in one of the government agencies is feeding info to Houghton's crew and his legal team."

"But he's already in jail. Why does he need a legal team?"

Ben set the folder on his bedside table. "The Feds are still trying to nail his ass for trafficking, but there's been some damaging information leaks, and they've already lost one key witness. Tony's team has been trying to help finger the mole, but there are so many agencies in on the action, they haven't been able to pinpoint where the leak is coming from. He wants me to look things over and tell him if I see anything that stands out."

"It sounds like he really trusts your judgment."

He couldn't help but smirk. "Believe it or not, there are some people who think I'm a pretty trustworthy guy."

"Oh, I can believe it," she murmured, moving so that she could throw one leg over his waist and straddle his hips, the crotch of her panties snugged up tight against his cock, which was already getting hard. "You're a pretty heroic one, too," she added with a smile, resting her hands on his shoulders.

Ben muffled a husky burst of laughter under his breath. "Christ, honey. You know that's not true."

"Like hell it isn't," she drawled, repeating one of his favorite phrases. Then she leaned forward and pressed her lips against the bullet scar on his shoulder. As a deep breath lifted his chest, she kissed her way down to the one near his heart, the tender touch of her mouth against his flesh the sweetest fucking thing Ben had ever known.

He'd already buried his fingers in her hair, pulling her face up to his so that he could capture her mouth, when he remembered she was probably too sore for where this was headed. "Damn it, woman. Stop tempting me."

"I'm fine, Ben." She brushed her soft lips along the hard edge of his jaw. "But are you comfortable with me sitting like this?" she asked, rubbing against him.

"Comfortable?" he choked out, trying to remember not to squeeze too hard as he clutched her hips. "That's not exactly the word that comes to mind when I've got a hard dick and your beautiful little ass is wriggling on my lap."

Reese was still laughing as he placed a smiling kiss against her temple. But the soft giggles turned into a gasp when he suddenly rolled her beneath his much larger body. She blinked with surprise as she found herself staring up at him, his stunning face right above hers. The guy had such freaking amazing bone structure, the bump on his nose only adding to his rugged appeal. And that warm, mouthwatering scent that always clung to his skin, seeping from his pores, was filling her head, making her drunk on the lust it inspired.

A small, wicked smile touched the corner of his mouth, as if he knew exactly what she was thinking. "You're hell on a man's system, you know that?"

"What do you mean?"

"When you get turned on, you show it so easily. You get all flushed and warm. Flashing eyes. Fuller, pinker lips. Pulse beating like mad at the base of your throat." His lashes lowered, the look in his eyes turning molten and hot. "It makes a man want to fuck you, Reese. Long and hard and rough."

She took an unsteady breath. "That's, um, not really been my experience."

His eyes crinkled at the corners as he laughed. "Like hell it hasn't. You've just never paid attention. You're good at ignoring things you don't want anything to do with."

Flicking her tongue across her lower lip, she said, "I'm not ignoring *you*."

"Only because I'm not giving you the chance."

He caught her mouth before she could respond, kissing her hard. When she started to tremble, her breaths quickening, nails digging into the bunched muscles in his arms, he started working his way down her body, rubbing heated kisses across her skin as he stripped her of her tank and panties. Then he settled between her legs and pushed them wide, his beautifully shaped mouth only inches from her sex.

"I love looking at you like this," he groaned, using his thumbs to separate her thick folds. "Your pink little cunt is already all slippery and swollen, dripping like a ripe peach. You are so fucking beautiful, Reese." Then he buried his face between her legs, eating at her like he was starved. She shivered, arching, so turned on she felt lit up. On fire. Glowing like a star in the midnight sky, pulsing with energy and heat.

"Ben," she gasped, her voice breaking. "I need you!"

Lifting his head, he wiped his wet mouth on his shoulder and grinned. "Good, because I need the hell out of you."

"Then get inside me. I don't want to wait," she said, compelled by some overwhelming sense of urgency, as if this was her last chance to hold him inside her. "I mean it. I want you *now*."

"Not yet." Lowering his head again, he lapped his tongue over her opening, collecting the moisture, and she could feel him smile. "If we're doing this, I need to make sure you're ready. You need to be really wet for what I have in mind."

"Oh, God," she cried, fisting her hands in the sheets. "Trust me, I'm ready!"

"You're getting close," he murmured, dragging his teeth over the swollen knot of nerves at the top of her sex. Then he gave a voluptuous lick from that hard little knot all the way down to her vulva, his lips moving against her slick, slippery flesh as he said, "But I don't want you sore tomorrow. Not after everything you've been through."

She gave a throaty laugh. "I'm always sore after a night with you. But I don't mind. It just reminds me of how good you make me feel."

He lifted his head again, his eyes heavy and dark, firm lips wet with her juices. "Don't ever forget it."

She felt trapped by the intense, visceral force of his stare, unable to look away. Not that she wanted to. "I won't," she whispered, knowing she would be happy to keep staring at this man for the rest of her life. Just so long as he never broke her heart. But that thought had no place being in her head right now, and she shoved it away as she said, "I couldn't ever forget the way you make me feel. I love it too much."

Ben swallowed and clenched his jaw as he came down over her, the way she'd said that, all breathy and soft, with that dreamy look in her eyes, nearly killing him. She was shocked wide open, all her shields blasted and broken, allowing him to see right into the burning, brilliant, blinding heart of her. And, God, what a view. It undid him in a way that nothing else ever had, his goddamn heart in his throat as he dug his fingers back in her hair and growled, "I want to fuck you in the raw tonight."

Reese's pulse raced. "The raw?"

"No rubber," he said, his eyes blazing. "Just you and me."

"Oh." She blinked, her throat quivering. "I'm not on the pill anymore."

"I know."

She wanted to ask *how* he knew, but he was already saying, "I'm clean. Healthy. I won't come in you. I want to, but it's too risky. I'll pull out at the end."

Her mind spun. "That's still taking a risk."

"Hell, Reese. I've been taking risks since the moment I first touched you. What's one more?"

Holychrist. The way he'd just said that was the sexiest freaking thing Reese had ever heard, because she knew he was talking about his emotions. But as incredible as it was to think he might be falling as deeply as she was, she was determined to have some kind of rational discussion about the possible consequences of not using protection. "If I got pregnant, you'd say I was trying to trap you."

His response, to her surprise, was steady and calm. "If you get pregnant, then it was meant to happen. I won't put any blame on you." His voice got softer. "And if it does happen, then we'll deal with it together."

For a moment, there was nothing but their rough, soughing breaths, and then she quietly said, "If you're sure this is what you want, then I don't want you to hold back this time. I want you to give me every inch."

The look in his eyes somehow got even hotter, telling her how much he liked that idea. But there was a frown weaving its way between his dark brows as he reached down and shoved his boxers over his hips. "Let's not push things quite that far tonight, okay? I don't want to hurt you." His expression tightened. "Hell, we shouldn't even be doing this in the first place. You were hit by a fucking car yesterday."

"And I keep telling you that I'm fine. You won't hurt me," she argued, knowing she could do this. That she wanted it. *Needed* it. "I want to know what it's like to hold all of you inside me. Just . . . just trust me," she pleaded, rolling her hips so that her slick folds slipped along the brutal length of his cock. He shook with a hard tremor, his expression sharp with things that were too carnal and hungry and desperate for words, and Reese knew that she had him. Reaching between them, she fisted her hand around his thick, ridged shaft, rubbing the heavy head against her entrance . . . and his control snapped so hard he flinched.

"Goddamn it!" he snarled an instant later, fisting his hand in her hair and yanking her head back, his tongue thrusting past her lips as his hips shot forward, shoving that massive cock inside her. She could feel the power building in his hard muscles as he pulled back his hips, then rammed back in, the kiss becoming something that was deliciously wild and explicit. Then he tore his mouth away with a hoarse curse and went onto his knees, pushing her legs out high at her sides, opening her right up for him. She could feel her sex pulsing as he worked himself in deeper . . . then deeper still, until she was taking as much of him as she had all the other times they'd made love.

"You're so fucking tight and wet," he growled, his voice slurred with the pleasure of feeling her skin-on-skin, without the barrier of latex. "Never felt anything this good in my life."

"I love it," she gasped, placing her hand against the center of his chest, his heartbeat thundering against her palm. "But I meant what I said. I want it all, Ben. Don't hold back on me."

"Christ, Reese." He flicked her a dark, worried look, and ran his tongue over the edge of his teeth. "You're gonna be the fucking death of me."

"Just do it!"

They both looked down. Her fingers dug into his bulging biceps, the breathless cry of excitement on her lips nearly drowned out by his harsh, serrated growl as he stiffened, then drove those last brutal inches inside her. Her breath caught, but he didn't stop, pushing inexorably deeper until there wasn't a fraction of space left between them, her snug entrance stretched to its limit, pressed up tight against his groin.

"Jesus, just look at that." He groaned deep in his chest as he ground against her, his dark shaft gleaming with her juices when he slowly started to withdraw. "You okay?"

"I'm great," she breathed out, mesmerized by the rippling of his tight abs as he shoved back inside. She was melting into hot liquid, his rhythm gradually gaining in speed, until his hips were slamming against hers again and again, and it felt like he was hammering into the very heart of her.

"It doesn't hurt?" he grunted, his dark eyes still shadowed with concern as he lifted his gaze.

Reese shook her head. "It'll take some getting used to, but I love how it feels. How full I am of you."

He made a low, rough sound, and came down over her again, wrapping his long fingers around her wrists and pulling them over her head, holding them there. Trapping them. Then he set about dismantling her reason, pumping his fever-hot body inside hers with devastating skill while his hot mouth moved to the sensitive tips of her breasts, each hungry, suckling pull mirrored by the clenching of her sheath.

Reese had no idea how much time passed, her thoughts in a sensual haze as he pounded into her, using his magnificent cock to make her scream and writhe and beg for more. They could probably be heard all the way down on the beach, but she didn't give a damn. All that mattered was this hard, piercing pleasure as he drove inside her, hurtling her into a shocking, explosive orgasm that burned its way through every part of her. With a low growl on his lips, he fucked her through the surreal waves of pleasure, his body moving faster . . . harder, until he finally gritted his teeth and jerked out of her. Fisting his cock in a brutal grip, he gave a guttural shout as he pumped hot, heavy streams of cum out over her stomach. Reese watched with wide, stunned eyes, completely fascinated by the beauty of such a raw, masculine act. It was the most erotic thing she'd ever seen, primal and violent and achingly intimate. His body shuddered as he braced himself on one arm, and she could feel the blistering heat of his gaze on her belly as he watched his cum slip across her skin, dripping into the dark curls on her mound.

His corded throat worked as he swallowed. "That's so fucking sexy."

"You're such a guy," she said with a soft snort.

"Damn straight," he grunted.

She grinned, too exhausted to move as she watched him hike up his boxers and climb off the bed. He stood there at the edge of the mattress for a moment, his hot gaze seeming to drink in the sight of her, before he finally turned and headed into the bathroom. She heard the water running, and then he came back into the room, his boxers gone, a gray washcloth gripped in his hand. Kneeling on the bed, he used the cloth to clean her belly, then lower. "I could have done that," she said drowsily.

"I know," he grated. "But I wanted to do it for you."

"Then in that case, I'll just say thank you for taking such good care of me."

His head jerked up, his mouth a hard, flat line. "You call fucking you to within an inch of your life taking good care of you?"

Hoping to ease some of his tension, Reese gave him a warm, happy look from under her lashes. "Well, there's good and then there's *good*, Sheriff Hudson."

His chest shook with a gritty, breathless laugh as he tossed the cloth aside, then stretched out beside her. She started to roll toward him, but he was already yanking her into his arms, holding her tight, his face buried in the curve of her throat. "I just want to protect you," he said in a low voice. "Take care of you. Make you come and laugh and smile. I can't get enough of it."

It was the most incredible thing anyone had ever said to her, and after the amazing day that she'd spent with him, Reese knew he meant every word.

She just didn't know for how long.

15

BEN FELT LIKE HE'D GONE FROM HEAVEN TO HELL. THAT BLISSED-OUT state of happiness he'd found with Reese the night before was getting the shit beaten out of it in the bright light of day. When he'd opened his eyes that morning, everything that he'd said and done since he'd brought her home from the hospital had crashed down on him with staggering force, his chest so tight he could barely breathe through the panic.

It wasn't that he felt any different. Fuck, no. He just didn't know how to deal with what he *did* feel.

Despite his bone-chilling fear for her safety, yesterday had been one of the best damn days he'd ever had, and now he was reeling. He'd never let himself need something or someone this badly, and he was scared shitless by the idea of losing it. He'd do whatever it took to keep some jackass stalker from getting anywhere near her—but there were so many other things that could go wrong. She could decide she wasn't ready for something this serious.

Could open her eyes one morning and finally realize that she could do a hell of a lot better than him. That she could have any man she wanted. That she didn't need to settle for someone who was terrified by the idea of feeling anything deeper for a woman than his driving need to fuck her.

And speaking of fucking—Ben didn't know what the hell he'd been thinking, taking her like that without a condom. He didn't do shit like that. *Ever.* But he hadn't been able to resist the temptation. Even now, as he pounded the shit out of the punching bag that hung in his workout room, doing his best to avoid her, all he really wanted was to go and find her. To get her in his arms . . . and under his body, where he could sink back inside that hot, plush little pussy all over again, feeling her melting over his naked dick while she held him tighter than a fucking fist.

Somehow, not even the idea of her swollen and pregnant with his child was enough to scare him off. He'd been thinking about it that morning when he'd climbed out of bed, and as he'd stood there staring down at her, soaking in the way she was curled up in his sheets, all he'd felt was an intense, bone-deep satisfaction and pride at the idea of knocking her up.

Christ. If that weren't enough to make a guy edgy, Ben didn't know what was.

Finishing with his workout, he grabbed a shower, pulled on a pair of jeans, and padded barefoot to his home office. The first thing he saw when he sat down at his desk and pulled up his e-mail was a message from Alex. His older brother had apparently run into Connie in town, and she'd told him that Reese was staying at his house. Now Alex felt it was his God-given duty to warn Ben not to get too hung up on her. He tried not to let Alex's shitty attitude get to him, but it wasn't easy. Especially when he had a lot of the same bullshit already looping through his head.

An hour later, Ben was still looking over the Houghton file that

Tony had sent him, when Reese came into the office, asking if he wanted any lunch, since it was already past two. He knew she'd picked up on his tension, but she hadn't pushed for an explanation. She'd just kept herself busy talking on the phone to her sisters and working on the laptop he'd collected from her place, along with a suitcase full of clothes. After she brought him a sandwich, chips, and soda, she sat on the small loveseat under the window and ate her food, while he kept his attention on the file. The silence was awkward and thick, but he didn't know what the fuck to say. Finally, she stopped picking at her food and moved back to her feet, her plate in one hand, her drink in the other.

"I should get back to my computer. I've got some classwork prep that I need to be working on," she murmured, heading for the door.

"Reese," he said gruffly, but she was already gone. Leaning back in his chair, Ben scrubbed his hands down his face, wondering what his problem was. He was acting like a total prick, and she didn't deserve it. Hell, he needed to have his damn ass kicked!

Ready to go and find her, he started to move to his feet, when his phone rang. Sinking back into his chair, Ben spent nearly an hour talking to Tony, then got wrapped up looking through some more documents that the detective e-mailed over to him. He was still too bitter to really give a damn about the Houghton case, but he needed something to keep his head busy or he'd end up going ape-shit worrying about Reese's stalker. Not to mention her accident and her trashed car and just how deeply the sexy little teacher had gotten under his skin.

By the time he was done reading over everything, the sun had set and it'd been hours since he'd seen Reese. With his jeans hanging low on his hips, Ben carried his lunch plate and empty soda can into the kitchen, then tracked her down in the dining room, where she was using the table as a desk. As she looked up from her laptop, her blue gaze lingered on his bare chest for a moment before lifting to his face, and some of the tension in his knotted muscles finally eased. He might screw up in the behavior department time and again, but there was always the chance that he could win her back with the sex. He was going to hold on to that bit of luck like a fucking lifeline.

"I'm sorry," he grunted, knowing damn well that he owed her an apology.

She blinked at him from the far side of the table. "For what?"

He braced his shoulder against the doorjamb. "For acting like a jackass and brushing you off today."

She gave him a tight smile. "Don't worry, Ben. You can brush me off and I won't crumple. I'm not as weak as everyone seems to think."

With a wealth of meaning, he said, "I don't think you're weak. I know exactly how strong you are."

"Good," she murmured, turning an adorable shade of pink. The woman still couldn't take a compliment to save her life.

Ben pushed away from the doorjamb and started making his way around the table. "Last night . . . things got pretty intense," he rasped, his dark gaze locked with hers. "I think I'm still reeling a little."

She turned in her chair to face him as he came closer, but she didn't say anything. Just tilted her head back and watched him with those big blue eyes, looking wary and hurt and probably even a little pissed. Which was no less than he deserved.

Pulling her lower lip through her teeth, she waited until he was standing right in front of her, then asked, "Are you worried about us not using any protection last night?"

"What? No!"

A little notch formed between her brows. "Then is it my being here? Did it freak you out to wake up with me in your bed this morning?"

Ben shoved a shaky hand through his hair. "No, it's nothing like that."

"Then what's wrong?"

"I don't know," he bit out, struggling to find the right words. "I'm just . . . I'm not good at opening up about shi— *things* with other people. But I *want* to be better at it for you. It just . . . It messes with my head, which is stupid, and I'm sorry you have to put up with my crap. But I—"

She cut him off before he could finish his rambling, pathetic explanation. "Ben, it's okay. I'm not mad at you for feeling that way." A small smile touched her lips. "I'd be lying if I said I didn't want to know everything about you, but not if it makes you uneasy. We can take things as slow as you want, okay?"

Reaching down, he grabbed hold of her and yanked her into his arms, his chin tipped down as he drank in the sight of her, wondering what the fuck he'd done to get this lucky. "You're pretty incredible, you know that?" he said huskily, sliding one hand into her hair, cupping the back of her head, the other settling against the base of her spine.

She choked back a soft laugh and smirked. "You're just saying that because you like the sex."

"I most certainly do," he rumbled, pressing a kiss to the delicate shell of her ear, then nibbling on the tender lobe with his teeth.

She moaned as she nuzzled her face against him, brushing her lips against the hard edge of his jaw. "That's still so surprising, Ben. The way that you want me."

Her quiet words sparked a searing rush of frustration inside him, and he pulled her head back, drilling his hot gaze into her storm-dark eyes. "When are you going to start getting it, Reese? *Want* isn't a strong enough word for how you make me feel. *Want* I could deal with. *Want* wouldn't leave my head spinning or have me acting like a jackass. *Want* I could shove to the back of my mind and walk away from. But I can't do that with you. I don't even want to fucking try."

Her throat worked as she swallowed, those big eyes startled and bright, shimmering with emotion. "It . . . it kills me a little when you say things like that to me."

"For God's sake, why?"

"Because I'm so afraid I'm going to lose you," she whispered, her voice trembling.

"Jesus, Reese. I'm not going anywhere," he groaned, resting his forehead against hers. "Don't you know how insane I am about you? Christ, any man would be crazy not to lo—"

His voice suddenly trailed off, his head jerked back, and Reese watched a stunned expression spread over his face as he realized what he'd almost said. That he'd been right on the verge of saying the l-word to her. From the look of panic shadowing his eyes, it was clear how horrified he was by the idea, and she tried to hide her disappointment. But it wasn't easy.

Pulling out of his arms, she turned and started heading around the far side of the table. "I'll see you in a little while. I just want to go and grab a quick shower before dinner."

"*Reese.*"

She didn't look at him—couldn't. Not until she'd had some time to get her emotions back under control. "We can talk later, Ben."

She was almost out the door, when she heard the text alert go off on her phone. It was sitting by her laptop on the table, the second alert making her flinch. "Ignore it," she whispered, dreading what the message was going to say. She'd been trying so hard not to think about the accident, or her trashed car, but her control was shaky at best. Yesterday, Ben had consumed her every waking moment, making it easy to bury the fear. But he'd left her out there in the emotional wastelands today, and she was feeling too raw inside. It wouldn't take much to tip her over, and she wished she could have just changed the damn number for the phone. But Ben had told her no, saying that it was best to know what the bastard was thinking.

His voice low, he said, "You know we can't do that, honey."

"Fine," she snapped, turning back and snatching the phone off the table. She clenched her jaw as she pulled up the message.

"What's it say?"

"That he *needs* me," she forced from her tight throat, setting the phone back down. She was so creeped out, she didn't even want to touch the thing.

Ben quietly cursed, then rubbed a rough hand over his mouth. "I want this jackass found. *Now.*"

With another hard swallow, she said, "Yeah. Me, too."

He started to respond, only to stop when his phone suddenly rang, the shrill sound coming from somewhere in the back of the house. "Shit," he muttered. "I'm sorry, but I've got to get that. It's our emergency tone."

She nodded, understanding that there were times when his job had to take precedence over everything else. And it's not like they could do anything about the creepy text. He left the room, and she heard the muffled sound of his voice as he answered the call. Though she couldn't make out any of the words, she could tell from his tone that something bad had happened. He came back into the dining room less than a minute later, dressed for work in jeans and a polo shirt, his phone clipped to his belt, a heavy gun in his hand.

"I have to go," he said, checking the clip on the weapon, before sliding it into his shoulder holster.

"What's wrong?"

He lifted his head and looked right at her, wearing his closed-off cop's expression. "We've got a dead body in one of the public parking lots near the beach. Just about a half mile north of here."

Reese blinked, unable to believe what he'd just said. "A dead body? Who is it? What happened?"

"I don't have all the details," he told her, and she followed after him as he headed into the kitchen, watching as he picked up his truck keys from where they were hanging beside the phone. "All I know is that the victim is female. Some teenagers who were skateboarding in the lot saw her body wedged under a car and called it in."

"Ohmygod," she whispered, slumping against the wall.

"I don't know how long I'll be gone," he added, punching a number into his phone as he walked out of the room and across the hallway to his office. She could hear him opening drawers in his desk as he spoke briefly to someone on the phone again, her thoughts too fractured to focus on what he was saying. She was still standing there, in the same position, when he came back into the kitchen a few minutes later. "I've called my brother," he said. "He's going to stay with you while I'm gone."

"What?" Reese shook herself out of her daze. "Ben, that's not necessary. I feel safe here. I don't need a bodyguard."

His jaw hardened as he grabbed his wallet, slipping it into his back pocket. "We're not going to argue about this, Reese. I'm not leaving you on your own."

She crossed her arms over her chest. "Fine. But please tell me it's Mike who's coming over and not Alex."

He slid her a shuttered look from under his brows. "You don't like Alex?"

"I don't really know him, but to be bluntly honest, he's always made me nervous."

He frowned. "He's pretty self-contained these days, but he's a good guy."

"I'm sure he is," she said, rubbing her hands over her chilled arms. "But he still looks like he could kill without batting an eyelash."

"So could I, if it meant keeping you alive," he muttered under his breath.

His phone started ringing again, and he went back into his office to take the call. It sounded like he was busy getting things coordinated for the investigation, so Reese went into the living room, curling up in a corner of the sofa as she waited for him to finish. She didn't think more than fifteen minutes had passed when she heard a vehicle pulling into the driveway.

"That'll be Mike," Ben said, stopping in the doorway to the living room. "Just give me a minute to talk to him, and then I'll say good-bye before heading out."

Ben watched Reese's lips form something that looked like *I'll be right here*, but his pulse was roaring in his ears too loudly for him to be sure of her exact words. He didn't know what his fucking problem was, but he hated the idea of leaving her here. This wasn't just fear. It was like a goddamn poison burning through his veins, and he didn't know how to deal with it—how to care this much about another person, to the point that it felt like steel bars were squeezing in around his chest.

If this was what getting twisted up over a woman was all about, then he sure as shit didn't know how to wear the emotion. It didn't fit, too fucking tight, too confining, making it impossible to breathe. He felt like he was coming out of his skin, everything shrinking in on him. He was half tempted to call Brit and talk it out with her, but knew he probably wouldn't like whatever she had to say. He rarely did. The woman had a way of seeing into him and digging out things he preferred to keep buried.

Standing at the end of his front walkway, he watched Mike climb down from the cab of his Ford F-150. Coming around the front of the truck, his brother asked, "Where's Reese?"

He jerked his head toward the house. "She's inside."

Looking curious, Mike lowered his voice and said, "I talked to Alex. He told me she's living here now."

Ben narrowed his eyes. "You gonna give me shit about it, as well?"

Mike gave a low laugh as he held up his hands. "Not at all, man. Alex can be as doom and gloom as he likes. But I think it's great."

Ah, Christ. All he needed was Mike trying to play fucking Cupid. "I like spending time with her, and she needs protection right now," he said. "But her being here doesn't mean anything more than that."

Mike looked vaguely surprised. "Doesn't it?"

"Look. I had an itch. So did she. For the moment, we're having fun scratching them. End of story," he growled, the shitty words shocking him as much as they did his brother.

Shaggy hair fell over Mike's brow as he shook his head. "So you're just gonna walk away from her when this stalker shit is over?"

Those steel bars started to squeeze in tighter, his lungs about ready to explode. "I'm not even thinking about the future," he bit out, sweating like he had a fucking fever. "What's so wrong with just enjoying the moment?"

Mike came a little closer, his expression taking on a hard, determined cast. "I'm gonna say something, Ben, and you're not gonna like it. But I'm doing it because I love you, so you'll just have to live with it. And let it go on the record right now that if you punch me, I'll punch you back."

"You're so fucking bat-shit," he muttered, turning back toward the house. But Michael grabbed his arm, jerking him back around.

"Listen. Just because Mom and Dad were screwed up, and Alex and Judith were like the couple from hell, you *do* know that it happens, right? That two people can make it work, so long as they love each other?"

A muscle started to pulse in his jaw. His nostrils flared. "You don't know what the fuck you're talking about," he said flatly.

"Yeah?" Apparently deciding to try a different tactic, a slow smile started to kick up the corner of Mike's mouth. "Then you won't mind if I make a play for her after you're done? 'Cause those sweet tits of hers get me every time. Are they freckled? Taste like peaches and cream?" Mike snapped his fingers. "I bet it's coconut. She always smells like—"

Before Ben even knew he was moving, he had his hands fisted in the front of Mike's T-shirt. "Keep your fucking mouth shut!" he snarled, lifting all six-feet-four of his baby brother off the ground and slamming him against the side of the truck.

"Why? What's it to you?" Mike shouted in his face. "You're gonna push her away, right? Send her off to have fun with some other guy. So what the hell? Might as well be me."

"You little shit!" he growled, slamming him against the truck again, before forcing himself to let go and staggering back a step. Breathing hard, Ben wiped the back of his wrist over his mouth, and tried to get a grip on his temper before he started a fight he knew he would only feel like crap about later.

"You might not like hearing it," Mike grunted, shoving his hair out of his eyes, "but you care about this woman."

"I never said that," Ben snarled, forcing the words through his gritted teeth.

Mike shook his head again. "I never figured you for a fucking coward."

"What the hell do you know? You've never been in love!"

"I know you can't turn your back on it just because you've seen some bad shit," Mike argued, tossing his hands up. "Jesus, Ben.

You want to end up like Alex? Be a miserable jackass for the rest of your life?"

"For the last time, Mike. I am *not* in love with her! So fucking drop it!" he roared, his deep voice thundering with rage.

Mike started to respond, but then he caught sight of something over Ben's shoulder and his eyes went wide. Before his brother had managed to pull his hand down his face and mutter, "Shit," Ben's heart had already lodged itself in his throat.

He ground his jaw and braced himself as he turned around. But he still felt like he'd just been kicked in the gut. Reese stood in the front doorway, ghostly pale except for the twin splotches of vivid color burning under her freckles. He opened his mouth, but she was already turning, disappearing inside. Feeling like the bottom of his stomach had just dropped out, Ben followed after her as she walked straight through the house, heading for his bedroom. She didn't stop until she'd made it all the way to the far side of the room. Then she just stood there in front of the window, staring out into the inky darkness of the evening.

Doing her best not to cry, Reese said, "I think it would probably be a good idea if I went to my sister's. I can ask Mike to drive me, since my car's still at the garage."

"No." His breath left his lungs in a sharp, frustrated burst. "I don't want you to leave."

"Why?" she snapped, glaring at him over her shoulder. "So we can keep scratching those itches you were talking about?"

He went rigid, shoulders looking twice their size as his muscles hardened with tension. "It's more than that and you know it."

"Just . . . don't. I can't take any more of your mind games right now." She looked back out the window, hoping she could just keep it together until he left. Then she could fall apart and cry like a baby, feeling like the biggest fool on the planet.

"What you overheard . . . that doesn't mean anything. Mike was just pissing me off. He loves to push my buttons."

Rubbing her stupid eyes, which were already leaking tears, she said, "Seriously, Ben. I don't want to talk about it."

"Damn it, Reese." His low voice shook with emotion. "Don't do this."

"I'm not doing anything!" She flung the words at him as she spun around, wondering what the hell he wanted from her. "I'm not the one pushing you away!"

He shoved a hand through his hair, looking haggard and pissed and so outrageously sexy she could have eaten him alive. "I'm not trying to push you away, either."

She choked back a painful laugh, her throat burning with tears as he went on, saying, "Please, Reese. Just talk to me. I don't want to fuck this up."

It was the worry and the fear she could hear in his rough voice that got to her, more than the words themselves. When he was open like this, she couldn't say no to him, no matter how much she knew that she should. "We can talk when you get back, okay? I just . . . I need some time to think."

He took a deep, ragged breath. "What the fuck is there to think about?"

She was trying so hard to stay calm, but it was impossible, her voice cracking as all the pain and hurt inside her suddenly spilled out, impossible to control. "Gee, I don't know, Ben. How about the fact that I've fallen in love with you?"

The instant she heard the words slipping from her lips, Reese knew he would react poorly. And she was right. His mouth went tight, lashes lowering to conceal the cold, panicked look in his eyes. But she couldn't stop now. She needed to get the words bottled up inside her out in the open, no longer willing to hold them back. Needed to make sure he understood exactly where she was coming from.

She sniffed, determined not to cower with embarrassment as she lifted her chin. "Do you understand what I'm saying? I love you and I want to be with you."

He pulled a shaky hand down his face, his breaths coming hard and fast. "I . . . damn it, Reese. I didn't think you'd be ready for something like that."

She took a step toward him, arms wrapped around her middle, trying to hold herself together as they barreled toward that brick wall she'd always known was coming, hoping like crazy that they could make it through to the other side. "I wouldn't be—not with any other man," she admitted, trying to make him understand. "But you . . . I think I must have at least loved you a little for a long time now, Ben, without even realizing it. Because now I love you so much that I can't control it or hold it back. And I don't . . . I don't want just a part of you. I had that once, and I didn't even love him. Not like this. Not like I love you. It's . . . all over me. Inside me. In my heart and my mind. It's like I've been cracked open, and now there's room for so much more than there was before. More pleasure, more hunger, more love. So you need . . . you need to take the time to think about what you want."

"What I want?" His voice was raw, the look in his eyes as terrified as someone facing a life or death situation.

She licked her trembling lips, and said, "I don't expect you to say the words back to me. Not now. I mean, I know that's not how you feel. But if you don't think that it's *ever* going to be something that could happen, then you need to let me know now so that we can end this before it goes any further."

"Goddamn it. Don't say that!" Ben paced from one side of the room to the other, his hands flexing and releasing at his sides. He couldn't function like this, ripped wide open, his emotions in chaos. This wasn't him. He didn't even know how to wrap his head around it. Sliding her a sharp glare, he growled, "Why the fuck are you doing this? We had something great going, and you're fucking it up!"

She looked confused, and hurt. "What's so wrong with falling in love?"

He made a sharp, cutting motion with his hand, as if he could knock her infuriating question out of his way. "Love is fucking bullshit, Reese! All I ever heard growing up was how much my mother loved my father, which somehow seemed to just give her the right to treat him like shit. Screw any guy she wanted, while he sucked down his misery in bottle after bottle, waiting for her to come back and tell him how fucking sorry she was." He gritted his teeth and tried to shut up, hating the devastated look on her beautiful, tear-stained face, but he couldn't stop. The words were being torn from some dark, savage place he always kept under lockdown. But the locks had been blown, and now all this shit was spewing out of him. "Then I had to watch Alex go through the same fucking thing. Watch his damn stomach get pumped while he begged me just to let him die. And all because that bitch he'd married thought it was fun to screw with his head. Fuck that!"

There was nothing but a breath-filled silence when he was done with the guttural tirade. Just that awful, heavy weight of things that were still unsaid and unresolved pressing down on him. He knew he needed to wait it out and finish this with her now, but there wasn't any time. He was already late as hell.

Drawing in a shuddering breath, Ben rubbed his hand over his mouth, then let it drop to his side. Forcing himself to look her in the eye, he said, "I need to get to the crime scene."

She nodded as she swiped at her tears with her fingertips, her voice a small, tight whisper. "Yeah, okay. I understand."

"I'll be back," he grunted. "Just . . . don't fucking go any-where." Then he turned and got his ass out of there, barking at Mike to keep his eye on her and to lock the door behind him.

By the time Ben had driven the half mile to the parking lot where the body had been found, he'd managed to get a grip on his temper. But he was still pissed at himself for acting like such a world-class bastard. Pissed he'd let Mike's taunting push him into saying things that had hurt her. Not to mention the things he'd said before he'd left.

He'd let his fear of one day ending up like his father or brother govern his behavior tonight. Not that he thought Reese would ever cheat on him the way his mother had cheated on his old man, or Judith had slept around on Alex. But there were other ways for a woman to fuck a man up. Love meant letting Reese have a kind of power over him. Meant letting her into every part of his life—not just as a fun accessory, but as the most important element. Meant opening himself up and keeping nothing from her, which was hardly his fucking strong point. But the alternative—watching her walk away from him—wasn't something he could live with.

Which meant he needed to figure out what the fuck he was doing, and fast.

Climbing out of his truck, Ben shoved his anger and frustra-tion to the back of his mind, and forced his thoughts onto the job. Despite the number of cases like this he'd responded to in Miami, it always put a cold feeling in the pit of his stomach. There was no way to describe the horror of seeing a woman or child who'd been killed. No way to describe how hollow it made you feel. How bleak.

Most of his deputies were there, along with the county's foren-sics techs who were collecting evidence beneath the bright glare of the parking lot lights. Robin and another deputy, a lanky twenty-four-year-old named Chris, were busy keeping the media back, as well as a group of beachgoers who'd wandered up to see what all the commotion was about.

Moving around the white screens that had been erected for privacy, Ben made his way over to the medical examiner, an older woman named Maria Surr, who was kneeling beside the body. The victim was lying facedown, her dark hair matted with blood, clothes ripped and stained. He knew from the last phone conversation he'd had that they'd found the woman's ID. Her name was Sylvia Smith, she was thirty-three, and she worked as a teller in one of the local banks. She was single, but her next of kin had already been notified and were on their way down from Orlando.

"How did she die?" he asked, noting the mottled bruising that covered her arms and legs. Her face was turned away from him, but it was obvious from the amount of blood in her hair that there had also been a significant amount of damage done to her skull.

Maria shook her head. "I can't say without doing an autopsy, Ben. She took a serious beating, so it could be any number of factors. But I think she was probably killed sometime late last night. I'll need to run some tests before I can give you any more than that."

"How soon will you have the results of the autopsy?" He knew there would be a lot of fluid and tissue samples involved, which would then need to be analyzed.

"Depending on what I find, it could be a few days. We're still short on staff in the lab and my assistant is out on holiday leave."

Frustration hardened his jaw. Improper staffing and funding was another legacy of his predecessor, and while they'd made significant progress since he took office, there was still a long way to go before the county was where he wanted it to be.

Ryder pulled up in his patrol car, then came over to join them. "Huh," the deputy grunted, after he'd crouched down to get a better look at the victim's face. "Is it just me, or does the vic look like she could be related to that girl who was attacked down on the beach last week?"

Ben got a bad fucking feeling in his gut. "They look that similar?"

Ryder gestured toward the woman's face. "See for yourself."

Ben was already making his way around the victim's feet, when Ryder's next words damn near knocked the air from his lungs. "Come to think of it, she also looks a little like Reese. They've got the same dark hair and blue eyes."

Another few steps, and Ben was staring down at Sylvia Smith's pale face, a low curse on his lips. Ryder was right. This woman hadn't been as pretty as Reese, but their coloring was definitely similar. And the same could be said for the teen who'd only been released from hospital on Thursday.

Remembering the woman who Reese had said was attacked in her building back in Boston, Ben left Maria and Ryder with the vic and headed back to his truck, where he had the copy of the police report he'd gotten from the Boston PD. Less than a minute later, he had his answer. The victim in her building had been a brunette with blue eyes, same as the others.

Goddamnfuckingsonofabitch.

What exactly was going on here? Two women with similar looks to Reese had been attacked . . . and now one was dead. Why? Was her stalker trying to frighten her? Or was this how he took out his anger with her? Did he feel slighted in some way? Rejected?

Leighton's rage-filled image jumped into his head, and it was a plausible theory. The jealous, possessive ex taking out his fury on women who reminded him of the one he wanted, but couldn't have. But Ben had been getting regular updates from the deputies who were watching the lawyer, and he hadn't left the Davis since getting to town. And even if Leighton had been paying some other bastard to do his dirty work, what would be the point of hurting these other women? If the purpose had been to scare her, then why hadn't Reese been taunted with messages about the beatings?

It didn't fucking add up. And the same could be said for the bitchy receptionist. When Ben had asked Ryder to do a background check on Lizzie Jennings, he'd been thinking that maybe she had some kind of weird hate thing going for Reese. It could explain the mutilated cat, and the threat that had been left with it. Even the text messages could have been the woman's sick idea of a joke. And like Leighton, she could have someone working with her, since they knew Lizzie hadn't been driving the truck on Friday. But again, how did the attacks on these other women play into it?

Fuck. No matter how he put all the pieces together, he couldn't get them to fit.

At the sound of someone approaching, Ben lifted his head, surprised when he saw Alex coming toward him, dressed in his customary jeans, black T-shirt, and black boots. "What are you doing here?"

"I called Mike. He said I could find you down here."

Ben set the file on the backseat, closed the truck's door, and looked at Alex. If his brother was here to argue about Reese, he was going to wish he hadn't made the trip. "What do you need?"

"I don't need anything," Alex told him, crossing his arms over his chest. "I just wanted to let you know that you've got a bigger problem on your hands than Reese."

"She's not a fucking problem," he ground out, wondering if his brother was ever going to stop being such a miserable jackass.

"Whatever she is," Alex said in a hard voice, "that guy you've had me looking for isn't her stalker. He's been watching *you*."

"What the hell are you talking about?"

"You're the one he's been running surveillance on. He's one of Houghton's crew."

Ben didn't say anything at first. He just stared back at his brother, hoping this was some kind of bad joke. But he'd known, in his gut, that something wasn't right. Ever since he'd first set eyes on that dark-haired bastard, he'd known there was something familiar about him. He just hadn't been able to pull it all together.

Lowering his arms, Alex reached into his back pocket and pulled out a folded piece of paper. "When you told me the guy looked familiar to you, I started thinking it might be someone you had come into contact with during a case. Some prick who might have a grudge against you. The Houghton case seemed the logical place to begin, so I started going through all the data I'd helped you collect on the son of a bitch back when you were investigating him." Unfolding the sheet, he handed Ben a copy of a grainy black-and-white photograph. "You can see that's your guy with Houghton. He shows up in a couple of other surveillance photos, as well."

Ben narrowed his gaze on the image, wishing that he could tell Alex he was wrong. But there was no arguing the fact that this was the man he kept seeing. The photo showed the bastard standing beside Houghton on the dock where the drug lord moored his yacht, Houghton's arm thrown around his broad shoulders. He couldn't make out the color of his eyes, but it was the same tall, leanly muscled physique and rugged, hard-edged features. The guy looked like he could kill without batting an eye, but then, that was a basic prerequisite of working with Houghton.

Christ. He didn't want to think about what this meant, his brain cramping as he tried to focus on the facts of the situation. "Do you have his name?" he asked.

Alex shook his head. "I can't pull any personal information on him. Whoever he is, Houghton's keeping his identity well protected."

Ben took a deep breath, then crumpled the paper image in his fist.

"Whatever he's after," Alex murmured, "you need to get Reese out of your house, man."

"Fuck you." His brother had made it no secret that he thought he was crazy for getting involved with her, but Ben wasn't going to stand here and listen to this shit.

"I'm not trying to get into it with you," Alex said, holding up his hands. "If you don't want to break things off, you could always put her in protective custody with the Feds."

"When Houghton already has a mole in the system?" he snarled. "We both know how hard it is to keep wraps on something like that. All it takes is one person making a slip and they've got her."

Rubbing two fingertips across his jaw, Alex's pale gaze was as cool as his tone. "Then you need to cut her loose. Publicly. Let them know she means nothing to you."

Ben didn't even bother telling him to fuck off again. The look on his face said it for him. But there was a part of him thinking *here it is, the perfect reason for you to cut and bail.* Then he wouldn't have to deal with any more of that infuriating emotional crap. Wouldn't have to keep walking around with his insides twisted in a fucking knot, trying to shake off who he was so that he could be the kind of man she deserved. One who could open his goddamn mouth and tell her how he felt. Who didn't get scared shitless when she told him she was in love with him. If he was going to end it, there wasn't going to be a better time than this— and yet, he couldn't do it. He'd just have to go home, sit her down, and tell her what he'd learned, and then . . . Shit, he didn't know.

Lighting up a cigarette, Alex took a long drag. "What are you going to do?"

"Not a fucking clue. So just shut up and let me think," he growled, walking away. He didn't want to think that Houghton would go to this much trouble to screw with him, but then, he was partly responsible for the man being in prison. Who knew what the jackass might do?

Goddamn it, he should have seen this coming. Should have made the connection days ago, instead of wasting all this time that could have been spent dealing with the situation. He sure as hell would have moved Reese to a different location, where he could keep her better protected. A lone stalker he was fully capable of taking down on his own. But if Houghton's man came after him, the odds were high he wouldn't be alone.

A chill slipped down his spine as he thought about Reese being back at his house without him. Yeah, she had Mike there with her, and he knew Mike could handle himself. But there was something about all of this that just didn't feel right.

Calling Chris over to him, Ben asked, "Where are the kids who made the call about the body tonight?"

"We took their statements and let them go. But the anonymous tip actually came in just before they called."

Ben narrowed his eyes. "What anonymous tip?"

With a shrug, Chris said, "Someone called in the body right before the kids found her. That's all I know."

"*Son of a bitch.*" Chris was asking if he wanted him to call dispatch to get more information, but Ben turned his back on the worried-looking deputy, already pulling his phone from his belt. Terrified this had been some kind of setup to get him away from the house, he called Mike's number, but there was no answer. Then he called it again. "Pick up the fucking phone," he snarled, but the call went to voice mail for the second time and Ben's stomach dropped.

Shoving the phone in his pocket, he started running back to his truck, shouting at one of the techs for them to inform Ryder that he was now in charge of the crime scene. Then he shouted for Alex to hurry and get his ass in the truck, telling him they had a problem. As Ben jumped behind the wheel, Alex quickly climbed in on the passenger side. Ben brought him up to date on the situation as he drove, taking the turns like a fucking maniac as he floored the gas pedal. He slammed on the brakes before he even reached the end of his driveway, jumping out of the cab while the truck was still rocking. When they found the front door of his house standing wide open, the fear in Ben's gut turned to lead.

"Wait!" Alex hissed, grabbing his upper arm when he started to rush inside. "You can't just go barreling in there! What if it's a trap?"

"I don't give a shit if it is," he snarled, jerking his arm free. "I'm not waiting out here when that bastard might be in there with her!"

They went in with their weapons drawn, and found Mike almost immediately. Their younger brother was lying facedown in the middle of the living room floor, the right side of his head wet with blood. Alex crouched beside Mike's body and checked his pulse. "He's alive."

"Stay with him," Ben choked out, his goddamn heart threatening to burst right out of his chest as he searched the rest of the house for Reese. But she wasn't there.

Standing in the back hallway, he turned and rammed his fist into the wall, plaster exploding in a white cloud, while his knuckles throbbed and bled. Leaning forward, he rested his forehead against the smooth surface and tried to get his fucking thoughts straight. His gut told him it was her stalker. If Houghton's guy had been trying to screw with him, he would have taken them both. But this was about Reese. The bastard had wanted her . . . and now he'd taken her. But where, damn it? Ben didn't have a clue. The only thing he knew with any certainty was that he'd screwed up so fucking bad. Damn it, he never should have left her! And why the hell had he driven away tonight without telling her that he loved her?

Like the stubborn jackass that he was, he'd fought it till the very end. But he'd known, deep down, where this was headed right from the start. There hadn't been any point in trying to avoid it. He'd just been chasing his own damn tail. But the truth was simple: *He loved her.* So much that it hurt. So much that it was driving him out of his mind. Making him act like a total prick.

And now he'd made the most colossal fuckup of all, and let some twisted son of a bitch get his hands on her.

"She's gone," he said roughly, standing in the doorway to the living room. "I'm going over to the Davis to question Leighton. Whatever it takes, I'll make him tell me everything he knows."

Alex gave him a careful look. "What are you going to do about Houghton?"

"I don't know," he grunted, holstering his gun. "Right now, I don't fucking care."

No, all he cared about was getting Reese back. Once that was squared, he'd deal with whatever else came his way. Stalkers, drug dealers, scum-sucking slime. Bring it on. He was ready to take on whatever the universe wanted to throw at him, so long as it kept her from getting hurt.

For a moment, he thought Alex was going to argue with him, and Ben gritted his teeth. Jesus, as if there were anything in the world he would put above getting back the woman he loved.

He actually felt a sharp burst of relief when Alex nodded toward the door. "I've got Mike, and the ambulance will be here any minute now. You go and find Reese."

"I'll call as soon as I've finished with Leighton," Ben said, tossing the words over his shoulder. But when he jerked the door open, he nearly plowed right into the jackass. "What the fuck are you doing here?" he snarled.

Leighton's mouth was pressed into a hard, flat line, the corner of his bottom lip still scabbed over from where Ben had punched him. "I hate your guts just as much as you hate mine," he said, "but I . . . I need your help."

Ben's right hand was already curling into a fist, when he noticed how fucking pale Leighton looked. Holding on to his control by a thread, he jerked his chin for the lawyer to go on.

Instead of saying anything, Leighton held up the phone gripped in his hand, turning it so that Ben could read the message on its screen:

You want her? Come and get her.

There was a photo beneath the text. An image of some kind of beach cabana, but he couldn't tell where it'd been taken.

"I know who it's from," Drew croaked in a thick voice, dropping his hand to his side. "It's Lizzie."

Fisting his hand in the front of the guy's shirt, Ben yanked him off his feet and slammed him against the door. "What the hell is she after?" he roared, getting right in the lawyer's face. "And who the fuck is working with her?"

Leighton shook his head, his bloodshot eyes panicked and wide. "I don't know. I swear I don't."

"Any other messages?" he demanded. "Did she send an address?"

With his feet dangling off the floor, Reese's ex spoke in a gruff, breathless rush. "She didn't need to. I already know where the picture was taken. I recognize the cabana."

"Then where the fuck is it?"

"The Twilight Bay Resort down in Islamorada." Leighton's eyes closed as he gave a hard swallow. Then he opened them . . . and looked Ben right in the eye. "It's the hotel where Reese and I stayed on our honeymoon."

16

WONDERING WHAT THE HELL HAD HAPPENED TO HER, REESE CARE-fully cracked her eyes open and looked around. Where was she? The last thing she remembered was thinking that she'd heard a woman calling out for help and then— *Oh, God.* It started coming back to her in painful, jagged pieces, her brain hurting from the explosion of data.

Jesus, she hoped Mike was okay. She could remember walking into the living room to ask him if he'd heard anything, only to find him slumped on the floor, blood pouring down the side of his face. With a sharp scream, Reese had rushed toward him, but then everything had gone dark. She didn't know what had been used to knock her out, but her head was pounding like a bitch and there was a searing pain burning down the back of her neck.

Taking a deep breath, she tried to study as much of her sur-roundings as she could without moving her head, not wanting to alert anyone who might be in the room with her that she was awake. She was lying on a bed in the middle of what looked like an expensively furnished, tropical-themed bedroom. There was a low light coming from somewhere behind her, and she could see a lot of swaying, moonlit palm trees through several of the long windows that covered two of the walls. The bed must have been positioned in the middle of the floor at an angle, because the other two walls were behind her.

There was something vaguely familiar about the room, but she couldn't quite place it, her thoughts fried by panic and fear. Knowing she needed to calm down, Reese tried to focus and take stock of her physical condition. With a sickening roll of her stomach, she realized her wrists were bound together with strong strips of plastic that were looped around one of the thick slats in the headboard, making it impossible for her to move off the bed. She was still wearing her jeans and T-shirt, though, and was thankful as hell that she hadn't been stripped. But every ounce of intuition she possessed told her that she was in a seriously bad situation, and a cold, slick wave of terror slipped through her veins, bringing with it a burning rush of tears.

"Finally," a man breathed out. "You're awake."

Pain ricocheted through her skull as Reese quickly moved her head from side to side, trying to find the owner of that low, bone-chilling voice. But she couldn't see anyone.

"Who are you?" she snapped, her own voice biting and sharp. "Where am I? What do you want from me?"

"Shh. Don't be so angry. No one's going to hurt you. I just wanted us to spend some time together."

He came into her field of vision then, and Reese's fear took on an entirely new dimension. He was probably only around twenty-one or twenty-two at the most; tall and tan and impossibly pretty. He had the kind of face you would see in those Calvin

Klein ads, with a body that was big and broad and ripped with muscle. But when you looked in his eyes, you could see that something was . . . seriously wrong. It was like the wiring hadn't been installed quite right, a kind of blankness in his gaze that made the tiny hairs on the back of her neck stand on end. And when he smiled down at her, his pale gaze slipping over her trussed up form, she wanted to vomit. It wasn't hard to see what he was thinking, his body responding swiftly, jeans tented with a massive erection as his attention lingered on her breasts. Beneath her T-shirt, she was wearing a thin cotton bra, the chill from the room's air conditioner tightening her nipples, and she'd never wished for something to hide under so badly in her life.

Just like with the room, there was something vaguely familiar about this man, though she knew she'd never seen him before. He gave off such an unsettling vibe, she definitely would have remembered.

"Who are y-you?" she asked again.

"His name is Rick. And he's my beautiful baby brother."

Whipping her gaze to the foot of the bed, Reese locked her horrified eyes on Lizzie Jennings. *Son of a freaking bitch!* Lizzie was dressed in a red halter top and jeans, her blond hair pulled up in a high ponytail, the straps of a colorful tote bag hooked over one of her bare shoulders. She'd have looked like a beach bunny getting ready to go out clubbing, if it wasn't for the murderous gleam in her eyes.

"Ben told me that your brother had died," Reese snarled, nearly choking on her anger. She couldn't believe this hideous woman was behind all of the crap she'd been through!

Lizzie laughed. "The authorities think Rick's dead because that's what he wants them to think. At the time of that fire, his doctors were trying to keep him away from me, and he doesn't do

well with that. So he found his way back home. Now I take care
of Rick, and in return he helps me with my . . . I guess you could
call them business dealings."

She took care of him? More like used him, from the sound of
things. "Exactly what kind of business are we talking about?" Reese
asked, cringing as Rick moved a step closer to the bed.

Lizzie smiled, but didn't answer her question. Instead, she cast
a satisfied look over the room, saying, "I chose this place because
you came here on your honeymoon with Drew. I know because the
idiot still carries a photo of the two of you on the beach here in his
wallet." Bringing her hate-filled gaze back to Reese, she gave
another soft laugh. "It'll be kinda fitting, don't you think?"

"Fitting for what?" she asked, understanding now why the
room looked so familiar. "What do you want, Lizzie?"

The blonde's wide smile instantly fell, her pretty face twisting
into an ugly sneer. The change in her expression happened so fast,
it was like a switch had been flipped. "What do you think I want,
you little bitch?"

Licking her lips, she said, "I don't know. I don't understand any
of this. What did I ever do to you?"

"It's not what you did. It's your entire fucking existence. You've
screwed everything up!" Lizzie shouted, slamming her hands
down on the top of the wooden footboard.

"I don't understand," Reese repeated, realizing Lizzie was
damn near as unbalanced as her brother.

"Trust me, I don't, either." Lizzie's top lip curled with contempt
as she looked her over. "I mean, what *is* it that has them so hung
up on you?"

"Who?"

"This pathetic brother of mine. And Drew. I had big plans to
get my hands on Drew's money, once you were divorced. But the
idiot wouldn't ask me to marry him because he kept thinking you

were coming back. I figured if I could just get you out of Boston, then he'd forget about you once and for all. So I had Rick start watching you."

"Ohmygod," she whispered, sliding her horrified gaze toward Rick. "Are you the one who killed that cat?"

Rick immediately blanched. "No! Never! I would never hurt an animal." He turned to glare at his sister. "That was Lizzie. She's the one who wanted to frighten you away. I wanted you to stay."

"In Boston?"

He looked puzzled when he brought his gaze back to hers, as if he couldn't figure out why she didn't understand. "Yes. So that we could be together." His eyes narrowed, the confusion in them replaced by some kind of chilling, visceral emotion. "But then . . . then I saw you out with that man, and I . . . I lost my temper."

"What man?" she asked, wondering how on earth she was going to get out of this. Did Ben even know she was missing yet? And once he realized, how would he ever guess to look for her here?

Rick's hands curled into massive fists as he answered her question. "You went out on a date after work one day with some guy dressed in a suit."

Reese cast back, trying to remember what he was talking about. She'd gone for a quick drink one night with Tim Driver, who'd dated Connie in high school. He'd remained a friend of the family over the years and had given her a call when he'd been in Boston for business. But it hadn't been a date.

Rick, however, had clearly thought otherwise.

"When I saw you with him, I lost control," he told her, the hoarse confession making her skin crawl. "That's when I found the woman in your building. The one with your hair and eyes, though hers weren't as beautiful. But I had to let the anger out somehow, and I didn't want it to be on you." Reaching out, he ran his moist fingertips down the underside of her arm. "You're . . . you're meant to be with me, Reese. I can *feel* it."

"Rick, you don't even know me," she pointed out in a quiet voice, hoping to reason with him. But his eyes burned with madness.

"That's not true. I know you so well. I've watched you. Studied you." He pulled a chair up to the bedside and sat down. Then he whispered, "I've even killed for you."

No, no, no . . . Please don't let him be talking about Ben or Mike. Please let them be safe . . .

Struggling to find her voice, she croaked, "Who? Who did you kill?"

Rick cocked his head a bit to the side as he held her gaze. "That criminal father . . . the one you turned in for abuse. He was watching you, too. Wanted to hurt you. So I hurt him first."

"You ran him over?" she asked faintly, unable to believe what she was hearing.

He nodded, and gave her a proud smile.

"And you . . . you wanted to run me over, too?"

"What? No!" he shouted, surging to his feet so quickly the chair flew backward, crashing against the wall.

Lizzie gave a bitter laugh from the foot of the bed. "Poor Rick. He really beat himself up over that one. He saw his chance on Friday and was hoping to pluck you right off the street, but that minivan pulled around the corner before he could make his move."

"I told you in my text that I didn't mean to hurt you," Rick said brokenly, but Reese was only giving him her partial attention. She'd just caught a flash of something at the edge of one of the windows. A second later, she could have sworn she saw a strong, masculine hand holding a gun, and she knew immediately that it was Ben. He'd come for her! She didn't need to see his face to know it was him. She could feel it down in places that were too primal and deep for explanation. Rick and Lizzie were both standing with their backs to the window, so she knew they wouldn't catch sight of him until he was ready to make his move. The thought filled her with terror for his safety. She didn't want to be in this room with these monsters—but, damn it, she didn't want Ben putting himself in danger to save her, either.

Knowing the best thing she could do was keep them talking, so that they were focused on her rather than whatever was going on outside, she looked at Lizzie and asked, "How did you get out of the hotel without being seen by one of the deputies? Ben's had them watching you and Drew since you left the hospital on Friday."

Lizzie rolled her eyes. "It wasn't hard. I just fucked one of the hotel's security guards and he let me sneak out a private exit."

Well, hell. If Reese managed to make it through this alive, filing a complaint against that incompetent jerk was going to be one of the first things she did.

She shifted her attention to Rick. "And those texts that you sent me. Did you get my number from Lizzie?"

"Yeah," he said thickly, staring at her chest again. She felt a fresh wave of nausea roll through her, the vile idea of his hands touching her in the same places Ben had touched making her want to scream.

As if he could read her mind, Rick whispered, "Why did you let him touch you?"

Oh, shit. This couldn't be good. Thinking a lie was probably the safest option, she said, "I haven't let anyone touch me."

Angry tears glistened in his eyes. "Not true! That fucking sheriff has had his hands all over you!" Sounding like a petulant child, he went on. "I've wanted to kill him for days now, but Lizzie said I couldn't because it would draw too much attention. But I heard the two of you together. Saw you. I was right outside his bedroom window last night."

"You were spying on us?"

He swallowed, sweat pouring down the sides of his face. "It made me so angry, watching you let him come all over you," he rasped, his gaze unfocused, as if he was going somewhere else inside his head. "There was nothing else I could do. I had to take it out on someone."

Oh, God. The woman in the parking lot. He'd killed her.

A relieved smile suddenly touched Rick's lips. "I thought Lizzie would be mad and that I'd be in trouble. She got angry about the woman in your building, and the teenager last week. Told me I make too many stupid mistakes. But when I told her what I'd done last night, she said it was a good thing. Said we could use it to get the sheriff away from his house so that I could finally take you." Staring down at her, he said, "She knew that even if he asked someone to stay with you, they wouldn't be as careful as he is. And she was right." The smile fell, and he quickly turned his head to glare at his sister again. "But I'm still angry at her for paying some punk she found in town to trash your car. That was mean and unnecessary."

With each word that came out of his mouth, Rick's psychological issues became more apparent. "How could you do this?" Reese demanded, looking at Lizzie. "He clearly needs help. Are you really so evil that you don't care about what's best for Rick?"

"I'm a survivor. I don't expect some pampered little snatch like you to understand. But everything I have, I've had to fight for. I don't have the luxury of worrying about his precious little feelings!" she shouted, then immediately took a slow, deep breath, as if trying to regain control of her temper. Some of the angry color in her face faded, a strange smile playing at the corner of her mouth as she purred, "And Rick has all kinds of *interesting* uses."

Oh, sick. Were they lovers? There was something so wrong

about this, and Reese didn't want to dig any deeper for details. This lady was fucking psycho!

Struggling to clear the lump of disgust from her throat, she asked, "So what happens now?"

A casual shrug lifted the blonde's shoulders. "I've sent Drew a message letting him know where we're at. When he shows up for the gallant rescue, you're both going to die."

"No! I told you before, only him," Rick argued. "Reese lives."

His sister gave a long-suffering sigh. "Rick, we've been over this. It has to be both. Drew's never going to marry me and it's all her fault. Now they need to pay for fucking up my plans. She *has* to die."

"Stop . . . saying . . . that!" Rick shouted, going red in the face.

Lizzie narrowed her eyes, her voice cracking like a whip. "I'll let you have your playtime with the little bitch, just like I promised. But we're not keeping her. End of story."

From the edge of her vision, Reese could see Ben signaling at someone outside. She hoped to God they were coming in soon, because the argument between Lizzie and Rick was escalating. They were screaming at each other now, but she recalled there being a lot of distance between the private cabanas here at the resort, and she didn't imagine anyone other than Ben and whoever he had working with him would be able to hear them.

"I won't let you hurt her!" Rick bellowed, the tendons in his neck bulging with rage as he took an aggressive step toward his sister.

"Fine. If that's the way it's going to be, I'm afraid you're no longer useful." Lizzie said the words without a flicker of emotion, the look on her face just as empty as she reached into her bag and pulled out a gun. Reese started to scream, but Lizzie was already lifting the weapon. A second later, she fired a bullet directly between Rick's eyes, and the back of his head practically exploded. The sound of the gunshot was deafening, the window behind him showered with blood as Rick crumpled heavily to the ground.

With her screams dying in her throat and her jaw quivering from shock, Reese flinched as everything suddenly happened at once, the explosion of action and sound like some kind of climactic movie scene. Ben came barreling through the blood-spattered window, the shattered glass still flying as he hit the floor and rolled. When he came up in a crouched position, he shot a bullet into Lizzie's shoulder, knocking her back against the opposite wall, the gun falling from her hand and skidding across the floor. At the same time, two other men busted in through the door. Reese didn't even realize one of them was Drew until he took in the scene with wild eyes and shouted, "You fucking bitch!" at Lizzie.

"Secure her," Ben growled at the other man, who was wearing some kind of law enforcement uniform, while he went to work on the plastic ties that were binding Reese's wrists. He was using what looked like a badass utility knife, and she couldn't wait to be free.

Reese could hear the guy in the uniform, who she assumed worked for something like the local sheriff's department, moving across the room toward Lizzie, but didn't watch his progress. She'd already tilted her head back, tears of relief streaming from her eyes as she stared up into Ben's strained, gorgeous face.

"I was so fucking scared for you," he ground out, his big hands shaking as he cut through the plastic.

"Ben," she croaked, her own voice choked with tears. She started to tell him how happy she was to see him, but was cut off when the other man started shouting.

"Get down!" he bellowed. "She's just pulled another gun off her ankle!"

With overlapping roars of fury, Ben threw himself on top of

Reese like a shield, ready to take a bullet for her, just as Drew launched himself at Lizzie. Ben was shouting commands at the guy in the uniform to fire, but the man kept saying he couldn't get a clear shot. Craning her head around Ben's broad shoulder, Reese watched Drew and Lizzie roll across the floor, fighting for control of the weapon. It fired once, twice . . . and then a third and final time a few seconds later. For an instant, there was nothing but an awful, weighted silence, and then Drew gave a pain-filled groan as he rolled himself off the top of Lizzie's lifeless body. He went up on an elbow, trying to get to his feet, but there were two crimson stains spreading across his chest, and he collapsed back to the floor.

Quickly moving off the bed, Ben told Reese to stay put and went to check on Drew. While Ben applied pressure to the wounds, the other guy called for the ambulance. Lucky for Drew, the local sheriff had already called one to the location, just in case it was needed, and the medics came rushing into the room just a few moments later. Ben let them take over with Drew and came back to Reese, lifting her into his arms.

Then he carried her across the grisly looking room, through the open doorway, and out into the comforting darkness of the night.

17

DESPERATE TO REACH REESE AS QUICKLY AS POSSIBLE, BEN HAD MAN-
aged to get transport for both him and Leighton down to Islamorada in the county helicopter, where they'd met up with one of the
local deputies. Even with the time it'd taken to get the flight coordinated, they'd shaved considerable minutes off what would have
been a gut-wrenching drive down to the Keys.

Fear and fury weren't strong enough words to describe the
emotions that had burned their way through Ben's insides as he'd
spoken to Harry Jackson, the local sheriff, while coordinating
Reese's rescue. And relief didn't come anywhere close to how he
felt now that she was sitting beside him in this cold, sterile hospital
corridor in the city of Key Largo, waiting for news about how
Leighton was doing. Lizzie had managed to shoot him twice in the
chest, before Leighton had drilled the last bullet straight through
her heart. Lucky for the lawyer, the bullets in the gun that Lizzie
had been wearing on her ankle weren't hollow-point like the one

she'd used on her psycho brother. But they'd still done some damage, deflating one lung and nicking an artery. He'd been in surgery for several hours now, but the last update they'd had was that he was doing well and would probably be transferred to the ICU within the hour.

Given any unforeseen complications, the guy was going to make it. Ben knew he should be glad, seeing as how Leighton had risked his life to keep Reese from being shot. But at the moment, despite his relief that Reese was safe and unharmed—except for a bump on the back of her head where one of the Jenningses had struck her—he was still too jacked up on adrenaline to feel anything but this tight, edgy restlessness.

He'd come so fucking close to losing her. *So. Fucking. Close.*

As they'd followed behind Drew's ambulance in the deputy's patrol car, Reese had filled him in on everything that Lizzie and Rick Jennings had said to her. Then he'd told her that they'd found a truck in the resort parking lot matching the description of the one that had caused the accident on Friday, which they believed was the vehicle she'd been driven down in. When she'd asked him why they'd waited so long outside the window before busting in, he'd said, "We couldn't see from our position whether or not she was holding a gun on you until she'd fired at her brother. No fucking way was I going to risk spooking her and getting you shot."

A wry grin had tilted her lips. "I think I was probably more worried about her shooting *you*. I kept trying to keep them distracted, so they wouldn't notice you were outside the window."

Ben had pulled her against his side, burying his face in her hair. "When she fired that first bullet, it was my chance to get in and take her down before she could get another round off." His voice had been gritty with emotion. "But I was so fucking scared I wouldn't be fast enough."

They'd reached the hospital then, and hadn't been able to finish the conversation. Reese had needed to give her statement to Sheriff Jackson, while Leighton had been taken straight into surgery. By the time Ben and Reese had wrapped things up with the local authorities, Alex, Brit, and a haggard-looking Mike had surprised them at the hospital. They'd driven down together in Brit's car, after she'd run into Alex at the hospital in Moss Beach. Brit had been checking on one of her patients, and Alex had been waiting outside the ER while they patched Mike back up. Ben knew from having spoken to Alex earlier on the phone that Mike had regained consciousness in the ambulance. The doctors had checked him out in the ER, where he'd received ten stitches for the gash on his head and some serious pain meds before being discharged.

After Ben had given Alex and Brit a hard time for not taking Mike straight home, where he could get some fucking rest, his younger brother had admitted that he'd threatened to take a taxi down to Key Largo if they didn't drive him. He felt like shit for what had happened and wanted to apologize in person. Amazingly, Mike could remember everything that had taken place before he'd been knocked out. He'd been watching a Mariners game in the living room when he'd heard a woman screaming for help outside the front of the house. Worried there'd been some kind of accident like a shark attack down at the beach, he'd gone outside to find out what was going on, and Rick had come up behind him, bashing him on the head. Then they must have dragged his body back inside the house, and gone after Reese.

To Ben's surprise, Reese had fussed over Mike like a little mother hen, assuring him that he'd only done what any decent person would do, while they all agreed, trying to make the guy feel better.

Ben knew his brothers and Brit meant well, and he put up with them for as long as he could. But after an hour of listening to the women coddle Mike, while Alex had gone into another one of his brooding moods, slanting the occasional dark glance at Brit whenever she wasn't looking, Ben had finally told them to go back home. Surprisingly, none of them had given him a hard time about it. They'd just wanted to see for themselves that everyone was okay, but seemed to understand that he needed some time with Reese. Brit told them both to call her if they needed to talk, and Ben had finally promised her that they'd stop by to see her when they got home.

As the group had started to take off, Ben had grabbed Alex's arm, holding him back. "What was that about?" he'd asked, keeping his voice low.

Alex's dark brows had drawn together. "What was what about?"

"Those looks you kept giving Brit." As far as Ben knew, his brother and Brit had never had much interaction. Certainly not enough to warrant Alex having a problem with her.

Alex had rolled his shoulder, his mouth flat with tension. "She just winds me up the wrong way."

Ben had given a skeptical snort. "You barely know her."

Alex's jaw had gone rigid. "I don't want to know her, either."

In that moment, it had all started to make sense, and Ben had had to fight back a shit-eating grin. After all this time, a woman had *finally* knocked Alex's blinders off and made him notice her. He never would have fucking guessed that it'd be Brit, but he couldn't say that he didn't like the idea. He just hoped to God his brother didn't act like a complete and total jackass.

"Are we done here?" Alex had snarled, knowing damn well what he was thinking.

Ben had held up his hands. "Go on. Get out of here."

That'd been nearly ten minutes ago, and despite having the first quiet moment together since he'd carried her out of that blood-covered cabana, he was still sitting there beside Reese in the hospital's god-awful plastic chairs, trying to figure out what the fuck he should say. Finally, he just went with what was in his gut. "You worried about Leighton?"

Her shoulder lifted in a tired shrug. "It'd be wrong not to be worried about him. What he did . . ." She blew out a shaky breath. "I never expected him to do something like that."

Well, hell. What was he meant to say to that?

You could try telling her what you should have told her before.

Yeah, as if it was so fucking easy. It'd been one thing when he'd been terrified he might never see her again. Another thing entirely to look deep into her beautiful eyes and rip his fucking heart out for her.

She did it for you. Had the guts to tell you how she feels. That she's in love with you.

He flinched as the words echoed through his head, making it pound. He was locking up inside, panic closing him down. He could feel it happening, and there wasn't a goddamn thing he could do to stop it. All he could keep thinking about was how close she'd come to dying. How pathetically useless he'd felt waiting outside that damn window, hating himself for screwing up and letting those psychopaths get their hands on her.

Jesus, he had to get out of there. He couldn't sit still. Couldn't fucking breathe!

"Where are you going?" Reese asked, when he surged to his feet.

Ben didn't even turn around as he replied. "Outside. I need some air."

He followed the signs for the hospital lobby, so pissed with himself he could have chewed nails. He stopped in the middle of an empty corridor somewhere along the way, his chest heaving, head aching so badly it felt like his skull was breaking apart. For some goddamn reason, his eyes were wet, leaking over his face, the salty burn of tears tickling the corners of his mouth. This was unbelievable. He was falling the fuck apart! He panted, locking his jaw as he scrubbed his face with his hands, but couldn't hold back the furious bellow that suddenly ripped itself up from the painfully tight depths of his chest, echoing through the sterile hallway.

A second later, someone walked by the far end of the corridor and stopped to look at him, before scurrying off. Shit. They were probably getting security. Time to drag his ass out of there. All this night needed was him getting loaded off to jail. Everyone at the station would have a fucking field day with that one. Not to mention how stellar it would look when it came time for reelection.

Forcing himself to move on, Ben worked his way through the mazelike hallways, until he finally reached the lobby and headed for the doors. Through the front wall of glass, he was surprised to see that the sky had turned a pearly shade of gray. He'd lost all track of time.

When he walked out into the sultry morning air, he caught sight of his brothers and Brit waiting in line for coffee at an espresso stand. He quickly turned and started heading for a little rest area set up at the far end of the building, making it clear that he wasn't in the mood for company. Hopefully they'd get their drinks and head on home, leaving him to sort his shit out on his own.

Making his way into the rest area, which consisted of a few benches and trees for shade, Ben propped his shoulders against the trunk of a thick palm, watching the way the hazy streams of sunlight shimmered across a small lake that stretched from the hospital into a natural mangrove. Leaning his head back, he closed his eyes and exhaled a ragged breath, enjoying the brief gust of wind that brought relief from the heat. When a slight sound brought his eyes open, he bit out a sharp curse, stunned to see the son of a bitch working for Houghton standing not five feet in front of him. The bastard was wearing a white dress shirt and dark slacks, looking like he'd just stepped off the cover of GQ. What the hell?

Reading the violence in his expression, the man held up his hands in a gesture of peace. "I'm not here to cause any trouble, Hudson. I'm a federal officer and I don't have a lot of time, so please just stay quiet and listen."

"A fucking Fed?" Ben gave a low, gritty laugh, his battered knuckles burning as he squeezed his right hand into a hard, brutal fist. "Bullshit. You work for Houghton!"

"That's my cover," the guy grunted, reaching into his back pocket to pull out a small leather case. He flipped it open, revealing a federal badge, complete with photo and identification number. According to the badge, his name was Damian Jacobs. "You can take the ID number and run it if you want. It'll check out."

Ben clenched his jaw. He was ready for some fucking answers and he wanted them now. "Why the hell has a Fed been watching me?"

Replacing the badge in his pocket, Jacobs said, "I was working undercover with Houghton's operation, until my cover was blown. I've got the mole he has working for him to thank for that. I thought it might be you."

"You thought I was the mole?" Ben shook his head, fighting not to laugh. "Before this weekend, I haven't had anything to do with that case in over a year. A fucking year!"

The Fed's dark gaze narrowed. "And that couldn't have been the perfect front? The disillusioned detective who wants nothing to do with a case that nearly got him killed?"

Ben scrubbed his hands down his face again, thinking it was a miracle everything had turned out as well as it had. As if it wasn't enough that the fucked-up, psychotic Jennings duo had been gunning for Reese, there'd been an undercover Fed out there trying to pin a perversion-of-justice rap on him.

Lowering his arms to his sides, he gave the jackass a cocky

smirk. "I hate to break it to you, Jacobs. But you've been wasting your time. I'm not the mole."

"I know. I'd finally figured that out."

"Then what the hell are you doing here?"

Jacobs rubbed a rough hand over his mouth, then shoved both hands in his front pockets. "I heard about what happened to your woman," he ground out, the low words sounding as if they were being pulled up out of him against his will. "I actually saw the brother a few times while I was running surveillance."

Ben took a step closer, his muscles going hard and tight as he held Jacobs' gaze. "You saw him spying on Reese?"

Jacobs was watching him carefully. "Only a few times. Started keeping a closer eye out for him, but he was good at blending in."

"Unlike you," he sneered.

"Fuck you," the Fed growled. "I only let you see me those times because I was trying to push you into making a mistake."

"And what the fuck did you think the bastard watching Reese was doing?" His voice got rougher, like he'd swallowed something gritty. "You could have saved her from going through this shit, you stupid fuck!"

A muscle started to pulse in Jacobs' jaw, but he kept his hands buried in his pockets. "I had orders from above not to act," he bit out.

Ben made a rude sound of disbelief. "And you always do what you're told?"

The Fed got right in his face, his voice hard and clipped. "I get that you're pissed, Hudson. And yeah, you have a right to be. But I came here to tell you that I'm sorry. I didn't think the idiot was for real."

"Yeah, well. Why don't you try telling that to the family of the woman he killed on Saturday night?"

"And if you'd been doing your job instead of fucking Little Miss Freckles' brains out twenty-four seven, maybe you'd have caught the bastard before he got to her!"

"You self-righteous son of a bitch!" Ben snarled, throwing a punch that slammed into the Fed's jaw, knocking him back a few feet. Stalking forward, Ben started to throw another one, but his brother was suddenly forcing his way between them.

"That's enough!" Alex shouted, shoving him back. "This isn't helping!"

"But it's making me feel a hell of a lot better," Ben growled, pushing Alex aside and shoving Jacobs against one of the massive tree trunks.

With a graveled curse, Alex wrapped his arms around Ben from behind and practically tossed him to the side. "Fucking chill!" he said, still shouting. "I don't know what's going on, but this isn't the place for this shit."

"He's a fucking Fed!" Ben snapped, flexing his hand.

Alex appeared as stunned as he'd been when he got that bit of news. "What?"

Keeping his attention focused on Jacobs, who was rubbing his jaw, Ben quickly brought his brother up to date. Just as he was finishing, the Fed's phone started ringing. Walking to the edge of the lake, Jacobs took the call, then made his way back over to them, appearing even more pissed off than he had before. "I've got to go," he said, looking at Ben. "But I meant what I said. I came here to tell you that I'm sorry I fucked up. If it makes you feel any better, I owe you one."

He wanted to tell the bastard to shove his offer up his ass, but Alex cut him off. "Take it, Ben. It's always good to have someone like him owe you a favor."

"Fine," he ground out, still wishing he'd had the chance to beat the shit out of the prick.

Jacobs started to walk away, then stopped and turned to face him again. "You might also like to know that Houghton's people have made it clear you're not a target. From what I hear, the man would personally thank you, if he could."

Ben scowled. "What the fuck for?"

Pushing his hands back in his pockets, Jacobs said, "Saving his daughter."

Alex snorted. "Has the jackass found religion or something?"

Jacobs shrugged. "Don't know, don't care. I just thought you might like to know."

"Well that was a fucking eye-opener," Alex muttered, after they'd watched Jacobs climb into a Chevy that'd been left in one of the emergency parking spots right on the curb.

"No shit," he grunted, shaking his head.

Alex slid him a curious look. "Why aren't you inside with Reese?"

Ben tried not to wince. "Because I screwed up."

"What the hell, man? You saved her."

"Not with that shit. I . . . ." His voice trailed off, drying up in his throat. Alex was the last person on earth he wanted to talk this out with. He'd have better luck getting relationship advice from the Manson family.

Alex's eyes crinkled at the corners as he turned his head to the side, squinting into the morning sunlight. "You really care about this woman, don't you?"

Ben gave a frustrated sigh. "Yeah."

Ignoring the NO SMOKING signs plastered everywhere, Alex shook a cigarette from the pack he had in his pocket, lit the tip, then took a slow, deep drag. After he exhaled, he said, "I never told Judith that I loved her." He rolled his shoulder a little, staring down at the cigarette pinched between his thumb and forefinger. "I don't know if it would have made a difference. But . . . shit, it couldn't have hurt. I don't think Dad ever said it, either."

"What? Of course he did."

"Yeah?" Alex lifted his gaze, locking his pale eyes with Ben's. "You ever heard him?"

He started to say yes, then realized that he couldn't actually remember ever hearing those words coming from his father's mouth when he'd been growing up. His old man had always been so gutted by his mother's cheating, Ben had just assumed he was crazy about her. But had his father ever actually told her how he felt?

Christ. Was that part of the problem right there? A piece of what had killed two marriages? The pathetic fact that a Hudson male found it impossible to open his fucking mouth and tell the woman he loved how he felt about her?

If so, Ben didn't want to be like that. Didn't want to follow in either of their footsteps. He might end up making a fool of himself, but damn it, he was going to go to Reese and finally lay it all on the line, telling her everything that he should have said before.

Slapping Alex on the shoulder, he murmured, "Thanks, man."

"For what?" Alex grunted, trying to play it cool.

"For everything!" Ben called out, already heading back toward the entrance. He gave a quick wave to Brit and Mike, who were standing and drinking their coffees near the stand, but didn't stop to talk, in too much of a hurry as he raced inside. He was moving so fast that people were actually getting out of his way, but he needed to reach Reese *now*, damn it. What if fucking Leighton came out of surgery professing his undying love for her? What if she decided to take the jackass back?

No. Hell no!

Driven by a visceral sense of urgency, Ben was practically running by the time he reached the hallway where he'd left Reese sitting in one of those god-awful chairs. But she was no longer there. After a frustrating conversation with the surgical desk, he learned that she'd gone up to the ICU with Leighton.

When he finally found her, she was coming out of Leighton's private room, and he was breathing so hard he sounded like he'd just run a fucking marathon.

"Ben, what's wrong?" she asked, shutting the door to the room behind her.

"Nothing," he panted. "Nothing's wrong, baby. Just . . . just tell me that you don't still love him."

Her eyes went wide. "Who? Drew?"

He had to swallow twice before he could scrape out a response. "Yeah."

"Of course I don't love him. I wanted to make sure he was okay, and to let him know that his family is on their way down, but I don't have any feelings for him." Her voice got softer, just like the look in her eyes. "I thought you understood that."

"Thank God," he groaned, dropping to his knees before her.

She gave him a startled, worried look. "Uh, Ben? What's going on?"

With his shaking hands clinging to her hips, he stared up at her precious face and said, "Reese, I'm so fucking sorry for letting you down, because I should have been there to protect you. And I'm sorry as hell for the fight that we had before I left, and for the things that I said. But I'm ready to do whatever it takes to make it up to you." There were a few muted gasps and sighs from the hospital staff who were working in the area, overhearing every word, but he was too desperate to get it all said to care. "I just . . . I need to tell you that I want you. Forever. I want to be a couple and I want us to live together—for you to move into my house and make it *ours*. Not because you need protection, though I'll always do everything I can to keep you safe. But because I want to spend every moment of every day that I can with you."

"Ben," she said shakily, wiping away the tears that were spilling over her flushed cheeks. "This has been a hell of a night, and you've been dealing with so much. You'll . . . you need to take some time to think, because you'll probably feel differently once everything has started to calm—"

"Bullshit," he growled, cutting her off. "I'm not some ignorant kid, Reese. I know my own mind. You may drive me bat-shit crazy at times, but I love you."

"What?" she gasped, looking like she might pass out from shock. She blinked, those soft, pink lips trembling as she stammered, "I . . . You . . . You *l-love* me?"

"Yeah," he rasped, feeling the tremor that moved through her. "I should have told you last night, only I screwed up. But I'm telling you now. I'm fucking crazy in love with you, woman, and I want us to live together. Is that something you want, too?"

Reese kept her watery gaze locked with Ben's, completely undone by the stunning wealth of emotion she could see burning there. Smiling through her tears, she managed a shivery, breathless "*Yes.*"

The normally quiet area immediately erupted with cheers and applause, both of them grinning like fools as Ben moved to his feet and pulled her into his arms, taking her mouth in a deep, deliciously hungry kiss that was over far too quickly for her liking. But when he put his lips against her ear, asking if she was ready to get out of there and go find a nice hotel room to hide out in with him, she couldn't say yes fast enough.

The local sheriff had left a Jeep in the parking lot for them to use while they were in town, and after leaving Ben's cell phone number with the nurses in the ICU, so that they could call if there were any emergencies with Drew, Reese asked Ben if they could stop by a Target on their way to a hotel. While he stood outside the store, trying to pick out a place for them to stay using the Internet connection on his phone, Reese hurried through her mental list of things they needed, grabbing toiletries and some clean T-shirts and jeans for them to wear. Despite the horrific night she'd just been through, she couldn't keep the silly grin off her face. She might look like the walking dead, with dark circles under her eyes, spatters of blood covering her wrinkled clothes, and raw marks around her wrists from the plastic ties—but she was happy, damn it. The happiest she'd ever been, actually. Not even the funny looks she was getting from the other Monday-morning shoppers were going to bring her down.

When she came back outside, she gave Ben back the debit card she'd borrowed and he loaded everything into the Jeep, then drove them to a beautiful little hotel he'd found on the Gulf side of the city. They got a few interesting looks during check in, but no one said anything. And really, they were too excited to pay much attention to anyone or anything going on around them. The ride up the elevator was annoyingly crowded, full of couples getting ready to go down for breakfast, reminding her that they still hadn't eaten. Reese was going to suggest they order some room service, knowing he must be starving, but Ben was on her the second he'd locked the hotel room door behind them and dropped the shopping bags on the floor, his strong arms holding her against his solid chest in an unbreakable hold as he did things to her mouth that probably melted a few brain cells.

"Wait!" she gasped, when he started undoing the top button on her jeans. "Shower first."

"Later," he growled, kissing the side of her neck as he pushed his hands into the back of her panties. "I want you in that bed."

"And we'll get there," she said with a soft laugh, pushing against his chest so that she could look him in the eye. "But I want to get clean first."

"Fine," he muttered, obviously realizing she wasn't going to give in. "But we shower together."

Less than a minute later, their clothes were strewn all over the bathroom floor, and they were standing beneath a powerful spray

of hot water, the sensual scent of the body wash she'd bought filling the steamy air as they lathered each other up. Reese pressed
her lips to the nicks on his face and arms from the window he'd
busted through, as well as the battered knuckles he admitted he
got from punching a hole in his wall . . . and then Jacobs. When
she asked who that was, he told her the bizarre story about the
dark-haired male he'd kept seeing on the beach, pressing gentle
kisses to the raw skin on her wrists while he spoke.

Reese had hung the bag with all the toiletries from a hook in
the shower, and after they'd rinsed off the soap, they used the
shampoo next. She had to be careful with the bump on the back
of her head, which was still tender, but it was worth any discomfort to feel clean again. As she lifted her arms over her head to
rinse the suds from her hair, Ben pinched her nipples with his callused fingertips, making her shiver and moan.

"I like showering with you," she said breathlessly, her sex
already swelling for him, going warm and wet and soft.

"I like showering with you, too," he offered with a wicked
smile, dropping down on his knees again for the second time that
morning. But instead of another stunning declaration of love, he
pushed his face against her mound, which was *almost* even better.
After nuzzling the damp curls, he lifted one of her legs over his
shoulder and put his mouth on her slick, wet sex, eating at her
with a hunger that was unlike anything she'd ever experienced.
He'd always been an incredible lover, but there was something so
much more powerful happening between them now. The sensations were sharper . . . deeper, the pleasure magnified in a way she
hadn't even known was possible. There was a new, breathtaking
possessiveness in the touch of his hands and mouth that said he
owned her ass . . . and it was his duty to melt her freaking mind.
Not that she was complaining. God, no. She was lucky enough to
be in love with a man who had the skill and equipment to make

her come so hard she forgot her own name. What was there to complain about? She was just going to hold on to him as tight as she could and be grateful as hell that he'd come into her life.

And she planned to do everything she could to make sure he felt the same. Not because she had to and was afraid of losing him. She didn't know how it'd happened, or why she'd gotten so lucky, but Reese knew he'd meant it when he'd told her he loved her, and she had faith in him. So she wasn't reciprocating for any other reasons than the fact that she wanted to . . . and because making him happy made *her* happy.

When she'd finally caught her breath after experiencing a lush, mind-shattering orgasm, Reese blinked the drops of water from her lashes . . . and smiled down at him. She lowered her leg and gripped his broad shoulders, telling him without words that she wanted him to stand. He watched her with a dark, avid look in his eyes as she motioned for him to get his back against the tiled wall. Then she leaned up on her tiptoes and stole a quick kiss from his damp mouth, loving the way she could taste herself on him. A low moan slipped past her lips, and he gave a soft, sexy laugh.

"Tell me about it," he said in a low rumble. "You taste fucking incredible. I could live with my face buried in your sweet little cunt and die a happy man."

"That's a lovely thought," she whispered, slipping down to her knees, "but it's my turn now."

"Reese, I'm ready to fu—" The rough words were cut off when she leaned forward and licked the flushed, heavy head of his cock . . . then started to suckle, and Ben knew those soft, plump lips were going to be the death of him. *Christ.* He'd been ready to blow his load the second he felt her breathe on him, and now he was too primed to hold back for long, her warm, silken mouth too perfect to resist. His back arched, hands fisted in her hair as he pumped himself over her tongue in hot, blinding bursts, knowing damn well that he'd never come so fast in his life. But he was more than ready to let her blow his mind and reduce him to putty whenever she got the urge. Which he hoped would be often.

Gripping her under her arms, he pulled her up and against his chest, then went in for a deep, eating kiss, getting off on tasting himself in her mouth. "I've never done this"—his voice was like gravel—"never kissed a woman after . . . But I like the way you taste with a part of me inside you."

Reese didn't like thinking about him with anyone else, but she wasn't going to let his past stand between them. And she liked that this was something new they could share, the way his tongue kept sweeping the inside of her mouth making her toes curl. The feel of his stiff erection rising against her stomach made it no secret that he liked it, too. She couldn't believe he was already getting hard again, but then, his recovery time was always impressive. And she knew exactly what she wanted him to do with this one.

Breaking away from the kiss, she was panting with excitement as she stepped back and reached into the bag again. Then she pulled out the bottle of lube that she'd picked up during her little shopping spree.

Ben's beautiful green eyes went wide, then hot. "Fuck, Reese. Does that mean what I think it means?"

She smiled as she laughed. "Considering how dirty your mind is, I'm pretty sure that it does."

It was sexy as hell, the way his breathing got a little rougher, his tough muscles bunched a little tighter under his skin. He was all leashed power and sexual, visceral hunger, just waiting for the moment when it could be set free. But instead of moving things forward, he gave a hard swallow and said, "As much as I want it, you don't have to do this now, honey. You've been through enough since yesterday. It wouldn't be—"

She shushed him by pressing her fingers against his lips. "I know I don't *have* to. But I want to. So if you want it, too—if you want me that way—then I'm telling you right now that I'm ready."

He ran his tongue over the edge of his teeth, his deep voice guttural and sharp. "Want you? I want you so much I want to fucking brand every part of you as *mine*, Reese. Do you have any idea what you're setting yourself up for? Because I can tell you right now that I'm going to give a whole new meaning to the word *possessive*."

"I can handle that," she murmured, staring into the dark heat of his eyes. "Just know that I feel the same way about you."

"I sure as hell hope so. Because no one else exists for me. No one. There's only *you*." His smoldering gaze was as sharp as a raptor's, reading every minute shift in her expression. "You understand what I'm saying?"

Her throat shook, chest so warm she should have glowed. "I understand."

"Good. Because I might drive you crazy at times, but I will always be true to you. I will not fuck around on you. That's never even going to be on the table, because you're the only thing in this world that I want. There's *never* going to be anyone else for me."

Oh, God. Who would have ever thought that the notoriously badass sheriff of Moss Beach County could say such outrageously romantic things? Reese was fairly certain she'd just melted into an embarrassing puddle of blissed-out happiness on the shower floor.

Flattening her palm against his chest, she tried to let every beautiful, breathtaking emotion she was experiencing show on her face, wanting him to see just how much he meant to her. "I love you so much, Ben."

"God, Reese. I love you, too." He pulled her close and kissed the hell out of her, as if to seal the deal, then pulled back and said, "Now ask me again if I want to fuck you in the ass."

"Do you?" she whispered, knowing damn well that she was blushing like crazy.

The crooked smile on his lips was pure, explicit sin. "Say the words, Reese. You know how much I love it when you talk dirty."

"All right," she murmured, teasing him as she fluttered her lashes. Voice theatrically breathy, she asked, "Sheriff Hudson, sir, would you like to fuck me in the ass this morning?"

Ben would have laughed at her playfulness, but his control was already shredded. Instead, he made a thick, serrated sound deep in his throat as he took the lube from her, set it on the shelf, and got her into position—hands braced against the tiled wall, legs shoulder-width apart, and that rosy little backside presented to him like the sweetest fucking gift he'd ever received.

"You have the juiciest little ass," he groaned, running his hands over the soft, pale globes. "We're talking so fucking gorgeous, baby."

She snuffled a nervous, but excited-sounding snicker under her breath, then gave a high-pitched squeal of surprise when he smacked his palm against her right cheek.

"*Ben!*"

"If I remember correctly, I think you're due quite a few of these," he murmured silkily. "You ready for another?"

"Oh, God," Reese moaned, unable to believe how much she was enjoying this.

"We're going to five," he told her, the low words husky with lust as he ran his palm over her burning skin. "And then I'm going to fuck you, sweetheart. Right in this tight little hole," he rasped, rubbing his thumb against the sensitive opening. "Ready?"

She swallowed, trying to find her voice, so excited she could barely stand. "Y-yes."

"Good girl." Then he smacked her left cheek, and she gave a throaty cry, feeling the burn seep into her sensitive skin, spreading through every part of her. By the time he'd delivered the fifth blow, she was panting for breath, her limbs shaking, her clit throbbing with a tight, hungry pulse, body on the very cusp of crashing into an orgasm she thought might damn well knock her out. But she struggled for control, not yet ready to go over, too eager for the next step in this dark, provocative, decadent interlude.

As she rested her damp forehead against one of her trembling arms, Reese could hear the rough cadence of Ben's breathing. Could sense the dominant male energy pulsing from his hard, mouthwatering body, and couldn't wait for him to take her. With one hand gripping her hip, he ran the rough palm of the other over her stinging bottom, then slipped his thumb into the crease and pressed against the tiny hole there, pushing inside. She breathed out a slow, shuddering breath, trying to relax and not fight the strangely pleasurable penetration as he kept pushing, going deeper than any of the other times he'd played with her there. She could tell he'd lubed his thumb, especially when he started working it in and out, fucking her ass with it. She was saying hoarse, shivery things under her breath, but they didn't make any sense. Just pleading phrases for more . . . for *everything*.

It wasn't long before he pulled his thumb back, a deep, throaty sound rumbling up from his chest as she felt the heat and width of his cock head pressing against her. His body tightened, both hands digging into her hips, and then he started to push inside the clenching ring of muscle. It was the oddest sensation she'd ever known. Painful, but so deliciously good. He didn't rush her, taking his time as he worked more of that massive shaft into her in careful degrees. One of his hands snaked around her hip, two of those clever fingers working her sensitive clit as he started working her ass with lunges that were a little rougher . . . a little faster. Reese wondered if he would come inside her or pull out, then had her answer when she could feel him getting even harder inside her. His fingers stroked her into a shocking, screaming orgasm just as it overtook him. With a sexy, guttural shout tearing from his throat, he wrapped an arm across her chest and yanked her against him, holding her off the ground as he blasted inside her, coming hard and thick and long.

"No one but me," he growled softly against her ear, when he finally lowered her back to her feet and carefully pulled out. "You understand?"

She nodded weakly, too limp to even be embarrassed by the sheer carnality of what they'd just done as she braced her forearms against the tiled wall, gasping for breath. It had felt so right, the way he'd staked his claim in such a raw, primal, dominant way. She never would have believed it, but she loved the way he took control of her body and its responses when it came to sex. The way he demanded she give him everything she had, reading her reactions as if they were his own, her pleasure his to create. And, God, but he was a master at it, wringing more sensation out of her tingling flesh than she'd ever imagined was possible.

Moving her hair over her shoulder, he leaned forward and pressed his lips to the back of her neck as he said, "I love you, Reese."

Her breath caught on a quiet gasp. "I don't think I'll ever get used to hearing you say that."

"You'd better," he told her, touching his mouth to the side of her throat. "'Cause you'll be hearing it every day of your life."

They finished in the shower, their movements lazy and slow, just enjoying the moment and in no rush to be anywhere but right there, in each other's arms. Ben dried them both with the hotel's monogrammed towels, then carried her into the bedroom and tucked her up under the covers, since she was cold. He put in a quick call to room service, ordering them both some breakfast. She laughed when he answered the door with nothing but a towel wrapped around his sexy hips and nearly gave the older woman who delivered the cart a lust-induced heart attack.

"I can't believe I was so stupid," he said, after they'd finished every bite of the pancakes and bacon, drawn the curtains, and cuddled up together beneath a fluffy duvet.

"About what?"

"You." He lifted his hand, brushing her hair back from her face and tucking it behind her ear. "Thinking I could get my fill of you, then cut things off and watch you walk away. It would have fucking destroyed me."

"I couldn't ever walk away from you, Ben." A crooked smile lifted the corner of her mouth, her tone deliberately teasing. "You keep me too exhausted."

His husky laugh filled her ear as he pulled her closer. "Sleep now, baby. 'Cause when you wake up, my cock's gonna be tiring you out all over again . . ."

With those breathtaking words keeping her company, Reese closed her eyes . . . and drifted away.

REESE WOKE TO THE SOUND OF SOMEONE WHISPERING HER NAME, A happy grin on her lips as she realized Ben was kissing his way up the side of her throat.

"What time is it?" she asked, unable to tell with the heavy curtains blocking out the sunlight.

"Probably middle of the afternoon," he murmured, his voice low and serious. He braced himself on an elbow beside her, and stared down into her drowsy eyes. "I told myself to wait and that you needed your sleep, but I can't. I've been lying here, watching you, and I just can't do it. I can't wait any longer, Reese."

She frowned, starting to get a little worried. "What's wrong?"

"Nothing's wrong. It's just that . . . damn it, I swore to myself that I wasn't gonna push you, but I need more. For the two of us."

"Oh." She blinked, definitely wanting to be alert for wherever he was going with this. "Um, what did you have in mind?"

His voice got even huskier, the look in his eyes stealing her breath. "You keep teaching while I chase bad guys. We build a bigger house together somewhere on the coast. Raise a few kids with your freckles, and hope like hell they turn out more like you than me. Get a dog. Fuck each other silly and grow old together."

With another slow blink, she said, "You're talking about building a life together."

His dark gaze smoldered with heat. "I'm talking about building a hell of a life together. The best I can imagine."

Running her fingertip over his brows, she said, "But you're not a settling-down kind of guy, Ben. You told me so yourself."

"That was just because I was too chicken-shit to admit what I really wanted."

Reese shivered, unable to believe that the big bad Ben Hudson was opening up to her like this. It was still too new, too astonishing. She half expected to wake up in some cold hotel room all alone, and realize the entire morning had been nothing more than a heartbreaking dream.

Quietly, she said, "Whatever you want from me, Ben. It's yours. You don't have to do something you're not ready for."

"But I am ready. That's what I've been trying to tell you." He grabbed her hand and brought it to his lips, placing a tender kiss against her palm, before pressing it against the heavy beat of his heart. "Reese Monroe, I know you're an amazing woman who could do a hell of a lot better than me. But if you say yes, I swear on my honor that I will do everything I can to make you happy."

"Ohmygod!" she gasped. "You're proposing? *Now?*"

He gave her a hard, breathtaking look of determination. "Damn right I am. I want to know we're legally bound together. We can go shopping for a ring in Miami before we head back home, because I want to marry you as soon as possible. I want to make you *mine*."

"I already am." Tears filled her eyes, catching on her lashes. She'd been so wrong about this man. About who he was and the things he needed—like love, tenderness, and devotion. And more than anything in the world, she wanted to be the woman who gave them to him. "Ben, I've been yours since the first time I ever saw you. You just didn't know it."

"I know it now, and I want all those other bastards out there to know it, too. I want it clear to everyone exactly who your sweet little ass belongs to." With a wicked gleam in his eyes, he caged her beneath him, bracing himself on his hands and knees. Then he gave her a devilish smile, and said, "Come on, Reese. I dare you."

She couldn't help but smile right back at him. "You know I can never resist your dares."

His expression was an insanely sexy mix of love and resolve. "Then say yes and let me fuck you."

"Yes. Yeah. You betcha," she whispered, her smile melting into a grin.

A deep, throaty laugh shook his chest. "God, woman. You don't know how good it feels to hear you say that."

Before she could even draw her next breath, his powerful thighs were wedged between hers and he was working himself inside her, their gazes locked together as he braced himself on his forearms and started to move. The rhythm was slow and thick and outrageously good. She gripped the strong, lean muscles in his back, loving the way they moved and flexed under her hands, his hips driving that beautiful cock into her hard and deep . . . but so achingly slow. She writhed, undone, able to feel every inch and ridge and pulse in perfect, explicit detail as he became a part of her. She started coming somewhere along the way, and then couldn't stop, the lush waves of pleasure rolling through her again and again, like riding the surface of an ocean. She made sounds she'd never even heard before: low, breathless cries for more . . . for all of him . . . for everything that he had. And he gave it all to her. His body . . . his heart . . . his soul. She could see it in the dark, glittering depths of his eyes. Feel it through that charged, emotional current that connected them . . . binding them together.

"I want to fill you up, Reese. Give you every drop of cum burning inside me."

Her eyes went wide. "I could get pregnant."

"I know." His voice got lower, rougher, sending a blistering rush of warmth through her veins. "But we've already wasted so much time. I feel like I've been waiting for this moment for years, and I don't want to wait anymore. I know it might take some time, but I don't want to put it off. So what do you think? You ready to start working on that family we talked about?"

"Yes," she breathed out, clutching him to her. "I can't think of anything that would be more incredible."

She only caught a brief flash of his gorgeous smile before he claimed her mouth in another one of those deep, deliciously drugging kisses that made her dizzy with pleasure. The instant she fell into another pulsing orgasm, he started riding her harder, his muscles rippling with power as he slammed his hips against her faster . . . and faster, a guttural growl on his lips when it suddenly crashed down on him. He pumped himself inside her with a savageness that was as beautiful as it was shocking.

When he finally pulled out, he braced himself over her on straight arms, that dark, glittering gaze focused intently between her sprawled thighs. "You look so fucking sexy with my cum dripping out of that pink little pussy," he groaned, moving one of his hands between her legs.

"What are you doing?" she asked, when she felt his finger pushing into her.

"I want to feel it inside you," he rasped, his attention focused hard and tight on her sex. "I've never done that before."

She blinked, more than a little surprised. "You haven't?" she asked, loving that this was another first they'd been able to share together.

Shaking his head, he said, "I fucked in the raw a few times when I was too young to know better, but I always pulled out. Never saw it through to the end."

"Well, you certainly saw it through to the end today," she murmured, her eyes slipping closed as she stretched her arms up over her head and smiled with satisfaction.

His chest shook with a breathless laugh. "Don't be falling asleep on me, sweetheart. I'm ready for round two."

She cracked one eye open and laughed. "Are you kidding me?"

He took her hand and wrapped it around his rampant erection. "You tell me," he said with one of those sexy smirks that made him look too gorgeous to be real.

"Hmm. You're an awful lot to take on, Sheriff Hudson."

His eyes burned with heat. "I know. But it'll be worth it, because I'm going to fucking worship the ground you walk on. Now, tomorrow, forever."

"You don't have to sell it. I've already signed on for the permanent package."

He gave another husky laugh, his deep-grooved grin the most beautiful thing she'd ever seen. "You won't be sorry, baby."

"I know."

"I promise I'll make you happy."

Reese pulled him close, and held on to him as tightly as she could. "You already do."

Epilogue

Three months later . . .

REESE HAD NEVER THOUGHT HER LIFE COULD BE SO WONDERFUL, BUT it was. She'd started her new job and loved it. There was a great camaraderie among the staff at the school, and her students were awesome. She'd had Ben come in and do some special safety presentations, and now all the kids kept begging for him to come back. They loved him, but she wasn't surprised. She loved him so much she sometimes couldn't believe that she'd gotten so lucky. After everything that had happened at the start of the summer, they'd come through even stronger than she'd thought was possible.

Thanks to Ryder, a lot of the questions they'd had about Lizzie and Rick Jennings had been answered in the weeks following that horrific night in Islamorada. The business dealings Lizzie had mentioned were con jobs she'd made her brother help her pull off.

Most of them had involved tricking wealthy older men out of their money, though Ben and the deputy believed the two might also be responsible for some violent robberies that had taken place up in Vermont the previous year. When she'd talked to Brit about the pair, Brit had said that both of the siblings were so unbalanced, there was no telling what kind of past had shaped them. It was an upsetting thought, but Reese was just glad they were no longer a part of their lives.

After his release from hospital, Drew had gone back to Boston, which had been a huge relief. He'd asked to see her before he left, but she'd told him there was nothing left for them to say to each other. Despite how badly their marriage had ended, Reese knew he'd never intended for her to be in danger, and she wished him the best.

And that was exactly what she'd found in Ben. The absolute best, most incredible man in the world, and one who had so many fascinating sides to his character she was still in awe. He was so deliciously rough and rugged, and then at times so endearingly playful, tickling her until she begged for mercy. And he could be amazingly tender, just cuddling her in his lap as they curled up on the sofa to watch TV or a movie. At those times, he would stroke his hands over her legs and hips, or the back of her neck. Little intimate touches that let her know he was aware of her, and that he enjoyed having her so close. It put a warm feeling in the center of her chest that she knew made her look blissfully happy all the time. But that's only because she was.

And tomorrow she was going to marry his fine ass.

Finishing with her mascara, Reese slipped on the slinky silver dress she'd bought especially for tonight. In an hour, they were having their rehearsal dinner at McClain's, and all their family and friends were going to be there. The only one who would be missing was Rachel. After their lunch that day at Casa di Pico,

Rachel had left town in a hurry, heading to Lafayette, Louisiana. Everyone who knew her hoped she was doing okay there and that she'd come back soon, even if it was only for a visit.

Reese had just put on a pair of strappy silver heels, and was checking her makeup in the mirror over their dresser when Ben came into the bedroom looking all studly and gorgeous. From his reflection in the mirror, she could see that he was dressed in black slacks and a gray silk shirt that'd been left open at the throat, the molten heat in his dark gaze as he looked her over nearly making her forget what she'd wanted to ask him.

"Is Ryder going to make it to the dinner?" She'd been growing increasingly worried about the deputy the last few times that she'd seen him. There'd been dark circles under his eyes, and he'd had those brackets that men sometimes got at the sides of their mouths when they were really stressed . . . or pissed about something. Whatever was going on in the deputy's personal life, he hadn't been acting like himself lately.

"He'll be there, but I don't want to talk about Ryder," Ben drawled with a sharp smile, coming up behind her. "Not when I could be telling you how much I love your ass in this dress." He leaned down, brushing his lips against her ear as he ran his hands over her silk-covered hips. "But then, I love it bare and covered in my handprints, as well."

Locking her gaze with his in the mirror, Reese gave him a playfully suspicious look. "Did you ask me to marry you just so you can act out your perverted fantasies on my ass?"

His crooked grin was ridiculously sexy. "Not just your ass, sweetheart. The second you're mine, I plan on debauching every beautiful little inch of you. So be warned."

The laughter spilling from her lips was husky, and full of joy. "I thought you already did that."

"Mmm, but just wait till we get home tonight." With a wicked gleam in his gaze, he said, "I went shopping this morning for a few things to help us celebrate."

Her eyes went wide. "Shopping where?"

"It's a surprise," Ben replied with a smile, imagining her face when he showed her the plug he planned on pushing inside her sweet little backside . . . and the nipple clamps for her beautiful breasts. "One I promise you're going to enjoy."

LATER THAT NIGHT, REESE FOUND HERSELF HANDCUFFED TO THEIR bed, Ben's hard cock buried deep in her body. He'd already done the most shocking, explicit things to her, and she'd come more times than she could count. But it was the way he was staring down at her flushed face, his gaze smoky and dark and full of stunning emotion, that completely undid her.

"Do you know why I'm going to marry you?" he asked in a low voice.

Her eyes went heavy. "Tell me."

"Because being inside you feels like my own little piece of heaven. Because you're the most amazing, wonderful, beautiful, sweet, funny, courageous person that I've ever known." His voice got rougher. "I'm marrying you because I love you, Reese. More than any man has ever loved a woman." Those dark eyes burned with need. "I'm marrying you because I can't fucking do without you."

"You won't have to, Ben. I promise."

"You're mine," he growled, thrusting into her harder . . . deeper.

Knowing in her heart that it would always be true, she whispered, "*Forever.*"

Read on for a sneak preview of

MAKE ME YOURS

A Dangerous Tides Novella appearing
in the anthology *Wicked and Dangerous*
by Shayla Black and Rhyannon Byrd.

Coming soon from Berkley Sensation.

DRIPPING WITH SWEAT AS HE TOOK A LATE-NIGHT RUN ON THE MOONLIT beach, Scott Ryder had a strange feeling burning through his veins, twisting its way into his bones. One that didn't have anything to do with his grueling pace or the miles of sand he'd already covered.

The feeling had been building inside him for weeks now, making him restless, leaving him in a generally shitty mood. He'd tried to shake it, but he couldn't. Damn thing just kept growing, pissing him off even more. People were starting to go out of their way to avoid him at the station, which was just as well, seeing as how he hadn't been in the mood for conversation. But tonight he'd been forced to attend the retirement party for one of the other deputies in the sheriff's department, and his nerves were still scraped raw. It wasn't that he didn't like Dwight Jones. Dwight was an okay guy who was looking forward to spending his days either out on the golf course or on his new fishing boat, and Ryder wished him luck. But Ryder's boss, Ben Hudson, had been at the party with his new wife, and for some unknown reason the sight of them had set his teeth on edge.

It wasn't that Ryder wanted the sheriff's wife for himself. Reese was more than easy on the eyes and had a killer smile, but Ben had staked his claim the moment she hit town at the beginning of the summer, so she and Ryder were friends and nothing more. But the way Ben kept looking at her during the party, as if marriage made him the luckiest bastard in the world, had made Ryder want to put his fucking fist through a wall.

He knew damn well that his reaction didn't make any sense. Christ, he wanted Ben and Reese to be happy. After everything they'd been through, they deserved it. He just couldn't stomach being near all that cozy, romantic bliss. Not when this itch in his veins wouldn't let off, his instincts constantly twitching, as if he were missing something important and needed to open his damn eyes. He'd had the same kind of feeling before, when he'd worked black ops, and it'd saved his ass too many times to count. But he'd left that life behind. He no longer had to live in constant survival mode. There was no danger here. No one gunning for his life or the people he cared about. Which meant he needed to calm the hell down and learn to relax.

Heading into the last half-mile of his run, Ryder repeated a familiar phrase in his mind. His personal mantra now that he'd settled down in the cozy little town of Moss Beach.

Nothing to run from . . .

Nothing to run to . . .

There was a peace and perfection in those simple words. They meant freedom. A new beginning. A new life.

Unfortunately, they were nothing but lies. Because while he might not have anything to run to, he was sure as hell still running *from* something. He might have decided to stay put in this scenic little beach town on Florida's Gulf Coast, but that didn't mean he wasn't fighting an internal battle every damn day of his life. He'd physically stopped, but his mind was still running at top speed, doing everything it could to forget about—

Shit. Don't even go there, he muttered to himself. And that thought was swiftly followed by a guttural, *Christ, I need a drink.*

He spent a lot of time these days telling himself what he needed to fix his head. A drink, a woman, or *women* when he couldn't be bothered to choose which one he wanted to take home for the night. If he wasn't careful, he was going to develop a reputation in town as the lawman who could screw his way through hordes of women without ever losing his breath. At the age of thirty-three, it wasn't a distinction to be proud of. It just meant that while all the other guys were getting on with their lives, he was still acting like an idiot who thought with his prick. Or one who would only touch a woman if she let him tie her—*No, damn it.* He wasn't going *there* tonight either. In his current mood, those thoughts wouldn't lead him to any place good.

Hitting the five-mile marker, Ryder finally slowed to a walk and pulled off his damp T-shirt, using it to wipe the sweat from his face. He headed across the sand toward the beachfront duplex he rented from an elderly couple who had retired there after living in New York for the past forty years. The house was designed with an entrance to each half at the sides of the duplex, bougainvillea-covered trellises creating two pathways that sheltered the entrances from the street, with matching archways in the back that you could walk through if coming up from the beach. The profusion of flowers was a little fanciful for Ryder's taste, but his sister had gushed about them when she came for a visit last month, claiming the trellises gave the house "southern charm."

Wondering if he'd finally be able to chill enough tonight that he could sleep, Ryder had nearly reached his front door when he sensed a slight movement to his left, in the shadows of the trellis, and he reacted before he'd even given conscious thought to the possible threat. That's what over a decade of black ops training could do to you, and despite being out of the game for a few years now, his reflexes were as lightning quick as ever. Dropping his shirt, he reached into the shadows, snagged a feminine arm, and yanked the woman into the moonlight, the shrill scream coming from her lips quickly shifting to an outraged snarl as she brought her other arm around to strike him across the face. He quickly blocked the move, catching her wrist and pinning both arms behind her back, while she flailed in his hold, kicking at his shins with her sandal-covered feet.

"Who are you?" he growled, quickly assessing that she wasn't a physical threat. Her hair covered her face as she struggled to free herself from his embrace. But despite her efforts, there wasn't a chance in hell she could break free. He knew how to counteract every one of her defensive moves, which only infuriated her more.

Narrowing his eyes, Ryder carried out a quick visual check on the female. She had her head down so he couldn't see her face—but what he *could* see of her made his mouth go dry. Waves of silky strawberry blond hair. Her miniskirt and short-sleeved, button-down shirt revealed creamy skin and a body that was slight but deliciously feminine. So familiar it was almost too good to be true. She had the right shade of hair. The right frame. The right shape. The right fucking everything, ripped right out of his goddamn memory to torment him.

He could hear a roaring in his ears, drowning out the rational voice in the back of his mind that was shouting for him to move away from her. Instead, he continued acting purely on instinct. On the raw, powerful lust that ripped up through his insides the instant he realized he had someone who reminded him of *her* in his arms. The very woman he never allowed himself to think about, let alone fantasize. But this was like a gift from fate. The bastard had never been kind to him in the past, but at the moment Ryder just didn't give a damn. The only thing he had to worry about was convincing the little hellcat that there was something a whole lot better they could be doing together than fighting.

His breathing got deeper, nostrils flaring as he pulled in her light, purely feminine scent, the autumn night warm enough that the air was still sultry and damp from an earlier rainstorm. His body had already reacted to the feel of her wriggling against him, a serrated groan on his lips when her belly brushed against him, making her gasp. She went instantly still, but not with fear. It was more like . . . surprise, and he knew the exact instant her anger flared into lust—and he was done for. In that moment he couldn't have walked away from her if his goddamn life depended on it.

For all Ryder knew, the woman was a thief who'd been getting ready to clear his house out, but he didn't care. She smelled like Lily, had that same gorgeous hair and sexy figure, and he was too fucking starved to resist. One second they were standing on the walkway in front of his door, and in the next he had her plastered against it, wishing like hell that he'd replaced the blown bulb in the outside light so that he could get a better look at what he was tasting. His mouth had instantly settled against the base of her pale, slim throat, his tongue fluttering against her hammering pulse as he grabbed the front of her short-sleeved top and ripped. By the time Ryder could hear the shirt's buttons pinging against the ground, he already had his mouth buried between her beautiful breasts. Any concerns he might have had that she wasn't on exactly the same page as him were shattered by the low moan she gave when he ripped the silky cups of her bra down and curled his long fingers around the firm, delicate mounds, then covered one of the hardened tips with his mouth. She cried out as he suckled her, her short nails digging into the bunched muscles in his shoulders, and it was like losing himself in a fever dream, her wild response to his aggression only adding fuel to the fire.

The nipple in Ryder's mouth was tight and sweet, the intoxicating taste of the woman's skin cranking his lust up to a primitive level. That irritating voice was still shouting in the back of his mind, warning him to snap back to reality and think about what he was doing—but he was too far gone, and she was too damn hot and willing. Her hands were already fisted in his hair, holding him to her as he switched to the other breast, her thigh riding his hip as she arched against him, as if she were as desperate for this as he was. And he was beyond desperate, his dick so hard he could have hammered through the fucking door with it. The longer he touched her, the harder he got. Not that she was complaining. The woman was grinding herself against the front of his running shorts, riding the hard ridge of his cock, the husky sounds spilling from her lips the sexiest damn thing he'd ever heard.

He didn't have a condom on him, which meant he couldn't fuck her until he got her inside. He might be desperate, but he wasn't stupid. He'd always been religious about suiting up with latex and had never screwed without it. But this hot little stranger made him damn tempted.

"We need to move this indoors," he rasped against the soft skin just under her right breast. Gripping her hips, Ryder dropped to his knees and kissed his way down her flat belly, until he'd shoved her skirt up and had his face buried against the silky front of her panties . . . then lower, between her legs. A rough, guttural sound crawled its way up from his chest as he caught the hot, mouthwatering scent of her cunt, the sexy underwear already damp with her juices. And then she had to destroy the whole goddamn thing with the soft, whispered sound of his name.

"*Scott.*"

Ah, Christ. No one fucking called him that but *her*, and it hit him like a bucket of ice water in his face.

He should have listened to his gut, to that damn voice that had been shouting in the back of his mind, because this woman didn't just *remind* him of Lily Heller. She *was* Lily Heller!

No. No way. Not her. Not Lily. Couldn't be. She was just someone who reminded him of her. Someone he could still touch and get his fill of. Someone he could—

Damn it! He tried, but he couldn't do it. Couldn't buy his own bullshit. The lie had been blasted into a million tiny fragments and now he was going to have to pay the fucking price for being an idiot. No doubt with his sanity.

Jerking back to his feet, Ryder gripped her shoulders as he locked his sharp gaze on her face for the first time in three years. *"Son of a bitch,"* he grated under his breath. Big green eyes with lashes that were long and thick stared back at him. Rosy lips parted for her panting breaths. Moonlight spilling down on those firm breasts, her pink little nipples still glistening from his mouth and tongue.

Oh, God.

He was shaking so hard she was jerking in his arms, but he couldn't stop, unable to believe what was right in front of him. The girl he'd left his life and career for—the one who had been the object of his most dangerous obsession for far too long—was trapped between his body and his front door, blinking up at him with those big, bright eyes while she tried to catch her breath.

Lily Heller, daughter of his ex-boss and goddamn thorn in his side, in the flesh, staring back at him as if she could eat him alive, with her perfect tits out and her skirt hiked up around her waist. *Jesus.*

Ryder rubbed a rough hand over his mouth, wondering how he could have let things go so far. What the hell had he been thinking?

He hadn't. Which was the problem. He'd shoved rational thought to the back of his mind and focused on what he wanted. Instant gratification would screw you over every time. Damn it, he knew that. Had an IQ that said he was way too fucking smart to make that kind of mistake—but his dick had apparently failed to get the memo. And now, thanks to this royal little screwup, he would have to go through life knowing *exactly* how right it felt to have her under his hands and mouth.

"Fuck!" he ground out through his clenched teeth, shoving away from her. At six-three, he towered over her, even though she wasn't a short woman. Maybe five-six or five-seven, though she seemed more petite because of her build. She was slim, but feminine as hell, and he wanted nothing more than to take her back into his arms and—

Shit. He couldn't do it. Because if he did, it was going to goddamn destroy him when he had to walk away. And he *would* walk. He didn't have any other option. He never did where this girl was concerned. Yeah, she might be twenty-five now, but he still thought of her as the gangly teen she'd been when he first met her all those years ago.

Before he could get his mind wrapped around this new reality in which Lily Heller had suddenly popped back into his life, she shoved her skirt down, yanked the sides of her shirt closed and glared up at him. "Do you mind telling me why you attacked me?" she snapped.

His jaw tightened. "I didn't attack you. You're the one who tried to hit *me*."

"Only after you yanked me in front of you," she shot back, as if he'd been the one at fault.

His voice was raw. "News flash, woman. That's what happens when I find someone lurking in the shadows outside my front door."

"I wasn't lurking," she argued, that bright gaze lowering to his

bare chest and shoulders for a moment, before she finally lifted it
back to his face. She drew in an unsteady breath, then blasted him
with a sharp, "I was waiting for you to get home!"

Ryder made a low sound of frustration in the back of his throat,
and this time her gaze drifted to the scar that ran from his temple
to the middle of his right cheek. Something he didn't quite understand moved through those green eyes, but she didn't flinch. The
last time she'd seen him the scar had been raw and fresh. It was
still ugly as sin, but looked a hell of a lot better than it had then.
He never even thought about it much anymore when he was with
a woman, but he quickly felt himself go hot under the skin, as if
he was actually embarrassed for her to see his face like this.

Fucking ironic, considering she was the reason he had the scar
in the first place. Not that he'd ever tell her that. But every time
Ryder looked in a mirror, he was reminded of just how dangerous
his obsession with this girl could be.

"Why are you here?" he growled, his nostrils flaring with a
fresh surge of fury as he stared her down. "What the hell do you
want, Lily?"

She bristled with irritation. "Wow. You're just all kinds of
kindness and warmth, aren't you? First you manhandle me, then
you maul me, and now you're being rude. Is that any way to greet
an old friend?"

"Cut the crap. You were hardly manhandled or mauled, and we
were never friends. Your old man made sure of that. So what the
fuck are you doing here?"

She started to pale, losing that pleasure-flush that had been in
her cheeks, the angry tension that had been riding her slender
frame gone as quickly as it'd come. "Believe it or not," she said
quietly, licking her lips, "I'm here because I need your help."

"Bullshit," he snarled, fisting his hands at his sides so that he
wouldn't do something stupid. Like reach out and grab her again.

"I'm the *last* person in the world you need to get near. Go back home to your daddy and leave me alone. Whatever problem you've got, he'll take care of it."

"I . . . can't."

"Why the hell not?" he exploded.

She blinked again, and this time a tear spilled from the corner of her eye. "Because he's dead."

Ryder shook his head, thinking he must have heard her wrong. "What are you talking about?"

She took a deep breath, then exhaled in a shuddering rush. "Heller's dead, Scott. Rado killed him eight days ago."

Rado? Just the sound of that terrorist bastard's name put an icy feeling in Ryder's gut. Of all the scumbags in the world, Yuri Rado-vich was the one he hated the most. But the man was supposed to be dead. Ryder knew, because he was the one who had killed him.

"That isn't possible. Rado is dead, Lily."

A wry smile twisted her lips, the raw pain in her expression making him flinch. "Yeah, that's the same thing my father believed. Until the monster waltzed onto our boat and slit his throat."

"Jesus." His head was starting to pound like a bitch. "You're sure it was him?"

She sniffed, and jerked her chin up in response.

A fierce scowl wove its way between his brows. "Then why the hell am I only just hearing about this? Why hasn't anyone informed the old unit?"

"Because I doubt anyone but me knows at this point, and I've been on the run," she told him, her tone tight and clipped and anything but calm. "I don't have my cell phone, but even if I did, I wouldn't have called you because who knows if your phone calls are being tapped and traced. I'm sorry for just showing up out of the blue, but it's not like I had any other choice. Even if I'd had a computer and could have emailed you, there's a chance he could be monitoring your account. You know what he's like—how extensive his reach is. And I didn't have time to come up with some other brilliant way to contact you because I've been doing everything I could just to make it here in one piece!"

"On the run from what?" he demanded, finally noticing how tired she looked. How shattered. "What happened, Lily? Why doesn't anyone know that Heller is dead?"

Her voice shook as she explained. "I was with my father and his girlfriend, Nancy, in the Bahamas when Rado made the hit. We were staying on a friend's boat, moored in some cove, when he and his men found us. He killed my dad and Nancy and had them thrown overboard." Her voice started to crack, but she took another deep breath and went on. "Then he tried to kill me. He actually took quite a lot of pleasure in explaining why I had to die and exactly how he and his men were going to do it. But I . . . I got lucky and managed to get away."

Ryder worked his jaw, guessing there was a hell of a lot more to the story than that . . . and dreading what he knew was coming.

"Do you understand why I'm here?" she asked, stepping toward him, those incredible eyes shimmering with too many emotions for him to name. "You're the only person I could think of who stands any kind of chance against him. The only person I trust. And I know I don't have any right to ask—I know you don't owe me anything—but I'm asking anyway."

In a flat tone, he said, "You want me to protect you."

It wasn't a question. Ryder knew damn well that's why she was there. He just didn't know what he was going to do about it. The situation was complicated as hell. One of his worst goddamn nightmares come to life.

Because while Ryder might be capable of protecting Lily Heller from Radovich, he didn't have a fucking clue how he was going to protect her from himself.